TRIANGLE BLACK

A Novel

JOSEPH MIGUEL

TRIANGLE BLACK:
A NOVEL by JOSEPH MIGUEL

First Edition

© 2020 JOSEPH MIGUEL

Visit the author's website at: www.JosephMiguelArt.net

For permissions contact:
J.Mig1982@gmail.com

ISBN-13: 978-1-7359926-0-0 (Hardcover)
ISBN-13: 978-1-7359926-1-7 (Paperback)
ISBN-13: 978-1-7359926-2-4 (E-Book)

CONTENTS

PROLOGUE
'THE 50S'

THE GRANDFATHER CLOCK ticked backward against its jaded self-will, settling into the year nineteen hundred and fifty-eight. The Cold War between America and the Russians was spicing and heating up. During that year, Russia gained an advantage over the United States in the overall space race by launching an impressive invention called Sputnik 1. Sputnik was the first-ever artificial satellite that orbited around the Earth's circumference successfully from space.

That was all before any human lifeform had been believed to have traveled to the Earth's moon. The two countries had also been sparring in the gritty contest of nuclear weaponry during that span. The US had already dropped two devastating atomic bombs on Japan in the 1940s during WWII; however, a nuclear form of obliteration became the prime directive for cost-effectiveness and bulk purchasing during the Cold War period.

The United States Air Force had developed a classified and top-secret covert mission titled Project A119. The project was also referred to as 'A Study of Lunar Research Flights.' That close to the chest mission's objective was to travel to the moon and detonate a nuclear warhead on the foreign planet's soil, with specific intentions to impose both dominance and power over the Soviets and any other viable threats that loomed in the American's rearview. It was also dreamt up to kill two trophy birds with one gigantic stone. To essentially win both races in a single blow, leaving the USSR behind to freeze to death in their beloved Mother Russia.

For the duration of recent history, Project A119 was considered blacklisted by the United States government. It was never even attempted, due to the loose fact that zero nuclear explosions could ever be seen from Earth or had been documented from the neighboring rock's orbit during the late 1950s, and for the key reason that numerous individuals on the project described such abuse of power as irrationally immoral.

Ultimately, Project A119 was, in fact, carried out once in 1958 and again in the early 1960s. However, neither mission was executed in full, and no nuclear warheads were ever detonated on Earth's intriguing satellite.

Most importantly, none of the two clandestine teams who made the journey to the Moon's illustrious face to carry out the secretive missions were ever seen or heard from again.

Two HIGHLY DECORATED United States Air Force astronauts with the last names of Wolfe and Kamisky attempted the first daring ascent to accomplish Project A119. The men had landed cleanly on the Tycho crater close to the initial darkest side of the Moon's never before graced upon surface. Humanity had been afforded the luxury of viewing its Moon from their forgiving Earth only by the half lighter side of the mysterious rock. The remaining dark void of the sphere was never offered visibility and remained hidden from an earthling's technological perspective.

That very void was where the thin black line of the Sphynx had resided for billions of millennia.

The mission had been running smoothly at the safe landing touchdown on Tycho, with the officers removing the warhead from their spacecraft, on the verge of wrapping things up to blast back homeward.

Wolfe felt the excruciating heat within himself while he stared off into the pitch-dark region of the alien landscape, becoming taken over by an ancestral thought-transference of mind manipulation that radiated from the ancient dark walkers. A horde of the prehistoric beasts was close, witnessing firsthand the devastating raw potential of man-made nuclear power that the disdainful mortal race had then become so dangerously accustomed to.

Wolfe fell as uncomplicated prey as the first-ever leviathan approached him from the Moon's chilling abyss. The tough astronaut was melted down in the murky weightlessness, silver space suit and all, and was replicated by the primeval Sphynx in a matter of minutes.

Kamisky had gotten smart and knew something was amiss with his comrade, Wolfe. Kamisky had been the more decorated of the two men, and he slyly attempted to go rogue and hop on board the ship to leave his unfortunate cohort in the space dust. He'd almost succeeded with his solo escape, as the shuttle's engines roared with vigor, while terrifying fear blanketed Kamisky's face through his white NASA helmet atop the exotic crust.

The only explosion to ever be seen or heard from the Moon's irregular formation was caused by the Sphynx, when an army of full-on abominations with oozy eggs for eyes swarmed the outside perimeter of the American craft. Kamisky combusted into fiery magma, moments before the entirety of his aircraft exploded along with him, in a certifiable display of sinisterly alien evil.

"I am become death, the destroyer of worlds…"
- J. Robert Oppenheimer

I

I T WAS ANYTHING but a run of the mill or innocent type of storm. The night had morphed into something sinister and unforgiving. The trees swayed violently as the wind howled. His chopper ripped into the rain like a steel vessel plunging forward through a chaotic abyss. The wicked climate showed face mere minutes from leaving the hospital after another draining spell of work. One more grueling shift spent offering his fervent zeal to the ever-pressing duality of his fellow mankind.

The deluge splashed the young man's face as he rode, practically blinding him; however, his troubled mind began to cool with the speed and unpredictable caliber of the newfound inclement weather. It was nowhere near ugly, that particular night. The moon perched ever full and was disgustingly scintillating, as the clouds above the magnificent Douglas firs and Ponderosa pines sat scattered just enough that the brilliant cylindrical sphere would occasionally rear its steadfast beauty before his wind-shocked eyes.

No other vehicles occupied that particular two-lane forest stretch of Colorado roadway. It was only Damien Winters and his custom candy and chrome Indian Scout 60, screaming through the dead of night after another punishing stint at Mason General Hospital.

As his burly machine pierced through the black, the man's ravaged mind fell away into a set of offbeat reminiscence. He pondered crucial life decisions and situations that swirled within his exhausted and worn-out psyche. Freshly turned 31 years of age, thanks to a nonchalant mid-October morning thirty-six hours ago, an image of hitting fifty and turning grey, while nevertheless slaving away for a decrepit medical facility that demanded so much of his life's original essence, made the melancholy flood downward into his brain's gooey surface.

Damien prided himself in his pressing line of work, but his extreme job duties had become increasingly more excruciating for his mind throughout the years. Now pushing ten solid years on the job inside the same demanding emergency unit, Winters' empathetic identity had begun to take a damaging turn for the worse.

He was more of a creative soul at heart, enjoying artistic endeavors like sculpting and drawing (however sloppy and off-kilter for that unimportant matter) as well as popping off an occasional black and white with his old Pentax film camera. His photography skills were amateur at best, with benchmarks such as framing and composition remaining primitive within his overall creative toolkit. However, film photography's olden art form never failed to fill his heart with an unbridled joy. The sweeping Montana landscapes while vacationing with Leigh, or the fraction of a moment to freeze just the right smile of a portrait subject's striking features were what the man truly lived for. Those expressive outlets were the aspects of an imaginative spirit that filled Damien's time outside of his troubling hospital career.

A lone ranger vehicle approached from up ahead in the gloomy distance, with its headlights lighting up the road like a movie screen's abduction sequence. He deliberated of the poor souls wasting away, day after day, at careers they wholeheartedly despised, one day snapping out of their collective coma to realize they'd made the grandest and most atrocious fallacies of all: they'd failed along their uneventful and oh-so merry ways to follow their inspirational and creative originality. Instead, opting to get all cozied and comfortable, while sledding through the shitty monotony of existence like it was some gushy security blanket to snuggle up to when the dark and stormy stuff began to creep under the bedroom door at night. Until one day, forty years down the road, they would yet come to realize that the blanket never existed in the fucking first place. It was only their fears and conditioned insecurities that held them back from what they truly desired in a challenging and, at many times, downright nasty realm of human consciousness. The petrifying unease to go against the grain and seek out something that had made them feel adequate inside, however hokey.

But, most of all, Damien wanted out of his unassuming little mountain town. He'd moved on once before, away from California for a fresh and invigorated start after a horrific tragedy for a shot at new beginnings.

His state of mind gave the riding man no clear objectives or splendid endgames. He craved only to get home to his darling Leigh and act entirely against his truest nature. Then just hit the ground riding, with her arms wrapped around him while they cut through the murky black. To never look back and be perfectly alright with that. The young man couldn't figure out or understand his strange and impulsive demeanor right then, but he knew he wished to be rid of Heatherton, Colorado once and for all.

Winters found himself operating in a state of autopilot, staring dead to rights into the dreary night. The rain continued to whack his face mid-ride, fogging up his vision in a dreamy sort of way. His shoulder-length chestnut hair peeked out from underneath his shiny black rider's cap, whipping to and fro behind him with some help from the gusting winds.

He then entered a bizarre nuance of psychosis that was not quite present. It was hypothetical in nature, neither being distant past nor future at all. The evening's workload had been jagged and rough at the old hospital, where, moments ago, he'd changed out of his usual work scrubs to gladly clock out and leave for the night.

Damien's unit had been functioning on a skeleton crew for over half the year, barely able to keep up around the clock, with twenty-four-hour dizzying demands and malfunctioning healthcare politics. The load doubled and tripled within the same time frame for his diminishing unit, with colleagues being gobbled up and spat out like gnarly steak gristle, or replaced like a decadent Mars chocolate bar in the mitts of some schoolyard bully on his first date night at the drive-in.

An emergency position within the medical system did suit several admirable aspects of the reeling man's intricate personality, but unfortunately not nearly enough. The stresses of grappling with life and death scenarios each and every day, along with being forced to think on the spot during moments of tragedy, took their damaging tolls over his lengthy tenure.

IN SHORT, THE aging care facility was going under. It was giving way to bigger and more sophisticated technologies throughout and across the Colorado state line. Grandiose and rapidly evolving centers had been running for decades within neighboring cities of the prestigious Centennial State. Big business hospitals with charming supremacy appeal and multiple locations, flaunting catchy and hotshot names were the flourishing entities within the bloated healthcare conglomerate. Those big organizations would continue to build rich and state-of-the-art buildings as if money grew on some poor chemo patient's withering away apple tree. Technologies would get topped, then replaced, and topped all over again. As Mason General became a relic by the current 2020 standard of healthcare operations, the cycle went on and on. The ripe facility was just over a hundred years old, yet had adapted like a fine wine during every part of the most extremist forms of business propagandas over countless trials and grueling tribulations.

The entire healthcare blueprint was changing across the board. Not just in his insignificant little dink of Heatherton, but also state to state that stretched countrywide.

Damien's mind, excruciated with distress, shifted a thought to a plethora of his former bosses during his long and uproarious career. There had been twelve of them in nearly a decade. They would march on into the unit with enthusiastic and lively spirits, get chewed up like Swiss cheese by their superiors or the insurmountable demands of a fresh and inhumane business model, then get shit right back out into the unemployment vat. Visions of their many faces danced around in the riding man's brain, giving way to each other; then they'd wash away and transmute into a new and confused look of a boss that never stood a puncher's chance from the jump.

Back in his rookie years, his team had consisted of twenty-two strong and brilliant hospital operators. In recent times, they'd been hammered down to eleven burned out and spiraling head cases. The workers demanded change, and so did he. When a fellow employee would run for the hills, or quit on the spot after a sudden mental breakdown, he'd be sure to inform the remaining lot of survivors to not hold their proverbial breath on getting a replacement any time soon. He knew that was precisely what the world was boiling down to, not only in his thankless world of mercenary healthcare but also within surrounding business models of various paunchy organizations that swept the nation. Juggernaut conglomerates were giving in to insatiable greed and the grossest extremes of skewed and alarming capitalisms.

Damien believed in ideas, such as pure capitalism, at its initial intention. Capitalism was what stabilized America and had allowed it to take off running for a beaming shot at a future of wonder and glory. He concluded that the twisted realms of decaying capitalism, powering the country in 2020, were anything but democratic. Quite frankly, it was more so a display of debauchery bordering on tyranny.

His frightening ruminations pained him much; however, he'd believed for the longest time that democracy never existed inside the "civilized" world.

Freedom sure as hell didn't, either.

He fought through several more clouded and shaky ideas, such as a great many people probably believed that if they prayed hard enough to their flags or their country, and even planted their red, white and blue spangled rags firmly gleaming on their spiffy porches to wave in the early morning sunshine, that they were safe and living that sought-after freedom they'd so desperately been promised throughout their lives. But stripes and stars and governments, and especially countries, never allowed their people to authentically ever be free. That mirage was a bold-faced lie, a farce in the blazing sands of a desert overruled by glorified and nasty scum.

The system only takes from its citizens, one way or another, and that was the vile human way of the slimy suits and ties that pulled all the strings from high up inside their glistening watchtowers. That same system always blinded the people on the ground with sexy slick jargon and late-night television loops, all the while wrenching and manipulating mind after mind into a non-productive shell of drooling conformity that had buried their spirits of infinite potential, choosing instead to settle down into a soggy midsection and an empty crinkled up bag of greasy potato chips.

It wanted its citizens to exclusively smile and nod, give up and give in to what they wanted and expected from "we" the people. Then, year after year, a tiny percentage of jelly-filled cretins would hoot and holler all the way to the bank while taxes blew through the floor, suicide rates shot down to hell, and home prices became laughably unbalanced in the most used and abused of American neighborhoods.

Damien had housed a skewed belief that raw freedom resided within the dimensions of one's own vivid mind. The abstract and perceived richness of the psyche's unique and complicated size was a human being's only reservoir of what could be coined as living freedom. One that did not conform to cookie-cutter ideals and decimated principles from the gluttonous masses' shadow puppet masters. Those random and piercing undertakings deemed the most troubling for Winters, as the Colorado storm cut through his leather jacket and settled into his grizzled and unsettled core.

Damien would have extensive and relatively enjoyable conversations regarding diverse types of deep-rooted human morality behaviors with his cherished friend and colleague, Kip Wells. Kip had joined the Operators Unit two years after Winters had gotten on the force. Damien had trained him for a full week out of the mandatory six weeks probationary period for the stressful job. The two men took some time to become unshakeable confidantes, but they worked wonderfully together when the hospital crap never failed to hit the bedpan metal. They were the same age, with Kip being seven months the elder. They had proven to be an unorthodox type of duo over the years, with

Damien being witty and charismatic, whereas Kip remained reserved and more awkward in personality and nature.

THE PHANTOM CAR passed by with ease, probably becoming startled by the charging roar of Damien's motorbike filling the midnight air with its mechanical thunder. He was back to being all alone and present within his ever-changing mental convictions: solitary with his log cabin nearly four miles up into the dark and melancholic, yet almost morbid and peaceful stretch of Colorado forest road.

As the rain mixed with his torrent rate of speed, hypnotizing every unconscious spectator, he'd only glimpsed the beast jump onto his path seconds before an inevitable collision. The thing entered as a blur and leaped out into the narrow highway right in front of his throaty pride and joy. In a last gasp attempt of desperate and heightened instinct, Winters lurched his motorcycle left, but with the slick asphalt and sudden change of trajectory, laid himself down sideways and brutally onto his left shoulder. The bike continued moving full speed ahead with no jockey at the wheel, sending it to smack kamikaze into a huge Ponderosa pine just off the narrow roadside. The man was fortunate to land on a greasier part of asphalt, to where he could shift his weight onto the full of his back and slide like a child at a waterpark straight up the two-lane blackness.

After the impact, he had no inclination that he'd shattered the bones in his arm in three clustered sections. As his waterslide maneuver came to a halt in the middle of the solid tar, a crack of thunder bellowed from high above, followed by a bright zigzag of lightning in rum succession. Before he could take a wheezing sigh of a labored breath to assess, the burst of skylight offered a shadow moving out toward the downed man's immediate right. It was indistinct and moved quickly, with Damien only catching a hazy glimpse from his fudged up peripheral vision. He managed to use both of his gloved hands to sit up from his back in the roadway, most likely due to the pure adrenaline rush from the harrowing crash, while disregarding his mangled upper limb.

Before he could turn to face his demise, the hulking thing was upon him. It launched like a lunatic linebacker gunning for a scrambling quarterback. He'd only had time to perch up half-way before being wholly afflicted. Before the bewildered mortal could even bat an eye of pure shock, he was on his back again with the crazed mass in full mount. The force of his sudden attacker was tremendously unexpected, causing Damien's helmet to smack, crushing onto the thick wet asphalt, rattling him down to his muddled existence. Winters had never worn a fully enclosed motorcycle helmet while riding his esteemed machine. He'd owned the cap version with the remainder of his head and face being exposed to the outside elements.

He finally realized what the bombarding creature was, but could not altogether fathom its absolute hatred for the human species. It looked to be some form of a mountain lion—the largest one he'd ever seen in real life or on the tube.

The possessed thing wasted no time with its bidding.

It savagely sunk a set of jagged grinders down into Damien's right side. His leather coat had been shredded during his initial slip and slide, with only his wet t-shirt laying vulnerable and showing around that particular area. The sphinx bit with such force that Winters could audibly make out a crunching noise, even as the sheets of rain continued to descend on top of him and his monstrous assailant. Again, the mortal man felt no pain against the ravaging. He just let out a deep and brutish grimace following the grinding of the chomp. Damien found himself working on sheer adrenaline at that point, fight or flight in the rawest of forms.

He had to do something fast, or he'd inevitably become one dead son of a bitch.

The wretched lion released the man's side and swung its giant cranium directly in front of his frightened face while attempting a kind of over-aggressive stare down. The beast had blood and flesh entangled within its chops, and Damien could physically smell the hot and steaming breath that blasted in waves from the cat's gaping death trap. The creature had become so close to the young man's face that some of his own dripping gore oozed from the thing's stew and onto his smooth cheek and forehead. Strangely, the feeling of his own lifeblood splashing down grew in him a wave of morbid and exotic excitement.

Suddenly, his mind flashed and flooded back to being a boy and having gruesome boxing matches in the backyard with his older foster brother at their childhood home. Vince had matured fast as a boy and had towered over the smaller Damien during their young and formidable years. They would strap on the red Everlast boxing mitts and slug it out like Ali and Foreman.

Truthfully, it was more like David and Goliath in that particular and nostalgic arena. Vince would never fail to leak Damien's nose within minutes of the brawl, but each time he did that, Damien would find clarity within the brotherly chaos and retaliate with a savvy style of vengeance. There were several occasions where Vince would be forced to cry mercy because little Damien would rally with a counterstroke in the heat of fraternal battle.

As Winters shifted his bending mind back to reality, the ugly thing outstretched its savage mouth, while it hovered above his face. The over-wild mammoth of a creature unleashed a heinous hissing sound, as its enormous head crept with a slithering grace toward the neck of the battered and confused human. In seconds, Damien would be choking on his own vital fluids. His jugular would be opened up, and that'd be all she fucking wrote. Dinner served warm to the hellish vile of a wretch.

At the last fleeting moment, he remembered his trusted Spyderco pocket knife. He carried the nifty blade everywhere. His mind had become so warped that he wasn't even sure he'd had it on him that time, or if he'd lost it during his insane motorcycle splashdown. While stuck on his back, lying more or less helpless, he dug into the usual jeans pocket and found the familiar blade.

A millisecond before the monstrous oddity grasped his throat, he pulled the carver, squeezed the release button to spring free the cut of steel, and sunk it hard and crudely with his left hand into the beast's right cheekbone. It howled something fierce and foreign in return, a dumbstruck evil yelp of surprise, but barely took notice of the unfamiliar display of human retaliation. Damien pulled his knife from the lion's skull and stabbed again. He found a home directly into the eye socket of the enormous and evil feline. When he yanked his blade back from the peculiar and yolky looking eyeball, the animal's blood jetted and spilled all over his face and eyes.

The overbearing orbs of depravity were nothing short of insanely irregular. It looked as if they had no retinas or pupils within them; just large, pulsating white discs as if no real eyes were in there at all. Before making full optical contact with the brutish sphinx, fear and adrenaline threw Winters into a crazed type of fit. Once the spilling ichor and gunk entered his line of vision, the man believed, for a fractured moment of plain absurdity, that the lion's face had somehow shifted on command. Almost as if it had changed into something else. It all but came off as passing for a human veneer, but that couldn't be possible.

The large cat managed a final biting attempt at his jugular, but at the last second, Damien sprung his right arm up in front of his face while the creature began to feast on his leathered and unfortunate other limb.

Winters stabbed and stabbed and stabbed!

The face, neck, and body, all in rancid succession, along with various clustered sections of the animal's furry right sidewall were being butchered by his knife-wielding left hand.

At last, the bulging sphinx withdrew its sickening grip from his shredded middle arm and collapsed in a heap, squarely on top of him. The man had slashed the puzzling tormentor thirty times with his faithful blade, and could barely believe the thing continued to breathe life while it rested its domineering frame on top of his wet and broken body.

The rain kept falling, as a burst of lightning lit skyward once again. Damien lay motionless with the hairy demon affixed next to him, listening as it gave a final labored heave that was both satisfying and gut-wrenching. Once Winters was sure the aggressive depravity was fully lamented, he tried to remove himself from underneath the dead and burdensome weight. The pain in his shattered shoulder screamed into his brain, a friendly reminder that adrenaline and a fight to survive only lasted on level invincible for so long. His shaggy hair spilled halfway into his chiseled face, as the man's entire housing remained consumed by the expired lioness.

The overtaken mortal made a final effort to free himself from the suffocating bulk as the rainfall toppled downward in tumbling sheets. He ultimately gave in to his feeble attempt, instead choosing to relax his entire body onto his back in the chilling cold of the forest drag. He turned his head to one side and lost consciousness.

II

'THREE DAYS BEFORE THE CRASH'

"**D**OCTOR BOUDREAUX, PLEASE REPORT TO THE OPERATING ROOM, STAT!" He had heard the overhead announcement twice in succession, but he'd missed the first pass of the three callouts altogether. He was fast asleep; not exactly snoozing on the job, but instead, lounged on his back in one of the MD sleep rooms on the lobby floor next to his office corner.

Gabriel couldn't recall the precise minute he'd conked out, but he knew it was the middle of the night. The well-detailed physician blinked several times in his laid-out position, the small sofa in the quiet hospital break room providing a loose bedding of comfort for the longer framed general surgeon. He'd been working like a madman during the recent months, but his mind never wavered from his meticulous civic duties of on-call hospital slice and dice.

Boudreaux finally sat up, allowing the black carpet sofa to give off a gentle squeak with his almost mechanical rising. He went to wipe his face but realized his glasses were still perched to his prominent nose. His pearl-coated lab trench remained glued to his athletic body, along with his favorite pair of formal white loafers.

He had just performed a minor operation for a gall bladder removal before scrubbing out around midnight to catch some much-needed shut-eye in the warmly lit sleep room when Damien's voice beckoned from the airwaves of dear old Mason General. He knew it was Winters, even while he slept soundly in wait for another call. Damien's voice was distinct, and it made the level-headed doctor rise from his slumber with a heightened purpose.

Actually, he'd liked Damien. The two of them worked for Mason like passionate bloodhounds. It was more of a professional curiosity, knowing that Winters was neither a fellow physician nor highly educated like he was. There was just something extra about the young man. Perhaps, it was the way they'd joke around in passing inside the blinding hallways during the strenuous nights. Or the fact that Damien seemed to take great pride in his work, always being a reliable source to assist him with any information needed pertaining to the usual hospital humdrum.

Gabriel made certain that his hair of slicked black was in perfect order before checking his wristwatch: it was well into the early morning witching hours. At least he'd gotten to sleep a few hours before being interrupted.

"This better be good, Damien," the tall and trim veteran mumbled to himself while rearranging his tie and gracefully stepping out into the hallway toward the nearby Operating Room.

It had been a gunshot victim. There were not many cases of that specific pedigree in little old Heatherton. He continued down the hall and practically ran into his charge nurse right outside the OR front door. She looked borderline frantic, but that meant nothing to the steely Boudreaux. Even after he'd found out that a teenage girl had been shot: with her own father's pea shooter, one that should never have been loaded inside the house in the first place, he'd gone away to scrub up as quickly as possible.

He washed his hands in a small room next to the OR, with steady calm and brilliant purpose. He was still slightly groggy from the power nap, but his mind was too precise and in control to be tired or unsharp. Damien interrupted him again while he prepped for surgery:

"DOCTOR BOUDREAUX, PLEASE REPORT TO THE OPERATING ROOM, STAT!"

"I'm already here, Damien. But it's so reassuring that you're always awake and ready for action," he said to himself before taking off his wedding ring and placing it in his dress pant pocket.

He finished washing and removed the Rolex his teenage son had picked out for him two birthdays ago. He was just about ready to go. All he needed was to mask up for the job he was designed to excellently carry out. Damien's even-toned resonance abruptly flooded his brain once again: never frantic with his overhead paging, but more so purposeful and with dignified reasoning, he thought. Just like him. Gabriel admired Damien Winters for his coolness under the pressures of his own demanding craft:

"CODE BLUE, 1ST FLOOR, OPERATING ROOM!"

Boudreaux heard Damien's voice four times back to back, but he was back inside the OR after the third bellow.

"We're losing her, doctor!"

A new Anesthesiologist was a bit too amped up for the late-night hour, perhaps not catching enough shut-eye of his own during the every-so-often hospital downtime.

Boudreaux, however, was perfectly centered and unmistakably at ease. He'd seen it all inside the walls of Mason General. He'd seen it, even worse, back in New York when he'd first started out after the treacherous years of medical school. He was the most decorated surgeon in the small-time Colorado medical center, and everyone knew it.

The girl on the table did, in fact, look more or less dead, even though his heart rate never spiked with the absolute realization of her dire predicament. The bullet had passed through the meatier section of her upper leg. It was an apparent accidental firing, the teenager not realizing the gun was loaded while she played with it after being awakened from a bad dream. She had lost puddles of blood, but blood was what doctor Gabriel Boudreaux pretty much lived for.

"Give me the paddles, nurse, if you please," he said.

Perfectly sound with his request, while he stood his sophisticated self over the damsel upon his operating slab. The youngin looked no older than his own teenage daughter. That didn't heighten his senses or trouble him in any way. It was only a quick notice. The patient had her pajama top on, but the bottoms had been stripped away to access the unfortunate damage. The nurse handed over the defibrillator after he unbuttoned her white and pink shirt to expose her giving up chest.

"CLEAR!"

The patient's dying body rocked and gyrated, but offered no life. A consistent flatline and a blaring Code Blue button greeted the recently awakened surgeon of authoritative conviction.

"I'm going to hit her, again" he dryly stated while staring through his spectacles at her closed down eyes and bloodied young veneer.

A single thought entered his mind before the second shockwave engaged from the heart resurrecting instrument. He flashed back to a patient that had gotten away from him during the snowier months of his rookie years on the East coast. It had been a boy, that time.

Only ten years old.

He was performing a routine hernia operation when the poor thing flatlined right in the middle of the procedure. Gabriel was fresh and new at his surgical artistry back then, and he'd never experienced a child stop breathing right before his eyes while under the courtesy of his steady knife. His team did everything possible to revive the patient, but the boy was not interested in the continuation of living. It was a tough pill to swallow for a year or two, but he had gotten over it. He had to. His mind was too detailed and precise, not to.

"CLEAR!!"

The second surge of electricity ignited the young lady, sending her heart jolting back to life. The Anesthesiologist looked green; perhaps it was something that he'd eaten, thought Boudreaux. The charge nurse remained behind him, grinning a wave of exquisite relief.

Gabriel proceeded, "I've got her back now, people. We're not going to lose this young lady. Not on my watch -- Nurse, a scalpel, if you please. Monitor her vitals. I'm going in to remove that bullet."

III

'THE EARLY YEARS'

DAMIEN WINTERS WAS a foundling child at the ripe age of two years and seven months old. He'd hardly known a thing about his biological mother, finding out much later in his teenage life that she'd died when he was around nine. The circumstances surrounding her death, given to him by his foster folks over a steaming meal on a March night, were vague. His nonfictional father was proud of being the local drunk wherever he parked his imbecilic ass and eventually settled down in a boxy California town called Rypon. He worked construction and banged sloppy barflies in his fermented spare time, finally finding the wherewithal to kick off from liver disease in Damien's early teens. Up until both of their deaths, his authentic parents had never reached out once to check up or inquire about their abandoned son. Damien barely knew a speck about either of them, only catching tidbits of their deaths from his fosters.

When Damien's adopted parents finally broke the news to him over the longest dinner of his adolescent life, on a gone but never forgotten Carmel, California evening in a buried and distant time, it had nearly broken him. They had tried their best to jazz up his loser parents and to make them out not to be villainous or malevolent deadbeats, but it was a tough pill to swallow for a teenage boy that had been continuously lied to his entire life. It was also difficult for his fosters having to break it to their long-standing son that they weren't his actual and genuine birthparents.

It was hard all around the table on that pivotal California evening. Damien had become upset over dinner at the news, while he stared down at a plate of his most favorite dish of pork chops and gravy with rice. He managed to compose himself, finally breaking his trance and gawking back over at the only loving people he'd ever really known. All of a sudden, they had come off as looking foreign to the honey brown-eyed boy. In only a fraction of a moment, he became confused, showing a shocking slant of perspective about them. The gut shot had skewed his brain in an alarming way that made him queasy and unsteady in his comfortable dining room chair.

Yes, they had wanted to tell him more of his mother and father at that cozy table back in the March year of something-or-other, but instead he'd risen from his chair and hugged them both, while a steady dose of tears flowed throughout the home. From that day forward, after only the age of twelve, Winters refused to mention or even inquire about his biological family ever again.

The fractured boy could've given less than two shits of what his genuine last name even was. Ernst had voiced it to him as he pecked away with his fork at the plate of brown gravy in the rich rice pool, but the oddball name went straight in one ear and right back out the other. He'd removed it from his spongy memory bank for the duration of eternity the second Ernst had uttered the word. His last name would always and forever be Winters.

Something's not right…

I don't feel well.

I think I laid down my motorcycle.

I'm scared.

I can't open my eyes…

Sue and Ernst Winters were Damien's foster parents, who had adopted him as an abandoned infant. They lived in sunny California where Damien was born, calling a sleepy coastal town near Monterey

Bay their home and shelter. They'd had a biological son of their own, Vince, who was three years Damien's elder.

The Winters had ultimately decided to adopt an orphaned child, primarily because they didn't believe in bringing another human being directly from their own genetic pool into the bustling world after they'd already had Vince, and also because there were so many other children already out there who were painfully desperate for love and a proper upbringing. There was a genuine and sterling level of nobility in such an approach, although misunderstood by the many masses of already living groups of mundane humanity.

Sue and Ernst had been classic high school sweethearts, picking up those garden-fresh sparks of young adolescence and holding on to each other for dear life from the infancy stages of their dizzying wonder years.

Damien had repeatedly found himself struggling while growing up, trying to comprehend how two people could stay together for so long from such a brutally young age. He wondered how two people could be together for such a long time when neither person really knew much about themselves from the beginning to wholly endure such a daunting and devoted journey. It was both a commitment and an absolute sacrifice to be wholeheartedly respected: one that Damien never had the pleasure of experiencing inside the confines of his own elaborately rocky life.

Sue and Ernst were very much the conservative and red-blooded American type folk, both politically and in their everyday lives. They were the exacting brand to always pay the taxman early, and aggressively resented being labeled as God-fearing people, even though they were just that. Not Bible thumpers or Holy Roller wackos, no-no. In other words, the Winters were all about their pride of country and ground things out to make ends meet for themselves and their two growing boys. They didn't have to rob Peter to pay Paul, but they also weren't crazily well off financially, either. They were a fearsome couple, one that knew how to pinch their dollars and piece together what they could after Uncle Sam came knocking in January and to also raise fine and rugged young men.

Ernst would've gladly worked his entire career for a large grocery spice plant, doing shipping and receiving; however, budget cuts and garbage politics kicked in one year and forced the plant to close its doors for good.

See, that was how Sue and Ernst Winters maneuvered throughout life. They may have been grossly predictable and maybe even boring to many rebellious standards, but they were consistent and ever-resilient working-class people. They had been there morning, noon, and night for Vince and Damien, and without question would reach out to the ends of the Earth to help instill upstanding values in their sons along the way. Sure, they may have played life a little too close to the chest, with working the same vanilla jobs, never daring to jump on an airplane in fear of crashing or terrorist hijack, making sure the neighbors' pools always stayed above ground, and religiously watching the local news stories for key societal intel every night.

The Winters were vintage American people, alright.

On the flippant and shadier side of the coin, which every coin in the human world absolutely has, Sue and Ernst were by no means perfect people. Ernst housed a short fuse and a sharp as hell tongue, at times, and Sue, being a full-fledged Irish woman, buried her fair share of a mean streak, which coursed like vinegar through her richly saturated Celtic bloodline.

Ernst Winters was, without a doubt, one tough as nails and a hard-nosed working man, rising up at the ass crack of dawn every single day for over forty years of his adult life. Damien was cursed with being more of a nighthawk and would be up a select morning or two while Ernst was getting ready to head out the door for work. Ernst's over deliberate mannerisms were like a display of timeless clockwork, always making his cup of Folgers coffee with a dash of hazelnut creamer while microwaving a bowl of fresh steel-cut oatmeal before settling down into a hot and long morning shower. A young Damien could vividly reminisce the invigorating smells of steaming maples and brown sugared oats sifting together with the black hot coffee. The alluring rich swirl of breakfast aromas would seep in underneath his bedroom door during the early weekday hours of his childhood. He had developed a mastery, over time, to love that invigorating smell. It had never ceased to remind him of starting a day off with fortitude and owning it for what it was. It also provided him with the fondest memories of his handsome foster dad.

However, off-top and random, Ernst also happened to be a mighty fine bowler back in his glorious heyday. There used to be a breezy alley down by the beach only a stone's throw away from their quaint one-story home, off the Carmel coastline. Island Lanes was the name; where every ball thrown was a strike, and the pinball machines in the airy speakeasy never jammed up or broke down.

No gutter balls were ever allowed that close to the beach!

Ernst must've taken the alley's slogan literally. Being stocky and compact in frame, Ernst would palm his customized Roto Grip boulder of pearly black shine and nail ten in the pit with an envious smoothness. Vince would inevitably joke around with his father and say he reminded him of Barney Rubble out there, strutting a few tight baby steps in his nifty bowling shoes, before setting his rock out on the boards with devastating accuracy.

Ernst had one of those professional bowler's hooks that could make Norm Duke jealous. The shimmering Roto Grip would start way out on the right side of the lane, while practically hugging the looming channel. Then, at the last unfathomable second, sweep back and demolish the entire rack with a thunderous shatter. Sue would lounge about in one of the little colored seats off to the side, with her arms crossed over herself, watching her dearest family carry on with the slightest smirk on her fair and freckled face. Happy and content was Sue and Ernst Winters' recipe for living—relentlessly clinging to the smallest joys of life's goofy shenanigans, such as checking out her husband and two boys ha-ha and throwing stones at wooden sticks out near the oceanfront.

DAMIEN SUDDENLY FOUND himself thinking of them, although he couldn't be sure if his mangled thoughts were past, present, or future in a jumbled sequence of scattered time. It felt as if he were caged or asleep in a screwy realm where time didn't quite make sense any longer. One morbid and powerful curiosity that did rush intensely home to the young man was of wonder, if from beyond the grave, his loving foster parents were watching over him then, somehow guiding his actions throughout what was soon to become the most punishing trials of appalling chaos.

I fought with something out there in the darkness.

I hear a distant voice.

Now more voices.

One seems more familiar than the rest.

He's telling me he's trying to save me.

It feels like I'm sinking...

I think I'm dying...

DAMIEN'S FOSTER BROTHER, Vince, was the typical all-clichéd big brother type. Being only a couple of years apart in age, Vince would regularly remind the world exactly who the eldest son of the Winters family was. There were the usual brotherly skirmishes, as well as plenty of admiration in between and along the way. But after puberty, Vince had become the high school jock, and Damien was reduced to the dweeby creative type, writing short stories at night after homework and enjoying an occasional deer hunt with Ernst in his father's boyhood town out on California's northern edge, a place where the freshly killed big bucks tasted like warm barbecued butter.

Damien had all kinds of friends in his screwy high school days in Carmel, but the boy had been cursed with being a severely late bloomer. He got along well enough with every scholastic group during those years, whereas Vince emphatically chose the "in" crowd. High school was not an enjoyable life period for Damien Winters. It was more so an oddity than anything else, a mundane and strange conformity of silly antics and thumbs twiddling in overpopulated and stuffy classrooms. Perhaps he'd found the whole ordeal a dull commonplace, longing to ditch the predictability of numbered educational practices and head off on his own way, as soon as possible. Vince ate the whole thing up, enjoying its hip and trendy structures and "cool" kid influences until the well-drained and dried up completely.

Vince had been a linebacker on the varsity football team. He was a scrappy one, at least to Damien's biased opinions. He would watch Vince from the stands and admire his brother, while he made smooth tackles on the glistening blades of green, forcing timid half-backs to cough up the pigskin under the Friday night lights of breezy Carmel.

When Damien finally moved to Colorado after Sue and Ernst's sudden deaths, the brothers had grown even more apart from each other. Vince had a stoic career as a fresh district attorney, working terribly long hours and climbing up the legal ranks of the structured system. He was married with adorable twin girls. Vince was the blueprint American dream kind of guy, much like his biological parents. He'd gobbled up the trophy wife fresh outta high school, and the twins along with the white picket fence shortly after.

Vince's life had become a picturesque Carlton Cards ordeal, postage stamp never optional. The glaring thing was, at least, what Damien had suspected in his unpredictable and off-kilter thought gatherings, that Vince had been lied to somewhere along the way. He was a supportive husband and father, but his work literally ate up his life. It was all Vince could ever talk about and seemed to look forward to. During off-hours, he'd drink with passion and carry on yelling at the girls and belittling the wife during holiday lunches and dinners. Damien owned this wacko belief that the cookie-cutter existence of living was never really all it was cracked up to be.

It was just a flimsy surface material.

Once you pierce through the initial layer of the glam, things don't look so nice and Pottery Barn quality underneath. Vince appeared to have lost a vital piece of his truest self to a forced and conditioned persona, a global standardization of what life should and needed to be for safe acceptance within the world. 'We order you to get married by thirty, have children, and make goddamn well sure your camper van with the toilet seat warmer has plenty of gas in it when you take a second mortgage out on the townhouse.'

I'm being taken somewhere else.

Another floor? Another place??

Things seem different.

Colder...

The familiar voice has gone away.

What's happening?

THE CAR ACCIDENT that killed their parents was horribly taxing on the Winters boys. It was viciously unexpected, with a drunk driver colliding head-on with Sue and Ernst, as they drove home from a dinner date in Monterey one unforgettable Friday night. A night that was long dead and forever buried. Some plastered orthodontist had crossed the median and slammed his piece of shit Mercedes right into the exemplary couple around the ten o'clock evening hour. The prick had been hopped up on white wine and pills, but he wound up getting off easy because he had a crooked district judge friend suckling at his bulging back pocket.

Vince couldn't do much during that painful time. He was just getting his feet wet with his own lawyer's gig, while the judge that Mr. Mercedes had sucking his prick happened to be a real hardass that loved all things money. Sue and Ernst were killed instantly, while the scumbag avoided any jail time whatsoever. Damien's twin nieces had just been born, and he was in and out of the hospital visiting with Vince and his wife, Marie.

During those years, Damien spent most of his hours as a struggling artist, selling paintings and sculptures here and there to make his own ends meet. He got in close with a reputable art dealer in Carmel, who'd helped him boost sales on larger art pieces while offering a low commission. He also worked part-time at a local Mexican restaurant called El Burro in the heart of Carmel by the sea. The food was always exquisite, and the extra income didn't hurt for his overly expensive art supplies.

He had rented a small loft several blocks from his childhood home near the beach. He enjoyed being close to Sue and Ernst. He would often visit for suppers and chit chats over a few beers and a relaxing ball game. Ernst adored the Athletics; while Damien had always been a Brewers fan. It was the hats he'd liked as a boy, not really caring who was winning or losing the affair. He merely enjoyed the friendly company with his parents. They'd discuss new drawings or artworks he'd been working on, with his parents beaming the proudest of smiles if he announced a big sale on one of his various creative masterpieces.

A few short months after their fateful deaths, Damien began to develop a grim and unpleasant assumption of the world around him while it remained dominated by the likes of humanity. The gripping trauma of losing them in a single blow tore the man limb from limb. His anxiety and paralyzing panic attacks spiked, while his strained relationship with Vince became increasingly distant. He took to drinking more often than he should, and began to pop a Xanax or Paxil, from time to time, to feebly mask the gaping open wounds he was carrying from inside. His deep depression periods would cause him to paint and create less often, but there were instances when he used his mind's festering darkness to materialize some undeniably incredible works.

ALL OF A sudden, he could feel the ghosts of his poor parents creeping into the heart of his brain waves, pleading for him to help them in a way he never could. They'd never planned on being snuffed out from the world, but then again, who ever did? Unless a person ended up lying in some bathtub with a razor blade and a bottle of Merlot nestled in their soapy mitts, judgment day probably always felt like a big old shocking surprise. Once he had packed up the little he had left in his oceanside loft and high-tailed it for a novel start in the mountains, he was hired shortly after at Mason General Hospital.

IV

'ONE DAY BEFORE THE CRASH'

"**E**MERGENCY OPERATOR, WHAT is your Emergency?" huffed Damien Winters in his curt and professionally aired tone.

That standard introductory phrase was the greeting that every on-duty operator within the hospital setting was ordered to state during any type of potential emergency situation. The night in question had been the Damien and Kip show, a usual recurrence with how Mason General had been doing business in the scintillating year of the momentous 2020. On many evenings, the pair had found themselves as the last remaining stiffs in their office around the midnight hour, just before the graveyard shift changeover.

The phantom caller on the other line had hung up with a forceful click in Damien's right ear. His headset went from a frenetic static to a comfortable and much needed dead silence. It had probably been some barely coherent nurse upstairs on an understaffed floor that had dialed the OSU emergency line by mistake, he'd thought. Scenarios such as those happened all too frequently.

"Why can't these nurses figure out how to use a frickin' phone?" bellowed Kip Wells from across the other side of the claustrophobic Basement office.

The men would usually station themselves at the very opposite ends of the laughably small office unit. It was a tactic that worked well for the tandem, being able to cover the entire floor plan of button panels and daunting alarm systems peppered throughout the tomb-like layout. Whenever the friendly colleagues needed to coordinate on a specific code or assignment on the fly, they'd meet up in the middle of the floor and talk shop.

There were six workstations in total, separated by a weak center divide between them. The blockade was an ugly and tasteless barrier, boasting half of a tan color with a rough felt carpet material, and the other side flaunted a thin cut of cheap and clear Plexiglas. The Operators' home base was dinky in unassuming stature, tucked strategically in the far west corner of the very bottom floor in the turn of the century geriatric medical center. In grimly ironic fashion, the OSU, or Operator Services Unit, was situated directly next to the Pathology department's boisterous front door. In fact, it was the Morgue door, a sub-divisional entity within general Pathology.

Damien finally responded.

"Christ, if I know, Kipper. Maybe they all switched to decaf up there. They're all moseying around half-cocked and shit."

The underground employees were wide awake, however. They had no choice in the matter. It was their utmost duty to respond instantly to any incoming transaction or code protocol, no matter how mundane or life-threatening in nature. If a patient suddenly switched from living to dead, several floors up in the Intensive Care Unit, the OSU was the first to respond by receiving a sounding alarm on a panel within their office, stating the nature of the code and the exact location of it.

If a crazed mental patient decided to snatch a fresh newborn from the wailing Labor and Delivery ward, a signal would ring out from a wristlet tag on the child that linked up to a specialized computer in Kip and Damien's office, one which would signal the exact location of the attempted kidnapping. It would then be their job to launch a set of detailed notifications and directive commands to hospital security and other designated staff on the labor floor. They'd finally all collectively work together in an attempt to rectify the pressing situation.

The Communications office, where the operators ran their command center, had to be entered via a five-digit numbered button code, which was also monitored by a surveillance camera attached to the access door around the clock. The camera's purpose was to record each and every individual who attempted access to the OSU.

For the record, Communications was also a secondary slang moniker for the Operator Services Unit. There were entrance buttons under each desk inside the office, with smaller cameras attached to customized phones connected to them, to buzz in personnel that came knocking at any unholy hour for a variety of business necessities. Doctors came by often to swap out pagers they had inadvertently dropped in a toilet upstairs or had misplaced somewhere throughout their grueling workday. Pager battery replacements was another off the cuff reasoning for a plethora of other hospital entities to demand entry into the multi-functioning basement workspace.

The Operator Services Unit was frankly the front line of defense for Mason General Hospital.

The chaotic life force, so to speak.

When the shit went flying, to any severity or spray pattern, the dwindling team was expected to be all and ever knowledgeable. Crises of sudden and intense severities were incredibly challenging to comprehend on the fly, and over time, took their unfortunate toll on the two savvy night shift employees. It also proved daunting to wrap an outsider's brain strings around the fact that highly educated physicians and brainiac administrators would phone down in practical hysterics, pleading for wacky answers to the most baffling and jarring questions from the minds of Kip Wells and Damien Winters. They were expected to have those intricate fuckshow answers, and ninety-nine out of a hundred times, they most certainly did.

A previous boss had pulled Damien aside one day and told him that the OSU was the metaphorical tip of the spear in a military man's realm of terminologies. His superior at that time had been a former Marine Corps veteran, so he liked to use that type of lingo with Damien behind closed doors. Winters had habitually believed that his unit was, instead, the face of the shield, not so much the piercing dagger.

The claustrophobic basement room lay scattered with multiple ear-splitting and obnoxious alarm systems. Fire panels, hospital generator monstrosities, an emergency code custom designed telephone, even a backup microphone to boom procedures overhead if the power ever failed within the facility, managed to blanket the walls on one main side of things.

The humongous generator affixed to the far back wall next to the tiny office refrigerator was frankly a sight to behold. The mechanism lit up sporadically with dozens of green, red, and yellow bulbs to signify any electrical malfunction going on anywhere within the hospital's body. Or when the Engineers decided to incredulously test the bastard thing, which was more often than could barely be stomached. It was the loudest alarm in the entire office and by far the most obnoxious. When the generator would inevitably come to life and initiate, it felt as if anyone unlucky enough to be working anywhere within a mile's radius of it were stuck in an airplane hangar with no escape, while a landing jet-liner barreled straight for the remainder of their shrinking sanity.

However, that office tune wasn't a gust of powerful winds from a majestic 747.

Instead, it was a probing beep of a constant boom that would rattle an employee's brain right down to their chattering shoelaces. There was a silence button attached to the bottom left side of the device, and each time it became active with an alarm, whoever was nearest would practically sprint to the son of a bitch to push the kill switch.

The fire panel next to the generator had been blaring like some half-assed form of POW torture for seven straight hours. Damien was sitting on the primary side of the office with most of the dangerous and intimidating panels and gizmos, with the main hub of the devices residing clustered on a wall closest to his right. The Engineering department had been popping off constant and choppily random state testing for the generator and fire panels for the last three months and running. During each and every shift, those over-tested alarms within the sterile square prison would absolutely pulverize the minds of Wells and Winters.

Being a hospital operator meant you had to somehow think swiftly at any cost, while basically being hit in the face from any direction with a sledgehammer over and over again for the duration of the shift, along with other treacherous chirps and chatters from demanding colleagues, as well as general public transactions that poured in on the telephone circuits from folks inquiring about sickly in-house patients or any other variation of graphic medical advice.

Imagine hearing a tornado warning for a fire alarm that pounded over and over in a worker's face for several hours, while trying to communicate with a screaming MD who was jabbering about their work schedule changes, a schedule they should already know how to change all by themselves. Then having a patient die in a bed somewhere on floor four, which then ignites another incredulous tune of the Code Blue alarm, which would have to be announced with pinpoint precision over the collective loudspeakers. And again, having to dispatch a team in an attempt to save the dying patient's life, then documenting the morbid transaction after the Nursing Supervisor calls you looking for the Morgue to indirectly state that your efforts were all for naught, and finally to conclude everything promptly on paper, along with software filing for hospital legality purposes. The complex job entailed executing all of those things in scattered pieces at the exact same time.

If a sick call happened to roll in and Staffing didn't want to squeeze out the precious OT for any additional help, a single operator would be responsible for each of those crucial duties single-handedly. The unit revolved around the clock like a pure dispatch enterprise, and if an employee happened to get stuck working alone due to negligent hiring freezes from the finance studs upstairs, they'd be shit out of luck when it came to breaks and lunches for that lovely day or night.

The OSU couldn't simply be shut down like some general medical reception office or main blood laboratory. The unit had to be monitored with fresh and able-bodied staff 24/7 for the rational fear that anything could go down. That also meant if a worker bee were stuck there working a double shift by themselves, they'd better kiss those same breaks and lunches they'd missed from shift one bye-bye for seventeen hours straight. Such spiraling practices not only haunted

Mason General, but had become the underground norm of operation throughout the majority of Colorado healthcare systems. In fact, the entire country was falling in line with similar legal and dicey slopes of insane malpractice within their working communities.

In an undeniably deranged and macabre sense of perception, being an operator for a hospital was basically to just wait around in defense of the place and to listen intently for death to come knocking inside their little realm of existence. And when it did, it was that operator's full responsibility to act accordingly and with the utmost precision. Lives are at stake, and there is absolutely no time for hiccups or scattered mix-ups of lackadaisical judgments.

The voices are gone.

Washed away.

Everything is different...

AT LAST, THE fire alarm cut off for a moment, blanketing the room in a much-needed silence that always seemed too damn good to be true.

Kip broke the sliver of quietude, "I mean, they call us for everything. They want us to fix their on-call schedules, use us to call out sick to their own staffers, and they ask us for directions to get to conference rooms on their own shitty floors. They act like we know everything down here in this dungeon that festers on inside this whole Mason crapshow. Like we're some all-knowing entity down here in the pit. We need a raise, D., or to get the piss out of here. I think going back to being a mechanic would be better off for me than this mess."

Kip rolled out in his chair from his mini cubicle. Damien heard him slide, and did the same from his main duty station. They looked down at each other at opposite ends of the dimly lit office. Whenever the men were on duty, they'd turn off most of the lights in the room. The reason being they could both barely stomach how bright the hospital lights would become while blaring on full power. The computer screens were bad enough staring them down for nine hours a night, but those Mason General bulbs on top of it all were a deadly combination.

"We're the Wizards of Oz inside this hospital nut house! But seriously, you've only been doing this gig half as long as I have, Kip"-said Damien. "Trust me, partner. I know this job isn't for the faint of heart. It's misunderstood, downright unrewarding, and the pay is for the crows. We're both better than this, but a job doesn't define who you are, ya' know?"

Without warning, a voice on Kip's main phone line beckoned in his ear.

"Yeah, uh, I have a Doctor Stat."

Answering swiftly and professionally, Kip followed. "You mean you have an MD Stat? We don't have Doctor Stats anymore. That verbiage of a protocol changed three years ago. Is this for an adult patient or a child?"

Confused, delayed response, retorted. "Child. It's in Radiology."

The time was 10:01 pm, technically hospital after-hours. Mason's protocol stated that all MD Stats were actually called Team Alerts. An entirely different team would have to be dispatched due to the later time window. The responding groups were broken down mostly for reasons of financial quarreling and hospital politics.

So, if the proper code call was actually an MD Stat for either an adult or child, the staff in the department should be fully aware that they needed the proper after-hours Team Alert squad. Also, the Radiology department was technically part of the hospital side of the facility, not the Medical Office Building portion. The Imaging ward was located on the invisible equator of Mason General, right in the center in an enclave section of the hospital's first floor.

Kip knew these facts like breathing and answered calmly, "Alright, this is actually a Team Alert, not an MD Stat. Due to the after-hours time window, the team you are requesting is no longer on site."

An annoyed and zombified response beckoned from the caller, "Can you just call a 'Doctor Stat' in Radiology, or what?"

Kip, "It's the completely wrong code procedure. You should know the protocol. What's your name and extension? I'm going to initiate the proper Team Alert command."

After reluctantly giving up the necessary information, Damien had been rubbernecking from the other side of the office.

Once the party hung up with Wells, Winters yelled, "Got it!" and launched the Team Alert from his blinking computer station in front of him.

The introductory part of a Team Alert was firstly the overhead page, where the entire hospital hears the voice of the announcing operator from the various loudspeakers peppered all around the ageless facility.

The wondrous voice in the sickly skies!

"Team Alert, Hospital 1st Floor, Radiology Department," bellowed Damien in his suave, yet unwavering and controlled demeanor.

Fellow employees would, at times, joke around with him regarding his overhead paging pipes. They would say things like he should be a shock jock or some radio show host with the distinct brand of rasp he carried while performing his job duties. Winters didn't appreciate such comments, but he went along with them mostly because he assumed deep down that they were some half-assed form of a shallow compliment.

"You always sound so smooth and collected over the speakers," they'd say.

Winters was reluctant to just let them have their assumptions. If they only knew how difficult it was to keep a level head when the announcing individual knew, at that very second, another human being was in a grave medical situation. Also, with the understanding that hundreds of employees inside the hospital were listening to his every breathing syllable for crucial directions, and most importantly, to the coded commands he announced as distinctly as possible.

After the overhead was finished, he went ahead with paging the proper on-call doctors and dialing cell phones, from Security guards to Nursing Supervisors, informing them all of the active code, in case they didn't hear his initial overhead command, and primarily to provide a friendly reminder to act according to their specific hospital procedures in response to the emergency.

Ironically, some of those parties would become upset with the OSU when they'd dial them in regards to an active or pending code transaction.

"Why are you calling me for this?!" they'd hiss from the other line.

"You're on the protocol list. Just doing my job," Damien or Kip would fire back while rolling their eyes to themselves.

After launching the proper Team Alert, Winters documented the transaction into the departmental code binder in a cabinet by his feet. That step was mostly for hospital legality purposes. Having as many records on deck for all completed emergency undertakings ensured that if somebody ever tried to sue the hospital for negligent care, Mason could pull as many reports and files as possible out of their rabbit's hat to try and debunk the case against the suing party.

At the very end of the day, it was all still just a business.

Souls danced into the stiff and sterile beds and eventually waltzed right back on out of them. Some walked out on their own vivacious steam, while others were rolled away on squeaky wheels down to the Morgue next door.

Of course, there were always levels of human decency existent in a dreary place like Mason General Hospital, but underneath that sanitary and forgiving exterior, the organization's money surpluses and overall reputation trumped everything else.

"Damn, she sure seemed confused, eh?" said Damien while writing his notes at his desk in the bulky code binder.

His left hand scribbled away with his head of brown eyes tilting slightly toward the right.

"Tell me--"

BING BONG, BING BONG BING!!

Kip was abruptly interrupted.

The added sound skewered through the men's souls like an ice pick sliding through a cylindrical clump of fused together ice cubes.

Damien shot his head up to the Responder 5 alarm phone that sat on the right side of his desk. The text on the shadow grey indicator read, 'BLUE, 4 W 4110.' That verbiage translated to a sudden cardiac arrest of a current inpatient on the fourth floor. A Code Blue was the most severe code to handle on the work list.

Without any slight hesitation, Winters tossed aside his writing utensil, clicked a few keys on his computer and launched the Blue command, all before his voice rang out once again into the dreary nightly occupants of rickety old Mason General, as if a smooth force from above had trickled down into a world full of bland chaos, "CODE BLUE, HOSPITAL 4TH FLOOR, 4 WEST."

Protocol stated never to announce the room number over the air because fellow staff needn't want to start a panic with family members or to have an unannounced audience flock to the room only to get in the way of the team whose job it was to try and save the patient's life.

Winters announced the Code Blue script four times in succession, with perfect clarity and sterling precision. He then went ahead with calling cell phones and paging physicians to direct them specifically to the dire straits 4 West bed of 4110. Kip's voice fought through the screeching symphony of alarm indignance and barked toward his prized friend and colleague.

"It's another PTSD kind of night, huh D?"

Damien didn't respond; however, the young man let out a long breath in a feeble attempt to compose his rattled and overanxious nerves.

V

'M DEAD WAS the initial jumbled thought that Damien Winters had when he regained some degree of lucid and present consciousness after passing out from the beast attack. Not a Heaven or Hell type dead, but more like an odd and perplexing state of psychosis. It was an off-putting, in-between kind of rancid feeling.

I'm paralyzed entered the confused man's fractured spirit next.

"Wha- why can't I move?" he managed to whisper aloud in the broken rasp of a deliriously fudged up slur.

With eyes half-open, he looked to his left then slowly inched his aching skull towards the right.

Winters found himself in a standard and unassuming bed with brightly unpigmented sheets and a thin crimson comforter. He peered around his surroundings and instantly noticed how sterile everything all appeared around him. He could almost taste the toxic odors of intense cleaning agents gelling with the mixed disinfectants. The wafting ensemble of stifling aromas nauseated the waking mortal to a near vomit. The enclosing wall space was a mint, pea-colored green, with snowy baseboards at the very bottom. An empty incubator nestled itself in vacancy among the far-right corner of the otherly peaceful room of sterile quietude. An IV ran clear liquid from a saline drip through a bulging vein along the middle portion of his left arm.

His busted shoulder and multiple bite wounds from the attack felt horrendous, but not as intensely excruciating as when he was laid out in the roadway underneath the hulking fiend. He remained in the same clothes he'd changed back into before leaving work on the night he laid down his bike, with his ratty t-shirt being attached like a bad habit to his lean and resting frame. His charcoal jeans were also on, along with his steel-gray riding socks. His beloved chocolate brown and leather motorcycle coat lay off on a simple chair near a sole window to his right.

"You're at work, Damien," voiced a stern tone that cut through the silence and resonated a vague familiarity, yet bore a strange twinge that echoed out from the opposite portion of the room alongside the entrance doorway.

The lights were on full-tilt fashion inside the simplistic and eerie quarters. The loathly display of illumination caused the hazy man's baby browns to shift in and out of a pained and groggy focus. Winters had never ceased to despise the relentless obnoxiousness of hospital lighting. It would constantly greet him with piercing tension and cluster headaches while working over at Mason.

He could hear the magnetic fizzing of the many fixtures above and around his sanitary ceiling for a sky. He was having trouble trying to adjust his sensitive blinking windows to the arrogant fluorescents, along with the strange-sounding voice that called out his name, but managed to gather a few paradoxical parts of scattered clarity back inside himself. His head throbbed, and his entire body felt sweaty and dirty.

He gazed down at himself in the flimsy bed and attempted to reach his other arm up toward his face to shift a tuft of dark hair from his over woozy eyes of warm sepia. Finally, the confused Damien responded in a tone of his own that wasn't so foreign, the only comfort so far in such a baffling and unconventional state of unraveling.

"If I'm at the hospital, then why the fuck am I strapped down?"

He had some wits about him, trying desperately to wrap his mind around the irregular situation that, all of a sudden, befell him. A chilling response met Damien's aching question.

"You're restrained because we're going to melt down your pathetic carcass to nothing but liquid and swallow down your God-forsaken soul. And that's not even the half of it!"

"Dr. Boudreaux?" strained Damien while very disoriented and unsteadily muddled. "I'm not following - Wait. I've got it... I'm dreaming, yes? Or you've drugged me to the point of paranoid delirium. Or perhaps, maybe I'm even stone-cold dead."

Boudreaux gawked before he replied from the corner entrance of the blindingly white room. He appeared as only a silhouette piece, a misty figure that Winters couldn't quite make out in his current shackled predicament.

The doctor swiftly replied, strange as ever. "None of the above. Wrong, wr-ONG, WROOONG. In time..."

Damien wriggled his head under the harshness of the skylight bulbs and craned his head toward the door, straining with desperation to clear the cloud that was poisoning his funky brain function. Boudreaux looked to be wearing his usual sweeping ivory trench coat with a black dress shirt underneath, and a solid noir tie to practically fuse into his smoothly pressed button-down shirt. A dark tan-colored pant was chosen along with a pair of pearly white dress shoes. Winters could never understand what Boudreaux saw in those goofy white foot covers, but he rocked the guiltless loafers early and often while on patient cutting duties.

Boudreaux's hair was always slicked straight back, with that night being no different, along with dark-rimmed square spectacles that never left his renowned veneer. Boudreaux was positioned in the doorless entryway, he practically blended in with the chalky white of his lab trench and was washed away with the searing bulbs of illumination that bore down from everywhere.

Damien eventually attempted a stabbing slice of his own charming spirit.

"Come on in, Doc. I won't bite... I mean, you've got me all shackled here like some bloodthirsty cannibal. I was the one who got attacked out there. By the way, forgive me, but before you commit me to a trial of your peers, I could have sworn you said something about feasting upon my soul? I really am delusional, right? From these painkillers, you've been siphoning into me? Or-"

Boudreaux cut him off and interjected smoothly with zero emotion, "Your hearing is satisfactory, Damien. Very good."

His voice seemed oddly uncomfortable, not quite himself. It sounded just like Boudreaux, but it wasn't really him. The overeducated man was undeniably off-kilter, a hollowed-out shell of his dapper former self.

Attempting to remain composed for Winters at that sinking juncture began to prove difficult for his overwrought reasoning. Being chained to a bed inside his own place of employment after a savage creature almost ripped his throat out, was frankly incomprehensible. Longing to pacify his cracking nerves, Damien began to loosely analyze his overall quandary: his left arm with the shiny bag drip felt more or less wretched, but surprisingly not as bad as a moment ago.

The bite wound on his side had been treated and bandaged up in a neat crisscrossed pattern, assumedly by a somewhat competent registered nurse. He again checked with his eyes and was assured that his same clothes remained on from the stormy and bloody motorcycle incident. He glanced over at his worked over, yet highly functional leather jacket, which rested in a draped over fashion on a steel chair to the right of his bed below the undersized window. The curtain had been drawn and sealed shut.

The fragile man began to feel claustrophobic and closed away from the outside world in his peculiar conundrum. He also paid heightened attention to the alarming fact that he still had some of his own blood along with the diseased big cat's fluids on parts of his beaten face and hands. He could sense the conflicting remedies encrusted within his wavy hair and stickily dried up on his defined and lengthy neck. He couldn't quite reach his face due to the sturdy arm restraints; nevertheless, he knew that the gunk was there. He laid his head back down on the cardboard pillow and turned it left to face his doctor friend who remained glued in the open doorway.

Winters gave a long and labored sigh toward him and managed the wryest of innocent smirks.

"Ok... you win, Doc. You've piqued my bloody interest. Why don't you come on in and tell me all about your intentions with my soul?"

Damien couldn't fathom how discombobulated he continued to remain, but the reeling man tried his damnedest to snap out of the outlandish comatose. Something frightening was going on, so he needed to think and act accordingly. Nothing, upon his painful awakening, made any rational form of logical sense. He'd felt as if he were stuck in a flipped over on its head dimension of dreamland, or the harshest setting of some chasm of reality; a murky place of bland and unsettling existence he knew all too devastatingly well. Hunkered down and tied up like a dog in some varnished pale purgatory from Hell, being antagonized by a doctor imposter with only malice for intent. Chained up like a heathen in the hospital he bled for on a nightly basis and gave his heart to from the very beginning.

To top everything off, at the distant doorway stood a highly decorated physician to whom Winters considered an actual friend and colleague, a rational MD who'd even treated him in the ER on the ground level for appendicitis back when things weren't completely falling to pieces. An enriching individual who'd had a wife and two children and enjoyed fixing up old cars in his spare time after grueling hours of hospital slice and dice. That exact same physician was fabricating deranged things that could only fit sanely in the underground comforts of a terrifying nightmare.

There's a logical explanation for all of this. I'm going to figure it all out.

"I doubt you'll be figuring out much of anything," chimed in the monotone masquerading voice of the debonair doctor.

Before blurting out an erratic scream due to the immediate assumption that the medicine man, no, thing, yes, thing, was then inside his head, Winters whispered back only with his mind.

You underestimate me, Boudreaux.

Only then did the doctor take a slick and snappy step inside the odiously hygienic 3rd floor NICU hospital room. Then another.

Boudreaux's movements occurred only slightly over controlled, but with a stiffness to him and a hitch of extra creepy rigidity. He almost advanced as some white coat looking puppet, Damien had thought, during his initial approach toward the bed. As if something that was not Boudreaux at all had been forcing the friendly doctor's hand, pulling every string attached to his usually analytical and sophisticated mind. Winters didn't pull his eyes away from Gabriel's progression.

With each cracking step of the doctor's bleachy tap shoes that collided with the snow-white linoleum, Winters' heart picked up its shuddering pace in his overly tense cavity for a heaving center mass. He tried to clear out his mind so that Boudreaux couldn't again gain access to his thought processes of unmistakable dread. With his head affixed to the left facing the door, the doctor finally took his final puppet shuffle directly in front of Winters' bed prison. He faced the window to the patient's immediate right, but then took a clunky pivot step with his right loafer and faced the bed straight as an arrow.

For a confused moment, Damien thought that Boudreaux might just even salute him. The doctor looked as inflexible as a fresh off the bus army private trying his guts out to impress his commanding officer on the first day of grunt camp. Instead, the puppet MD folded his steady hands in front of his crisp beltline and stared into the very essence of a panic-stricken and frightened to the core Damien Winters.

Boudreaux was absolutely grotesque looking from up close. The whites of maleficent oblivion resided where his pupils and retinas used to be. They bulged from his chiseled face as bloodshot, puss-filled pucks ready to explode out of his human-appearing mass of a skull. The milky globes leaked down his usually personable face, dripping something thick and unholy all over his trusty black spectacles. Then Boudreaux's whole face shifted into something else.

Just like that.

It transitioned from a fanciable doctor with egg yolks for eyes to an incomprehensible abomination. Winters didn't cry out in response to the unveiling; however, he squirmed within his cranked to their limit shackles. Within his thrashing fit, he ripped the IV from his arm and leaned forward in bed for a mad attempt to work the restraints with his gritting biters.

Boudreaux then chimed in with a suave degree of steely coolness, "Lie back now, Damien. Your human vessel needs to heal before I can fully take advantage of your piteous little meat sleeve. We don't want you wasting any more of our precious and infinite dominion. Now, look up at me, boy."

Damien continued to wrench and twist, causing the dinky bed to make a screech and shift on the slick flooring below.

"Go fuck yourself, doc!" he continued his thrashing.

Boudreaux abruptly raised his voice two full octaves in the overly sterile confines, "LOOK at ME!"

The voice was absolutely soul-piercing, with nothing human belonging inside it any longer. Nails on an invisible chalkboard that the strapped down patient wanted nothing more than to shatter into a thousand powdery slivers to force a reprieve of much needed silent innocence. His gnawing ceased to no avail, so he laid back down reluctantly to check out the standing physician. The villainous face remained gawking down right in front of him. Eyeless, alien, and utterly reprehensible. The thing owned bone-colored horns that bulged from each cheekbone area. The unfortunate surgeon's mouth wrapped violently in a wide kind of snarl, with hideous teeth that were obviously created only to consume the very souls of anything human and remotely righteous.

"This is merely but a glimpse of Our truest materialization," boomed Boudreaux before settling into a steady monologue.

"You see, Our kind was around well before you humans were ever even a forethought. We were also here before your God ever existed. We created Him; then, He decided to go ahead and create you, with all of your human fallacies and pitiful inadequacies, to nurture all the damage your race has already caused right up until this inevitable moment. We existed when this system you call Earth was nothing more than a black-less void of a pleasant nothingness. And we resided over that void. Not only your measly speck of a planet, but as far as your hollow-brained scientific minds could ever wander with your numbers and frivolous equations. If it weren't for you humans, stuffed with your wicked imaginations and diseased qualities of intention, this realm would be a thriving atmosphere of rich serenity and exemplary tranquility. Rather than clinging on the verge of catastrophic collapse, whether it be by your man-made war weapons or sorrowfully archaic ideals. Your God may have spawned your fellow mankind; however, we will finally correct His nefarious and foolhardy mistake."

VI

BOUDREAUX AGAIN ENTERED the gray matter of the helpless young man. The invasion was perverse, a telepathic attack on Damien's most intimate thoughts and fears. It felt like butchery, as his entire existence up until that moment was being poked and prodded inside his writhing skull. It almost felt as if the crazed physician was making hollow incisions, ripping out parts of the defenseless human's origin story that secured his vividly creative spirit. He fought the overpowering mental onslaught, digging into the finer crevices and darker confines of his own mortal intellect.

He somehow shook off the invasive barrage and raised his own deep voice to a bold and intensive wrath. "Cut the shit, Gabriel. No more mind games. Converse with me man to man, or whatever God-awful thing you claim to be. Doctor Boudreaux, please. I know that you're still in there. You can fight this…"

Boudreaux fired back with an even, yet domineering force field. "You listen, you pathetic overfeeling micro-organism." Gabriel took his right hand and neatly adjusted his favorite squares of glass to the center portion of his sharp and distinguishable nose before continuing.

"In a nutshell, humanity has been doomed from the very beginning of your ever-expanding consciousness. The God that you and so many others of your kind grovel and pray to throughout your insignificant lives did not truly want you to become this way. He does exist. Your idea of a God is no enigma or figment of your diseased imaginations.

He wanted your kind, mostly perfect as He is — Ever knowing, but not overly sensitive. Not selfish, destructive, or corruptible. That's precisely how We made Him at the beginning of all things. However, He grew greedy along the way with His own design for Mankind. His biggest mistake was allowing you the ability of free will. To create and do things how and when you see fit. When He gave Man an ever-evolving consciousness, you gradually took that gift and did nothing but destroy with it. Your race of humans has actually de-evolved as your time has drawn forward."

Damien stopped squirming in his sterile cage and stared down the eyeless monster squarely in its detestable eyes of oblivion.

The doctor proceeded, "Your Hitlers and your Stalins, your out of control technology that is destroying this planet's supple environment in gloriously negligible waves. Look at what's become of your world today, you pathetic good for nothing pawn. He gifted you the ability of His own free will. He gave you a choice to make up your own minds, decide with your own hearts, do the right things with all your supposed powers of originality, while so very many of you have folded your hands over to the deepest pits of the satisfying dark. You end up leaving your world worse off than you found it. We've been watching from your neighboring Moon for thousands of your manmade years. Within those years, it's been a steady decline into chaos and despair for the entire conglomerate of human existence. Your greed, your lust, your step on your neighbor's mentalities to get ahead inside your selfish and overindulgent flesh prisons are all cataclysmic. Believing that each and every one of you pitiful ingrates is actually something more than fresh meat to a superior and dominant legion of civilization."

Boudreaux's monologue continued while his white lab coat with a physician's badge, framed in a red rectangle plaque on his breast pocket, antagonized the powerless Winters.

"Your reproduction rates are astronomical, and your population as a whole is off the charts. Corrupted and diseased personalities with the heaviest anxieties and mental instabilities produce offspring at dangerously high levels, since this has become the social acceptance in your culture up until this breaking point. Then those children inherit the same genetic shortcomings their elders have passed down upon them. The mothers and fathers don't consider this before bringing another one of you damaged menial beings into this ravaged world. As a result, the population becomes more fearful, angrier, and resentful toward their fellow humans. Your laughable ideals of governmental control are more mockery than ever, with your current supposed leader acting aloof as another sociopathic marionette in the grand scheme of eventual judgment. Well, Damien, those days are now over. Just like the ancestral dinosaurs of the Mesozoic era, who roamed freely well before your kind ruled this planet, it's now time to pay the authoritative piper in full."

Remaining incapacitated and motionless, the battered Winters cracked the faintest of innocent smiles and aimed it up toward Boudreaux's fucked up face.

"I think you've thoroughly misjudged some of us, doctor."

Without warning, Boudreaux locked his deadlights deeper into Damien's mazed expression. Winters again struggled to avert the excruciating offensive; although something held him there against his will. A force, presumably alien, pulsated from the vile thing's domineering and bygone cerebral cortex. The real Boudreaux was long dead and erased. Winters felt that horrible truth down to his chattering bones. The creature was weakening his thoughts, along with his sterling individuality, while attempting to delete every one of his lifelong trepidations at a dizzyingly torrent speed. For the briefest of sequences, it all felt to the twisting man like slipping sideways into a steamy warm bath. Troubles all washed away clean, rub a dub dub.

Damien defended himself against the sphinx doctor's appalling albino brights, while managing to fully close his own, deciding at the last moment to crank his shaggy head hard left, in an attempt to bury his face within the stiff hospital's bed pillow.

The break off from the stare down infuriated the incredulous entity. Boudreaux suddenly hunched down low at the foot of the bed and placed his surgically pristine hands of clay to the crystal clean tiling. He sprung up from the ground, lab coat and all, and landed on the same side of the mattress where Winters had his eyes glued shut and cowering. The sphynx grabbed the man by his hair with a heavy right hand and slugged him directly in the face with the other.

"Oof!" moaned Winters in a surprised display of heightened anguish.

Blood trickled down from his left nostril, he then had no choice but to open his eyes out of a defensive move of absolute primal instinct.

"Look at me NOW, you deplorable waste! Our leader will drain you for..."

CRACK!!

Out of nowhere, Boudreaux was sent sprawling off the bed and onto the hard floor. The doctor didn't make a sound, and the usually glued-to-his-face spectacles were sent flying from his devilish head as he hit the hospital linoleum brutally hard. Damien looked around wide-eyed and flummoxed with blood still draining from his bruised nose. The shackled man finally rested his darting eyes upon Kip Wells. Kip was holding a fire extinguisher in both hands while he stood over his defenselessly tied down comrade.

"Happy to see me, old buddy!?" he managed to utter in a frightened shitless tone, but forced a grin while peering down at his feeble friend and colleague.

They both shot a glance toward Boudreaux, as the white coat began to rise up from the initial blow from the large smoke can.

"Fucking hell," huffed Winters.

Without hesitation, Kip pulled the pin on the bright green extinguisher and let the creeper surgeon have it. The doctor's face was blasted first with the aggressive shooting mist, drowning out his chalky monstrosities for tragic onlookers.

Boudreaux was spilled again to the floor as the room filled up with a thick blanket of white fog. Kip emptied the entire can on the villain, taking a full minute to drain its contents bone dry. After the room became engulfed with extinguisher mist, Damien heard the apparatus thunk coarsely to the tiling below. The square NICU room remained saturated with the fog-like substance, and it caused Damien to choke on its potency along with his own flowing crimson. He could barely see an inch out and in front of his own swollen face.

Another agonizing moment progressed blindly, seeming nothing short of a dreadful eternity, when Winters felt a hand grab for one of his legs. He squirmed with fury at first, but realized it was only his friend.

"Time to go, Damien," exclaimed his saving grace.

Kip went to work on the sturdy arm straps, freeing one of Damien's arms with a trying effort.

"These things are a real bitch to get off," exhaled Kip.

Damien started on his other arm as his left became freed, while Kip clumsily worked around and down with his leg shackles. The two men fumbled with the buckles in the murky abyss of the barren room, barely able to see much of anything at all.

Kip stopped working and made a healthy break for the door, thinking Damien had been fully set loose from his prison for a bed. Winters frantically tried to unearth himself from the son of a bitch sack, but realized a fraction too late that his right foot wasn't fully unhooked out of its unruly restraint. He twisted the ankle and fell halfway off of the bed with his foot remaining attached to the cuffed confinement.

As he righted himself back on the frame while he flimflammed around with the last strap, Boudreaux came flying out of the white night and landed squarely on top of him. It was still the doctor in relative human appearance; but those eyes, those dreadful humanless eyes, gawked straight through him even in the thickly overcast environment. Boudreaux was seething from the gape as if a rabid dog were on the guilty pleasured cusp of slathering up and consuming his nightly meal of prey. Damien grabbed the doctor thing by his boldly colored necktie, extended his arm out, so Gabriel's face was slightly away from his, and slammed a solid right hook across the poor surgeon's ugly skull. Boudreaux took flight once again, tumbling backward over the left side of the bed frame and disappearing from view into the foggy medical meadow.

Winters reached back down by his foot and finally got the bastard thing all the way loose. He darted his head around the room for Kip, but couldn't seem to locate his friend. He jumped from the bed with a massive charge of adrenaline and bolted straight for the open doorway.

At the very last second, he remembered his boots and jacket were still laid out by the window in the other corner. He wanted to just forget everything and continue his mad dash, but thought better of such a hurried and incompetent rash of decision. He blindly scurried back inside the guts of the room by the closed curtain window. He found his jacket with luck and kicked one of his shoes in the process, which were resting underneath the wimpy hospital chair. He grabbed his things and turned to make a second attempt for the door.

Boudreaux remained in a heap down on the surface someplace; but there was no way of telling exactly where with the smoggy and reeky conditions. He tripped right over the doc with socks on his feet and jacket with heavy boots cradled in his grasp, sprawling like a half-assed superhero completely outside the welcoming entranceway.

The hallway proved clear and fogless, as the man could see with a solid degree of clarity once again. He yelled for Kip and took one last look inside the Mason General Intensive Care room that was only seconds away from finishing him off. He threw on his coat and danced around while hopping on both of his boots, ultimately standing tall and anew in the desolate hallway. Boudreaux was nowhere in sight. Winters let out an exasperated breath of fully panicking air before taking off, running down the 3rd-floor hall of emptiness.

VII

HE STOOD ALONE by the elevator bank at the end of the eerily quiet NICU ward and pressed the button to go straight down. Damien couldn't withstand and fell backward into his mind for a deep sequence of intense deliberation. He couldn't possibly imagine that the entirety of Mason General was being overrun by the exacting and precise monstrosities that had done something so despicable to Dr. Boudreaux. Kip had obviously been fully himself and unharmed, which was, in and of itself, wonderful news. He'd scampered off somewhere and out of sight, though.

With the same thrashed attire he'd worn on that earth-shattering midnight, where he crashed his bike and fought to the death with a member of the Sphinx, the unsteady human managed a small degree of shaky wherewithal to assess his assaulted physical condition. His body remained tender and sore all over, but he'd been treated satisfactorily before the eyeless creations came knocking at his hospital's gates. His dislocated shoulder was stiff and rigid, but he could tell the arm had been reset while he was out like a light. The lengthy limb worked well enough, and that was all that really mattered in his desperate condition. He stared ahead at the closed elevator door and rotated his mangled section in a gingerly fashion. The bite on his sidewall and the cuts and bruises that covered the rest of him remained existent, but they'd been cleaned up a bit with various sutures and other forms of hospital dressings.

All in all, he was in decent shape barring the horrendous predicament. The button light on the up and down in his direct line of vision shot out a red shade of indigo, offering an antagonizing glow in the eerie quietude of the empty hall. He decided to break for the stairwell at the very end of the mid-level floor.

As Winters came up to the far staircase door, the elevator behind him gave a ding and hitched up, opening with a dry metallic sound. Three savage looking beasts then burst out onto the vacant arena: two of the wretches were operating on all fours, while the other was on a pair of distorted stalks, giving it the appearance of a bizarre and animalistic humanoid. The ungraceful towers of stinking flesh practically sucked the oxygen straight from the hallway on sight. They appeared to communicate with each other, but in a more primitive display of incessant grunts and growls. He could barely believe what he was seeing, his legs turning to jelly and his heart practically giving up in his chest.

Were they only hunting him?

Was the entire hospital completely overrun by these vile creations?

Damien opened the door carefully and slipped into the side stairwell, closing it stealthily behind him. The scene grew darker all of a sudden, but it managed to offer the quaking man a dimly lit milieu. On each floor level was a warm-colored lightbulb in the very cornered section of the wall. The bulbs housed a yellow metal casing that surrounded each unit. It made the entire staircase's setting look ghostly and spectral to the naked eye. As if he'd stepped back in time along the way someplace, or perhaps it could have been forward in the program, having to decide whether he wanted to go up or down the moody steps to nowhere.

Mason's 5th floor was officially the top and final deck of the small-scale Colorado medical center. Winters was still on three. The 4th floor bore the general Intensive Care Unit, not the Neonatal ICU, where he'd recently escaped from, along with multitudes of other high-risk inpatients. Above that was the gaudy Administration wing. Last, but not least, was the roof.

He decided against going up and instead went downward

toward floor number 2. He gave up on entering that floor due to an overwhelming instinct he couldn't solidly interpret and trekked straight down to the 1st-floor lobby. He opened the stairwell door with a jolting display of suspect forcefulness. He didn't mean to act so recklessly with the approach, but overly spiked nerves were toying with the mixed-up man's rational and primary senses. Once the door swung open in full, a figure darted right out in front of it. The shadow disappeared from view and headed off by the main hospital cafeteria. Frightened beyond belief and certain it was another diabolical minion prepared to strike, he sheepishly peered his head out and noticed the fleeting figure resembled that of his fellow human.

It was Kip, thank Christ.

"Kip!" Winters whisper-yelled.

Wells stopped and looked back at Damien. His sneakers squeaked on the lobby floor with his abrupt ceasefire. He looked petrified while donning his usual midnight black scrub work suit. His curly hair perspired off his brow, and he looked to be fighting straightforwardly for an easy catch of normal human breath. Kip finally turned all the way around and ran back toward Damien and the side staircase.

"Weren't you gonna wait up for me? Or are you trying to get your ass killed in here all on your own?" Winters exclaimed while placing a hand to his friend's shoulder.

"Sorry, D. I'm scared shitless, here. We all knew you had been attacked out on the main drag on your bike and were recovering up in Intensive Care. A few hours after you came in, crazy shit started happening all over this place. When these white-eyed things came knocking, most hospital staff just took off running like scared rabbits. Abandoned fucking ship. I stayed in our office and turned on the T.V. I tried to assess what was going on around here. The news says it's some terrorist cell, and the threat is subsiding. I just had a feeling I needed to check up on you. I first went up to ICU, but what I saw up there, I can't ever un-see. I saw one of those creatures feasting on an inpatient. Then one of the nursing supervisors was there, and another animal looking thing just dissolved her body down with its eyes and then like ate her up. Just like that! I almost lost my shit, Damien. I! I..."

Damien reached out and hugged the delirious man. "Easy there, old friend."

He pulled away slowly and stared his colleague right in the eyes. "Thanks for finding me, Kipper. You saved my ass up there. As long as we stick together, I think we have a shot at getting out of here."

"Yeah? Well, I think we're all screwed, personally" voiced Kip in a quaint retort.

"There you go, Wells. Always the shiny bright and stoic optimist" a sarcastic tone exuded from Winters.

"Yeah, yeah," Kip followed up.

They finally stopped the chit-chat and took to looking around their hospital's distressed 1st floor.

The particular stairwell entrance that the two men had crossed paths in was virtually positioned in the invisible equator splice of Mason General's lobby floor. The cafeteria sat dead ahead with the Emergency Room being planted off to their farthest right. The outpatient Pharmacy and Radiology departments were staggered to the opposite left. The lights decided to give up on floor one, with the usual piercing brights taking a seat and transforming into a near blackness. The main backup generator kicked in on command, supplying dim floodlighting of red and yellow, offering a chillingly warm complexion throughout. Damien had always been mesmerized by how many ordinary people were frightened to death of good old-fashioned hospitals. The irrational phobia of such a sickly joint was called White Coat Syndrome.

Ironically, Winters himself used to have recurring nightmares while growing up by the oceanside of California, repeatedly finding his dreaming mind being chased down by a sadistic deity in an empty geriatric institution, with blinding fluorescents high up and all around.

The tousle-haired Winters had no choice but to reminisce for only a moment, as the standard luminance gave way to near dark, at how venomously sardonic his and Kip's current circumstances had transgressed. If there was any light left at the end of their night-marish tunnel, it was the fact they were both still together and knew Mason General exceptionally well from inside her ageless walls. They had become two soldiers trapped inside their own dismal stomping grounds. A place of past times, which they both undeniably loathed, but also an environment they strangely sort of cared for, all wrapped up in a haphazard and bizarre conundrum of festering hate and ignorant admiration.

Without warning, the two huskily large and closed Emergency Room doors, with their ugly two-toned flaps, burst open with an authoritative swing. A lab runner, an Environmental Services janitor, and an ER physician all came barreling out and toward the standing Wells and Winters.

The three new beings were clad in their respective on-duty regalia, all laced with a piercing dread on their surprised and, more importantly, all the way human faces. Then, closest to the swaying ER assembly, two soulless entities entered the hallway in a heart-pounding sulk from the cafeteria entrance. The rancid pair were dressed in matching hospital gowns, one a middle-aged man and the other a younger-looking female. They entered out of thin air like stiff ghosts, devoid of humanity and replaced, instead, with bulging and ravenous bulbs affixed to their otherworldly mortal looking heads. All three of the unsuspecting staff, who'd fled from ER, froze in their skittish tracks, while the two former invalids turned to face the mortified trio of running scared employees.

Both the physician and the lab runner began to liquefy where they stood, their clothes and skin actually going up and catching a sweltering fire in unison. The shattering screams were blood-curdling and loaded with agonizing terror as they both hit the floor, flailing for mercy. The sphinx patients then opened their gapes in a crude succession while muscle and cartilage gave way from the two inferior hospital workers. Once the screeching bodies turned to nothing but charred ash, the cinders rose on command and projected into the gowned demons mouth traps, as the floating souls of their fragile spirits shot mystifyingly into the dastardly dead lamps of the unfathomable Sphynx.

Damien and Kip remained scarecrows in the dead center of the hall, frozen solid in a piercing mortification at the unfolding scene up ahead. Once the EVS worker attempted a second dash for freedom, he was tackled from behind by a full-on monster that must've been chasing the three people throughout the ER. The poor janitor stood no chance at survival. The animal sphynx's jaws latched with a crunch onto his thin and veiny neck, spilling fresh blood everywhere. The flooring and nearby walls, even the sizable decorative faux plant that stood cozied close to the Urgent Care, were plastered with the toilet cleaner's wave of gore. He twitched and squirmed in the grasp of the hulking organism, with the thing quaking its beastly lion inlay with vigor by its perfectly timed death strike.

Wells and Winters stumbled away together in the opposite direction by the main Pharmacy, just as the gowned devils, who'd only seconds ago swallowed up two living people, lashed out their destructive gazes toward them. The two colleagues averted the insidious leers from a distance, which flashed sinfully from the inconceivable forms of ancient wickedness.

The final sequence both men could hear before crashing through the Pharmacy door at the other end of the hallway floor, was the gurgling death chime of the ill-fated custodian they'd watched gruesomely perish.

VIII

"THESE THINGS CAN consume multiple people within a single host?" Kip was hunched over while trying to remain upright as he met up with Damien's gaze of absolute dread.

Winters couldn't speak or even respond to his closest colleague. He could barely even think any longer in a straight line of working order. The man stared forward in the pale pill haven, hardly rational. His head began to swim on his shoulders, and he felt he'd pass out right then and there. His heart thumped like a hammer inside his suffocating sternum, drumming a heavy metal tune that beat wildly out of control, with his arms and legs becoming as numb and heavy as syrupy molasses. Damien's entire lengthy frame began to shake; a full-blown panic attack was striking the ill-fated man like a bolt of sinister lightning. He tried never to fight or tango with his afflictions, those periodic episodes of crippling trepidation. He'd suffered from intense bouts of anxiety and PTSD that started at a very young age. The overwhelming and downright frightening exploits began to hit him even harder later on in his adult years, increasing with morbid severity once he'd begun Emergency duties at insensitive Mason General. A trick he'd learned, overtime, was never to quarrel with the panic—that trying method of fighting back only stacked resistance onto resistance. Instead, Winters would challenge his episodes in a completely accepting and almost loving way, practically calling out for more physical sensations and terrorizing ruminations that infected his mind. Egging on his own psychosis, so to speak.

Keep beating Satan's throttling fucking tune, heart. Beat even harder for all I care. Bring this shit right the hell on.

Damien dove into his psyche for a severe pep talk. After losing reality for the sake of his fleeting right-mindedness, he heard Kip's voice off from somewhere close by. His buddy was still with him, standing at his side.

"D, you still with me?" a concerning look was affixed onto the surface of his medium complexioned face.

Winters finally responded without even looking over at Kip. "We don't stand a chance, do we. Us, I mean. People in general. We're an egomaniacal and overzealous breed of primal fuckery. We've officially met our match, eh Kipper? All these years, we've had this infected notion that we were untouchable. Now, look at what's become of us."

Winters sank down to the floor against the initial inside wall, while Kip shut the Pharmacy door behind them, locking it from the inside.

"You're the toughest sucker I know, Winters," said Kip in a sincere implication, while he peered down at his collapsed colleague before turning round to scan the micro outpatient Pharmacy.

Damien appreciated the compliment from his running mate, but the man still could not pull himself together. He sat with his head buried into his hands by the shut and locked door. With a shaky reluctance, he looked up and past his colleague to scan the quiet Pharmacy. The lights were damn near on fire up in there. They made him squint with force during his initial eye sweep. A sturdy cash counter was positioned squarely in front of them. Behind it, shelf after shelf of prescription drugs lined the walls in the shallow back. Every Big Pharma tasty nugget from under the hospital rainbow was behind that counter.

To a seasoned pill freak, whom Damien and Kip dealt with on a daily basis over the phones, Mason's Pharmacy was their almighty hog haven. The scrumptious place of goody gum drops and fun-sized pieces of glitter sprinkled candies to wash away the pain and bury the dark memories.

Winters felt deeply for a society in the harshest stranglehold of a pharmaceutical epidemic. He could personally relate to having delved into the world of prescription medications in times of intense mental trauma. There were always exigent circumstances where medication was the only option for a person's survival; however, the darker side of the happy equation was frankly abuse. A pill addiction of any kind was never pretty, and more times than not, had the potential to end in utter disaster for the sorry patient who was tumbling down the spinning rabbit hole.

Damien ceaselessly clawed with his conscience regarding such topics. It was crazily ironic that his career had settled for so many years within the healthcare sector, although he tirelessly questioned its methodologies and questionable practices. The all-mighty Big Pharma was a juggernaut he'd pondered over maddeningly.

The brightly lit room looked empty, perhaps even safekeeping for a quick hot minute or two.

It was not.

A full-fledged sphinx daemon crashed through one of the shelves at the back and leaped to the countertop in the blink of an eye. The deviant obscenity was covered in blood, definitely human in alarming and dripping origin. The creature was hairless and muscular in its dastardly build of slender bulk. It stood atop the counter with a form of leviathan grace and towered on all despicable fours. The mutant appeared to be female, as its floppy breasts sagged down unevenly from its smooth animal chest. The head was utterly shorn and had razor-sharp horns protruding from each cheekbone.

Before Damien's eyes could lock mates with the sickening monster's deviance, Kip grabbed his shoulder and yanked him up by his jacket to his feet.

"Go! GO!!" Kip squealed.

They unlatched and escaped the Pharmacy and stumbled back into their initial meeting hallway of destruction. Damien slammed the door shut behind them, attempting to make a minor barrier between them and the loathsome outlander on the other side.

"The Basement! Let's try and make it to our office. Maybe we can still call out from the emergency phone down there," exclaimed Damien.

He had no clue where his cell phone had gone. The brain-altering brick had somehow become lost in translation from his stormy smackdown to his shackled bed situation on infamous floor 3. Kip dug around his dark scrub pants pocket and yanked out his old as time goofy flip phone. The murky green illuminator offered no bars whatsoever and had been doing so for hours, zero service to be had from the infernal machine. The internet and cell towers were probably toast by then anyway.

Inside the OSU, there was a special red telephone that hooked directly into the local police station in uptown Heatherton. The local smokeys of the sleepy mountain abode were only numbered as four relaxed officers, but the shiny badges were led by a decorated and purposeful chief with the last name of Snell. Even during a major power outage or a severe Code Triage, which was a form of internal or external disaster to any degree that involved the hospital, the special dialer would remain operational and patch in with Snell's dispatch.

Wells and Winters scampered off down the 1st-floor hallway, away and toward the other stairwell door at the very end beyond the main outpatient Laboratory. They completed the frenetic scurry, as Damien swung open the door. Acting with extreme caution, a caution that pulsed uncomfortably with primal petrification, the surviving hospital workers made their way straight down.

IX

THE STAIRWAY WAS illuminated in bright red, more so a hazy magenta due to the one fizzing bulb cemented in the top corner crevice of the space. It was only a nine-step jaunt, then a hard turn backward, and another nine to the basement door. Damien was the leader while they both stopped as they approached the dark wooden entry divider with a thick white 'B' imprinted in the center mass, embossed by a black squared tile. Winters reached for the handle, but that time, he used extreme forethought. He wrenched the knob delicately, unveiling the floor's contents with only a cracked inch or two. Eerie silence met with him from the other side; nothing raucous or crazy seemed to be stirring. Becoming a little braver, he opened up just enough to pop his shaggy-haired skull through the wooden doorway.

"Coast looks clear," he whispered after turning his head back through the door to face Kip, who'd been standing down a step.

The leather-jacketed man took a grinding breath of stifling air and opened up to the fullest extent. The mortals then stepped out onto Mason General's all-too-familiar catacomb underbelly.

The basement level's lighting system had also been impaired, but thankfully, the backup generators were assisting enough to liven up the darkness. The illumination matched the stairwell in sinister hue, offering a blood-red glow mixed with a thin, silvery haze throughout. There appeared to be no one in sight. Mason's cellar consisted of the Pathology lab, which included a morgue, two other neighboring autopsy rooms, and a smaller blood Laboratory with a blood bank. There was also the main Engineering chamber to which touted every toxic gas and electrical systems equipment known to what was left of the civilized world. Lastly, was the Operator Services Unit, which was manned at least fifty hours a week by Kip Wells and Damien Winters. The staircase they'd come down from was luckily on the same side as their office, with it being situated up ahead of them and on the right.

Kip approached their office door with Damien following, doing his best at keeping a firm set of eyes on their six. Wells punched in the digital code sequence on the electronic buzz box attached to the top of the door handle. The device made a faint screechy sound, while the men hurried inside after nearly barreling through their familiar office base. For an initial few seconds, they'd felt almost a hollowed sense of irrational security, like slipping back into friendly surroundings where they'd spent years of their waking lives keeping an eye out on the lesser fortunate souls of a tarnished humanity. They'd endured so many insane work hours inside that very bottom space. The darling wave of nostalgia quickly foreclosed, with the men abruptly feeling suffocated and entombed inside their shitty home away from home.

For years, Operator Services had been loosely nicknamed "The Dungeon" by a healthy portion of varying hospital personnel. Strangely enough, they weren't even the specific group of workers who'd coined the little moniker. It had been given to them by other departments and differing floor units throughout Mason General. They would often come down for pager swaps or other intricacies of miscellaneous types of procedural information. They'd scan the room before exiting, then religiously ask how the operators on shift managed to survive down there in "The Dungeon."

Damien's panic-stricken mind suddenly fell back in time for a scattered duration, where he recalled a particular time an Anesthesiologist had the audacity to waltz in one evening and verbally state he'd probably lose all of his remaining marbles if he had to work down there each day and perform an Operator's specific job duties.

THE OBNOXIOUS SCARLET backups had also kicked on within their department, filling the paper secured claustrophobia with a fittingly haunting luminescence. Winters darted for the 911 corded telephone by the first workstation next to the majority of the office's major alarm panels, the one that was specifically designed to withstand any form of meltdown and provide the ability to radio Snell and his cowboys if the power had been severed from the failing facility.

To his chagrin, their one single lifeline had been ripped from the cluster fucked wall. The phone was strewn out on the floor in pieces and looked as though someone had stomped and smashed the SOS into another realm of oblivion.

"What are the odds that this piece of shit thing..."

Damien's voice trailed off into nothing as he looked underneath the desk near the disintegrated and unusable dog and bone.

It was Clara.

Clara Jenkins.

Clara had only been part of the OSU team for one tumultuous year. Winters had trained her off and on for several weeks during the infancy stages, while she toughed out her taxing probationary period. She had been struggling with the demanding nature of the job, but was a steady and valued asset to the diminishing first responding unit.

Clara had been savagely ripped to shreds: one of her arms severed from her body, her face half gone and eaten clean off. Her head had been turned around and twisted in full 180-degree savagery, with her mouth agape and eyes glued shut, frozen like a stone in a horrific death pose. The woman was barely recognizable, warped up and contorted underneath the table like a human jigsaw puzzle that would never be quite finished. The half-gone part of her face crawled with maggots and forced Damien to gag while he gawked at the soupy pulp of a mess. The truest authenticity of confirming that it was Clara was her hospital name badge. Doused with her blood, and yet it remained pinned up and affixed to her purple workers' union t-shirt.

"Jesus... It looks like Clara maybe went for the phone? But one of those sphinx things like you call them got to her first?" said Kip on approaching the scene to take a close stance behind his friend.

"Maybe," said Damien in a surprisingly smooth guile, while he stared down at the mess with eyes wide and a genuinely shocked transfixion.

He finished, "That's no way to die, Goddammit."

With the phone officially out of commission, Winters and Wells needed a serious brainstorm. They mulled around the familiar room in search of anything they could readily use—a weapon, a working cell phone, or Security walkie-talkie: anything to assist in the current nightmare. All the men could muster up was a sand wedge golf club that their in-standing boss had brought in one morning to help relax the unit's overcooked morale.

"Just use it as a putter and take turns hitting some golf balls into Dixie cups during slivers of downtime," said the boss the day he brought the wedge in hand along with a box full of fresh donuts in the other.

The OSU manager position had been a constant and troublesome revolving door for well over a decade. None of the poor and unsuspecting schmucks during either Damien or Kip's tenure had managed to last longer than a full year without getting shitcanned or dashing for the hills due to blistering job stress. Bill had been the 2020 boss man, and he only had a year and several months to go before retiring off into the sunset that would unfortunately never again materialize for him or anyone else. Bill was a decent chap but played an even better punching bag for the grisly politics of the healthcare company. He had been, more or less, tailoring Damien to take over management duties up until his soon to be golf games and cigar dates finally came true on his retirement gravy train.

Winters waltzed to the door leading into Bill's side office. It was positioned in the far opposite corner inside the OSU. He swung Bill's door open with authority and took a quick gander around the tidy enclosure. No Bill. Damien was quick to assume that he was probably already dead, or scorched down and replicated into one of the soulless fucks that roamed the residual Mason halls. He left Bill's space and closed the door behind him, finally resting his eyes on Kip, standing in the middle of the room holding the office's silly sand wedge.

"Take it easy, Tiger. Don't even bother with that stupid thing," said Winters sarcastically.

Kip shrugged a look his way and took an awful little swing with the club. He eventually dropped it to the carpeted floor in front of him.

"I'm thinking the roof," sighed Damien.

He went on, "Listen; we should eventually head for the highest point of Mason. Take the stairwells, stop at each floor. Have a cautious look around, then keep climbing. If we get to the Administration wing with all their fancy lattes and tasteless wall paintings and shit, then maybe we can get out through the roof. I'm fairly certain the one door leading outside up there is locked, but we can always bust through a window in a random office, someplace, to get outside. Once we're higher up and have a better vantage point, maybe we can see what the hell is going on out there. Reassess. Signal for help. Something..."

"What have we got to lose besides what's left of our ravaged and crumbling minds?" sighed Kip.

"Poetic... Fine, let's move," asserted Winters as they huddled out of their infamous hospital dungeon.

X

THEY HAD TO traverse five full flights of stairs, but it had technically been six, including the climb back up and out of the basement. The Administration and IT teams sat comfortably on the 5th and final floor of Mason General, which led out to the roof access the two listless men were hoping for. Damien and Wells hurried back to the stairwell they'd just come from, which entered the bottom floor. They climbed, with Winters leading the ascent, and arrived at the 1st-floor closure. The wavy-haired man palmed the handle and opened up.

Screams and shrieks boomed in immediate proximity, somewhere slightly off and jarringly near. Damien nearly slammed the barrier shut and bolted out of mortified instinct, but he managed to gut up instead and peek his head through and take a timid and shivering look. The lights had begun to flicker on floor 1, a maddening one-two punch of crimson and black with barely enough red to illuminate an eyeballed perspective of the incredulous scene.

Two lengthy sphinxes were clashing with three human and ordinary-looking unfortunates. The revolting creatures towered over the inferior humans, collectively outweighing the trio by hundreds of massy and muscular pounds. One man wore a scuffed half to death lab coat, the single woman was blanketed in a pattern spotted hospital nightgown, and an on-duty security guard's usually bright white shirt was splashed heartily with a sanguinary ooze.

The been-around the block officer locked his human eyes with the devil's orbs off to the side of the skirmish, then his grunged out upper garment instantly caught ablaze. The sorry sap spun around like a five-foot-seven geriatric kind of top. Moments later, his entire body was engulfed in a firestorm. The young woman patient in her nightie had been the shrieker of the bunch, while herself, along with her new lab worker ally, flailed and thrashed with desperation to fend off the putrid assault. As a sphinx took a heavy swipe of its clawed meat-hook towards the hysterical lady, her head was severed off from her thickset shoulders. Her continuous wailing ran deftly silent, with her lab tunic friend ceasing his defense in a stone-cold stupor. Her body continued fighting where she stood, totally headless. She attempted a hitched little jab with a jittering right arm, then her legs buckled hard and gave out all the way.

As a volcanic eruption of steamy hemoglobin spewed upward from where her noggin used to be, she crumpled crudely to the linoleum floor. The sphinx that applied the guillotine move turned toward the wide-eyed and defenseless worker, ultimately striking another blow with a heavily clawed scrape, gauging and opening the chest of the puny medical assistant. As the guy began to howl for all the heavens and all the angels to come running to his safeguard, Winters slammed the staircase door shut and staggered up with Kip toward floor number 2.

With Kip remaining in the follower's position, the 2nd-floor stairwell door was upon them. Damien reached out for the handle, but only touched it with a lanky middle finger. He looked down at his hand and noticed it trembled violently. The leather-jacketed man was terrified beyond rational comprehension. As his arm quaked with vigilance, he timidly turned the knob and opened things up about halfway. It looked clear, but right when he popped his head out fully into the hallway, an army of wretches and human imposters alike, all eyeless and devoid of humanity's fragile essence, cluttered a majority of the hall at the far other end.

Some were full-fledged animal sphinxes; others were mostly human in nature, except for the eyes. A select few wore hospital scrubs of different colored variants, while another handful was dressed in other mixes and matches of funky street attire. One villainous thing even simulated a half-human, half-sphynx hybrid theory of blasphemous proportions. It lumbered this way and that, sticking out from the crowd inside the dramatic hospital doomsday, wrangling horrifically to figure out which ghastly form to settle itself into. The group of aliens smelled of absolute death, even from the shielded shallow distance.

Winters was stuck dead at the scene; his unbelieving eyes practically bugged from his skull while he peeked out the slivered crack from the heavy staircase door. Kip reached an arm out and pulled him back into the gloomy safety net, making certain the door closed stealthily behind them. The peeking man's olive skin had literally turned white, a ghostly complexed face blanketing a paralyzing dread. He gawked a look through Kip to the shadowed dark wall behind them.

"W-we gotta go up. I… it's…" Damien trailed off from himself.

With a swift and violent shake of his swimming head, Winters commandeered the ascent upward to floor number 3, home of the NICU and Labor Delivery units. It was also the exact same floor where he had regained consciousness to fully enter his newest and unfathomable terror. He pondered backward to Boudreaux for a morsel of a fleeting instant, praying to anything worthwhile that the swallowed-up physician wasn't scouring the halls up there.

"Here we go. What's behind door number 3?" he then whispered in a dry performance of silly sarcasm.

Kip couldn't believe how his colleague could retain his sense of humor during such a time, but then again, he actually seriously could. Despite his troublesome and unfortunate mental shortcomings, Damien Winters had aggressively projected a pure calming aura during chaotic shit storms. It was both his gift and a throbbing curse all in one goopy sandwich of a tumultuous life.

Winters opened stairwell door 3 and an alarming creak rang out, showing off Mason General's gritty wear and tear, as he finally stepped out into the Labor and Delivery ward. Kip could hardly fathom how brazen of a move that was, and out of his own intense petrification, remained planted in molasses in the dank staircase aura, staring out at his friend on the unpredictable Mother and Baby unit.

The hall looked vacant and desolate, but before Damien could turn back toward Kip, a nurse shot out from a nearby patient room, holding a fresh as springtime newborn infant. She seemed to be perfectly human in overall creation, except for her rancid and seeping milks for eyes. The baby cried helplessly in her worse than possessed arms of barren amber.

"Give me the kid, you bastard," huffed Winters with an outstretched arm of rugged leather.

The nurse's bulbous ovals lined up with Damien's; however, he refused to stave off the piercing attack. His entire anatomy began to sinisterly boil from the inside, a skin-crawling feeling that was both intensely painful, as well as perversely intrusive, yet he hoped to fight for mental clarity against the classical and warped methodology of psychic torture. The nurse vessel snarled, then voiced in the most chipper Filipino accent with a hint of broken English.

"Come un owt, ladies!"

Before the man could dart over and snatch the exposed child away from harm, a dozen other former staff nurses filled the hallway in front of him, all cradling fresh human souls within their warped clutches of doom. The nurses were literal clones of one another, with uniforms pressed and dressed with dripping dastardly voids for seeing windows. The little ones squirmed and whimpered throughout, giving the scene a surreal and unspeakable sense of otherworldly chagrin. For an odd moment of skewed clarity, it all appeared normal and natural to the standing man. The night crew was simply caring for the restless newborns on spooktastic floor 3 over at creepy old Mason General, waiting patiently for the tiny tots to tucker out so they could place their fragile frames back to their mini incubators for beddy-bye time.

Without a second's warning, the entire baker's dozen of changed and rapscallion nurses projected their forceful fixations straight down at their respective newborn child, goggling at the distressed and writhing babes of guiltlessness. The innocent bundles went up like little match-sticks, turned instantly into squalling marshmallows, barely given a chance at human life, forever destined for the blackest abysses of screech worthy purgatories. Forced forever into a realm absent of any degrees of emotional states or future dreams, only mindless puppets to serve a foregone form of viciously controlled tyranny.

Before Damien could manage a maddening howl or an agonizing bellow, the floor's fire alarm boomed to life. Bright greens and ambers joined the symphony of fire lighting on the melting and shrieking Labor floor. All thirteen babies remained in flames and smoldering within the mitts of their prehistoric captors. Winters could literally smell the burning flesh of the perishing tykes in front of his crumbling self. It was a rancid fragrance tossed with the blanket fabric they'd been wrapped up in for their sphynx transport to a bloody and fiery inferno.

It flooded the appalled man's nostrils and instantly caused a violent dry heave. The nursing crew held their ogles steady and continued to crane downward on the popping little flame balls they relentlessly continued to smother, lacking the faintest of human emotions or remorseful expressions. The sprinkler system decided to kick on with a jolt, spraying a cool hydro mist everywhere, in meager defense of the mini-human s'mores.

Damien dropped to his knees, where he stood racking and aghast, managing to crawl back and away to the doorway and into the staircase he'd wholly just come from. As the hearty 3rd-floor stairwell divider made its creaking shift to a settled and secure close, Winters was on the floor at his friend's feet, sobbing uncontrollably.

XI

H E COULD ONLY weep for a moment. His glazed-over browns eventually stared up at Kip in the gloomily lit evanescence. Wells was staring off straight ahead and was gorgonized on the closed door that deemed their only flimsy protector. Kip's mouth was slightly ajar, a disbelieving shock blanketed throughout his boyish veneer. Damien wiped his face with a left leathered sleeve and mindfully rose to his feet.

"Kip? Yo, Kipper?!" he peered over at Wells in the morbid stair lights.

"I watched them all go up, Damien. The children… I can't take this anymore! I'm getting the fuck out of here!" Kip's tone was bordering on hysteria, a frantic tune of fleeing dementia plunging its jagged hooks into his ravaged soul. He turned to run back down the stairs toward floor number 1, operating on a primal fight or flight for any sense of relief from the current scenario of suffocating doom. Before the scrubbed man was all the way out of reach, Winters lashed out and grabbed his friend by the arm with a sturdy and gripping force. His bummed shoulder pained him with the sudden burst of effort, but he dug deep inside for an added strength of genuine moxie. He corralled him and yanked his colleague back into him.

"LISTEN, and listen good: if we split up, we're dead. We don't stand a chance against these fucking things. Understand? We need to see if we can either help anyone else left in here or get up to the roof. It's the only chance we've got right now."

In a swift and angry reply, Kip hollered back psychotically, "To hell with you, Winters! I'm better off on my own. I'm not risking my neck for anyone in this shithole. I'm getting the fuck out of here."

After sweeping a sweaty tuft of dark hair from his water-logged eyes, Damien studied his friend's frightened hazels with a gripping intensity.

"You did for me, Kip. You got me out of that bed. Don't you go quitting on me now, Goddammit," replied Winters with a raspy set, yet sublimely smooth tone, a tone that could never be taught or instructed.

A demeanor like that was something one was simply gifted with at birth. It was inevitably peculiar how in the face of horrendous evil and violent devastation, there were always a select few and far individuals within the overall human collective that chose to face such nefariousness with noble and authentic intent. With a clear mind and an honorable spirit for a destination of overall good. More often than not, it wasn't even the human beings you'd ever expect it to be. Especially not from some shaggy-haired orphan who'd fled for a new life in some pint-sized mountain town several years ago. Damien upheld his position on his colleague's upper arm until Kip finally succumbed whilst in the domineering grasp of the taller man.

"Alright, Damien. You win. I'll stick around for this hero shit."

With tired mirrors for eyes and snot draining down from his slightly swollen nose, the chocolate orbed Winters said, "It's not hero shit. It's the right thing to do. Now, move your ass."

They continued climbing toward floor 4, accompanied only by their horror-stricken demeanors and the oozing scarlet illuminators of the staircase. Hospital floor 4 was home to the general Intensive Care Unit and a handful of other special triage wings within Mason General. The most high-risk and seriously ill patients made themselves at home up on 4. When the men finally transcended the stairwell door, Kip snuck past Damien and took his place in the lead.

"I got this one," he said softly as he turned back and gave his comrade a calm and confident expression.

Damien nodded and waited as the new wingman in a gripping state of writhing tension. Before Kip could even grab for the handle, the hinges swung open in a flash, revealing a half-human, half-sphinx mishmash of despicable proportions. The sphynx side looked female, whereas the human region remained that of a common man. The beastly portion owned an eye of vile and diseased death, a sickeningly yellowish lamp that pussed and oozed in search of immediate, primal satiation. The other half of the face owned a plain Jane sky blue-tinted human eyeball. The man section was stark naked along with its detestable side of the scoundrel's body of the Sphinx. The sphinx region was noticeably larger in dimension, causing the entire mass of contorted flesh to sag lopsidedly in the open space. The entirety of the being seemed to glow in the hallway, appearing like some gigantic rubbery mountain of sturdy and grotesque wax. The man side looked absolutely mortified; however, the sphinx part wore a devilish grin that protruded rigorously from its revolting lion face.

It grabbed for Kip's throat with its mixed entity and pulled him like an unruly teenager straight through the stairway door jamb with exemplary ease. When the door quickly slammed shut behind the pair, all of a sudden snatching Damien's cherished friend right out of sight, he fumbled crazily for the stupid handle.

He opened up and plunged forward onto the floor with no authentic regard for the general safety of his own brittle mortality. After taking three healthy steps onto hospital floor 4, the man slipped suddenly on something wet and slick, causing the gangly Winters to go sprawling clumsily onto his back. Not understanding how he'd fallen, he gazed upward towards the ceiling, then over to the surrounding area within his initial line of vision, then back again at the ground where he lay.

Everything and anything in immediate view was consumed in a dark and bloody gore. Fresh ichor poured from the rafters, while the walls were thoroughly splashed and speckled, with the dull flooring being completely ingested in the blobby foreign goo. Damien tilted his head upward in a desperate attempt to locate his friend. Kip and the beast stood several feet ahead of him. The sphynx still had him by the neck with one human appendage, grasping him entirely off the ground in an exhibition of incredible and freaky charisma.

Winters kicked his legs and arms a little, creating some distance between the pair, while trying with vigor to rise back up to his feet. He finally righted himself in the midst of clicking and clacking his rugged boots generously into the slimy muck. He splashed the icky liquid all over himself in the scrambling process. His hair and jacket were literally covered in the coagulated sea of sloppy jelly. With the rose matter lighting in perfect tune with the gross fluids all around, it was an outright overload of hospital red death—a scene pulled straight from Hell itself. Or perhaps, even a place that existed long before Hell was ever a creative forethought. A feeding ground where the legion of the Sphinx owned the totality of the dark and didn't give two substantial shits what a human-derived God thought about any of it.

Kip had his eyes closed tightly in the clutches of the monster, not wanting to mesh forces with the grotesque soul swallower. Winters couldn't help but take another jittering look around at what had become of the dripping ICU. An empty wheelchair rested off near the sidewall closest to him. A severed human leg was pleasantly situated in the empty rolling seat. It wore a tattered and ripped mint-colored hospital scrub pant. A blurry tattoo of a dagger was printed around the bloody calf region. The image came off as a fake to him, maybe a mockery to his overwhelmed and pulverized imagination. Perhaps a prop that had been set out on a neighbor's porch to scare the sugar starved minions on a brisk Halloween night back when the world was in a somewhat more confident swing in favor of Mankind.

However, his current scene of absurdity was all too authentic.

He reeled forward and focused back on his colleague and the hulking daemon that owned him. In a jarring flash, the thing whipped Kip from its human hand side to the opposite sphinx claw, clenching him by the good of his throat with the intimidating beast duke. Kip's hazel eyes remained sealed, baring wrinkles around his forehead and above his cheekbones, due to the strained intention not to meet with the terrorizer.

The half-lion began to shake Wells in midair with its angry right hand, as if the man were a rag doll being bullied by an enormously rabid hellhound. The heavy rocking made Kip's eyes come alive and open, reluctantly greeted with dread in light of the incredulous leviathan. The sphinx continued to offer one pulsating lamp, while the other remained smaller and very much human. The sole yolky cylinder was more than sufficient to begin the horrifyingly fatal process.

Wells began to writhe violently and grind his teeth in the seizure of the ageless creature. A white vapor broke out on top of his twisted bed of curly and glistening hair. A moment ago, he'd been drenched with frightened perspiration, but all of a sudden, Kip's entire body was on the verge of smoking to the point of fiery human combustion.

While Damien witnessed the dire progression from his shallow distance, he sprung forward without even thinking. With his messy steel-toe motorcycle boots striking the crimson covered hospital tile, the man charged full-steam and weaponless straight for them.

The moment Kip began a gutted showing of a dying scream, Winters crashed into the sphinx, head-on, leading with his bummed and freshly set shoulder to apply a maximum charging force. His adrenaline was spiked through the roof at that juncture, a feeling of near invincibility, and all engines running on absolute infinity. Upon impact, the beast fumbled significantly and lost its satisfaction upon Kip, dropping him like a limp noodle to the soupy hospital deck.

The leather jacket and the hybrid impurity went careening to the floor as one, sliding across the ICU against the fleshly slip and slide it had sickeningly become. When they finally came to a messy halt, Damien found himself lucky in a mostly top position against the monster. He brought a bare hand up and plunged a long and rugged finger into the dazed bastard's bulbous and hoary marble of albino white. It trembled in agony, belching a human scream concocted with something even more ungodly. The eye exploded inside the lion thing's stew, shooting a milky ooze all over itself and on the man's embattled, but always faithful dark bomber's jacket. It swung a large sphinx paw up in response, catching Winters on the whole left side of his face, causing the scrappy mortal to catch air and slam into the adjacent wall several feet away from the scuffle.

Only slightly dazed, he peered over at Kip.

Wells appeared alright and somewhat coherent. His body had stopped sweltering, and he was trying to move his arms and legs on the floor. Damien scrambled to his feet and rushed over to pick up his wounded companion from the ICU bloodbath royale. Winters huffed and wheezed with exhausted lungs, while he dragged both of their standing weights back toward the stairwell door. Before it was again slammed shut behind them, he gave a quick double-take to look back and fire a frightening scowl at the clodhopping predator. The sphinx crossbreed was sprawled out on its uneven anatomy, convulsing profusely in the muck with its alien breasts flopping about its nude body, all the while becoming saturated in all variants of vile and ichor.

The thing never stopped screeching.

XII

"**L**ook at me, Kip. Say something. You still with me?"

A concerned tone escaped from Winters that he didn't display often. While remaining deathly silent, his friend stood shivering and facing his immediate direction. Kip's eyes of grayish hazel were wide with a gripping anguish that was buried deep inside his wrenching marbles.

The recently attacked man eventually broke free from his muted agony, "I, I think so... I can't describe the pain," he tried to go on.

"We can't discuss it right now, old buddy," interrupted Damien, "We gotta keep moving. We're almost there. Can you walk?"

Kip attempted an unassisted move up a step in the moodily lit stairs, but staggered and nearly went down with a thud. Winters caught him and wrapped a right arm around his dazed and confused fellow mortal. Arm in shoulder, they carried on skyward into floor number 5.

They could be seen as two battered soldiers ascending a series of divine steps in search outbound from a diabolical purgatory, wanting nothing more selfish than to desperately reach a morsel of warming essence at the higher end of the pitiful dark. Damien hoped and prayed in continual thought for any scrap of relief in the hospital of insanity that his counterpart and he were thoroughly engulfed in.

Another minute passed as they trudged the slick steps, nearly there and face to face with the floor 5 stairwell door. Kip seemed to have recovered somewhat from his ordeal back on 4, and again managed to take his place on his own two feet behind Damien. When they neared the eminent hatch, Winters noticed that the door was already completely open, propped wide and ajar by a hinge at the bottom corner of the rectangular assembly. The lighting system was fully illuminated and shimmering like a beacon up on 5. The warm fluorescents slipped through the open doorway, shooting a longing brilliance of pyrrhic warmth that poured down and over the wounded young men. It looked like home, the glowing phosphorescence at the end of the nightmarish tunnel—the illustrious way out—the break in the God-forsaken madness. Winters and Wells both smiled upward at the open space, with exhausted emotions taking center stage over the rugged hospital employees.

While acting supremely on the side of deliberate precaution, Winters turned back around and gave a steady look at his damaged friend. "Let me check things out first. Stay put and relax for a bit. I can tell you need it."

Kip gratefully complied and slid down to the floor in his grey-black scrub suit just before the doorway entrance. Damien turned away reluctantly and headed up the last remaining steps, finally entering the brightly lit and prestigious floor number 5. His honey-brown eyes demanded a moment to adjust with the normal and constant flow of overbearing ambient dazzle. He peered left down the sparkling hallway, then right. The whole region of the floor within his reeling view seemed utterly unscathed. The walls were plastered with a thick and fresh coat of forest green paint, and richly lit photographic art prints lined the general perimeter.

The loftiest story of Mason General Hospital featured the Administration gang and a handful of Information Technology personnel, otherwise known as the Help Desk in hospital slang terminology. Except for Damien and Kip, who'd over the years coined them the Helpless Desk for significant reasons, and multitudes of other CEO's, CFO's and hospital Nursing Supervisors.

In Winters' nearly full decade tenure on the job, he'd only been up to the Administrator's wing a single time. Part of an Operator's training protocol during initial hiring was to take a complete and thorough tour of the whole facility. The reason being that each OSU employee had to fully understand and physically lay eyes on every nook and cranny of the care center's layout they'd been chosen to watch over. Touring the grounds inside and out gave each employee a better guideline of how to direct traffic in a centralized hub without actually seeing an important scenario unfold firsthand.

With being stationed down low in the basement, the team had to envision certain situations that doctors and nurses would demand of them while relaying from the witnessing source material. It was just another odd part of the job, an absolute requirement of an adapted skill that was crucial to the core of that specific profession. Even in the most severe circumstances, such as a life-threatening code procedure, those specific codes were broken down depending on where certain departments resided within Mason.

All the gaudy and bougie knick-knacks remained in top-notch order on snazzy floor 5. Luscious plants were littered in office doorways, a giant sprawling display of foliage covered a sweeping section of the wall just off the closest elevator bank. When Damien had visited nearly ten years ago, he was blown away at how quiet things were up on the final floor of Mason General. He could frankly remember hearing a pin drop; that's how silent it was.

No angry telephones rang out incessantly, the smell of rich and foo-foo javas soaked through and sifted around the copious offices and corridors, and there hadn't been a single living soul in sight. He'd presumed that the staff was all scattered inside the confines of their cozy and spacious office spaces. Hidden away from the death and dying chaos from underneath the decomposing floors below.

While standing alone in the same hall, the cynicism of everything that had transpired up until that second flooded violently through Damien's entire body. In a clouded moment inside his own ripping psyche, everything before him appeared mundanely vanilla. He could almost taste the wafting coffees and delicious pastries from years prior, and could actually visualize the hotshot executives staring off into space at their mammoth desks of thick mahogany, along with their fizzing computer screens, conjuring up sly new ways to save a buck or two when bonus time rolled around.

WINTERS BREATHED IN deeply, held it for a firm six-count, then exhaled with a shutter and decided to give himself another quick once over. The man remained sore from root to stem, his shoulder throbbed fiercely, and his beloved leather jacket was immersed with both sphinx and human forms of carnage. His charcoal jeans and motorcycle boots were all sprayed with red, along with his slender face and shoulder-length hair dripping with exhausted perspiration. Damien was plainly grateful to still be alive. Knowing that Kip was close by and enduring the same atrociousness alongside him made the young mortal feel like a luckless card shark with a desperate, yet familiar ace in the hole.

After his micro reminiscence, he listened for anything that stirred on the esteemed upper floor. Not so much as a peep greeted him, so he hustled down the corridor a way. He hung a right at the end of the forest green section of walls as it opened up serenely into a blue steel coated set of evocative palisades. The acrylic was slathered roughly and with a raised texturing, giving the imposing medium a thick impasto appearance of rousing boldness. The walls gave off an incredibly modern and artistic appeal.

A lofty photographic metal display of the Rocky Mountains at a snow-covered dusk was affixed marvelously on one of the chunky walls of blue velvet. It had a ghost backing, which made the piece appear to float all by itself right up on the wall. The landscape image was tack sharp throughout the foreground and background and was heavily saturated with breathtaking vividness. Damien remained silent during his frenetic investigation, not uttering a word and keeping his booted steps as muffled as humanly possible. He roamed around the joint, looking for an office or enclave that could give Kip and himself an easy window to break for their planned rooftop access.

Just before reaching the conference room bank up ahead of the picturesque straightaway, he heard a thud ring out from conference room A-13, which was positioned in front of him and to his left.

He then heard voices.

It sounded as if an ordinary business meeting was going on and in a heated discussion, with human opinions being intermingled with jumbled banter of this thing and that. The man became overtaken with a naive sense of sudden aspiration.

What if he'd finally found a band of humble survivors in the Mason house of pitiful chaos?

He then stutter-stepped into the ample and open A-13 door frame, and took a whopper of a step squarely in the center of the large entryway. Winters bore the faintest of boyish grins on his mug, one that exuded an ecstatic relief that couldn't possibly be helped. It settled upon his chiseled features out of some misplaced sense of blind optimism, thinking only that it had to be a shimmer of an answer or a fraction of solace to the frothing festering down below. The smile faded and was washed away in a sharp snap of a calloused instant. His mouth dropped open with only a slur of barely audible coherency, which managed to escape from his quivering lips.

In the thickly set room before him, were two mighty oak office tables aligned with contrasting metal chairs positioned around and underneath them. A humongous window was affixed at the very back of the room, and a smaller stimulating one was situated sheepishly off to the left. If broken, the smaller aperture on the left would wind up on the Mason General rooftops. The more obnoxious glass display in the far back region was a sheer drop of nearly a hundred feet to the aforementioned Promised Land.

The lights inside functioned on full steam and with their usual eye-splitting intensity. The shadeless back window, however, gave off an uncanny unveiling of incredible outside scenery. Darkness fell consumedly with rich and assertive splendor, while a blueish-green mist weaved in and out of the scattered clouds on the outskirts of the grand hospital chamber. A sequence of lightning bolts blasted off fittingly behind the group of attendance goers, although no thunder of any kind could be heard from the eerie tower confines.

Roughly seventeen or so collective participants ceased their jabbering and looked toward the entrance area, all staring intensely at the down but never out Damien Winters. Each and every one of them was dressed in a variation of silky business attire. Some were pressed and situated inside dark suits and jackets; others donned charcoal patterns with solid pastel ties, whether bow or full Windsor in maneuverable fashion, while the remaining bunch settled their night of reckoning with colorful pinstriped threads of showy fancy. The noblewomen of the group were snugly fitted into curvy dresses or white and black business suits of impressive crisp.

A secretary type was presented like a charming Christmas gift in a flattering white top with a checkered shorter skirt, dark grey, and white in shade with silver and red lining to break up the symmetrical and clashing squares. She wore thickly rimmed black rectangular glasses and sat stiffly off to the nearer side of the loaded gathering. She had her legs wrapped tightly and crossed over herself, revealing silkily long stalks to shamefully lust for, ones that snaked all the way down to a pair of black velvety leather pumps.

A handful of the others were seated in chairs during Damien's interruption, while the remainder stood standing with an overconfident dominance. A cluster of the occupants showed several signs of being very crushed and normal looking, especially the secretary lady with her seductively striking appeal, except of course, for her rancid and swelling globes of rotten impurity. Each and all of the meeting's gatherers flaunted the ancient eyes of milky unpigmented death. Only the whites bulged sacrilegiously from their human appearing skulls, pulsating in a frenzied fever at the very sight of the grief-stricken and shit out of luck Damien Winters.

The fetching secretary broke the brief silence ever so alluringly.

"Hello, Damien. I've been expecting you. We've ALL been expecting you."

She had obviously, at one time or another, been a former Mason General employee. However, Damien never had the pleasure until that unfortunate meet and greet. He did recognize some of the other swallowed-up and impersonated skinsuits. Her voice was laced with soothing and inviting undertones, executed with a variety of skills that could bring a grown man fully down to his knees on command.

The only word Winters could conjure for a reply was a distasteful, "N-o-O-o," in a broken hypnotic dread of shattering disbelief.

His legs nearly buckled and gave up from under him, but he managed to grasp the door jamb in a lasting effort to reinforce his crumbling balance. The mortal staved off his gaze from the sea of faceless puppets, all decked out and dolled up, with no place really worthwhile to go anymore. The secretary uncrossed her sultry and vivacious stems, revealing starch white panties that barely covered what was left of her lost and gone humanity. With the brandishing maneuver, her buttery legs gave way to the shortness of her skirt of checkered appeal, hiking up insanely toward her while simultaneously offering nearly all of her healthy and vanilla-coated shanks.

Then, she rose stiffly to her feet. As she stood fully erect as the leading commander of the bunch, the remaining seated drones followed in perfect order. As a harmonized unit of bygone Sphinx degeneracy, the things forcefully projected their powerful white marbles directly at Winters, while he could barely stand upright by his own accord in the generous front entrance of conference room A-13. While he was beckoned to join his alarmed humanity with the secretary vixen of damnation, Damien felt a massive head rush of biblical proportions that surged straight through him. It almost sent the leather-coated man flying right out of his boots and fully backward. The sudden heat was deathly unbearable, as his most intricate thoughts and clever human ideas were beginning to get attacked and tinkered with, as if a sadistic ventriloquist were yanking at his brain's metaphorical life strings.

At the ruthless moment, where he felt his mind going off the rails and being handed over to something grossly foreign and undeniably bone-chilling, he rushed in a slew of his own off-kilter and imaginative processes of thought. The attacked man conceptualized his ludicrous artworks and rough pencil sketches, honing every brain cell of attention he could call on to every nuance of detail within his creative and original intellect. He forcefully switched gears from the inside and mused of making zealous love to Leigh by a crackling fire at his cozy cabin on the outermost edge of town.

He even brooded over God, how if He truly did exist, He could quite seriously be a precious ally right about then. They were continuous and elaborate ruminations, mostly detailed depictions of his life's short stories frozen back in a careening box of swishing time. Highly original brain activity was the only thing keeping the tortured soul somewhat together in defense of the primeval invasion on his mind.

Right as his plain dark jacket began to practically breathe fire, Damien slammed his forced eyelids emphatically shut. A collective shriek erupted from the assaulting group in front of the ravaged young man, a mixture of disgruntled former humanity peppered with a pulverizing force of inexplicable rage. Winters staggered away from the soul piercers with his eyes glued closed and his jacket still smoking, on the verge of going down hard in a suffocating heap. His body started to hit the floor just outside the conference room entrance, but he flung out a hand at the last possible second to stop him from going down all the way. He managed to get to his feet again, and with a gritted gasp of breath, he opened up his umber eyes.

He could instantly feel the majority of his truest self, along with his infinite lusty passions flooding uncontrollably back into his unsteady human vessel. All his pain, his joys, and graphic memories of life, all came gushing back in a shivering wave of raging intensity. Damien lumbered and ran during the lengthy spasm, stumbling like a pinball back down the steel blue atrium, somehow knowing to turn left and stagger back down the initial forest green section of the Administration hallway. He broke into a full sprint as he crashed through the stairwell door where he'd left Kip to rest easy.

"Kip!?" he said in a frantic daze inside the ill-lit gloom.

His friend was nowhere to be found.

XIII

WITH ALL HOPES unfairly dashed, Damien found himself alone and reeling in the bloody fluorescents of stairwell floor 5. His psyche remained scrambled and fudged-up due to the conjoined attack from the uniformed clan of disgraceful blankness, with crushing defeat beginning to claw its way into the jellied portion of his cerebrum, to settle in heartily like impenetrable cement. He was visibly quaking as yet another panic attack attempted to pulverize what remained of him. His legs and arms went frighteningly numb and tingly, with the temples of his skull seeming as though they'd been gripped with impunity inside a hellacious vice grip. A primal fury began to boil within the central core of his ravaged being.

From the hallway he'd just escaped, he could make out human-sounding sphinx snarls and ramblings in thirsty search of him. They'd most assuredly been angry that they'd let him escape their vacuumed eternity. By then, hopefully he and Kip were the remaining human suckers left within the festering walls of Mason General. The anger intensified, bubbling to the point of dangerous overflow. Winters stood unyielding in his position in the murky stair coffin, finally whipping his head toward the capped heavens disguised as the rank medical center ceiling, and howled an absolutely violent scream.

"AAHHHH!!"

A conundrum of everything volatile and human that coursed within him spilled forward and out. Fury, desire, wrath, and overthrow all twisted up in one sinister melody. Another blistering cry out from the mortal rang true like an explosion within the doomsday confines.

"AAAHHHHAAHH!"

The emotional charge sent tears down his cheeks and shockwaves smashing straight through his heart, providing a choked-off sensation deep within his straining esophagus. The ravenous beasts in their dapper monkey suits were nearly at him. Another squeal from the posse rang out as if indicating the game was just about done. In an instant, the barrier would be flung open, and Damien would simply just give up. He'd let the prehistoric bastards melt his body down to soup, then allow the fiendish degenerates to gobble up his fractured soul right up off the fucking hospital deck.

In a timeless and fleeting tick of an instant, the young man reminisced of everything that he'd ever done or cherished within his short and undeniably rocky existence. Mostly being fancied a pessimist throughout his usual waking hours, he could all but barely stomach how at that very moment, in the deepest ruins of his ghoulish desolation, that he was forcefully bombarded with beautiful thoughts and wonderful sensations he'd encountered throughout the entirety of his troubled life.

A literal nanosecond before the floor 5 stairwell door burst open with the hungry faces of the soulless horde, Winters whispered one small phrase to himself before galloping like a wounded banshee down the semi-dark hospital tread boards.

That phrase was "BURN IT ALL."

XIV

T HE BASEMENT.
IT was the one floor to which the man knew with utmost certainty.
His entire hospital career had resided down in the lowly bowels of
Mason General. There were intricate treasures, such as chunky tanks
of oxygen and carbon dioxide gases, even nitrous oxide used to fuel
various degrees of hospital power and to, most importantly, provide
special medical treatments for special patient needs. Basically, any
highly volatile chemical under the medical universe called the basement
level their home.

In Pathology, one of the two autopsy rooms consisted of countless
variations of noxious mixtures and loaded chemistry vials for anatomical
dissection purposes. Next came Biomedical Engineering, and finally
standard Engineering, which in fancier terms was named Facility
Operations at the opposite end of the underground wing. Bio-med had
all sorts of gadgets and devices that were to be used in the technological
dealings of the medicinal branch. Highly complex computers used for
pricey x-rays and MRI's, EKG machines for Cardiology and transplant
patients, even electronically powered wheelchairs were jammed up and
pressed with authority into the large square plan for a room.

Damien danced the Basement floorplan throughout his worn-out
mind, while he haphazardly lumbered down the narrow steps to
nowhere. He descended to floor 4, blowing right past it and lurching
his way down to 3. He paused at 3, breathing open-mouthed, all the

while frightened to his mortal wit's end. He listened for any infected sounds from above and craned his head that way once or twice to check up if his ghastly entourage of sphynx suits were hot on his tail. He couldn't hear them in the stairwell, so he kept on hustling into his bottom destination.

Down, down, down: under what was left of his shattered and crumbling world.

The stifling darkness in the stairs only lit up red every other second or so, providing Winters just enough illumination to watch his feet and continue his dive. The backup lighting system seemed to turn lazy at that particular point, on the verge of sputtering out under the apocalyptic circumstances. He floundered beyond floor 2 with wobbly legs and a chagrined spirit that swam with the weary and desolate uncertainties. He flew right by lobby floor 1 and stared down the last remaining steps of dark crimson until the Basement door was upon him once again.

The man sucked in a huge and deliberate heap of stale oxygen, with the sole intention of feebly trying to get a slippery stranglehold of what was left of his fleeting sanity. Not knowing what to expect, besides probably the utmost worst, he tramped the final remaining stoops and put a shuttering outstretched hand to the closed-door handle of smudgy chrome. He turned the knob shakily as it opened with a creaky form of disquieting delight.

The first thing he noticed was there didn't appear to be a single thing in sight, neither dead nor alive. Damien also quickly realized that the lighting had switched on a dime down there. The reddish fluorescents had given way to a rich and vivid blue, casting a cold and spectral chill upon everything Basement. His own shadow brooded before him in the vacant hallway, casting a graphic undertaker of his shaky and remaining self-worth.

There was one specific room in the Mason General cellar that he wanted to avoid like the plague, but was well aware he'd eventually have to entertain the option to execute his elaborate action plan. He carried on steadfast, traipsing his way toward the Morgue/Autopsy rooms. But before he could engage the circular Pathology door handle, a black-hearted boom echoed out of nowhere.

A gunshot, presumably.

The blast spun the lanky man around right there in his boots, spilling him to the Basement ground in a shocking instant. Winters wound up on his side, clutching at a higher section of his better-off shoulder. The phantom who'd fired from his right blind spot stepped into view and stalked over the fallen man. It was a woman, as feminine and as human could undeniably be. She stood right over him in the chill-factored abyss. Even from his grounded view, her posture appeared smallish in overall nature, if not even petite, and she wore a pearly white lab coat that came to settle down around her knobby knees of dark material. Her medium brown hair was pulled back in a tight-locked ponytail. She had a name badge that dangled off her coat pocket, one which offered an aqua white hue to it in the creeptastic illumination. The badge read, 'BIO-TECH' in bold red lettering.

Only fear had consumed her oh so human eyes, the tiny dark circles gaping down at her surprised victim. The injured man went to say something in defense, but was interrupted by her gun manufacturing a grinding clicking of a noise in her delicate hand. She had fired again toward his skull, where he lay wounded, but the handgun had locked or jammed on her brazen attempt. She shook the firing piece violently over him, trying to right the weapon again for proper bang bang. The handgun looked to be some sort of Glock pistol, dark charcoal in color with sufficient amounts of plastic parts. The extension of her hand appeared much bigger than she did in his skewed and secondary perspective, with its blue steel thrashing above him while it chomped at its bit to execute a final death shot. Damien couldn't believe that she had intended to continue with the shooting, knowing full well that she and he were both very much still human.

While clutching his newly damaged shoulder, he tried desperately to do something, or at least to audibly say stop, but with all her fumbling she got the pistol ready again. Before she could pull the trigger to release another bullet, Winters swung his right boot out stiffly, catching the technician in the shin. She gave him a weak screech in return as the pistol fired a second hollow point, narrowly missing Damien's face and settling into the linoleum flooring only inches above his head. The woman went crashing to the floor with her Glock ricocheting out and off in an unknown direction. After losing interest in his punctured through and bleeding arm, the man got to his knees and leaped for the white-coated executioner. She had landed on her side, as Winters met her in a wrestling match on the blue floor of satin.

"What the shit, lady? I'm on your side!" he pleaded in the heat of the scuffle.

The Glock had landed to the right of the lab worker, as she reached around herself to look for her deadly toy.

"Fuck you!" was her only response.

Her left hand found the gun with the man still on top of her. She tried to aim it in a grizzled attempt to uncork a third and point-blank shot, but Damien swatted the pistol away with his right palm, sending it careening again into the frosted ocean of noir. She tried to knee him good where the sun doesn't shine, but managed to miss altogether and instead strike the inside of his jeaned leg. Regretfully, Winters then gristly slammed his right elbow down into the Bio-technician's furrowed face. She went out cold in an instant, as blood swelled from both sides of her cute button nose.

Out like a crazed little light.

He rose from her lifeless body and went searching in the aqua for the missing handgun. He found it resting up against the wall, several feet from him. He picked it up with a wheeze and studied the assembly with an intriguing curiosity. He was more than familiar with handling firearms, owning two registered weapons for himself. He had only shot that style of Glock once before in his lifetime, but he felt confident it was fairly self-explanatory. He removed the magazine and noticed that ten rounds remained inside the slender bullet clip. He then checked the chamber, which somehow managed to be hollowed out and empty. He slammed the magazine back into the piece, swiftly pulling back the slide to snap and load the chamber with a hot and heavy round, and gave a quick glance back at the insane technician lady on the basement bed of blue. She remained on her halfway mark while facing away from him, still very much unconscious.

"No hard feelings, little missy. But I think this is where we officially part ways," stammered the slender man.

Being dominantly left-handed, he moved the gun from his secondary hand into his more comfortable southpaw. It felt incredibly relieving to finally palm a weapon for the pure self-defense purposes of his own remaining life. The inanimate object of plastic and metal was officially controlled by him, and he knew exactly what to do with it if need be.

With the slightest sliver of a newfound confidence, Damien had almost forgotten his fresh bullet wound. His endless reservoir of adrenaline was nevertheless continuing to fire at an impressive sky-high. He was headed to the morgue anyway, and it would be there where he'd both reassess his plan and take a concerning look at his recently shot through right shoulder.

XV

THE MORGUE WAS a short trek up the frosted tunnel of a hallway, positioned directly adjacent to his own office of Operator Services. He arrived unharmed, barring the sinister circumstances, and crashed through the swinging double doors with authority. While gripping his right shoulder with his gun-palmed left hand, the man scanned the room in front of him.

It was pitch black inside the cadaver's lair, so he tried for the light switch on his left. With surprise, the lights flickered on at their own accord after the flicking effort. The bulbs began slowly at first, giving quirky popping noises of scattered illumination to help brighten and warm things up a bit. Eventually, the full set of long ceiling tubes switched on completely. Damien blindly assumed that certain wards and random offices would still have some degree of functioning power within off-beat sections of the old-timey hospital. Mason General's morgue happened to be one of those rooms. The layout was organized with six metal corpse beds positioned in the center region of the airy space. The beds were all empty and thankfully, lifeless. To the left was the cold storage fridge. It consumed an entire wall from root to stem, towering an overbearing credence of inescapable mortality within the cube. To the right, a multitude of surgical instruments and laboratory equipment lay out on a table, indiscriminate.

Winters shifted to the right side of the dead room, sifting around different tubes and vials that were strewn out all over. Some of the glasses were filled with assorted samples, others with tough-looking chemicals of unknown severities. Several sharp scalpels were peppered here and there. Under his frenetic investigation, that particular area of the morgue was left chaotic. He figured someone had already come looking for anything that could have been useful to retaliate against the insurgence of Sphynx.

His arm throbbed while he rested his weary burnt siennas on a tuft of gauze and a bottle of alcohol on the cornered edge of the cluttered work surface. He removed his jacket and placed the Glock on the table with it, like a paperweight but for coats. Damien's ripped t-shirt was tarnished with his own vital fluid, but luckily, the bullet had only grazed him. It barely even nicked the skin. His almost black coat of leathered armor had taken most of the punishment, possibly deflecting the round, giving it just enough trajectory to only scratch the shoulder's meat. It did bleed a little, so he doused the bloodshed with some bottled alcohol from the table, and stamped a crumpled piece of clean-ish gauze on top for crude measure. He rummaged like a monkey for some tape and found a full roll, finally giving himself the world's worst hospital field dressing.

Satisfied enough with the amateur effort, he pulled his jacket back on and palmed the lightweight and handy Glock pistol. The man strained to focus his scattered attention to anything flammable that resided in the room of the recently deceased. Above the disorderly surface was a semi-large glass case with a yellow skull and crossbones stamped in the bottom right corner. It was packed to the gills with several long and clear cylindrical liquids. There were clear pipe-shaped vials and a select few cloudy fluids, along with blue and piss colored ones.

They would have to suffice.

He took the butt of his gun and smacked it in the center of the glass enclosure, being extra careful not to pierce any brimming potions in the process. The shards fell away cleanly, revealing his dangerous scientific prizes. The morgue lighting system buzzed to life while he removed five different tubes from the busted through glass case of chemistry. He wanted more than five, but that was all the man could carry safely within his grasp. Winters needed both hands for the job, so he placed his firearm behind his back and tucked it down into his scuffed jeans. With hands loaded completely with imprisoned and volatile chemicals, he turned away and stalked back out into the azul basement world.

The first thing that struck him was the deranged gunslinger had disappeared right up off the floor. No matter, that wasn't very concerning to him just then. He had her gun, and she had a busted snout. Winters then headed down the corridor a ways, coming face to face with the main Engineering nucleus.

OH, THE MASON General Engineering department!

Those choice men and women fancied a slew of menial tasks for the hospital's overall standard operations. Some jobs were as frivolous as changing a bathroom light bulb; however, the bulk of their duties revolved around and were designated to the fire alarms and poisonous gases quarantined in the facility's intestines. The Engineering entity appeared to thoroughly get their rocks off with testing the fire panels for days, weeks, and even months, consecutively. The Code Red indicator would sound off maddeningly within Operator Services for hours and weeks at a time, causing mass hysteria within the unit for lack of a better term. Before the world had thoroughly begun to implode, it seemed to Damien as if the Engineers had absolutely nothing healthier to do with their "valuable" work time but to tinker with the offline system at all hours of the day and night.

Things got so bad, it even became a running joke within the OSU, a rather sick one at that, causing a handful of the crew to hypothesize they were all rats in an overgrown maze, and the Engineer pricks were the monstrous humans with the shock treatments and squares of cheese. Winters and Wells would envision the overpaid screwballs gawking down from the rafters at their measly OSU unit, while they guffawed and laughed and button mashed the alarms for no rational reason, except for downright lunacy. They'd high five each other and carry on with pushing and pulling, glaring down at their pet rat Operators and cackling like hyenas, while Winters and his team lost their most functional marbles on the underground surface of front-line hospital defense.

Of course, that was more so likely a fictitious claim spawned from an evocative and deranged imagination of the mind, but then again, who the hell really knew anymore? Especially with what was transpiring within the walls of old rickety Mason General, nothing short of ludicrous was wiped clean off the corroding fucking table.

XVI

INSIDE HIS SLENDER hands that nearly overflowed full of volatile liquids, he bent down and tried the Engineering handle with two long fingers.

Locked.

The door was pretty flimsy, so Damien decided to try some good old-fashioned ultraviolence. With chemicals cradled in hand, the man front kicked the barrier with a steel-toed boot. The hinge gave way only a smidge, inviting another invested wallop. Winters complied, sending his right foot smashing into the thing with all his might. The aged door flung open against its will, revealing the illustrious contents of the intricate and dangerous space of cluster.

Way back during his training days, he had only passed by the Engineering hive. The door had been locked then, as it was a moment ago before he caved the lightweight sucker in. He was unfamiliar with the innermost layer of Facilities land.

The area was set up in an L-shape design.

Straight ahead was a whopping generator panel, even more monumental in stature than the one glued to the wall in his home of Operator Services. Red, green, and white lights filled up rows of numerous and sequential squares on the titanic electronic device in front of his eyes. Each square had a label attached to it, with an easy to translate inscription that read things such as, 'CO2 Reserve Full' or 'O2 Level Low.' The individual boxes were quarantined off, with each one owning their own color. It looked like a ginormous rectangular Christmas tree with its different neon chessboard lights carousing across the wall in hypnotic variance. To his left were clumps and tumbles of thick exposed wiring, each hooked up to miscellaneous electrical circuits inside the wall. The hub where he broke in powered the full entirety of Mason, everything from vital breathing devices in ICU patient rooms to mundane cafeteria light fixtures.

To the right of that were the tanks—dozens of them. The majority were hooked up to hoses inside the drywall, where others weren't interested and remained more or less sprawled around the surrounding circumference. The menacing tanks were unlabeled but could have been topped off with anything from pure oxygen to highly volatile nitroglycerin. The lights happened to already be on in the Engineering world, but they did, in fact, bleed shamelessly dim in overall credence. It wafted a white fluorescent wave, a cool white at that, but managed to spill over the area in frustratingly low capacity. The entire space gave off a buzzing churn, which radiated from inside due to the massive levels of electrical currents and over-exhausted devices that were scrunched together like stinky sardines.

Damien walked to the corner region of the L-shaped factory-looking room, then made a hard right, and stopped glacially in his booted steps. He dropped the entire lot of colorful chemicals he'd held so preciously, with them all splashing and fizzing to the concrete floor below.

In the farthest cornered slice of the L-shaped territory, stood two Engineers and one chalky lab coat. Each was alien, with the Engineers appearing pretty much all the way human, but the other dwarfish employee in her bleached trench was nowhere near. She had horns protruding from each cheek in coordination with a lioness's outstretched mouth. The trap was bent in a grimace, and her miniature posture was bizarrely contorted, providing Damien the sight of a half woman and half something unspeakable. He soon realized it was the gunslinger he had tussled with earlier in the Basement frost. She had fallen victim to being transformed into a soulless fright of an unfortunate thing.

The lurking Engineers beside her were both males, with Winters recognizing one of them. They stood at the same height and stature of one another, wearing dark blue jumpsuits with their first names stitched into the thick material. The mechanic style uniforms were worn as formal attire for all Engineering personnel while on duty at the hospital. On Damien's front left was Stan, to whom he barely knew, and the other next to Stan was Marc. Marc was the sphinx imposter that Winters had known in a previous life. Marc had never been particularly friendly while he belonged to the land of the living; although, he was much worse off all of a sudden. The two Engineers swayed upright and were frothing, actually foaming at the mouth in despicable hopes to eyeball Winters into submission, and to intrude upon his splintered down and fractured soul of deranged humanity. The lab coat was struggling in some sort of degree or process of sick transformation. The she/it writhed at close range in the shadiest cornered enclave off and to the side, nearly snuffed out in consumed shadow.

With petrified mortification, Damien pulled the Glock from his back jeans pocket. Instead of attempting mind control or battling for eye supremacy with the average man, Marc and Stan both lunged at Winters in jarring unison. While executing a tight hand over hand grip, three shots blistered out into the dank Engineering L-space. The first bullet struck Stan right between the eyes, sending him careening to the floor with nothing but a whimpered gurgle. The remaining lead ended up in Marc's chest and in one of his eggy sphinx lights. The chest shot barely slowed him, but the round to the murky window made his entire oversized head instantly explode on impact. Brain and puss flew all over, with some even making it to the firing man's already ravaged and grimy getup. The body kept running forward a couple dancing steps, totally unaware its head was in a fully detached million pieces. The skull-less jumpsuit fell chest first to the surface in a seizing fit at the bootstraps of the defending young man.

Only the half and half technician who had shot him earlier remained upright, occupying the noir slivered section supplying an utmost abhorrence of horrifying visions. Her transformation was nearly complete, as the thing's posture became more lifelike with the shadows playing through and on her conflicted meat bag.

"I should have ended you when…" she began to hiss in a chilling flavor of a foreign tongue.

Her comment ran cold as a fourth shot rang true from the Glock handgun, sending the former biomedical technician rotting to the dirty floor in a cursed heap.

XVII

DAMIEN DESPERATELY DEMANDED a moment in an attempt to rally together his broken-down bearings. He stood in the derelict Engineering sanction with three corpses strewn out in front of him—three heaps of flesh that he had just put down to save himself. With his breathing labored and choppy, he took his left arm that held the freshly discharged firearm and wiped it across his salty sweating forehead. Nausea crept over him while he tried with diligence to keep his guts from splashing to the surface.

Think. Think - It's not your fault. They were worse off than dead. Don't quit now.

Basic and primitive motivation entered his tormented brain, urging the sinking mortal to snap out of his intensive state of overwhelming shell shock. While stalking in his exact firing position, he looked around the uncomfortably silent room. He then noticed the fragmented mixture of his chemical stash that he'd accidentally dropped while stumbling upon his three villainous chums. An obnoxiously large pool of the flammable fluid snaked a path towards the inordinate generator right up and nearly on top of him. Winters stalked over to the sizable gas tanks near the right wall of the narrow functioning space. He studied them in a fluttered frenzy and settled his optics on a grainy encrusted propane tank. It was hooked up into the wall by a thick and beefy tube of material. Before the assembly entered the foundation, a small digital meter was connected closer to the tank, which read 87%. That meant the flammable tank was in use and nearly 90% full.

He took two generous steps backward, pushing himself up against the generator at his rear. He couldn't be sure if his next move would blow him all the way and straight to Hell, but he mustered up the guile and went for broke.

Damien raised his gun and fired a single shot at the nearly full gas tank. The round pierced straight through the silver housing's upper region, sending a plume of white smoke shooting out into the L-shaped underground. The emetic fumes spilled with emphatic rapidity, choking the man's lungs nearly half to death. He then looked down at the substantial vat of raw chemistry he'd created in a passionate act of frightened distraction. His boots were planted inside the stuff. He stepped out of the toxic mess, slanting off nearing another cluster of stacked arrangements of hearty gas cylinders. He raised his right hand to his face and mouth, trying to shield his vital areas from the putrid cloud of noxious spray. He suddenly realized that he had no matches, which made his already nerve-racked heart skip a lurching beat to a tune of fuckery. Kip was the smoker of the two and always had fresh fire on hand.

Nonetheless, Kip was gone.

He'd scampered off to Heaven only knew.

Damien was on his own down there in the diabolical hospital cellar, attempting to pull off the crazy and unthinkable. He gawked at the unpredictable puddle on the cracking concrete floor a final time, then pointed his weapon towards it and shot. The swirling liquid sparked instantly and whiffed ablaze. The flames opened up and climbed the far wall, while consuming the overbearing generator unit with a cruel display of heated smoothness. The embers pranced, and the fire crackled, inching its way into the perished clump of sphinxes at the edge of Engineering headquarters. All three of the flesh caskets went up delightfully, with their lifeless masses adding fuel to the makeshift bonfire Winters had just manifested. Once extreme sparks began to flutter in all directions inside the narrow alphabet space, the crafty human turned away and bolted for the door.

He blazed through the smoke and flame-filled entryway, opening up again with the neon blue atmosphere of the Basement hall. Damien yanked his head left to break like fuck for the stairwell he'd come from; however, that escape route had become infested with gnarly sphinxes. A small army of the monsters was huddled there like a diseased cluster. The clan of deadites then converged on him at top speed. Full beasties snarled and foamed from their ugly jowls, hungry as ever to capture a little taste of the one soul that'd so far been a thorn in their older than time sides of degeneracy.

He shifted his weight to dart right, thinking the other staircase at the end of the corridor by Biomed would be free and clear. To his detriment, a handful of matching jump-suited Engineers slithered forward. None were left human, but all had somewhere along the way become consumed and grossly defecated into insidious displays of suffocated darkness. Winters was being boxed inside two different directions, with all remaining options nearly bone dry. The beasts on the left lumbered more deliberately, making sounds of scratching hoofbeats on the icy linoleum.

In a last desperate effort, he bounded straight ahead for the single elevator on his subterranean hospital corridor. It was right there in front of him, positioned off toward the side of the converging Facilities crew. The elevator door was open all the way, assumedly a sign from a Higher Power that was with him in the fiery frost-colored catacomb when all hopes were nearly lost. He dove into the claustrophobic apparatus with Glock firmly in hand, then made a turn sharply around and whacked at the circular button which read, 'Lobby-1.'

Damien was aware that the power was cut in multiple areas of Mason, and that neither himself nor Kip had attempted elevator access until that point, but the clunky up and down had become his last and only chance of a possible escape. There was nowhere left for the hapless worker to run.

With the gun remaining gripped in his shaking left hand, he peppered the blasted button with a long index finger, until it seemed as if the quarter-sized disc might justifiably explode into pitiful dust. A multitude of audible expletives escaped from him while he gave the

Lobby circle switch a crazed beating for the sake of his own human survival.

At the very last second, the clinking silver door began to close.

It stammered and inched along in no real hurry, shutting just as the more famished of the horde almost reached inside. The arrow above his head switched on, illuminating an orange arrow pointing upward that gave off a wave of exhausted glee, which was frankly indescribable. The rustic moving cube buckled and rocked in place, then began its bumpy ascension. It buzzed and creaked the entire one story up, creeping slower than an uncomplaining snail's pace. It finally rested on the Lobby deck and belched another sound at him while he quaked alone in the stifling enclosure.

The door slid open with a jarring stutter.

He exited in a blitzing dash, almost tripping over his own two feet while flailing out and onto the vestibule main hospital corridor. Nothing too horrendous appeared to be left brewing on 1, except for the lighting, which had also changed from red to blue as it had done downward in the steely cold of the infamous dungeon. The whole hallway was thrown into a blanket of chilled aqua, frosting the area with a hauntingly supernatural glow.

At last, the frosted over luminescence had become irrelevant.

Winters sprinted for the exit double doors while bolting right by the main cafeteria. As he galloped along, the scrappy hospital employee could taste his inevitable freedom. He could feel the stifling grip of his hospital of horrors begin to ease up a bit and surrender its toxic pressure. He even fumbled a stupid thought out toward Valhalla to thank the forgotten Viking paradise for his harrowing escape from hellish perdition.

With only fifteen miserly steps away from the airy outside world of Mason General prison, Damien's bloody kicks crunched and ground to a screeching halt. His hefty boots made a squeak and scratch as they skidded with hot friction against the linoleum surface.

Standing between the hollow hero and his single way out, was none other than the dashing and now eyeless Dr. Gabriel Boudreaux.

Winters flipped his script and felt like cursing the same bastard heavens he had just offered a thankful breadcrumb to only a second ago.

The dapper surgeon held a hostage at close range.

It was Kip Wells.

XVIII

"How's THIS FOR some fucked up nostalgia, eh Doc?" Damien almost maniacally chuckled in his slickest display of whimsically cool acting.

From deep inside, he was both fuming and petrified, mostly for his companion's dire predicament. Beyond all that, the battle-hardened Winters was worn down to the weary bone, barely able to stand unassisted on his own two boot straps. Boudreaux stood ever tall and dominant as a towering presence that loomed inside the double doorway just inside the Mason General exit. Kip was in front of him, being clutched with a repellant intensity and locked inside a sturdy bear hug. He looked vanquished with his straining marbles of full-blown humanity standing front and center aisle. Wells owned his personalized hazel eyes, which darted and stared back at Damien with a mortified intensity of sheer desperation. Boudreaux had positioned Kip as his personal human shield, but the doctor remained much more imposing than his captive, where Winters could plainly make out a substantial silhouette from behind his friend.

Boudreaux wore his same pearly overcoat from earlier in the melee, along with his black as midnight necktie that screamed all business. The surgeon's hair remained in perfect working order, not a slicked follicle out of its impressive situation of envious sheen. The sickly doctor's face was very much his once upon a time veneer, with the horns on his cheekbones back from Damien's shackled bedtime being erased like a marvel of black magic.

Gabriel did not look well, however. Large boils covered his forehead and consumed the hand he was using to provide the naked chokehold on Wells. The physician's skin had, over time, become scaly, covered with thick veins that pulsed sinister and angry magma. The degrading albino's fore eyes were bugged so far out from his domineering skull that Boudreaux appeared oddly surreal to scrutinize from a fully human point of view. Bizarrely enough, Damien couldn't help but take notice that the doctor had misplaced his reliable pair of usual spectacles. In nearly nine years on the hospital workforce, Winters had never seen Gabriel without the fancy glasses glued to his snout, until then.

"Why do you continue to resist your inevitable fate, you shit heel, nonexistent little human?" Boudreaux sneered in a chilling tone, which could have turned a genuine nobleman to a piece of Medusa's splitting stonework.

Winters shakily raised the Glock with a heavy left hand, bringing his right over-under to assist with the rock-steady grip of mostly fear. The man stood with his legs spread apart, aiming his pistol at the horrid organism as if he were a patrolman attempting to take down a bad guy who held a scrubbed hostage in a world not so long ago. The pistol's intimidation made no impact on the sphynx disguised as Boudreaux.

Instead, the doctor shifted his weight a touch and hardened his corral around Kip's neck and shoulder line. Kip choked and gagged in response to the heightened intensity. Once satisfied, Boudreaux carried on in a curdling tone of vile inflection. "Don't you see that your God has failed you? Most of all, your own kind has failed you. Look around, you woeful ingrate of a meek pawn. Our kind has come to right the continual wrongdoings of your despicable race, along with your faulty Holy Spirit, once and for all. There is NO escape. Our oblivion is purely inevitable," Boudreaux almost trailed off in a hollow snicker, while a wackily satisfied emotion exuded from the damned creature that ruled over the chilling black.

"If you don't let him go, I'm gonna send you back to whatever disgusting hell you came from!" replied Winters from his distance, with a booming vengeance filled with primal aggression and mixed with gooseflesh dread.

"Hell?" whiffed Boudreaux. "Hell was a created afterthought long after our kind had been existent. The thing you humans call a God manufactured your Hell. The Hell you speak of does exist, most certainly. And WE helped to create it. We were everything and all-everlasting well before your puny interpretations of what you believe Hell is in theory, and your intricate Earth and infinite worlds of vastly complex galaxies, beyond which you could never even dream of comprehending, were much better off beforehand. Now, look into my eyes. I'm going to devour the noteworthy prize of this miserable and trite little town."

A face-off of sorts between Damien and the boisterous surgeon ensued in the aqua cold remaining lightshow of Mason General Hospital. With the Glock pointed around the grotesque physician's head area, Winters was nearly shot out of his boots by Boudreaux's attacking discs of decay. The palmed handgun fell down by his side while the man's entire body took a freakish hovered flight several inches above the icy linoleum. Damien was downright locked in midair like stone, transfixed into the gazes of the ancient alien's piercing brights. The initial contact heat that the young mortal's body began to produce proved unbearable, causing the hovering slender man to cry out in a terrible pitch of horrendous agony.

"Just let go, Damien. Free yourself from your meager and meaningless affliction."

The voice that entered his head was Gabriel's telepathic charm, or more so the thought transference of the vile beast that had gobbled up the unfortunate doctor during the earlier hours of endless mayhem.

Other brain games were craftily conjured from the deranged sphinx cutter, ones that knocked at the frontal lobe of Damien's rugged psyche, forcing the defenseless human to question his very own reasoning of overall clarity.

"Your species is insubstantial, and your time has come to an end. You can't resist the benevolent temptation of the obligatory deletion of all your

mortal pains and primitive despairs. Just exist, Damien. Exist with US, surrounded by the totality of our absolute nothingness. We are the first and righteous order of all things."

Damien could painfully feel the most sacred regions of his thought processes becoming maddeningly jumbled, invaded with scrutiny by the bombarding foreign evil. A blitzkrieg of his own authoritative memories would rush toward the surface of his powers of reasoning as a symbol or shield of defense; then, those same thoughts would begin to be plucked away from him against his will. It was a chess game of wits between a distressed and inferior mere mortal, clashing against an overly advanced enemy that was as old and callous as time herself.

Winters found himself losing the lopsided battle, while his most passionate convictions were being taken away from the board and erased from the boundaries of his knowing existence. Such a feeling was both hypnotic and sheepishly relaxing in a strangely satisfying discernment of human regret. The man could sense himself starting to give in all the way, willing to surrender every nuance of control to his most personal and dearest impressions.

A fleeting second before his olive skin began to sizzle, the overruled man flashed a vivid abstraction of his own accord into his gouged mindscape, one that catapulted him forward throughout time. It resided in a semi-distant future that was somewhat possible, but confined solely to a land of his own make-believe. Trouble was, he couldn't be assured if it was made up by him or something more menacing. With all of the chaotic cerebral torture, he couldn't be positive if he was witnessing the imposter's realm of forethought, or if the imaginative vision remained confined to his own personal volition.

The thinking scene was of purely unmixed destitution, a vast abyss of absolute nihility. Zero human life forms existed, and a single cognitive thought could barely be scratched into fruition from his overwrought earthling consciousness. The single thing that remained sharply consistent was the immersive amount of deep anguish from within himself. The pain was not imminent from Damien's nearly combustible human skin; however, the source festered somewhere inside that was both terrifyingly close and alarmingly intimate. His flawed human essence was being stolen away and consumed into the miserable black of the prestigious Sphinx.

He looked down at his body floating indiscreetly, suddenly finding himself stark naked in an endless barren of a black hole inside an unforgivable realm of dead space. The man was all the way lost to time within an endless force of desolate purgatory, where nightmares continued without question, and never as much as ever faded away from anthropoid recollection. The overpowering mental sorrow began to take over the more physically painful aspects.

However, Winters rallied and managed to grasp hold of the somatic and earthly forms of treacherous punishment. He peered down at his physique that swirled within his personal whirlwind of forced trans-fixion. He shook his head and clapped his godly hands together with one striking move, shooting himself back into his earthly body and into the heartless realm of present time.

As his wavy brown hair began to singe from above ground on top of his sweltering skull, Damien lurched his head left while remaining in midair, averting the profane scrutiny from the insidious Doctor of Death.

Boudreaux seemed to not quite absorb such a strength housed inside such a puny and insignificant mortal man, and growled a beastly tune in response while Winters was slowly lowered back to the floor. The insatiable boil from inside subsided while he shook out the sticky cobwebs of the primordial onslaught. Once his riding boots hit the hospital linoleum again, his balance had been pushed severely off-kilter, sending Damien down to a single knee. He placed his right hand to the hardened frost and opened his eyes in a bewildered daze. He breathed heavily and locked his sights to the cerulean-flavored tiles at his feet. He could feel his raw humanity creeping back to him in a feverish passion, providing the man with a sharp vulnerability only a red-blooded human being could ever truly experience.

"I don't know, doctor. I'm not sure I'm a fan of what you're shoveling over here," heaved Damien with an alarming wince while down on a knee with his face aimed at the floor. He managed to find a degree of bodily coordination and gingerly rose to his feet, again pointing the pistol at Boudreaux in a one-handed leftish fashion.

Without further ado from the overly aggravated and disgruntled bowels of Mason General, a thunderous explosion echoed from the underneath Basement that shook the very foundation of all things hospital.

"Perhaps your little buddy here will be more cooperative," heckled Boudreaux in an icy inflection that could stop the chivalry of time. The doctor swung his malignant glare into Kip while he continued to writhe in the sphynx's powerful hold. Boudreaux yanked Kip's neck with a twist, to the degree of something one might see only in the spirit realms of demonic possession. His face was tilted up in the pathway of the mad physician's hideous pustules. The scrubbed man's eyes shot open with the rough wrenching of his devastatingly human extremity. Wells began to scream bloody murder on sight, a sort of sick moaning sound you'd expect to hear from a dying animal that was recently shot through the abdomen for sport.

Winters remained rigid with fear while holding his gun several feet away, practically white-knuckled at the scene. He was no longer sure if he had five shots remaining in his scored plastic weapon or only four. The statistics felt irrelevant as his cherished friend had nearly run out of time. With Kip thrashing in despicable agony, Boudreaux provided a small window of exposure for a scarily dangerous, but somewhat clean shot.

Aiming only for the eyes, Damien squeezed the trigger. The seeking bullet erupted from the pistol and missed the intended target, instead ripping a hole through the shady side of Boudreaux's offensive face. Angered immensely for such an interruption, the beast doctor snarled and with a flick of its wrist flung Wells like a ragdoll fifteen feet across the Mason General flooring and out of frame.

Boudreaux then launched in a single bound, catching flight as quickly as a heavy jetliner using its wings to separate from the Earth's crust. The rotten physician's destination was runway Winters. With his white coat flailing behind him in the aqua-kissed atmosphere, as if he were some yolky-saucered caped crusader, Damien crouched to a knee in defense and gripped the Glock with two strong hands.

POW! POW!! POW POW!!!

He emptied the weapon's magazine into Boudreaux as he flew, catching the doctor twice in the center mass and once in the neck, and again in the ear, exploding it clean off his human sphinx mug.

Just as his trusty handgun clicked empty, Boudreaux smashed squarely into Winters, where he sat hunched in an absurdly powerful descent. The surgeon was stronger than ever, quickly pinning both arms above Damien's head with the man ending up on his back. The empty firearm went ricocheting, never to be seen or heard from again. The mortal lurched with all his might in an attempt to release the straddling sphinx from on top of him, but it was no use.

"Die, you miserable waste. We will savor your juicy soul for all eternity!" salivated the nemesis white coat as he came nose to nose with a nailed to the floor Damien Winters.

The surgeon's yolks for peepers were microscopic inches from the human's frantic and worked over face of grit. With his brown eyes protectively shut, causing his sterling face to wrinkle up and strain, the Boudreaux daemon reared its head back and sent it down hard into Damien's nose, issuing him a powerful head-butt to the very front of his already battered mug. It stung like the dickens, causing a strange "Oof" reaction on impact, forcing the mortal's eyes to flutter open in frightened defense.

The bulbous and puss-filled saucers of Boudreaux held the man's petrified gaze yet again.

Damien kicked his legs in a fury, but they settled down as his most prized understandings began to wash away from the confines of his being, becoming the stolen property of the degenerate sphinx doctor. He could smell his leather coat heating up and getting ready, seconds from going ablaze along with the rest of him. Boudreaux leaned in another half-inch to practically touch with Damien's face, unworthy common man to ungodly and morose dominant, for the single purpose of intensifying its uncanny kill stare.

After the bold offensive maneuver, Boudreaux jolted rather suddenly. Instead of progressing with the inevitable melt session, the doctor looked up into the ceiling with terrible disbelief and wailed a deafening howl toward a God that was nowhere to be found. Kip stood standing over the both of them; his breathing scrutinized and very much intense. A hearty fire ax came into Damien's view that protruded ghastly from the poor sick doctor's lengthy spinal column. The wound opened up on impact, spewing a rank display of human appearing magma, along with a puss-like and unidentifiable goo. Boudreaux then opened his soul catcher for another malevolent shriek, but instead, vomited all over Winters horror-stricken front. The chunky upchuck was grey-black in coagulation and resembled a thick tar-like substance to the naked human eye.

It stank of bile and deathly rot.

The screeching and oozing Boudreaux released its grip on Damien's tormented mind, along with his pinned down arms as the man slammed a left-leathered elbow into the sphinx's chops, forgiving the mount in full payment.

Kip fell to his knees in the distance by the front doorway entrance. He appeared injured somehow, but Winters had no time to assess his friend's unknown damage. His boots scrambled upright with shaky confidence, as another monumental blast rocked out from below the hospital, causing the elevator he had just arrived from to blow up in an intense fireball behind him. The aluminum door flew right off her hinges, sending it smashed like a boxy torpedo into the adjacent hospital drywall.

Boudreaux was laid out on his stomach with the heavy ax plunged into the square portion of his back. The thick chopper handle was a matte black of healthy impressiveness, and the shiny base of the imposing instrument remained visible at the split open entry gash of the surgical guy's newly destroyed snowy overcoat. The Boudreaux sphinx went to grab for the boot of Damien while he stepped over him. With a satisfying response, he savagely sunk a weighty toe into the temple of the messed-up anomaly.

He moved onward toward Kip, who remained down on his knees and butt near the hospital's main entryway.

"Get the fuck up, soldier. This place is coming down. Up you go now, Kipper." Damien grabbed at his confused colleague and pulled him up to his unstable sneakers. Arm in arm again, the two heroes stumbled for the double-doored exit.

They burst through them, just as Doctor Gabriel Boudreaux screeched the final scream of his damning and dual existence.

XIX

W ITH DAMIEN PROVIDING most of the heavy lifting, the comrades continued their journey out of the Mason entrance doors. Fifteen or twenty feet outside, another roar belted out from the way past its prime hospital. The ground shook hard underneath the fleeing men. The institution was exploding from the basement floor up, her grizzled and spent guts pleading with a heightened showing of elderly dismay. The entirety of the first floor suddenly churned firestorm and detonated with a passionate ferocity, tumbling the gritty survivors to their faces by the ambulance bay, a stone's throw beyond the patient drop off rotunda area.

A transport bus was parked straight up ahead in the otherwise empty lot of the psychedelic night, with its front and back doors all projecting wide open. It was one of those original models from an innovative and embryonic ambulance company called, 'DRAGON.' The newfound company's buses were painted a reflective black all around, with an imposing green hologram dragon on the rear side of them, introducing a fresh and fancier attempt at transport for patients who would be charged up the wazoo for requesting a medic back when the world was still the world.

Damien again unearthed Kip from the cold outside concrete, moving him another few feet to safety behind the sleek dragon bus. He managed to peek back over his shoulder to have one last look at what was becoming of Mason. A series of unmitigated blasts from the structure erupted furiously on command, trembling the entire bedrock of the once-thriving facility. The groundwork underneath her gave way and sunk inwards, forming a massive crater in the very spot where it used to stand stoic and unflinching. The remaining floors crumbled and cracked, then began to sink ploddingly into the magnificent hole. A sizable amount of the third-floor windows shot to pieces, sending molten shards and fireballs showering down onto the asphalt near the bay.

Damien shrunk away with each new explosion, but never took his eyes away from the collapsing medical vessel. His and Kip's bodies remained shielded by the dragon. However, his disheveled head sat exposed and out in the open, taking in the entirety of his handy work with an insatiable level of dizzying awe. The leather-jacketed man's eyes shimmered dancing jewels while the steel and concrete became one colossal rage fire, sending the entire healthcare hub of his little Colorado town plummeting basement first into a cratered oblivion. From his covered vantage point, with the last remaining section of his crashing down Mason General becoming fiercely consumed, it appeared as if the once spirited center for wellness had sunken down and away into the eternal depths of Hell itself.

XX

'JUST AN OLD NIGHTMARE... OR?'

SHE HAD COME to him often; but that night in an obscure echo, had been the very first time. Damien was nearly three full years into tackling steady swing shift hours over at the hospital. It had been just after 3 am, the darkest and liveliest of the witching hours. He fantasized most nights, but that particular dreamscape felt different from a chilling drudge of nervous anticipation.

He tossed and turned in his cabin bedroom, offering occasional expirations and incoherent ramblings during his wild incubus cycle. His dark hair had been moist, and along with his lean and naked body, soaked through with sweat underneath the cool sheets of gray satin. On any other night, those behaviors would have been passed off as usual job stress. However, that particular realm of comatose was something different. It didn't feel like a dream or even a night terror. It was as if he'd been awoken as an intruder inside his own safe space, somehow sticking his nose unknowingly into something unsavory that he had no business prying his humanity onto.

He'd been sober for three solid months, with not even a lick of alcohol or anxiety pills helping to impede the man's sometimes conflicted mental stability. The job at Mason tended to be brutal and ragged around the edges without the crutches of self-medication, but

Damien did possess a resilience within his spirit that was unmatched when pushed to the ultimate brink of rational sanity.

The young man was jarred awake suddenly. Alone without Leigh that night, he had been sleeping on his right side facing the large frosted over Colorado bedroom window. In the corner section of the darkest pitch of black, she appeared plainly as a mountain's silhouette in the palest of moonlight. It was a woman with flowing hair of sable and a thin white nightgown, crouched in the farthest region of the room that Winters gazed upon when he was racked awake for no apparent reason.

After acquiring a fully conscious vision, his blood ran frigid and instantly cold. He'd wanted nothing more than to avert his frightened eyes or to, at least, let out a scream, but all he could manage was a stern glare into the unbelievable horror. He was frozen in bed, never taking his orbs off the uncannily real lady crouching in his sights. She rocked back and forth in his spacious chamber with her knees pressed up to a shadow for a face. At first, she refused to look his way, or even up from her lace-covered and halfway bent legs of muted ivory. She continued to see-saw in place on the floor, appearing like some ghostly human recliner chair with a blanket of raven hair.

Moments before he could finally blink his dried out umber eyes, her head shot up from the depths where she sat curled in the darkness. The only visible part of her face in the moonlit windowed pitch was her eyes staring straight back through him. They sat in her skull as large white ovals, appearing more like satisfied shark discs in the process of feasting upon a fleshy limb of an unsuspecting night fisherman off the coast of holy shit. Then what looked to be jagged and crude horns began to protrude from the cheek area of her phantom and disquieting silhouette. He could hear the crunching as they inched their points to the surface of her defined shadows of slender bone.

Damien's powers of observation began to slowly adjust to the darkness so he could make out the loose structure of her shocking real surface. The room instantly transitioned from icy cold to a raging sear, as her possessed eyes latched onto the waking man's mortified soul. He struggled and managed to blink several more times in succession while forcibly shaking his dazed head with complete disbelief.

As quickly as she'd materialized, the entity vanished into thin air, retreating to the farthest cornered void of his cabin bedroom. Winters was left panting in the lonely dark, staring out into the abyss of his log house with heightened senses bordering unhinged.

Fear was nothing new to the trauma filled man. He had come a long and tumultuous way throughout his life, enduring both tragedy and addiction in their ravenous strangleholds of overzealous extremes. He wanted nothing more than to jump out of bed and make a frantic break for the medicine cabinet in the bathroom next to him in the capacious area, open it up and grab an orangey-red pill bottle. He thought for a moment what he'd look like if he palmed that psych bottle and slammed the cabinet door. He envisioned how he'd probably just stand there staring at himself in the little square mirror of frost, buck naked and doused to the bone in his own defeated fear. He'd then look down at the container with his name and prescription number imprinted on it and feel an instant form of shame and awful fucking regret.

The elaborately foreshadowed vision made the young man think again before actually acting out of primal stupidity. He continued only to lay there, rolling over onto his back and staring up at the popcorn ceiling in a silent huff. There was just enough moonlight visible that night, with most of the illumination being offered by the alarm clock radio on the nightstand close by.

Before falling back into a scattered realm of slumber, he'd almost been confident it was all only but a dream. Another vivid panic of sleep or a product of some strange medium between the dream world and mundane reality, where he'd found himself crossing paths unexpectedly.

It couldn't be real.

She couldn't be real.

It was all insanely preposterous to pass on as truth or fact.

The uneasy Winters sunk backward into a puzzled doze on a random and forgotten September Thursday, with a chilled encrusted heart and the rocking ghost girl with her yolks for eyes burnt deep inside his haunted mind.

XXI

"**G**OOD SAVE WITH the ax in there, Backdraft," Winters had turned around to face his confidante. Kip was pushed up to the back tire of the nifty ambulance truck, sitting down with his knees slightly arched. Damien followed suit and slouched down beside him while letting out a series of painful groans and grimaces. Remaining in his usual dark scrub suit, from his own historic on-shift interruption during the unforeseeable apocalypse, Kip Wells appeared to be very much in a state of overall shell shock.

"Let me look at you a minute," Damien said while reaching a right hand over to inspect his brother in arms.

Kip seemed to be holding up well enough, for the most part, barring a few minor cuts and bruises around his face and forearm areas. The jacketed man locked eyes with him for several drawn-out moments, only to make sure his usual muted hazels hadn't manifested into the loathsome chalks of ancient ruin. They had not, as his familiar secret windows jumped around in his head and mirrored an exhausted overwhelm.

Damien took a look around while seated, realizing they'd finally made it alive and somewhat well to the outside world. He heaved in a victorious whiff of Colorado fresh mountain night air. The sun was nowhere to be found; things had become destined only for the dark.

On a brighter note, the skies gleamed like an otherworldly spectacle from high above them. They craned their skulls up to face the captivating light show, staring in reverence upon a burst of rainbow sherbet-colored airspace. The forecast in view showed partly cloudy, while a few greenish-yellow puffs swayed by in the wacky psychedelic twilight. It was almost as if the Earth they had known their entire living years had been turned upside down and shaken like a pretty snow globe, with every illustrious saturation known to Man bursting from inside it to be set back upright again. The stars sparkled with pride and glistened in their stationary positions from light-years away, but were visible to a human's untrained eye. Other comets and meteor showers shot through the stratosphere and disappeared into the above nothingness. The Moon found itself exposed and out in the open, a full cratered cookie rubbernecking with amusement at what was becoming of its neighboring Earth. The hazy and bizarre atmospheric rings that surrounded the satellite planet proved terrifyingly hypnotic in a beautiful style of powerful intrigue.

"What say we hop inside this Mickey Mouse reptile bus and rest up a minute," Damien insisted, as he ushered his old buddy to rise up and stand tall.

Kip complied, with them both entering into the backside of the ultramodern first responder's truck. Each door attached to the dragon remained open, so they went around closing and locking everything, providing a temporary sense of selfishly craved security. There was an empty gurney in the back of the bus, along with ransacked equipment that every other ambulance carried onboard at all times. The main lights in the rear cabin were out, so they sat on the floor in the obscurity. The strange psychedelics of the forever night glimmered through the tinted windows here and there.

"Why the hell did you leave me up there on 5?" a burning question escaped from Winters.

Kip continued staring off someplace, not willing to turn to face his colleague's question.

He finally replied, "I just had to get out of that place. I just had to... I couldn't take it in there anymore."

"Yeah, well, you're out now," Damien chimed back with agitated undertones, which were peppered in with usual satire.

There was silence for several minutes while they remained exhausted, but more so, frightened halfway to death. Winters sat and pondered what kind of absurdity was destined to pop off next for both of them. A cluster of time went by as they listened in the dimness of the contemporary transport machine. It felt wonderful to have the luxury of finally being able to take a small breather and relax; although, they were aware that they couldn't just dick around and loiter there forever.

"What now?" Kip turned his head left to face a shadowed Damien.

Winters responded immediately, "Suppose we should try and find the keys to this jalopy and see if we can start her up. Then maybe head on over to Thelma's and see if she's got a bead on all this crazy."

He shifted his frame toward Kip, while his silhouette came into focus, blanketing the man fully in an orange hue before proceeding. "I need to get back to the cabin and check in on Leigh. Jesus Christ, I hope she's still there and alright."

Kip interjected dryly, "You still got that shotgun and revolver, right? Your cabin is on the other edge of town and pretty well secluded, D. Maybe these things haven't made it over there yet."

For several crushing moments, Damien's throbbing conscience was bombarded with horrible hypotheses. Losing his precious Leigh in all that was happening would deem a mountain of devastation he didn't for once think he could ever endure. The wrenched through man rallied up enough grit to say what needed to be said.

"Let's first get over to Thelma's. She's a friend, and she's closest to us. I'm sure she's got her own firepower up in that diner. Wouldn't be surprised if the old kook had a rocket launcher or some shit pinned up in that squeaky-clean kitchen of hers."

They both managed hollow smiles, but nothing more.

Damien lost himself momentarily in a scattered translation of reeling mind while nestled away in the dragon rig. The important fact that he'd made it out of the leveled hospital with both his life and his colleague's was unimaginable.

His cerebrals picked up speed with his body resting and insisted on bending unforgivingly to dabble in both the past and future, all at the same time. The present was washed away like rain, and he began to rehash the grisly ordeal he and his counterpart had endured up until his unwanted mind split. Winters brooded over all of his taxing years inside the living and breathing walls of Mason General, some filled with goodness and others festered with absolute ludicrousness.

He reminisced of the first time he'd met Leigh in the hospital cafeteria one late night in another busy October, while he worked a double shift almost five years ago.

His mind twisted again and switched to the spectrum of a vividly hypothetical future sequence. The man's brainbox was bombarded with graphic forethought of what the world could become if the attacking sphinxes finished their obliteration on his fellow humanity. He also pondered if his own kind were holding their own out there and across the earthly globe, or if they too were being methodically exterminated like insects in a grander carbon copy of his own puny town.

His mental onslaught offered up a rather strange review regarding the present moment in the overall art of living time. Human beings seemed to rarely settle their full attention spans within their present moments, unless maybe their very survival had been dependent upon such a commitment. People could go most of their waking lives living in the past, churning their realities between previous traumas and painful hardships from grueling years long ago.

A person could also become swallowed up by their own made-up and devised scenarios of the future, ones that were based upon personal perception, which were nothing of a true reality at all, and would more than likely never occur in the exact same way they had envisioned. Those human clarities of flawed and skewed perspectives, along with owning a rare ability to contort storylines and possible events into their intricate realms of conceptualization, had the perfect potential to become increasingly damaging on one side of a person's psyche, or instead, a powerful gift in others on the varying outer side of the overall mental spectrum.

Becoming morbidly consumed with olden regret and life's prior shortcomings had the utmost ability to destroy the very essence of lively imagination that the human species had been innately created to produce. The freedom of reasoning and thoughtful originality had the grand potential for a purist form of intent, which possessed the ability to conjure up the most striking beauties within the civilized world.

The ironic reality to Damien's jigsaw puzzle of suppositions was that the present moment was more times than not a mundane frame of relative existence. The deep-cutting gemstones that made human life forever grossly intriguing were, in fact, the hyper-stimulated perceptions of each individual's raw and evocative imagination. The scintillating visions and various endgames that one could dream up to associate with the present and other infinite timelines throughout one's own personal lifespan.

The swerving man's brain had again become stuck inside a possible realm of the future. He was affixed there against his will to resist. He mentally chewed over a world without a single earthling man or woman on the absolute face of it. The entirety of humanity had become completely nonexistent.

He presumed, strangely, that the more luscious and glorious things, which were left on his planet Earth, had never been touched or tarnished by the messed-up essences of his fellow Man. That rumination saddened him, with a cold chill followed by prickly goose-bumps flooding through his chest and arms, blanketing inside his warm leather coat.

Winters did not loathe his fellow people, but he was hip enough to own a grip of understanding as to why the world had come down to such atrocious disarray. One could only place their filthy little mitts inside the loaded cookie jar so many times before they scraped the bottom of the barrel, providing nothing left to enjoy but scraps and crumbs of a once bountiful kingdom of plentiful sugar. Another could stick their hand in a tiger's mouth so many times before the said tiger took a whopper of a bite, leaving nothing but a soggy and useless stump.

Perhaps the ancient Sphynx had indeed grown tired and fed up with the predictable destructiveness of the dark side of human behavior. Maybe they had become bored and exhausted by looking down on such a race from a closer than comfortable distance, while watching them ruthlessly rape and plunder their savory indulgences into gross overpopulation, diseased political platforms, and dried up and befouled bodies of oceans.

The falling man couldn't control his spiraling reminiscent ideas of how human beings tended to be very foreseeable creatures throughout their living lives, almost like moths to a hungry flame. It had become a follow the leader mentality of overall existence for most, instead of an original idea of a truly noble and thriving being. Fathers tended to have similar lives and afflicted tendencies with their sons, as did mothers with their immaculate daughters. It was a rare breed of person that ended up branching off from their preconditioned mold and becoming something of their own drawn-out and fought for volition. The man's dying planet craved more of that up until the very end of the civilized world.

Damien got caught up in a whirlwind of troubling thoughts regarding the sensitive topic of human procreation. He questioned the overall intentions of all parents that had children of their own. He puzzled if they ever came to a point in their lives where they regretted their decision, realizing that they were selfishly bringing another fragile life that was an imperfect extension of themselves into a world full of chaos and dismay. He wondered what all parents thought when that earth-shattering day arose, when they glared into their children's wondrous eyes on a random sunny day, and watched their fleeting innocence wash away from their unsuspecting souls like a distant and unforgiving storm. The inevitable giving in and surrendering to all the hardships and tragedies of everyday human life. The blatant switch in the game, where the offspring could relate to the broken sided truths of all things life to which their human creators had known about all along.

"Let's seriously try and find the keys to this lizard hunk of shit," echoed Damien while climbing into the front cockpit of the dark dragon.

"Twenty bucks says we're royally screwed," snapped Kip in his ever so usual optimistic tone of conviction.

Winters ignored the comment and continued his quest for the keys. Kip joined in, opening drawers in the back of the rig and rummaging through high-tech medical gear by the empty bed gurney. They searched high and low, but the starting mechanism was nowhere to be found inside the dire straits endeavor. Damien opened the driver's side door and stepped out of the ambulance. Kip popped the back and also hopped out.

Both men feasted another glance at the enormous crater, where Mason General had once stood for what rationally felt like more than an eternity. The area in scattered sections remained in flames, darting around in a sort of laughing inferno close to the sizable sinkhole. Wells and Winters stared at the monumental scene of molten rubble, affixed with a piercing degree of powerful shock at the fact they'd simply endured the collapsing pitfall that Damien had engineered on the incredible fly.

"The hell's up with this goofy weather?" Winters said as he snapped out of their rubble coma and applied his own original divulgence, referring to the ultraviolet setting currently shrouding the above space and time.

From an orange sherbet section of supremely saturated space, two fighter jets roared past them at a low and dizzying tempo, nearly deafening the two grounded survivors. The persevering hospital employees hooted and hollered for an inconsequential sequence, while desperately trying to capture the attention of the military aircraft. It all, however, proved to be of no real good use. Kip did most of the hooting, with Damien following the majestic machines into the sopping sky until they disappeared like uproarious ghosts out of their blurred lavishness.

"The cavalry!! Hope that's a good sign!" Kip turned back toward his leathered friend while barking with a substantial smile after stopping his little happy dance.

"Yeah," was Winters' only reply.

XXII

ID THE HUMAN collective deserve such a sudden and bestial threat of extinction? Was it as inevitable as the predestined art of death itself? Part of Damien's broken demeanor wanted to turn against and spite his believing God, for just sitting by and twiddling His thumbs while the armies of the Sphynx came roaring in like ravenous hyenas. He also wanted to smite his Lord for supplying him with such a gift. The gift of pain, suffering, and the ability of remembrances to a magnitude of all things dead, gone, and forgotten.

On the tough other side of his hatred, the damaged young man did realize down to his sturdy bones of unnerved calcium, that without his gifted curse of a vivacious and hyper-stimulated consciousness, he wouldn't be Damien Winters at all. In an even stranger realization, he attempted to understand the sphinxes' primitive motivations behind their forceful annihilation on his world. If the soul swallowers had truly been the initials of everything existent and enjoyed the peaceful nothingness for God only knew how long, then humanity unknowingly assisted in royally fouling that up. Even if the sphynxes had created God Himself, as the bedeviled Boudreaux had touted, their legion should be going after Him personally, not a lesser organism like the human race.

Damien struggled to wrap his honorable intellect around the fact that, possibly, an ancient biblical struggle, one which transpired millions of millennia ago, had been the precursor to the boiling down of the very night he and his colleague were savagely enduring. Winters didn't believe in a notion such as blind fate, but he did know that nothing was made to last forever.

Or was it?

Does a soul really go on to a better place after a customary human death, if uninterrupted by a rebel force whose sole objective was to suck up and consume their God-given humanity?

Does a dead soul wander and find peace out yonder in the deepest trenches of the forever cosmos?

Does it reincarnate into something else, sightlessly remembering a previous life or lives while perhaps only in a dream state?

Or was the human spirit only destined for nothing more than a damning pitch of black, a dominion of oblivion that strangled the shifty entity forever and ever?

The sphinxes singular objective appeared to be that of a complete takeover, to ingest each human like some thirsty bloodsucker, only an ancestral form at that, with infinitely more ruthless malintent.

Damien had a loose belief that once a soul was consumed by a member of the Sphynx, the endless and despicable void that every human being was petrified to even think of throughout their entire living existence was cast upon them—there was no turning back. They were simply gone, erased from the chapters of overall time and space. There was room no longer for candy-coated pipe dreams of pearly gates and ordered judgments under the chimes of harps that clinked away in the clouds. Only the endless pit was imminent, the inky hole that devoured hearts and never hesitated to look over its shoulder to ask for filthy seconds. Perhaps the lion beasts were jealous, even unnerved somehow that God had given mankind so much power of raw creationism. The hollow-spirited demons were insatiably famished for fresh slices of humanity because maybe, just maybe, they didn't have actual souls of their own.

For all Damien knew, a soul was only an invention that was molded in the hands of God Himself. What if He had entrusted the human race to make such arduous and difficult decisions of mind in a time ageless years ago? The sphinxes obviously craved the Earth for themselves and their own wrath, because according to them, the mortal-dominated planet would remain a bountiful paradise, if not tampered with any longer in overextending and sloppy human hands. Or perhaps a God that even Damien had trouble believing in for himself, was the single creator of his Earth and other bouquets of lavish planets, and the sphinxes wanted a taste of God's creativity because they couldn't create anything of elaborate value any longer for themselves.

Up until that dreadful night of reckoning, the Earth did manage to valiantly remain a wonderful rock of a place, one which had been beautifully crafted by something broader than any human being could have ever created.

XXIII

AFTER THE HARROWING escape and the staggering demise of Mason General, Wells and Winters aimed their sights toward Thelma's. Thelma's Diner was a shallow quarter-mile hike through the Colorado forest, adjacent to where the ashes to ashes care facility they'd manned for nearly a decade used to perch. Both men would visit the hip diner after hours and on a steady basis, spending many nights together after a numbing swing shift slinging coffee and listening to one of Thelma's assorted stories or intriguing tales. The chic little eatery was open for business until 2 am every waking night, and opened back up again at 6 am sharp, accepting no substitutes. It was refreshing for such an off the grid town like Heatherton to have a staple close by on the payroll, where a local could stop in for a quick bite after the watering hole closed up on Main Street for the night, or to satiate the evening's workers after a grueling shift on the job.

They shot through the woods on foot like two frightened fugitives on the run. Within the density of the enriching foliage, the landscape surrounding them grew much darker in domineering intensity. The weirdo atmosphere became consumed by the immense Colorado pines. Wells and Winters were utterly exhausted, tripping over hidden branches and intrusive twigs while they worked through the wild night terrain. They ran with no tangible plan, except only to make it to the diner unharmed. They ran out of a heightened desperation for basic human survival.

The good news was that Thelma's had been a familiar and homey setting for the blood-soaked hospital employees. The men also wanted to check up on the old bird, and they knew she had a weapon or two at her friendly disposal.

HECK, FOREVER SPRY 82 years young full-blooded Portuguese Thelma Louise would carry a snub-nose .38 in her girdle every day while she manned her treasured Colorado establishment. She'd even used the thing on some poor son of a bitch back in the early 1990s.

The guy had come in one night after dark and ordered everything on the left side of her restaurant's menu. The two cooks on duty back then slaved away in the kitchen, whipping up everything from hash browns to eggs benedict with sourdough toast slathered and topped with mixed jellies and jam. It had been the breakfast menu the slacker was interested in, which took up a half portion of Thelma's light blue-colored all-day menu. Biscuits with chunky and savory gravy followed the eggs and sausages, along with bacon and fruit medleys on the side.

Throughout the guy's nightly feast, he'd not for once been interested in any sort of beverage during the entirety of his ravishing. Thelma had offered him coffee or juice or plain as day hot tea, even generic tap water with lemon that he wound up turning his nose to. The dude just wolfed down the grub like it was his last day on planet Heatherton; drinking had never been in his shuffle of cards. The glutton finished up with two Belgian waffles and a small Dallas omelet that gushed with grilled hamburger, onions, and tomatoes with an extra sharp and flavorful cheddar cheese. He'd sat alone in a large booth that could have housed five and didn't drop his fork for over an hour and some change. The fat body decimated every last crumb of the comforting midnight grub.

When it came around to pay up time for a substantially inflated dinner bill, the trucker type with his flimsy trucker hat got up from his seat, let out a juicy burp for the ages, and sauntered for the diner's front door exit. Old Thelma was behind the counter up front, of course. She lived in that very spot, being it was where the one and only cash register had rested and hopefully still rests. The Portuguese owner had been unflinching at first, politely hollering after the reject's marbled back to inquire if he ever thought about paying for the twelve pounds of saturated fat he'd just mopped up like a gourmand.

"Not especially, you old witch," was what the soggy tough guy bellowed in response.

With his back turned away from the mini diner landlord, almost all the way outside of the front door entrance, he'd heard the little mechanical click of her pink revolver's hammer. He stopped in his tracks and turned around to face the dainty poof of silver-gray hair. .

"Do the right thing here, sonny. We all gotta make a livin' 'round here. This is my establishment. Don't make a fool outta' me," she'd said.

In the blink of an eye, the dummy instead went for his own gun. He'd had it all along tucked away into his too-tight overall pants in front of his breakfast belly for the duration of his midnight jollification. Before his firearm could even raise, old Thelma planted three .38 specials into the poor sucker's chest cavity. He gurgled out a shriek of terror, a quick and surprised yelping kind of sound, only to stagger backward and crash through the front door glass onto his back at Thelma's front stoop. He'd pissed his grungy jean suit before he'd even hit the ground.

Dead as a frickin' doornail.

"BEING DEEP IN the woods like this, things almost seem normal again," Damien broke the silent scampering.

He knew his comment was hollow and contrived, mostly stupid optimism kicking in while his lungs screamed bloody murder at him. Safe and normal didn't exist.

Not anymore.

Winters had always been aware of that grim and honest truth. Once someone or something was born into the world, the unpredictable roller coaster ride started with a lurch. No payment was necessary, and the amusement park machine fired right up with a rocky anticipation from good old-fashioned jump street. Followed by the inevitable bumps and bruises from the rigid seat of slivers along the way. There were no freebies once you were chosen to ride, either.

Not for any human creation.

Everything during that ride inevitably came with a steep and daunting price for general admission. A person had better learn to take their thrashings with a smile glued to their pretty little face and to let those black and blue bruises brush right on off, only to continue on trucking the clunky park tracks along their merry little cotton candied day.

If not, the world had an unforgiving ability to swallow someone right the hell up. It owned a relentless potential to take everything moral and righteous from a person if they let down even the smallest of guards while inviting the curious little prick in for a hot cup of soup.

All of those unpredictable possibilities had always been possible when humanity reigned superior. It had since transformed into a chaotic fight for survival, between trifling mortals and the dominant alien Sphinx. Not only to exist as a surviving species, but to keep one's very soul from being ripped from them and torn apart for all eternity.

DAMIEN AND KIP cleared the dreary woodlands. The brush opened up into a scene of newly unfamiliar hallucinations. From the above night bright, pods of fresh sphinxes lined the unreal atmosphere. They were crashing down from the heavens and hovering in mid-flight around various sections of town. The foreign pods were giant rectangles and clear as sparkling glass, appearing like floating cosmic Pandora's boxes of heathenish malevolence that streamed down on the usually cozy

Heatherton settlement. A few rogue boxes crashed into the wooded foliage behind the men, and another set deflected off towards the east side of their under attack Colorado mountain borough.

Thelma's Diner was right in front of them, a beacon gleaming steadfast on one very edge of town. The establishment rested all by its lonesome, with the woodlands tucked in behind it. The lights were warmly inviting and powered both inside and outside the joint, with its bright sign of neon clichély reading, 'Thelma's Diner' in a seductive and classical green cursive font. The sign looked like a friendly hankering of sorts on the surface, just what they'd been looking for in a house of yearning refuge to escape from the gripping confines of pulverizing terror.

They both broke for the door.

Kip got there first and entered with the famous sound of the silly cowbell that was attached to the top corner of it. Wells entered with a jingle, with his dirty black hospital scrubs catching a reflection in the newly manufactured dazzle.

Damien followed behind, but before he stepped in, he was suddenly plagued with a dreadful intuition that coursed through and tapped at the rawest deposits of his calcified bones. One of his powerful feelings of unexplainable insight had just come knocking. To the blind or untrained eye, the familiar stomping ground resembled a safe haven and shelter on that never-ending evening of dread.

Winters shook off his overpowering senses and stepped inside.

XXIV

To Winters and Wells, Thelma's Diner was the quintessential Colorado staple. Thelma provided most of the hometown intrigue, with her vintage sense of humor and priceless after-midnight chin wags with her more loyal patrons. The restaurant had unwaveringly remained spotless at all times throughout the dining area, even with crowded customers enjoying the small-town comfort cuisine at unholy hours of day and night.

The bar table in the center stretched long and wide, with swivel-style chairs lining up one after the other, affixed by sturdy poles to the spick and span floor top. The impressive desk bar was the darkest of grays, while the trendy chairs offered a booming bright red for a killer contrast. Their leather sparkled in the warm ambiance of the charming mountain establishment. A single row of booths on each side of the entrance door were all empty and clean as a whistle. The table surfaces were black with sturdy shines, while the glossy sitting booths were infused with a shimmering white leather material. The floor was sprawled out like a marbled chessboard with the smoothest white and noir tiled squares. The single restroom in the very left corner owned an overbearing magenta light fixture with side by side stick figures of a man and woman above the door. It glowed broodingly with spooky confidence.

"Looks like nobody's home," huffed Kip with an almost sad sigh in his demeanor.

"This may sound insane, but I'm absolutely starved. It feels like I haven't eaten in two bloody weeks," Winters said while hunching over next to Kip with his hands rested upon his sides.

"Thelma?! Anybody home?" offered Kip.

Not even a peep followed in response, or a clink of a piece of silverware, or even a shuffle of feet on the checkerboard floor. The two men glared at each other while having their own human type of brain gelling sequence, then Damien finally spoke with a shrug that made his leather jacket sound off in a crunching crinkle.

"Fuck it."

He jumped the mid-height bar counter and entered the kitchen door at the back of the cozy and scarily desolate Heatherton eatery. Winters never had the pleasure of taking an intimate tour of Thelma's back cookery, yet he was abruptly struck with amazement at how that particular plot of land had managed to remain unmolested by destruction courtesy of the abominations that were infesting the town. Thelma's kitchen was in perfect and unspoiled working order, with the knives all hung high, strikingly clean and symmetrically organized, while hovered up next to each other on the wall near a bulky sink planted near the back left.

The huge oven stove where all the magic happened was full of growling prestige on the right side of the equation. Thelma would have never once dreamed of disgracing her patrons' breakfasts, lunches, or dinners with a new age electric stove. She owned a gas unit, and it was a real beauty. It was an old Wedgewood timepiece that cooked the meanest eggs benedicts and fancified omelets in half the state. It glistened in a rich and industrial ivory coat of acrylic, while sprouting six sturdy burners, all charcoal in general dark color. The Wedgewood didn't have a spot of food on the thing and bore a deep double oven with glass doors resting below the cooking burners.

A haughty walk-in refrigerator with hundreds of pounds of delightful perishables stood bonded in the other cornered section of the cookhouse. The entrance door to the hefty ice locker was a sterling gray steel. The chrome framework was wiped so supremely that Damien could almost see his reflection in the burly alloy as he approached.

"Hey, Kipper! Brew up some coffee out there! I'm gonna whip us up a mean end of the world breakfast of champions. Hopefully, Thelma has a rocket launcher or two back here that we can use against these bastard shapeshifters."

"Roger that!" said Kip with authority, as he began to fumble around in the main dining area.

Winters offered at the sturdy chrome handle and opened the meat locker door. A burst of frigidly hazy air struck him in his sapped face. It felt ravishingly welcomed, as it consumed his beaten up and over-anxious life vessel. The young man had been in a continual state of fight or flight for what felt like an eternity. For half of a second, his entire body unwound and relaxed with the inviting chill; however, he was then turned upside down inside himself and became hardened as an overstuffed piece of taxidermy.

In the dead middle of the illustrious fridge, packed with all the savory breakfast goodies under the sun, the same exact sun that had given up on rising any longer for the pleading sake of mankind, was little old Thelma Louise.

Her frail hind was pushed toward Winters while she stood swaying in the arctic confines. She was hunkered low in a strange way, almost cocked to one unnerving side. The entirety of her frame appeared to be warped in a freakish texture of loosely twisted sinewing. In the gentlest of tones that the man could deliberately exude, he barely above a whisper said, "Thelma, it's Damien. Is everything…"

His question ran colder than the locker's icy temperature when the restaurant owner turned around to face him. Thelma stood humanless, of course, while her fresh and pulsating whites protruded from her timeless and elfin face. Thelma was a spry 82 years young, tinier than ever, and weighed 103 pounds soaking wet. She was dressed in her usual work uniform, which consisted of a long white skirt with black frill at the bottom, and a triple small black t-shirt top and doll-sized little black shoes. The entirety of Heatherton knew Thelma like a grandparent, but she would always wear her same work badge with pride while operating her immaculate and original eatery. 'THELMA: Owner' was inscribed top to bottom on the plastic button pinned right above her petite and adorable little heart. The small rectangle was white in shade with black embossed lettering. Thelma's Diner was inscribed in a baby blue cursive on the badge's modest header.

Winters was glued where he stood in the entranceway. He raised a hand toward his mouth to stifle an urge to vomit when he realized what she had been doing in her own meat fridge. Dear Thelma was holding up two plentiful handfuls of raw and semi-frozen hamburger chuck. It wasn't entirely frozen because juices ran down her face and snaked along her usually squeaky-clean business attire. She chewed loudly while chunks of the purple cow flesh slithered wayward from her precious mouth.

She stared right through him with her newish set of evil and raunchy peepers, as the mere mortal man felt his overburdened soul being crushed with authority from far and deep within. His entire life's story began to drain from his slender frame, nearly causing the strong human to hit the floor in an impish writhing of meek surrender. Come hell or high water; he hacked it to avert his mortified eyes, narrowly avoiding the full impact of the death glaze from bite-sized Thelma Louise.

Before he could turn to run away, Winters heard the jukebox kick on from out inside the main dining hall. Kip had started up the record player by booth number seven. It was positioned by the bathroom at the back and only played vintage saucer vinyl records. The juke wasn't anything too fancy to look at, but it scored all the proper artistic and unfading classics. It was a Crosley Rocket that held 70 or so records within it, a real old-fashioned piece of neat-o antiquity. The machine geared up some golden oldie by the one and only Johnny Cash.

Something about falling into a burning ring of fire.

Going down, down, down, and the flames going higher.

Thelma all at once sprung for Winters with a crazed form of despicable delight. She took flight in a gravity-defying double leap. Thelma

Louise's new sphinx carcass snapped, crackled, and popped with the unfathomable effort; nevertheless, the bound was undeniably precise.

She smashed into Damien as they both went hurling to the floor as an unorthodox mixture of age and beauty. The human youngster could barely believe how imposing the new Thelma had become. The sphinx impersonating the elderly biddy was shamelessly sinister with alien intent. She, no, "it," hissed and spat at Winters, drooling on him with her raw flesh dinner clutched in hand and mouth. Damien grabbed his former friend by the throat and lifted with all his might, flinging her backward and off of him. She landed on her feet as gracefully as a figure skater splash downing a triple axel at the Olympic games on a mild afternoon.

Winters regained his footing and staggered for the organized knife rack on the kitchen wall. He snatched an overzealous meat cleaver and turned with it outstretched in his dominant left hand. Thelma ran smack and square into the sharp chopping utensil. It sunk into her stomach as easily as slicing through a rare medium cut of juicy steak filet with a dull butter knife. Thelma's dwarfed frame seemed not to notice the human retaliation, and instead turned skyward to the lanky man at dangerously close range. Thelma then opened her mouth extra-wide, but not to scream.

Damien could feel his entire body temperature spike from perfectly normal to holy shit. It felt as if he was burning up from the inside, about to combust like a balloon that had been prematurely popped by a snot-nosed little shit at his 6th birthday party. He yanked the cleaver from Thelma's gullet, spilling blood to the once pure kitchen floor of sterling gleam. He swung the dangerous instrument again with a short and forceful stroke, entering the side of the restaurant owner's veiny neck. Upon entry, a dark soupy substance sprayed without caution in all directions. The defending Winters was blinded by the filth. It covered his face and jacket, but the Thelma sphinx held up her gripping stranglehold on his human and inferior consciousness. He slugged her with the cleaver hand right in the teeth, spilling the little lady to the tarnished kitchen canvas.

He jumped on top of her in more or less a side mount position of his own frenzied attack. He reached out and grabbed Thelma by her snow-white ball of hair, the same snowy tuft she'd always been so proud to say she could still flaunt, and proceeded to saw at her thin neck with the overbearing kitchen instrument. He cut and scraped through flesh, cartilage, and bone until the eatery owner's entire head broke loose from her frail and gyrating body. Pools of chunky discharge overflowed the area around the two scrappy kitchen fighters. The divot where her head used to be overflowed and spewed a blackish flood of darkly saturated magma.

The heat ceased from Damien's body, while he at last relaxed his primal display of incredible wildness. He remained on top of the Thelma sphynx, while heaving breaths both choppy and agonizingly profuse. The messy cleaver was still clutched in his left hand, with her dripping severed head grasped with vigor in his right. He dropped her crown to the soiled floor, along with the sharp object he'd used for the job, and stumbled crazily out of the messy cookery to inform Kip that Thelma Louise was forever dead.

XXV

DAMIEN STEPPED OUT into the dining area of the homey sit and stay, with his clothes and face doused with the putrid fluids of the delicate old bird he'd just hacked to bits. A changing tune took a poised revolution around the stylish old juke by the john. It switched from Cash to The Doors as Morrison echoed his sultry jam titled, *Touch Me*, a song, which Leigh loved to croon out with pulsating seduction in nothing but her sexily thought out bra and panties ensemble of the evening, while parading through his candlelit cabin with incredulous curves, along with saccharine honey dripping from her come-to-bed desires.

"Kip?!"

Nothing.

He walked over to the restroom and whipped open the door. Even the toilet's layout was clean and shimmering, but all the same, there was no Wells. He had vanished once again. There must've been a reason; Winters attempted to assure himself while burying a sucker punch to his sinking abdomen.

Truth be told, Kip was more or less that brand of guy, and Damien had always known it. Kip Wells was the type of chap that had the fullest of potentials to be a reliable and decent friend, and could succeed in saving a life if he got a little shamrock luck on his side every now and again, but mundane reliabilities had never been a strong character trait in the man's overall genetic makeup. Kip was regretfully the breed of man that folded under the everyday pressures of ordinary life, withering like an autumn leaf to the menial and tedious efforts of the necessary tasks of model citizenry, such as showing up to work in a timely fashion. Or finding himself a stable life partner to settle down with, or maybe even reaching some level of genuine human happiness.

Right up until the sphinxes came knocking, the two colleagues had a mostly off relationship. There were no hard feelings; they were just different kinds of hospital officers. Damien had always taken a gritty sense of delusional pride in his daily work ethic at Mason General, although that same determination proved taxing on his overall mental stability. Kip, on the other hand, faltered with the pride aspect; he never seemed to really have much of the trait in anything he worked at or did during his usual day to day.

They had begun to lose touch with basic friendship things over the last couple months, like hanging out after work to grab a beer, or to fire down a witching hour omelet at the unfortunately headless Thelma Louise's. Kip had seemed to slowly transform into a closed book, seeming to shrink away from Damien with no tangible reasoning.

Kip had been more of a fleeting personality, running away at the first signs of trouble. He was grossly predictable with that specific part of his mortal fabric. Damen relentlessly continued to exist as a fighting spirit throughout life, digging his heels into the dirt while attempting to grapple with any storm that tried to sink him.

Winters slumped over and sunk into one of the sparkling diner booths by the door. He gave a sigh of exasperation after the surrendering effort. The booth and table became fudged up with the icky substances he was covered in from the kitchen murder scene only moments ago. He arose again while staring off into nothing and voicing audibly to himself. "Yep, fuck it."

He returned back to the kitchen, stepping over what was left of Thelma's dismembered corpse, and made himself a God-forsaken breakfast omelet for the dying cause of the fucked-up year of 2020. He'd watched Frank work the old Wedgewood for years and morphed into quite the on the fly natural at whipping up his own impromptu apocalyptic egg concoction. He scavenged some onions and peppers in the iron-fisted fridge where he first spotted the restaurant's micro owner, along with a few linguica links and a fresh brick of jack cheese. A single tomato was laid out on the floor. He picked up the green-ish-red vegetable, while uttering another brand of to all hell with it, and mozied on back to the timeless gas grill.

With not really giving a damn about who or what could traipse through the front door while he remained preoccupied, Winters cooked up that meal with a smile on his chiseled and stubbly face of young grime. He took an unbloodied knife from the orderly wall and diced up his foraged lot of fresh vegetables. He gave the four brown eggs he'd found in the icebox a crack, and made Frank the once upon a time nightshift grill man of Colorado nights past awfully proud. After plating his food, he again stepped uncomfortably close to Thelma while trying every trick in his mental notebook to block out her mutilated carcass, and finally dropped the steaming dish at the empty booth he'd originally dirtied up.

Before sitting back down, he waltzed over to the coffee pot at the foot of the bar counter window. There was bold black java still left in it, probably days old and left to die. It appeared as if Kip didn't get around to making any before running for the hills and away from everything that mattered. Winters switched on the warmer and stood waiting by the countertop with a halfway lean of his athletic build. He did a quick turn around and gave an innocent glance toward the diner floor of shine.

Lined up behind the bar was a series of Thelma's signature coffee mugs. They were painted in a shiny black hue with 'Thelma's Diner' scrawled out in her favorite baby blue cursive. The mugs were dignified in their overall construction. It was a cup designed for a seasoned coffee drinker. All that foo foo la la sweetened and milked to the moon crap had no business in a mug like Thelma's. He grabbed one from the underneath area with a brazen clink and turned it over, knowing exactly what he'd find next.

On the white bottom of the brash cup for coffee was a little spaceship. It hovered alone in the albino bottom and had two kickstand legs to signify it had landed somewhere inside the ivory nothing. A little green fella stood next to the out of place aircraft. The Martian gave a silly wave and came off looking more like a puny stick man with an oversized head than anything else. See, Thelma had this thing about extraterrestrials. She'd gotten a huge kick out of the whole phenomenon. The quirky old-timer would quote some black goo X-Files episode reference on occasion, or blather on about Area 51 during countless early mornings over pancakes and coffee, when Damien would take to her place after working a loathly night over at the hospital.

"There's definitely something going on around those parts, that Area 51," Thelma would declare as her poof of silver hair blotted out her own counter lights at her itty-bitty back of ageless splendor.

"We gotta storm that joint, Winters, and get past all them turkey government no-gooders, and get a real good look at them aliens!"

Damien had admired her unconventional company and had spewed out his plain black java once too often during their silly and casual midnight back and forths.

Oh God, poor Thelma!

What have I done?

Did I save her, or did I brutally kill her?

Was she already dead?

For Christ's sake, please help me!

Will this endless nightmare never cease?

Pleading desperations of shameful thought danced and toyed through the ravaged mortal's murky gray matter, as he got the coffee up to snuff and poured himself a heaping amount in one of Thelma's UFO mugs of piercing black. He brought the piping hot lava back to his breakfast booth and sat forever alone in the empty fluorescents of his crumbling town's most famous outskirts eatery.

He ate his custom omelet and stale hot brew, with the only other customer left in the place to keep him company being the sphinx corpse disguised as the diner's lovable owner, which was decomposing on the kitchen floor due to the alarming brutality of his raving self-defense.

XXVI

AFTER FIRING DOWN the makeshift breakfast like it was his last meal before the electric chair, Winters glazed a gawk at his quarter full mug of coffee that sat on the shimmering tabletop. He got lost in the java's steam while it rose provocatively from its liquid confines, reminding him that he was very much still alive, along with providing the only authentic peace he'd had in what felt like a decade being right then and there.

He worried agonizingly for Leigh, hoping, more than anything, she was boarded up in the cabin with his shotgun by her side. She had a tiny one-bedroom apartment of her own right there in Heatherton, but she worked for her father's local bank several towns over that he managed like a purposeful hawk. Leigh would stay at her own place here and there, but most nights, she was at the cabin with Damien. The man's cellphone remained nowhere to be found, and the phones in general seemed hopelessly obsolete right then, anyway. Thinking of his lover initiated a charging force of delicate strength, fueling his cells with a heightened energy that mixed with both hope and suffocating panic. With all of the carnage he'd been involved in, his mind shifted only back to her.

How she'd be sitting in a chair in any old place on a hot August night, wearing the skimpiest Daisy Duke jean shorts hard-earned money could buy, without having an urge to ravish every square inch of her. Or her almost raven hair being situated in straight loose pigtails while resting on her various rock and roll crop top of the day. He'd study her with his mahogany eyes and rave with excitement as she crossed her long legs over in her seat, bulging those toned quads and thigh muscles, providing the man a compulsion to just wither away and perish right down to her feet of angel's dust. Or noticing a glisten break loose over her neck on a Sunday afternoon, while he BBQ'd the meanest hunted elk in the entire great state of mountain town Colorado.

He'd loved her through and through from the beginning, although the tormented man couldn't help but loathe himself for not saying those three clichéd, yet vitally important words often enough throughout their young and mostly carefree years. He was shot back to reality in a blitzkrieg of force, left staring zombified at his remaining quarter cup of no longer steaming black joe.

Damien had to get home.

He had to save Leigh.

HE UNEARTHED HIMSELF from the warm diner booth, playing a satiated sole survivor who was hunkered down for a precious moment in his favorite eatery on one edge of his devastated town. Before making his way to the front door exit, he took to the men's room. It was a universal toilet, being only one room for both the ladies and the gents in Thelma's liberal restaurant agenda.

He relieved himself and walked towards the sink to wash himself up a bit. With the lukewarm aqua flooding over his strong and slender hands, the man took a long and hard look at himself in the squared mirror that stared straight back at him. The walls in Thelma's washroom were of the brightest green, and the lean light fixture above the sink gave off extra cool tones of a subdued ambiance.

His miserable and bloodshot eyes darted to a black and white newspaper cutout of a familiar midget wrestling scene, of all things. It was pinned up to the right side of the mirror, almost above the one and only frosted black toilet. Damien never ceased to manage a laugh followed by a healthy head shake at the image whenever he locked onto it, knowing full well it was none other than Thelma's zany sense of humor at work in her nifty little food realm. The eight by ten clipping was framed in a plastic gold material, with two little people in leotards squared up in a royal rumble of sorts during an odd circus wrestling match. He could never get a straight answer from old Thelma as to where she'd cut the newspaper photo from, or why the hell she had it up as a monument in her customers' only restroom.

His patchless chocolate brown motorcycle jacket was scuffed to the max and covered in Heaven only knew, as were half of his distinguishable facial features. Coarse stubble had broken out on the surface of his olive skin. With usually being clean-shaven, Damien had gone days without a blade to scrape on his healthy jaw. His shoulder-length hair was oily and matted, also owning blood both foreign and domestic. The young survivor felt dirty and vulnerable, with his problematic, yet steadfast mind nearly shattered as a result of the night.

He bent down and began using his hands to splash over his face and hair, doing a stopgap job at tidying up his brutalized appearance. His newest shoulder wound seemed in good enough shape in light of the shit circumstances, as the dressing he'd applied back in the Basement morgue was holding up just fine. His injuries during the initial motorcycle crash would have to suffice at that stage of the game.

The enduring human could ill afford to be operating at half speed right then. He needed to dig deeply into the chasmic trenches of his willpower and heighten every last one of his remaining gifted and primal senses. He'd simply have to, or he wouldn't survive the night.

The water turned hot as steam began to rise from the sink with his head bent down, inviting the lava stream to run over the back of his skull, crawling up towards the forehead region and running down his face and neck. Once satisfied, he postured up and took another look into the icy window. It had fogged up from the smog, so he took a hand and scraped over the glass, revealing a slightly more sanitized version of himself.

He glared broodingly at his reflection, getting momentarily sucked within his own brunette eyes. Damien was barely holding himself together. He wanted nothing more than to lash out toward the spirit realm again, not understanding how it had all come down to his insufferable nightmare.

Had the infamous Dr. Boudreaux been correct with his taunting lectures?

Was the unstoppable race of the Sphinx the beginning of everything and all?

Does God know of this?

Were the sphinxes the most powerful of all the gods, and are rightfully out to correct the wrongdoings of an overreaching and zealous race of humanity?

Winters lost control and couldn't help but delve even deeper into his intoxicant reflections and ponder.

Did Jesus or God or the Holy Spirit make the gravest of mistakes with giving human beings free reign here on Earth? Providing us with His free will and ever-evolving imaginations is the utmost and rarest gift of handed down power. A power that can be used for either good or evil, but which side has really been winning the war up until tonight?

He dove headlong into reminiscence, abandoning the monologue approach, and abstractly contemplating the very art of a human soul. For most of his adult life, Winters had trusted that a soul didn't authentically evolve with material earthly possessions, or even favorable circumstances or unchallenging factions of mortal existence. Having children, wearing fancy suits and ties to the skyline office uptown, or owning the yawn-worthy picket fence gag of conditioned life were never the mighty skeleton key to the blueprints of human evolution.

In a more skewed sense of consideration, he hypothesized that the plunging forward of a soul to a better and advancing realm of body and spirit could only be attained through deprivation and painstaking grief throughout life. By making and owning the toughest decisions while knowing that those choices would hurt and cause massive amounts of suffering along the way. It was within those dismal settings of going against the conditioned grain of inflicted decision making, to instead believe in oneself and their own moral gut instincts, where the abundant reservoir of growth and healing lies dormant, and to all intents and purposes, resides completely untapped. To cease the chattering matrix of all the distracting bullshit and to just shut the fuck up every so often and look around at what's really going on.

But not just look, to see.

See what the hell is manifesting underneath the shit encrusted surface of all things human. Feel it, listen to it, and understand that not everything is as it seems to be. A reservoir of such elaborately prepared magnitude was shacked up inside the darkness, the cornered trenches of mind that few ever dared to enter and most never had the audacity to entertain.

To never conform to a basic system of passed down standards, or a colorful and pretty flag, or a flashy poster saying that was how one should live their fucking life or else.

He pondered, while woefully sinking, that that was precisely what had become of his kind, the human condition. The common people were losing their very souls right there on Earth, long before the sphinxes even began to careen down from the skies to kick off their insidious incineration show. Everything seemed to be coming full circle, with the eyeless reaper swooping down to rear its ugly and horrific head, to collect on the debts of a wilted and used up species. The bygone Sphinxes appeared to possess the abilities to, in some sense, duplicate a human body, to steal the soul's mortal essence, and bury it from the purest fleeting forms of existence, which included everything or anything the taken over host had ever known or would never become again.

The bastard creatures were just plain old hungry, gobbling up human beings for only that purpose.

To feed on a prehistoric need.

The alarmingly imaginative man whipped back to himself in the fogged-over mirror while staring straight forward, his watery eyes providing him with an outwardly human grief he wasn't all the way used to, and could be felt as indescribable.

The murky basin water ran throughout, so he shut it off at last with a squeak of the windmill shaped handle. He wiped his face and wrung out his thick mop of mane with two lengthy bare hands. Winters took one last look at himself, then marshaled up an unsteady courage that only a human being could remotely conceptualize, and stomped his heavy boots to the floor, aiming straight for the diner exit door.

XXVII

ONCE HE WAS finally back outside of Thelma's, the atmosphere had slanted and shifted in a puzzling way. The sky above had become the brightest of yellows with smacks of lightning busting loose in scatter-brained pieces of the forever pitch. There were no clouds to be found, causing the airspace to appear breathtaking and unworldly, all at one gripping speed. Empty sphinx pods laid strewn around the surrounding grounds, up that way and down the other. In the farther-reaching distance, Damien could make out full Pandora's boxes armed with the dreadful shapeshifters descending like a plague to other unfortunate sections of his world.

Without a second's warning, the foliage where he and Wells had scampered through to reach the more or less abandoned diner began to rustle and swish with heightened ferocity. The dense Colorado forest whipped and slashed with a charging vehemence, followed by a thunderous mechanical roar that seeped straight through.

In another instant, the woodlands appeared to open up, revealing a colossal gunship that hovered like a schoolyard bully from a great distance above. It entered the scene like a majestic crossbreed between Airwolf and a stalwart branch of a military helicopter. The machine levitated over Damien, causing the overpowered man to retreat back to the main doorway in the restaurant of bloodied neon. He was forced to shield his eyes while he peeked up in the direction of the thrashing chopper marvel, but he did so with an ecstatic smile glued to his bruised and freshly cleaned veneer. The floating apparatus of mighty bulk was covered in a full shade of camouflage, obviously a special branch of military unit, and owned an impressive machine gun on one side of its hull. A whopping rectangular box that looked from Winters' perspective to be a kind of rocket launcher, loomed threateningly and was attached to the other.

As he began to wave his hands with fury at the pilot, who remained hidden by the craft's tinted windshield, a rocket blazed free from the armed launcher. It smoked and flamed on release, slicing through the yellow night at a psychotic torrent. He followed the smoldering rocket until it collided headlong with a cluster of packed sphinx pods that were barreling down behind the diner. It was a gang of three degenerates, while the seeking bullet made a piercing impact with the middle craft, causing the full trio of alien bastards to explode in a Herculean skyward fireball.

Damien returned his thunderstruck look toward the aircraft, watching it descend slowly to the ground, just out a bit in a shallow clearing several long yards up in front of him. The blades churned with terror, causing a deafening roar at what could most likely be heard from a quarter-mile away. When the war machine touched the surface, Winters beat his feet for it. There were no doors anywhere on the aircraft, so he jumped through an open side of the framework and landed inside.

There wasn't a single person on board except for the pilot. She turned around in her seat with the intent to study her battered new passenger. The woman looked somewhat small in stature, appearing slightly dwarfed while manning such a brilliant machine free solo. Her long blonde hair was swirled into a tight braid, snaking its way down her own camouflage uniform, which matched colors with the incredible mongrel she was commandeering. The officer wore a low brimmed hat with the same soldier girl camo scheme, paired neatly with aviator sunglasses that nearly swallowed up her face.

With a gloved hand, she waved for Damien to come up and join her in the front passenger seat of the crazy loud battle machine. Once seated, he stared over to his left at her. The lady pilot was striking from up close, with her fair face of milk radiating a natural beauty that tried its best to hide under her stealthy military attire. He wondered what branch the flying soldier was occupied with. He hesitated to ask such a question at first, but assumed it might have been the Army, even a Green Beret or some type of Ranger. She wore her name stitched on the left breast of her form-fitted clothes of multicolor. The name read, 'WOODS.'

"Can you believe all this shit!?"

Damien hollered in an excited, yet almost overthrown tone of voice. The she-wolf disregarded his question altogether, "I'm Woods!"

Assuming that was a last name, he replied back, "Winters!!"

She continued her glare, fixated on the man in his bloody motorcycle jacket and scuffed half to death Levi jeans. She went on, "You're the first real human I've seen for miles! This town and a large chunk of the whole state is under heavy attack!"

Damien stared at her shielded face, along with her curved brim hat that hung low with her mirrored glasses, which provided the graphic pilot a wall of shameless reflection.

"You mind taking off your sunglasses a minute?!" he yelled.

His constricted body remained in full flight or fight, and rigid as a tree stump, praying to anything that the albino-haired commander would not unveil a vile and disgusting secret. Woods complied, removing her oversized mirrors and revealing two icy blue eyes. Her jewels of beautiful glass were uncannily human, giving off a frightened determination of powerful confidence that was vivaciously alive within her glimmering frost.

Woods and Winters remained grounded for another half minute while the blades lashed full-blast straight from above them. It was dark inside the craft; however, the gauges in the cockpit threw a greenish hue over the two human beings.

Woods proceeded, "I saw the hospital come down back there! It was a real shit storm to see from the air! I was headed back to base about 50 clicks from here until I stumbled upon you! You know what happened back at that old hospital?"

Damien turned away from Woods and placed his dirty mane down toward his boots. "Indeed, I do… Listen!! My cabin is on the other edge of town! I need to make it there right away!"

Woods frowned and retorted, "Negative! It's too dangerous. Your tiny town is completely overrun! For all I know, my own base is, too!"

In a raw and desperate inflection, Winters responded by turning his entire body left to square up with the admirable mini pilot. "Please! I barely made it out of that hospital alive! I have to go check on my girlfriend! I know she's still there and alright! I just know it! Woods, PLEASE?!"

The officer hesitated a moment and scanned around with her head as if it were on a swivel, while surrounding her immediate area that they were grounded inside, then finally giving a darting look at one of the copter's control panels in front of her face. She turned back to Damien with those phenomenally animated and organically chilled eyes and hollered, "Alright! Lead me to it! But after, we get out of here!"

With a passionate wave of relief, the distraught man only smiled and nodded, sinking down into the rocky passenger seat with anticipation for the leviathan to take off.

With two daintily gloved hands, Woods slowly edged the stick of her rumbling helicopter. They began to rise slowly, lifting a few feet off from the majestic Colorado earth.

Out of the wind torched timbers from nearby and behind, a herd of messy beasts bolted from the clustered thicket. They ran on all fours and emerged absolutely ghastly, near blurs of famished death barreling headlong into the ascending camouflage. They dismounted one after the other, with two attaching themselves to the landing gear and the other gluing its abominable frame right up and on the main front windshield of the lifting craft.

Woods cried out over the near-deafening sound of her Airwolf, a surprised shriek that escaped her highly trained and determined state of being. She had placed her aviator mirrors back on for takeoff, but that meant nothing to the pasted-on fucker attached to the window in front of her.

The clinging and gruesome spawn was covered in hair and bore the head of an almost rabid looking lioness. It spewed drool and mucus from its stew, while it defiled the military vessel's reinforced windshield glass. The others remained on the landing gear mechanisms, scratching and clawing their alien way with ardor, attempting to climb up and in to have their horrifying feast with the two mortal passengers. The hulking helicopter didn't appreciate the added weight, and proceeded to sway from side to side forty or sixty feet from the looming ground below. Woods attempted to jerk the scoundrels free with a maneuver of her own, but to no avail.

Before Damien could yell for his pilot friend to not look at the malevolent demon in the eyes, it was too late. The thirsting yolks of the abysmal lion had become transfixed with the female commander's shielded orbs of decadent frost. She froze in her seat as the mirrored spectacles exploded right off from her fetching face. Woods removed both of her hands from the cyclic control and moaned in a horrific nature of disbelieving anguish.

The helicopter swayed even more, suddenly on course with a breath-stealing descent. The wind picked up a bit while helping to assist the titanic warmonger toward the daunting Heatherton floor. Winters tried to reach over and steer the out of control vessel, but they had already passed the point of no return. The chopper went sideways in the eerie yellow night, with Winters holding on to anything inside for literal dear life.

Woods remained lifeless and seated in her main cockpit's perch, slouched over and strapped in at the front of her multiple gauges and gizmos. He unbuckled his seatbelt and reached over towards her, but it was all too late.

Before the inevitable crash down, Damien lunged from his seat.

The ejection was hearty and unbelievable, however narrowly survivable. The man hit the ground and performed an awkward barrel roll maneuver on impact, somehow getting to his feet in a crisp flash of agile effort. He lumbered back toward Thelma's, which remained very close in proximity. He was practically still on top of the joint.

While nearing the front restaurant doorway entrance, he lurched his frazzled head back at the insane scene, just in time as the valiant chopper and its vivacious pilot smashed into a hellacious heap to the Heatherton cement near the front parking lot of the old town diner. The group of sphinxes persisted like cockroaches and remained stuck to the assembly, while the moving propellers dug hard into the rocky terrain, causing one to break off like a match stick and careen into the black woods in back at a deathly rate of speed.

The crash was hellacious, nearly sucking the very wind right from the man while he watched it unfold in a delusional state of unbelieving slow motion. He turned and sprinted back into the direction of the downed craft with a complete indifference for his own general safeguard.

He could still see Woods hunched over in her seat while he ran for her, just as the entire application sparked and ignited. It went from nothing to a combustible eruption of fire in a fraction of a moment. The powerful explosion sent Winters flying forward, launching him headfirst into the trajectory of the crashed service hell storm. He landed on his face, smashing his forehead and right ear jaggedly into the rough parking lot asphalt. He was laid out on his stomach and managed to cover his head, right as a second explosion greeted the atmosphere, sending a sonic boom and a multitude of mechanical debris and fleshy sphinx parts cascading throughout the vicinity.

When all that was left to be heard was the out of tune cackling of a smoldering holocaust, Damien looked up from his sprawled-out position to which he was thrown. The cremation was a safe distance away, but it was a little too close for comfort. He glared outward once more at the flaming cockpit, with hands still clenched to the back of his skull, and could barely make out the fiery silhouette of what remained of the beautiful, icy-eyed pilot named Woods.

XXVIII

HE WALKED ALONE like something undead back into Thelma's empty restaurant, not quite understanding how yet again he'd been allowed to survive. He arrived at the inside bar counter with his mouth ajar, fuming at what he'd laid witness to right outside and up until the totality of his waking insanity.

Damien smashed his fist on Thelma's sprawling table, sending a mini shockwave throughout the hollowed-out arena. A stack of unsullied and squeaky-clean dinner plates at the end of the bar took a crash onto the checkerboarded floor. The sound echoed throughout the place, even with the burning mayhem raging right outside the door for entry.

Winters had to get back to his cabin.

But how?

He was weaponless, injured, and pretty much out of any viable options with zero transportation in sight. Thelma did indeed adore her firearms, with the NRA probably admiring her even more so in return. There had to be something inside the diner that he could take back out into the pungent yellow inferno of affliction. He wanted nothing to do with the kitchen any longer, being that was where the elderly owner had met her secondary demise at his blood-soaked hands.

The job, however, had to be done.

He jumped the counter with an unusual swiftness for a taller than average man, and again, infiltrated the restaurant's cooking area in the rear portion of the establishment. He gingerly stepped around what was left of Thelma Louise, which frankly wasn't much. Her flesh had rotted away completely, exposing a mini-skeleton of unbelievable sinews, with bleached white bones piled up on the floor in a pool of boiling and dripping sludge. An uninviting steam-like substance rose from the gunk, which wafted a pungent burning aroma. It entered Damien's nostrils while he held back the bile, instead spitting a rocket of mucus across the usually crystal undertow, several feet from what was left of the beloved proprietress.

"Come on, old Thelma girl. Give me something I can use in this fucking lunacy," he spoke out loud to himself while turning circles in the initial section of the lit cookhouse.

There was an American flag situated on a wall in one corner of the room. It was stretched out and pinned up with eight nails surrounding itself, along with a steel sink below the flag for dishwashing and rinsing usage. Without really knowing why, Winters kicked his boots over to the sink. He stared at the red, white, and blue cloth, with its stars and stripes chuckling down on him, all the while finding it grimly ironic at how many of his kind fell so hard for the misperceived rationales of state and country. How someone could give his or her life for such a cause, but never really knowing about the authentic root reason to why they were committing to such a thing, or what they were actually fighting for.

Many would have probably gushed the all too familiar word called freedom, but was freedom ever really free in the United States of America?

Has it ever been?

Were the drawn-out battles and political skirmishes after WWII even necessary, except strictly for governmental and financial appeal for the triple-chinned pricks that were perched like neatly dressed slugs atop their golden thrones?

Damien had once believed there was a short window where he would've made a decent soldier out on some ugly battlefield somewhere far away, one that was cleverly fueled by cock-eyed and unjust blood propaganda, but it was the conforming part of the whole ordeal that had proved most difficult to justly buy in to. He could never imagine carrying out an agenda that he didn't honestly-to-goodness believe in, only because he was ordered to do so, whether it be killing or telling someone else to kill, strictly for expendable governmental delights.

He thought of Woods for a bleeding moment while his mind split away from the present, at how brave the soldier was to touch down in all his Heatherton hell to try and save him. She should've been the one that was still alive and breathing—not him.

AFTER COMING BACK to his demented senses, he inspected the basin. It was clean as a whistle, providing a glistening reflection of his tattered self around the bottom nearside of the drain. He knelt down and felt along underneath the steadfast water trough. The sink was rather large, more of a rectangle in shape than a symmetrical square. While sifting blindly, the man's slender hand finally touched on something foreign. It was long and cold as he grabbed for its center mass and gave her a good yank. The object gave away easily, with it being rested on two custom hinges underneath the unassuming washing station.

In Damien's grasp, he then held a rifle, an old classic piece to be precise, a kind of Wild West special. It was a Winchester that wore a touch of honorable wear and tear around her edges, and flaunted a speck of rust here and there, but nevertheless a vintage beauty.

His inspection of the scavenged prize continued.

It was a lever-action repeater with a cobalt stock and a rosewood grain finish. He cocked the lever underneath, half expecting a round to eject from the rifle's deep chamber.

No luck.

Thelma had, without question, been an all the way old-fashioned licensed gun owner. The adorable old kook did everything by the book.

She would've never allowed one of her sterling babies to just lay around locked and loaded in her precious diner. Winters then went down to his knees after placing the weapon gently on the floor beside him. He cranked his head up and peered underneath the bottom region of the basin.

Tucked in the wall on a hidden ledge, which where someone aloof would never have known to be existent, was a square box of loosely stacked ammunition. The man pawed for it, pulling the stow out all the way into the kitchen fluorescence. The box was custom made and bound by brown leather and a wiry twine. It looked about as old as the rifle. The rounds inside were larger than he expected, assuming they were more of a powerful buffalo type bullet. He then checked the model of the tired looking firearm. It was a Winchester 1886.

Damien began to perspire a bit while looting around and fumbling about on the floor. He gripped a round at a time from the custom bullet box, plunging them into the gutsy chamber of the mature repeater.

Chick, chick, chick.

Nine rounds in total as the weapon became fully loaded and ready for action. A dozen or so silver bullets remained in the ensemble, so he emptied the load into his right leather coat pocket and discarded the box altogether.

A new hope surged through the fractured man as he rose from the floor with his rustic rifle, courtesy of the boiling bag of bones on the restaurant deck only feet from him. Winters exited the kitchen, and again broke for the front door, throwing himself out into the endless derangement of chilling night.

He would never set foot into Thelma's Diner ever again.

XXIX

HE COULD ONLY think of Leigh.

The eldritch yellow sky seemed to bleed downward, giving off a semi-thin fog of the same suffocating color. The young man's cabin was nestled in the complete opposite direction of town, so running on foot in heavy boots wasn't an option. He looked around hopelessly for anything or anyone that looked remotely human, only finding a resting place for his coppery eyes on the exploded helicopter that entombed the stouthearted pilot named Woods.

An overwhelming dread flooded his lungs, in coming to grips with the only way back toward a shot at getting home was another blindfolded jaunt through the darkly lit forest. It was the last place he wanted to trek at that luckless instant, but his spirit provided a broken reverence of flimsy guile for the wearily unpredictable hike.

He took off in a trot, allowing the Colorado woodlands' rich sable foliage to downright consume him. The Winchester felt comfortable inside his grasp, while he headed on with both hands clenching the rifle at the ready. He came upon a clearing that spread apart the trees, somewhat closer to the other side of his destination, back near his pummeled and destroyed Mason General Hospital. Towering Douglas firs sat like a wall all around him, but luckily, he could still see faintly in the blackness with the bright, atmospheric mist seeping through the dense tree line.

Winters stopped in his run at the black heart of the wooded clearing, catching an unsettling rustle of sound bearing down on him from a probable due east. He turned that way while huffing like a trembling madman. From the west, more oddities sprouted from the darkened thicket of shadow and shrubs. The south followed suit, as if in every direction there was a convergence of unknown origin coming right for him. Damien had become his own ground zero with no chance of possible escape.

Off nearest his gloomy right, a couple of shady figures popped out from foliage nowhere. From behind them, another handful made their presence known out of the blinding density of trees. They were all human in form, with some dressed up in engineering jumpers, while others donned tattered hospital coats and garb. One wore an inpatient's nightgown that was dipped in foul and gunk.

The armed survivor swirled around in a 360 maneuver, despairingly trying to study his stalkers in the suffocating endlessness. They were all former employees and a solo inpatient from Mason General. They must've been the stragglers that had made it out alive before it all came crashing down. Although they weren't actually alive any longer—none of the wretches were.

Each of the sorry hunks of meat slithered toward the tense man with peccant and unwholesome eyes, filled to the brim with nothing but famished doom attached to their swelling skulls. Piercing and damned near bursting whites with no pupils was the menacing theme of the darkly lit forest. A select few of the circling horde's deadlights were so bloated within their human appearing heads that puss along with a thick milky substance ran down their faces, manifesting within the confines of deliciously wicked grins. They moved just like ordinary people, not communicating amongst themselves due to the human conquest before them.

Winters found himself boxed in and surrounded. From an aerial view, he could be seen as the unfortunate eye of a storm, the very center of horrid chaos reincarnated. The leather coated cavalier mustered valiantly to not lock eyes with any of the oncoming legions of sphinx.

"Keep away from me!"

Winters howled into the woodland abyss with a raspy and chaotic nucleus, but his human senses remained operating quite flawlessly.

One greedy disgrace for an Engineer bolted from the pack first, breaking up their offensively dominant full circle. Damien had to turn his body hard right to zero the charge. He raised the Winchester and brought it up into his right eye for aim. The man was ambidextrous by nature, being more comfortable firing a handgun with his left hand, but a rifle or a shotgun feeling at home in his right. He prayed that the ancient artifact was still up for the task of shooting bullets.

He fired off a shot at the storming maniac, striking the bag of ancient torment right between its billiard balls for eyes. The Engineer's fucked up cranium exploded on impact, a barbaric result from the powerful buffalo rounds inside the stoic mortal's mighty relic. One of the white coats came next, barreling with a wild head full of hungry and demented steam. A swift cock of the rifle was followed by a thunderous BOOM!

A shoulder strike caused the closing demon to spin around like a kind of top and twist down to a fall in the crunching leaves of a blackened Colorado. The remaining group advanced in a collective effort, anticipating to gobble up the ever-pesky hero. The single former patient bent down from the rest, in a contorted and sickening posture, then proceeded to run on all fours. Her longish hair swept over her face in stride, swaying up, then down, and side to side with the despicably possessed motion of vomitus quirk. Winters unloaded on the freak, striking what appeared to be her human hand, and blew the clawing thing off her swinging arm. She kept coming, so he cocked and fired on the monstrosity a second time. The round hit home on the very top part of its forehead, causing the gowned corpse to face plant only feet in front of him.

He had to run, and he did just that.

He tore off into the other side of the clearing he had intended for, leaving the remainder of depraved hospital goons to give heightened chase, but they were thankfully slower and couldn't keep up the certifiable human pace. Damien broke free from the dreary woods and popped out close to the ironically familiar Mason General ambulance bay.

He only paused for a second, reflecting on the appalling doom he had survived moments ago. The crackerjack mortal cocked his rustic rifle once again on shaky legs, as a round discharged from the spicy chamber and was replaced with a fresh one, and lumbered his way deeper into his ravaged little town.

XXX

FOREVER ON FOOT, Winters jogged for several blocks. He stayed hidden often, laboriously zig-zagging his way through the familiar Heatherton streets, occasionally using a fuel station or scattered liquor store for a purpose of feeble cover.

He passed right by Chuck's ice cream parlor on Main Street. Chuck's was fondly considered a higher quality staple of mom-and-pop sugar joints throughout the great state of Colorado. A proper frozen cream kind of place, none of that tacky froyo junk. At least, that's what Chuck would emphatically inflict upon any customer that would waltz through his creaky parlor door. His advertisement sign on the outside rooftop of his cramped-up business had been fitting for its simple name. Up above the dearly petite box of a parlor, was a flashy and glittering neon sign with a woodchuck holding an ice cream cone.

The color palette of the display was fairly accurate to the inclined depiction. The browns and whites of the bulbs lit up the fuzzy chuck rodent, while the flavor of cream the lucky devil was holding in his silly little paw looked to be strawberry, or maybe it could have been raspberry. Under that, in a soft pinkish hue, read, 'CHUCK's.'

For as long as Winters could remember, Chuck had the darndest of times keeping his own name lit up on his catchy shop's welcome board. The smiling woodchuck and his flashing tongue that protruded out in a wag, with his plush cone of sugary freeze, were forever constant, never burning out even for a second year after year. It had repeatedly been the "C" and "H" in "CHUCK" that would die out often and provide the goofy owner fits. More times than Damien could count, he would stroll by Chuck's place on any whatever evening, and catch a glimpse of an ecstatically fluorescent neon marmot enjoying a flavored cone with the pink name of 'UCK's' shining bright like a diamond directly underneath him.

He would head in every so often and inform Chuck that his eyegasmic waymark had gone AWOL for the umpteenth time. Chuck would usually thank him dryly and offer up one of his famous waffle cones in his thick as molasses Japanese accent. Chuck was a character that never seemed to age a single day in all the years that Winters had known the ornate freeze keeper.

Damien could remember from the time he took off from California and moved to town, way back in his twenties, that Chuck hadn't aged a lick in over ten years. They'd both joke around about trivial small-town matters, things such as how the Rockies were doing that particular year, and how the team was never the same after Larry Walker hung up his bat and glove. Then Chuck would gloat over how his waffle cones smelled and tasted the finest in all of the endless realms of splendid ice cream wonderlands. Damien would never dream of arguing such a claim because he thought Chuck's cones were mighty fine, but Kip would sometimes give Chuck a hard time for his megalomaniac and boisterous declarations.

Along with his wife, Chuck had literally built and personally owned the sleepy Heatherton parlor for over 50 years. They were quite the Rocky Road and Mint Chip scooping tandem, until sweet Clancy died in her sleep one January morning back in 2016. Her death devastated Chuck, but he kept scooping flavors for all the locals and glassy-eyed tourists who passed drearily throughout the town. Chuck stocked all of the most decadent and exotic ice cream flavors, such as Cookie Monster Blueberry and Oreo Bliss Supreme. Damien would frequently inquire with Chuck about how he managed to consistently create such delicious and off the cuff flavors of sweet splendor, but the Japanese ice cream legend never once showed his hand.

He'd, nine times out of ten, give a wink instead to the scruffy headed Winters while placing a rangy finger to his mouth in a shhh'ing manner at the frequently asked question. Damien was a solid pistachio fan and never wavered from it because Chuck's indeed was the best in the business. There was just something different about it, a loving richness and vibrant zeal that fused together like a symphony with the fresh pistachios inside the green melt.

Chuck always knew what Damien was primed to order whenever he walked in, and each time he'd request his usual pistachio cone, Chuck would say, "Oooh, that's a good one!" or, "Yeah, I like that!" while combing his scraggly silver goatee with a spotted hand and rearranging his four-inch-thick bifocal spectacles.

More times than not, Chuck would be sporting a hat while he scooped alone behind his fun counter of sugar tubs; usually, one of those painter style sorts that old mobsters used to wear before robbing a bank or two back in the '20s.

As HE PASSED by Chuck's micro parlor back inside his own abhorrent present reality, the woodchuck sign was completely switched off, and the front window of the nostalgic place had been smashed to pieces. Winters peered inside from the black sidewalk, but nobody looked to be home. He prayed that Chuck had gotten out and was somewhere safe; although, a painful realism crept up inside his tired and disoriented skull that washed away the flavor of his sugary sweet reminiscence.

The fiery mortal continued his spirited operation throughout the central smorgasbord of town, hurrying past Maple and Frost Streets, respectively. A section of buildings on Main appeared to be burning from up ahead of him, one of which, from a distance, looked to be Marty's Drugstore and Tackle.

He continued onward, to walk some here and sometimes enter into a mild running trot there, all the while armed and ready with Thelma's Winchester repeater. He began to lose steam out on his own in the dangerous wide open, mostly for the unfortunate fact that he remained entirely on foot. His heavy boots clicked the midnight town's asphalt while he gritted his teeth to keep up the rough and ready pace toward home.

He decided to give up the double-fisted grip on the heavy weapon, and instead began carrying it in his left to loosen up his upper body while he pressed forward. He proceeded with vigilance and was on the verge of passing Montgomery Street, but first, he decided to duck behind a horribly shot up pickup truck on the edge of the spookily blanketed street corner. The tires were all the way flat, and the machine was leaking every fluid known to what was left of civilized Man.

While plowing on, with nothing left but downright determination toward the flame-riddled establishments a few blocks up, the sky became unexpectedly vicious. Up until then, it held its yellow haze with minor wisps of cloud coverage in a nonetheless beautiful and starry vision of supernatural sky. The full circle moon shifted from the brightest of whites to a muted magenta, as more clouds rolled in at an other-worldly speed. The Earth's neighboring satellite became swallowed by the incoming density, as sharp thunder rang out, causing the battered human being to grimace against his will where he stood huffing in the chilled, open street.

He darted for cover and hugged a brick wall in a nearby alley, then cozied up next to a Heatherton cigar shop named, 'Twilight Smoke.' He looked up with hesitation into the new and threatening abyss, watching the swirling clouds turn into puffy cinnamon rolls and forcing a blueish-green lightning show to cascade with savagery throughout the preternatural universe. Clustered roars of thunder strikes beckoned out from above his shivering frame, rattling the breathless man to his bones out in the open downtown.

Suddenly, bizarre particle fragments began to fall freely from the treacherous display of unpredictable heavens. The stuff crept down like snow; however, it was mostly black in color. It glowed the same dark shade and almost looked like a type of ash that could have been touched by the angels, or maybe on a night like the one in question, something even more rotten than the devil's rejects.

For a horrifying flash of realization, Damien stifled a thought that the falling debris could very well have been the remaining particles of his fellow Mankind. The majority of his town's occupants drained dry and melted to nothing but dust by the superlative sphinxes that he himself was barely surviving against. The abnormal discharge continued to trickle down hypnotically while slicing through the air during the last night for human superiority on what was left of a dying planet Earth.

The winds then picked up their own relentless momentum, screaming and whipping throughout the devastated Colorado settlement. Winters panicked at the unforgiving gusts and sought the largest and most stable structure in his general vicinity. Adjacent to the forgiving brick wall where he stood huddled and cowering, stationed only a hair westward up Main, was Alpine Bowling Alley.

It stood untouched from an outsider's perspective, with Damien having a dry comfort in knowing the place pretty well from the inside. He took another look at the churning whirlwind above him and conjured up a steely and forced suck of the contaminated night air. The hollow hero sprinted across the street for Alpine with a primal daze of frightened tunnel vision. More lightning screamed out halfway to his destination, causing multiple flashes to light up the murky boulevard of small-town black. One rogue bolt sliced right through a solo fire hydrant up the next block on Cherry, causing the ivory watering hole to rip from the ground and land like a giant cartoon anvil on the hood of a rusted through Dodge Challenger that was parked illegally near the corner. A deluge reservoir shot from where the hydrant used to live, causing a mini blowhole in the concrete sidewalk on a usually discreet Heatherton thoroughfare.

As another rumble of raucous thunder caused the dismayed Damien to crumble down and duck for cover in the middle of the stormy asphalt, he dug even deeper and pressed on into the intended safe zone. At last, he reached the main front door windows of the rock thrower's alley. It was a sliding glass deal, which usually opened up by motion sensor all on its own, but not on that incubus of a calamitous evening. He tried to pry it open with his bare hands, but the effort proved nothing but futile. Winters took the butt of the Winchester and gave it all the strength he had left in his draining human tank. He exhaled a minor, "Uhh," sound with the move as the glass cracked in a spider vein pattern after rifle butt met bowling alley door. Another whack with the old shooter sent the entire panel shattering to the floor at his boots.

He turned back toward the street only to hone in on a full beastie lion sphinx operating on two gnarly legs chasing down a frail person in yet another Mason General lab jacket. Once the fiend had tackled him in the doomsday stretch of street, the guy's fancy overcoat went up in a sublime fireball.

It wasn't until the degenerate with no eyes sucked up the remaining ash of the melted down hospital worker, who shrieked nothing short of bloody murder throughout the assault, that Damien turned away from the carnage and wobbled inside the bowling alley doors.

XXXI

H E COULDN'T EVEN make out a hand in front of his own face on the initial entry to Alpine Bowl. The establishment's outside lights and the branded sign had all been dark, while the main drag he tiptoed through offered zero visibility. Damien hadn't been to the alley in a few months, as right then, the dark entrance felt off-kilter to him. The initial hallway was usually carpeted with a thin dark blue pigmentation of confetti and colorful star patterns that wove throughout the sea of floor. The ground his boots met felt harder, like a concrete surface or tile.

He inched forward in the washed-out pitch, clutching the Winchester so tightly it felt as though it might break apart in his bare hands. The main cashier's desk was up ahead somewhere and off toward the left. He could only gauge the setup from a previous memory of times less sinister. While inching closer, yet remaining blinded by darkness, the brave soul continued forward. He listened for any peculiar variation of resonance, but all his ears picked up were his own steps gently rapping on the unfamiliar undertow with each nimble footfall.

He fumbled around without the liberty of sight and got to the desk where a revolving door of underage receptionists usually lounged sporadically, while they sprayed rainbow patterned bowling shoes and held up the counter with their lazy frames on Colorado Rock 'n Bowl Friday nights. Bowling alleys had a specific kind of smell to them. A distinct must consistent of mixtures of lane oil, grease, and potent cleaning agents. Gooey nacho cheese and doughy French fries would also seep through toward the lanes from the snack bar on drafty occasions, along with wafts of golden pitchers filled with clashing lite beers and pepperoni pizzas.

Winters adored the collective aromas of such a place, because it never failed to remind him of rolling mostly gutters as a kid with Ernst.

He sightlessly maneuvered all the way around to where he believed the main cashier's counter area was, creeping his way to the very back region of the space. He smacked his right elbow on one of the desk corners in the process, almost causing him to drop the rifle, while sending a stabbing sting that fired up his damaged and overworked appendage. He felt around the far partition where he knew the light switches were stationed together. By an act of something holy, he found them in the blindfolded confines. There were three switches, side by side, that were positioned on the overall wall area.

He turned his large hand upside-down while cradling the rifle and switched them all on simultaneously. The entire alley section in front lit up all at once. Twenty empty bowling lanes of shining wooden boards and perfectly placed pins of paint revealed themselves with an old-school prestige of sporty confidence. The lighting out on the lanes was a pure purple fluorescence, throwing bizarre shadows further into the way back portion of the oiled wooden strips. The remaining fixtures took their sweet time and eventually ignited the oversized bar off to the right side of the enterprise.

Alpine Bowl was nowhere near a colossal sporting arena — more like, the polar opposite. The place fancied itself as a friendly bowling experience, featuring only the twenty chic lanes with galaxies and planets painted on the walls in a grandiose mural behind the pin pits. The snowy Rocky Mountains were the majestic foreground, of course. The summits and peaks of the icy range tied into the background galaxy theme perfectly, adding depth and distance to the overall august backdrop of landscaped surrealism. In embossed white lettering read, 'Alpine Bowl' stretched across lanes seven to fourteen.

Believe it or not, the speakeasy happened to be the most groovy aspect of the whole place. The lights continued to flicker alive at their own expense over that way, sweeping the barkeep with a neon orange sheen of brilliance. The bar area appeared to be the most appealing scene under the conditions, so he entered the constructed drinker's den nearest to his right.

There were no paying customers or soggy mid-sectioned stone-throwers to be found on that insipid evening in question. The combine looked completely abandoned, a relative theme of things since his unfortunate hospital awakening. The whole place had a feel to it as if news of the apocalypse had broken a short while ago, sending everyone running like frightened banshees for the jagged ranges of nearby mountains.

Damien soon realized that the floors were different there, as well. It was a newer looking hardwood, with some boards being light in color while others deemed dark, making generous 'M' sized shapes underneath his overworked motorcycle boots. Winters concluded that Alpine must have been recently under some kind of interior reconstruction before the devilish Sphinx onslaught.

The paint was different than what he'd remembered, and the brick wall at the back, behind the bar top, had been transformed into a white and black combination of inviting stonework. The two side by side bathrooms in the lounge were covered with large wooden boards out front, an obvious sign of a project in its infancy stages of never gonna happen completion. The orange neon blistered the watering hole's layout from the ceiling, with thin and sleek tubes making lengthy X's across a majority of the confines. It gave off a dramatic frame of wholesale complexion.

While scanning the human emptiness, the man began to feel isolated and as alone as ever out there in the brunt of his gripping madness. A Boxer Glove gaming machine made some noise off in a corner, occasionally singing little blips and lighting up scattered number sequences on its screen, waiting to be sucker-punched by an overconfident drunkard that would never again exist. A Dirty Harry pinball machine was next to the boxer, lit up and flashing with the intent to entice a glazy-eyed patron to come on over and make its day.

There were three pool tables in the center of the airy room, all with red felt linings and a dark wooden rim with golden saucers for table legs. A few generously sized drink tables lined up around the velvet pool slabs, tall standing with round tops and four rings and a long pole to support your feet while sitting, but most importantly for the overall table weight itself. The chairs were eccentric to the eye, bar top in style with a shiny booth leathered material. They were orange in color to match the intriguing ceiling bulbs, with a white stripe in the center that was supported by thick and snazzy legs of chrome.

As Damien stood studying the funky new layout of the place, he had totally forgotten how many buffalo rounds he'd already spent while battling the outside army of the Sphynx. He reached inside his coat pocket and pulled out a fresh handful of thirsty lead. He armed them into the shooter with a smooth degree of primed precision.

Once the weapon was fully loaded back to a sweet and steady nine, he contemplated sitting down and having a God damned beer.

The ludicrous thought inside the confines of his current predicament broke out a wry and evil grin to his still boyish, yet nevertheless seasoned veneer. Winters then peered back behind the liquor counter to see if Alpine still carried his favorite brew on tap. The elixir was called Boont, an Oregon based amber concoction that the man adored the taste of. His brown eyes sifted through the orange and scanned the various beer taps, coming to terms with the one with a grizzly bear head thrust into a full growl attached to it.

That was the one.

He picked out a glass from the neat and organized quarter behind the barkeep, not giving two shits if it was crystal clean or filthy and mangy, and poured himself a pint of Boont.

He sipped his beer in a fragmented euphoria of broken peace. Damien was the lone customer in the unbridged house, and he acted as his own covetous bartender. The feeling was peculiar and hit him in an outlandish kind of way. He couldn't envision the last time he'd truly been in a soothing and authentic state of being, except maybe with Leigh.

Many nights after an ugly shift at Mason, he would suffer illicit bouts of anxiety and stifling post-traumatic stress. When things really got sticky, mundane tasks of everyday life, like taking a shower or going to the market for groceries deemed daunting and difficult, causing a panic-stricken psychosis that strangled the ravaged man out of delusional thin air. Winters had endured so very much since the initial insurgence upon his town. Perhaps all the adrenaline and stressor fear had finally been maxed out within him for a short window of churning time. The well had drained dry as Damien found himself in a satisfied and straightforward morale, an exotic sense of bliss, knowing at the very least in that very second he was alive and painfully human despite staggering odds. His present moment was all that mattered, then more than ever, in the tumultuous complexities of his rocky mountain life.

His elaborate mind had relentlessly been prone to wander from past to future, or what if this and oh no that at a blitzkrieg, always adding creative fantasies and wacky scenarios as cherries on top to the present mark of humdrum existence.

But right then and there, in that very minute, Winters sat up at the Alpine bar in the middle seat and stared down at his half-gone pint of Oregon's finest draft beer.

As he raised the glass up into his face, orange and white reflections danced off the thickness of it, giving him a cheap ticket of a light show to entice the onlooker, only if they happened to be focused down toward it before drinking. He watched the beer bubbles rise and pop at the surface within the glass while admiring the dark copper color of the growling bear elixir. A light froth rested above the bubbles, dressing the liquid like snow on a frozen-over lake in the colder months of his decimated hometown.

Thelma's rifle lay close beside him, resting butt down on the ground with a forward lean at the counter. He took another sip of the chilly crisp brew, listening with heightened vigilance to his overall surroundings, with senses infinitely keen inside the fleeting aura of inner peace. He was ready for anything that came knocking inside the forever night. The copper water went down nicely, and all the young man could recount for the shallowest drag of a tick-tock, was that particular beer was the most satisfying cold one of his entire life.

He chugged the last quarter of the grizzled Boont and offered up an indignant belch, settling his eyes on a mirror at the very back of the counter behind the hard spirit liquors. It was his own reflection that startled him, a tired, yet joyous posture hunched over on an island at the long tabletop of vacancy.

A burning rage that was never gone, but at no time ceased to churn from deep inside, began to creep up to the surface while he glared through himself in the dark mirrored glass, wanting nothing more than to vex anyone and anything who'd assisted in bringing about the devilry of his nefarious predicament.

For all Winters knew, he also had a hand in the inevitable destructive efforts of his fellow humankind. He was nowhere near a hero, or anything close to being perfect, and he'd fucking well known that from the very beginning of all things him. Since a young age, Damien had realized that he would never have all the answers to life's many mysteries, or even half of them for that pressing matter.

Also buried deep down, inside the endless pit of his tensing stomach, may have been a deciding factor as to why he'd never wanted to have children of his own. There were other reasons, such as malignant overpopulation and a downright scary world in his current year of 2020, but he also couldn't make sense of another human life that he'd helped create for his own selfish reasons, being forced to endure his shadowed hardships and painful inferiorities throughout their own lives.

Winters had accepted that human existence was fucking hard, and the idea of bringing about another innocent being that was a substantial extension of himself, to clash with the inevitable pitfalls of the human condition, never sat well within his skewed and unorthodox moral foundation.

The plummeting man then found himself scowling at his own hellish reflected self in the dirty bar mirror, while he picked up the rifle acting as his only bar companion, to whom was perched fashionably on the floor by his knees.

He palmed the empty beer glass he'd just consumed and threw it into the tough Alpine mirror. The half reflection merely danced a little shimmy, but the drinking cup exploded into numerous sharp fragments and careened into a bottle of Jack Daniels on a nearby shelf, causing it to combust and bleed out to a draining death.

He took one last look at his disintegrating self-worth and wiped the dark brown hair from his sulking, but handsome overlay. He grabbed for and raised the Winchester rifle, a little higher upward and into his chest, and barged out of the orange crushed ghost town of Alpine Bowl's permanently under construction watering hole.

XXXII

With the fiery fluorescents and pool tables at his back, Winters took to the main alley. Thunder from the outside storm ricocheted with another sublime fury, shaking Alpine's guts like something relentless. He was on the verge of heading back toward the front door to offer up a quick look outside.

Maybe another survivor was running for their life, or perhaps the storm would break apart and come to an end soon.

The atmospheric elements since the sphinxes first landed had been incredibly unpredictable. It was wrath and rage one moment, then baffling serenity transitions and jaw-dropping psychotropics, which were deemed nothing short of marvelous the next. He turned to make his way back into the direction of the exit, when a heavy thud rang out from a distance behind him.

He discerned the abnormality of resonance only once.

It wasn't quite a crashing noise, but more like a rummaging around somewhere deeper within the place. He stopped in his boots and turned around to face it. All that was to be seen were the black lights bouncing off the haunting denseness of all twenty Alpine lanes. There wasn't a pin out of place out there, with each glistening wooden track presented uniformly and perfectly untouched. He listened while craning his neck to one side, offering his stronger ear a small degree of extra assistance, causing his fatigued eyes to become wide and darting. Only silence responded, giving back nothing satisfactory.

His perception loomed as if telling the hollow thud had come alive from the very rear, way out beyond the long rock pits. He wanted to forget he'd ever heard anything, and instead continue out to check up the storm, but what if it was Kip back there?

What if he was alive and managed to get to Alpine first and was pinned down like a frightened dog waiting for help just as Damien was?

The spent mortal scavenged a little extra bravery somewhere in the cobwebbed section of his remaining mind and crept over to lane one in the very far corner of the dark purpled bowling arena. He took to the narrow pathway at the left of it, metaphorically walking the bowler's plank to reach the stern situated machine room area.

The smells of fresh resin and lane oil spilled into his nostrils halfway down the strip, which neared the silent chasms. He breathed in the mixing odors through his nose, allowing his senses to soak up the wafts of comforting nostalgia. The fluorescents grew dim as he proceeded, offering darker light the further he trekked down the lane. He paused right before the skinny open entrance to the mechanical chamber of Alpine's intestines. Another deep breath escaped from him as Damien ducked into the unpredictable opening of blackness.

He turned his entire anatomy to the right where he stood and peered into the familiar theme of richly pure sable. Again, he couldn't see one foot in front of him, but he knew there had to be a light switch near off or close by somewhere. Placing the bulk of the Winchester in his left hand only, he reached around the wall nearest him in the rectangular pitch of noir.

Nothing doing, but as he reached his hand back toward himself, it nicked a string dangling from higher up. He swiped through the black for it, flailing his leathered arm in heightened desperation. Another attempt floundered in the void until he finally caught it. Damien pulled the string as a warm, yellowish light flicked on from straight above his head. He looked up to catch the metal dish that the bulb was affixed to doing a twirl and spin from the upper region, giving the back area's new guest an overall chilling milieu.

As he turned to face the heart of the room, the figure was already charging at a bellicose speed. He raised his rifle instinctively towards the oncoming blur, no longer concerned if it was all the way human or full-on sphinx, but his time had run pitifully barren. Winters fired off a shot right as he was collided into, causing the round to spray off somewhere into bowler's oblivion. He was slugged in the face with a blazing fist, causing the slender man to slam down to the sooty floor with the rusted Winchester spilling off behind him.

With a stinging jaw that he believed might have been broken with one punch of absurd power, he stared up at his incredible assailant. The figure lurked above him, open-mouthed and full of spite. The single swinging light above their heads cast shadows then highlights onto the overaggressive attacker's shifty silhouette.

It was Bud.

Bud happened to be Alpine Bowl's longest and finest standing house porter. He had worked at the small-town alley for as long as Damien could remember, running into Bud frequently when he'd come down to throw stones with Kip or Leigh on a random Heatherton day. Bud was an odd little dude; however, Damien had thought of him as having a kind-hearted aura that select few people had the ability or patience to distinguish. Kip tended to jolly around with claims that Bud probably lived back behind the grungy Alpine lanes.

"That screw loose Bud guy's got a bed back there, someplace," he'd say after taking a swig of a random bottled cold one following a 6/7-10 spare pickup.

Bud looked young for his age, although he was one of those individuals who someone could never pinpoint their actual authentic age. He was average in height and general stature and could've been anywhere from ages 21 to 47, give or take twelve years. Bud was a dandily committed bowling alley porter, always picking up the deadwood on the lanes when asked by his reception team of teeny-boppers, and was eager and quick to assist with the scoring machines and overall house maintenance.

As the years wore on, Bud began talking to himself a little bit more around the place, scampering about the establishment in his all over the joint sort of world, mumbling away to his own misunderstood intrigue.

Winters could recall one time where Bud had approached him one night while he bowled on his own, getting some practice in while Alpine was free from bursting at the seams families and screeching unsupervised rugrats. Damien had remained respectful and cordial with Bud, usually asking how life had been treating him while chatting around intricate bowling tips and the latest professional gimmicks.

On the night in question, a single human tooth somehow made it out on one of the shiny approaches, two rows down from where Damien happened to be bowling. It had most likely fallen out of some ten year old's trap while they chomped down on a tray of runny nachos in between sheet cake and punch during a glorified birthday bash. Bud had picked up the tooth and scampered over to Damien with a grin to show off his scavenged prize.

The only thing Bud had said after holding out his hand to reveal the tiny piece of mouth bone was, "I like teeth," then he turned right around and headed off on his merry way, pocketing the tooth and mumbling sweet nothings to nobody in particular.

Winters just shook his head where he sat in one of the attached plastic chairs in front of his scoring machine, giving off a creeped out little chuckle and got back up and kept on bowling.

But that was Bud!

Trouble was, it was no longer Bud at all.

The hovering mass gave off strictly human vibes and deemed unassuming in stalking form. The standing thing resembled the former lifer bowling alley porter, except the new meat carcass that contained him felt callous and diseased to Damien. The new blob that stood over him in the bowels of Alpine Bowl was something straight out of an unimaginable and prehistoric hell ground. A realm that existed well before a human idea of Hell ever came about and was manifested, a playground done right the first time because it was that much worse in spiteful and dastardly appeal.

Bud wore his usual porter's work clothes that consisted of a grunged out and faded black shirt, paired with scruffy and even more washed out black jeans. He was sweating profusely while his shirt stuck to what was left of his familiar skin. His eyes of mortality were completely gone from his closely cropped head of hair, replaced only with soupy off whites primed to melt and sickeningly consume. The bulbous jawbreakers attached to Bud's skull were bloodshot and swelling, draining chunky liquid down his face that seeped straight into his crooked and wide-open stew.

The charlatan's mouth was agape, all the while drooling and slobbering down his chin and work polo. Bud's tongue wagged in a reptilian slither, inside then outside the main meat and potatoes of his compact shoulder setting. The porter stood see-sawing over the fallen man in the homicidal back room lighting.

"I don't care about teeth anymore, Damien," Bud spat up and wheezed as he spoke. "I only like souls now. Human souls!"

The floored Winters was incapable of speech as he laid sprawled out and vulnerable on his leather back. His jawline screamed from the initial sucker punch, but he realized his face was not busted. He felt around for the Winchester but couldn't manage to find the elusive relic. Bud jumped for Damien and landed right on top with the dazed mortal man coming face to face with another set of vengeful saucers of Sphinx. He attempted to shield his face with a sterling leathered arm, while Bud dripped down snot and mucus on his chin and neck.

The Bud hellion was savagely strong, a new and improved firecracker that easily handled the longer-framed man named Winters. In a move of frantic desperation with the intention to not look, Damien pulled his head hard right and smacked that side of his face grudgingly into the cold ground, as Bud attempted a fixation of a close-quarters scowl upon him. An old wooden bowling pin sat resting on its side by the machinery by lane 1. It hadn't been painted the usual white with a red stripe yet, its light brown rawness coming forward in the man's watery-eyed view.

Damien reached out for the under-construction bowling pin, but even with his long arm, it remained a hair's length out of his reach. Bud writhed and clawed at Winters with human-looking hands from the creature's dominating position. The man outstretched again, getting an index and middle finger to only graze the heavy and naked chunk of lumber. He lurched his body with everything he had towards the slice of shaved wood, only budging a few inches with the Bud monster all over him.

He then stuck out his arm a third time, managing to grasp the pin's head with a full and blood-encrusted hand of flesh. Bud postured up, creating a small window of distance between the two savage fighters. The desperate man looked right up at Bud, locking horrified human eyes with ghastly sphynx globes.

"Not tonight, Buddy boy!" as Winters swung the pin up and sideways like something inhuman, striking the house porter in the temple.

The sphinx uttered a disgusting gurgle on impact, as its tongue drooped with a limp instead of a wag. Bud remained in full attack mode, switching instead to attempt a telepathic brain onslaught upon the fallen down Winters. Before the maddening tactic slithered inside his shattering brain, Damien swung the pin again, even harder than the first strike.

With a direct hit in the same vicinity on the atrocity's gut-churning noggin, both yolks for eyeballs popped straight away from Bud's head. They turned to a jelly slime and spilled over Damien's jacket and onto the calloused flooring underneath them. Bud's bashed-up face then shifted from human to an eagle at a dizzying speed of light, abhorrently owning a bird's face in a disgusting human meat sleeve.

A third blow with the wooden weapon caved in the whole left side of Bud's atrociously fowl face, forcing a hemorrhage on that immediate section of horror. The area ballooned to a point, then burst. With only half of a face no longer human in the slightest, Bud leaned forward in a heavy collapse while still affixed to the maniacally defending and fighting mortal. Winters shouldered the dying degenerate, sending it tumbling with force off top of him.

He looked over at the body, as its legs kicked and the hands pawed at nothing but stale back alley air. He righted himself in a standing position and approached the seizing abomination. He came down hard with a black boot heel on the remaining side of Bud's profile, pulverizing it to a splattering pulp. Only then did the headless porter cease his convulsing outrage.

That was the gruesome ending of Bud, the Alpine Bowl porter.

Damien slowed his rapid heartbeat while choking through lengthy and deep heaves through his nose, releasing them from a quivering and open mouth. His jawline continued to sting like the dickens, but all he cared for then was the missing rifle. He looked around and down toward the ground behind him and found it. It had managed to skirt near the wall when he was leveled to the floor. He grabbed the weapon as relief drenched over his panicking soul.

With the saucer light continuing its sway to and fro from the ceiling in the sky, he peered deeper into the back-attic room of the undersized alley. All the intricate workings of all twenty pin racks were visible there, manifesting itself all of a sudden into more of a factory than a functioning sports center. He moved further in, while creeping past lane after lane.

About halfway through and around lane 10, he nearly slipped on something watery. He looked down by the rack and noticed a hefty pool of thick and coagulated hemoglobin. It had found a home underneath the pin pit on 10, with splatter covering the impeccably situated pins of 7 thru 9. Entangled in the mechanism of the rack was a human arm. The mangled thing appeared to have once belonged to that of a common man. Damien then assumed that it was ripped clean off before the remainder of the poor sap's body was liquefied down to soup.

It looked like Bud had been busy back there before stumbling upon the scrappy sphinx killer named Winters.

He looked back left, even deeper into the entirety of the backside alleyway as a collective whole. Tucked away in the very rear next to lane 13, existed a smallish and makeshift cot. It was no larger than a twin-sized bed. There was a dusty white comforter tossed on it in a crumpled and disorganized fashion.

Damien approached the dusty area and studied its begrimed surroundings. There was an arrangement of scattered photographs on the wall by the teensy sleeping quarter. They were spread out in no particular order, just dirty polaroids solidified in a simpler and more carefree past time. The man scanned the images with his brindle orbs that fluttered in the machine room doomsday essence.

They were all of Bud.

Bud, as a baby.

Bud, with what looked to be his parents.

There was even a faded black and white with Bud and a pretty girl, written on the blurry camera paper while perched hand in hand. Bud wore an innocent and cheesy grin, along with an even bigger smile from his fetching counterpart. The passionate porter was in his usual faded work getup, while they both stuck out in time by the main front desk of Heatherton's Alpine Bowl.

Winters scanned over the scene for another moment, as he swallowed down the onset of his own sodden eyes. He wiped the melancholy away with his grizzled coat of leather, all the while shaking off the goose flesh that had ravaged over him, and walked back around toward the way he'd come.

He stepped over what remained of the Bud monster and turned off the not moving old-fashioned light fixture that dangled from the cobwebbed ceiling. He cocked his rifle with purpose and made his way back out of the room, which led into the bowling alley's forefront.

XXXIII

ONCE EXITING BUD's World of Blood, he was back out on the lanes. The pure purple fluorescents longingly met Damien's eyes. He looked left and peered all the way down at the very end of lane 20, seeing nothing but usual desolation. He kept moving toward the main lobby floor, halfway down the side plank next to lane number 1. From up and around the snack bar area, just off to the right of the official reception desk, he picked up some movement.

Next came the scream, a piercing resonance that shrieked a feminine timbre. The cry sounded painstakingly human, and it caused the man to rumble off in a sprint straight for it. He jumped the two unassuming steps to land back on the central floor and stopped on a dime right after he passed the line of bowling ball racks on the cruddy unfinished floor.

In a beeline in front of the snack bar window was a young girl. She couldn't have been more than 15 or 16 years of rhapsodic innocence. She had neck length deeply natural red hair and was wearing a baby blue knee-high dress. She had lost her shoes along the way, while she stood cowering in bare feet in the open restaurant aperture.

Almost entirely blocking her from Damien's vantage in the youngster's path was a maintenance gardener from the seemingly forever alive and kicking Mason General Hospital.

It was Cliff, in fact.

Damien and Cliff had never really spoken during the grind 'em out human years, but Winters would pass by Cliff many nights outside the perimeter of the hospital, catching glimpses of him pruning the surrounding bushes and tending to the flowers and decorative plants. The gardeners were a bite-sized crew of only three employees in full charge of nursing the entire care facility, but they were a diligent bunch and worked well together.

Damien was amazed at how the trio never stopped moving, always picking up something around the place or blowing leaves away from the sidewalks near the ambulance bay. The gardeners even specialized in windows, washing and scrubbing the Mason glass until the clean sheen was so clean you could lick the coolness off from it.

He looked upon Cliff from a distant side view, catching sight of the left-angled portions of his stout profile. Cliff wore his tan work shirt and matching pants, along with black comfortable sneakers and a yellow reflective vest for when the cutting crew worked night shifts. Cliff was built on the heftier side of things, and he talked with a peppered accent of unknown origin to Damien. Although they'd never spoken one on one, Winters would overhear Cliff conversing with one of his team while dishing out hospital orders, always wondering where he'd hailed from. The gardener's extra tan skin and short dark hair were oily and glistening in the violet-black Alpine lighting.

Cliff charged for the girl and went to raise his meaty right arm up toward her face. The aggressive move made the orangey redhead in her blue dress squeal again in a grinding display of maddening terror.

Out of the near distant shadow realm, Winters boomed a, "HEY!?!" as both Cliff and the young woman stopped and looked into the direction of his beacon for a voice.

It was only half of the real and actual Cliff.

The other side of his body was an ungodly mess, a beastly deformity of odious and malevolent Sphynx. The eye on the unspeakable side was the powder-coated soul swallowing bulb, bearing a hairless lion's face with thick whiskers projecting from the one cheekbone. Cliff was clothed on the shameful half of his body, and the putrid section emerged mutated and strangely dressed up in human working man's threads. Cliff's lengthy pair of pruning shears still hung from his belt, dangling a shake from his insufferable side of alien death.

The half-bred disregarded Winters, and instead, turned his rotten attention back to the cowering shoeless girl in her plain aqua frock. The man-beast raised his right paw, a muscular animal hand with curled black and bent claws, and came down for a scrape.

Damien shot a round from his rifle toward the attacking blob, but the attempt missed poorly and wildly inaccurate. The bullet whizzed by both parties and exploded a large mustard container sitting on the snack bar counter just next to them. Cliff then landed his clawed deformity onto the innocent unfortunate, ripping her chest and shoulder region-wide open with a single rip. She yelled out again, but that time in a different way. It was gut-wrenching and painful as the sound spilled out into the airwaves, no longer only a heightened fright of scared intimidation.

The firing man knew the difference all too well.

Her fresh fluids painted the wall behind her, gushing out like a sudden wave of red connecting with a sturdy rock on a choppily bloody shoreline. While keeping his standing distance, Damien cocked the Winchester repeater's lever, projecting a spent casing right in front of his appalled young face. He again unleashed a booming effort, proving accurate and true in the heat of revolting battle. The buffalo round connected gloriously with Cliff's left leg. The bullet pierced right through the muscular stalk, but barely slowed down the sturdy shocker.

Cliff pounced again toward the injured woman and began to feast menacingly on a thin region of her frail midsection, before she went down all the way to the floor. The leathered man blasted again from his classical weapon named Thelma, plunging a round into the hearty meat of Cliff's marbled back. The girl and the gardener both went down to the dusty canvas.

With unbelievable disregard for Damien or his thunderous boomstick, Cliff only gawked at his injured prey with his one soulless sphinx light. The young woman shrieked bloody murder at the horrific initiation and began to convulse violently from underneath his sturdy weight.

BOOM!

Another explosion from Winters met Cliff in the lower region of his thickly stern. The sphinx gardener continued with its salivating glaze and merely flinched with being shredded by the heavy animal rounds.

Damien set down the rifle and scrambled towards the bowling ball rack to his immediate right. He grabbed the first round stone he saw, a scratched and scuffed dark blue 15 pounder. He rushed at the crazed sicko and his unlucky victim with the ball cradled hand in hand. When he reached Cliff, he kicked him in the side with a sturdy toe of his boot, removing the shredded thing off the young lady and putting the fucker on its putrid back.

The Cliff sphinx was livid at the human's audacity, snarling and moaning its own form of primeval incessancy. Damien then vaulted on top of Cliff and his unsavory exhibit of appalling depravity. The man scowled down at the thing's nightmarish face and noticed that it still owned one human eye along with the one full-fledged bubble of dismay. Cliff had become a disgusting gel of a heinous and bullet-riddled hybrid theory.

With both hands gripped and fueled by a maddening rage, Winters pulled the heavy boulder above his head and brought it crashing down to the floor in a sickening manner. The bowling boulder met the good side of Cliff's head, causing the infested creature to forge a repugnant popping babble upon impact. Uncontrollably exasperated, the mortal rose the stone and brought it down again toward the revolt.

And once again!

As Cliff was left with only a murky pulp for a brainpan, Damien tossed the bowling ball aside. The clodhopping hospital gardener moved no longer; his reign of terror officially snuffed out by an angry wrath of human justification.

The out of breath man rushed over to the injured youngster's aid on the floor beside him. She was down on her side with her back facing him, and when he got close enough, he reached over and turned her over onto her slight and soggy back. She was spilling from the initial claw wound; the devil had gotten blessed from the beginning and struck a major artery somewhere crucial inside her.

Her blood poured like wine as he reached out both hands and applied pressure to her gaping laceration, sealing it with his slender and powerful dukes. He pressed down fiercely on the gash with his instinctive efforts, causing the girl to moan in agony ever so gingerly. He gazed up at her face with a frenetic and concerning display of raw and desperate humanity. Her fiery auburn hair was behind her head, resting on the messy floor where she was laid out bleeding and dying. She had freckles on her cheeks and owned a full set of her own honey brown windows of raw human sight.

"It hurts," she cried out.

"You're gonna be just fine," Damien said gently on one knee, hunched over her body while pressing shut the overflowing injury with valor. "I'm Damien," he said with the cheesiest wink and grin that the man could conjure from above her trembling frame.

"R-r-rose," she could barely manage but a whisper.

They stared straight through each other for a short sequence, with Damien never letting up on the seeping tear in the woman's chest. She broke eye contact and looked around with a glazed over expression.

"I g-got away. I-I saw you break in here. I came in after y-you to see if you could h-help me. I…"

"Try not to talk," the reeling man interjected warmly while she ground her teeth in mortal anguish.

"I couldn't.. f-find," as her eyes began to close.

"Stay with me, Rose. I'm here. Stay awake for me," he uttered in a trying voice that nearly sucked all the remaining life force from what remained of him.

"I couldn't find... y-y-you," and then her eyes closed down forever.

Blood spewed through her fatal mutilation, rushing through the trying man's clasped down hands. He never let up his endeavor, continuing to seal her wound so vigorously that the grip began to cramp his bare and overworked bony indicators. They'd become numb with the demanding effort of the job.

"Rose!? Rose, honey? Please, stay with me!!" he pleaded.

Her head turned to the side and away from him as she choked on a final and unwanted earthly breath. Winters grasped her split-open chest for a good for nothing lasting moment, staring sympathetically down at her young and darling face of scattered pepper flakes. After checking for a pulse and finding nothing but silence, he knelt down further and cried in her blood and tears.

XXXIV

THE NEARLY BROKEN man scrounged a napkin and pen that barely bled ink in the simple alley snack bar and scribbled a rough and ready note, all the while sitting Indian style next to the remains of young Rose in her baby blue sapphire dress.

When he finished, he placed the handwritten letter beside her, removing himself from a state of inexplicable grief, marching out of the Alpine entrance with a burdensome heart unto the forever trenches of the grizzly night.

> *I'm so very sorry, Rose. I tried but could not save you. I'm painfully uncertain if I could have done something more; however, I will never forget you. It saddens me deeply to think that perhaps this was a better path for your unfortunate and untimely destiny. You died a lovely and vibrant being. One that was both innocent and completely guiltless. You never have to experience such unfathomable fates as so many others in front of you now must endure. Keep an eye out for me. I need all the help I can get out here.*
>
> *Your friend always,*
>
> *Damien Winters*

XXXV

H E COULDN'T BE aware of how much longer he could endure the never-ending nightmare. Back outside the front entrance of Alpine, the man looked around his person and then skyward. The atmosphere had cleared up altogether and morphed into a condition as eerily stagnant as a fancy showing of California earthquake weather. The cloudless ether offered streams of shooting stars that whizzed about over and yonder. The Moon became visible again off in the darkest distance. The dashing sphere almost appeared normal within the madness, like he'd always remembered it looking his entire life, except for the alien solar rings that surrounded its distant crust.

There were two of them, giving off the very whitish color palette as the planet it encircled. The sky's totality had an aqua hue; however, no fog or mist joined the cosmic bash. It suffocated the street almost dreamingly with extra cold frost.

Damien craned his neck into the upper regions and thought of Rose one last time in his crumbling state of mind, taking one last peek over his shoulder at the broken in entrance he'd been guilty of creating one hour before. He cocked his trusted rifle and lazied on alone toward the flaming structures deeper within his crushed and withering mountain town.

After passing Cuthbert Street with Baker Auto on the right, the first property on fire down Heatherton's Main Street was Gypsy's Mind Reader and Tarot Cards. Upon meeting up with the prancing inferno, the man's brain fell backward into a past variation of fond remembrance.

Winters had loosely fancied himself a mysticism enthusiast for several years, along with a passionate case for off-beaten stories regarding the occult, and had walked into Gypsy's one night a year or two prior after a shit night over at Mason, which was followed up by a spiced rum over ice with the giant squid on the bottle drinking binge. It had been pouring rain that lamented evening back in time, with Damien coming in soaked and mellow after making a punch-drunk kind of love to Leigh at the cabin, then heading back out for a nightcap after she'd fallen down to sleep next to him.

The decked-out individual who'd greeted him when he entered the quirky little place was a middle-aged man. A bell affixed to the door signaled Damien's drenched arrival, and Gypsy appeared from a funky looking room at the back, behind the counter. Winters had been drawn into the inviting neon sign that was attached to the front window of Gypsy's far out business establishment. It depicted a large yellow triangle with a lit-up black eyeball in the very center of it. There were two other separate signs next to the triangle that read, 'Fortune Teller' and 'Mind Reader.'

One was red in color, the other green. Damien was taken aback when he'd found out that Gypsy was, in fact, a real name and also not a nuts and berries clone of a psychotic hippie person. Gypsy had materialized from behind his eccentric counter space, looking like a 40 ish-year-old genie on a groovy Halloween night, with muted grey long hair and tie-dye bracelets on each arm.

Never being one to judge a book by its peculiar cover, Winters paid for a reading and found a way to actually enjoy the unconventional experience. They both settled in back and sat in the candlelight of Gypsy's whimsical shrine studio, discussing strange phenomena and off the rails theories regarding humanity and other energy marvels of mysterious distant powers.

That was one special and defining memory that cascaded to the front of the jacketed man's mind while he stared at the building engulfed and burning. He shook off the memory and pressed on toward home, hitting the next corner of Pine Street, stopping to lean up against Mel's Antiques to catch a breath and snatch a quick view of what was up ahead of him.

From a distance, while he lumbered further back on Main, he'd believed that another structure was aflame, although his assumption proved to be untrue. It was actually a bus of some lineage, the large tour kind of transportation jazz. It was lying upside-down in the intersection of Pine and Stone streets, overtaken by reddish-orange magma. The smell of melting tires and steaming rubber socked Damien in his tender and swollen nose.

Beside the blazing bonfire sat a hefty police motorbike. At first glance, it looked to belong to the Colorado State Patrol, one of those bulky and boxy cycles with a broad windshield and two metal saddlebags on each side of its body. It rested on its side, with the lights still flashing, a red and blue symphony amongst the incandescent backdrop of fire.

Off to the side of the abandoned bike and in front of the burning tour bus was a group of what appeared to be lined up and positioned human people. There were four of them in all, and they were dressed in different clothing and common garb. In front of them were two figures decorated in full neo-noir military or police riot gear. One held a large assault rifle, while the partner carried what could be seen as a new age series of flamethrower. A pack was affixed to the soldier's upper rear side, also black, with a tube of the same color running down to a long thrower gun. The sable weapon in the dark gloved person's hands was lit by a small flame at the tip, begging to erupt.

The trooper types wore helmets with tinted shields affixed to them, making their identities an absolute mystery. Damien peered across to the four street clothed individuals at the very front of the fiery tour bus. Three of the sorry suckers were degenerate, human imposters on the hunt for more of God's unworthy creation, to suck down and swallow with morbid delight.

The fourth and closest person to where Winters was standing out near the street corner, seemed to be that of an ordinary man. He looked no older than Damien with his confused, broken-down eyes proving spirited and forgiving. As the flame toting soldier raised his torch at the group, the only soon to be marshmallow that threw up their hands in a defensive fit was the young man.

Without thinking twice about what he was seeing, Damien fired off a shot into the air where he stood at the corner. He then entered the middle of the intersection, gaining ground on the eldritch apocalyptic scene. The action stopped for a second as the assault rifle spotter swung his weapon on Winters. They drew first blood, whizzing multiple bullets around and past his slender coated frame.

Winters fired while continuing to stalk forward, striking the psycho soldier in the chest, dropping the body straight backward in a shocking blink. As the one human innocent noticed the hero's objection, he attempted to sprint away to safety from the rest of the sphinx pack. The other assassin in black then raised their flamethrower.

Damien tried to shoot off another bullet, but old Thelma jammed up good on him, locking a buffalo round halfway in the chamber while he cocked the weapon to fire.

That was all the time the inferno wielding individual needed.

The commando opened fire on the group, spraying a glorious burst of flame at the three human sphinxes and the one full-on mortal man. The four of them lit up in unison, as the sphinxes stood firmly in position until they went down without even a whimper. The poor fella screeched a psychotic melody, running and flailing around in the reflective street while ignited and lit up like a log, until he sat down by the bus after his hair and face scorched away and quit moving forever.

Damien stood flabbergasted at the brutality of the scene where his denying eyes were seeking to somehow process. The masked murderer then turned the thrower toward him. Winters remained stuck, standing in the middle of the intersection, trying to unjam his fossil for a rifle. He finally fixed the jam, sending a clean round into the Winchester's hungry chamber. His time had run out, though, as the blacked-out soldier unleashed their smoldering flame straight at him.

The man turned and dashed hard left in a breathtaking display of a maneuver, narrowly avoiding his own hot and heavy Viking funeral. He somersaulted on the hard asphalt and popped up to one skinned knee, with the burst of fire missing him by mere inches. The commando seemed surprised by the sudden agility, while all they could manage was to turn their helmeted head toward the acrobat as he unloaded a kill shot straight to their black-uniformed heart.

The flame of the thrower went out cold, as the soldier crashed to the asphalt as if they'd just been struck down by a bolt of lightning. Damien eyeballed back over toward the burning horde of bodies by the bus. The sphinxes were all toast, and unfortunately, so was the other young man.

Winters, again, readied the Winchester to fire and approached the first masked gunman. They were both laid out on their backs while he crept up near them with heightened and extreme caution. He reached down and pulled off the helmet of the first commando.

It was just another average looking commoner, nothing more and nothing less.

His eyes were pulled wide open in a fixated and surprised death glare. He was completely human in a dead on arrival dynasty. He moved on ahead to the next soldier, the one who'd controlled the unreal heat rifle. He first nudged a padded leg with the rusted repeater barreled straight down on them, a clever precaution under the spine-chilling moonlight. He knelt down and removed the tinted riot mask. Long and dark tresses spilled out from underneath the shielded helmet of gloss.

It was a woman.

Her eyes were pursed closed, but her mouth was open, and a drool of blood flowed from it. Damien reached in with his right hand and opened up one of her eyelids. Also undeniably human, as her organs of sight were all but settled in some realm of undetermined eternity.

"This is insane," is all that Winters could voice to himself in the chill-factored street.

He thought quickly, attempting to shake off what he'd just seen and had to do. There laid two human beings primed and ready to barbecue another man for a reason he would never be able to comprehend. When pushed up to the very brink of existence, the human race tended to unrelentingly show off their truest and most authentic colors of inten-tions toward one another.

The ongoing rumination that continued its cycle throughout the man's swirling brain was the fact that the two crazed super-soldiers he'd just gunned down were in all likelihood better off dead.

XXXVI

DAMIEN APPROACHED THE heavy police motorcycle that was pulled down on her side in the Colorado night street. He placed the Winchester to the ground so he could use both hands to pick up the weighty two-wheeler.

The way the bike had been discarded reminded him of a child jumping off from their BMX bicycle and refusing to use the kickstand. They'd been in too much of a hurry to get to somewhere else after the ride over to the candy store, so they'd dumbly let the cycle keep moving forward until it careened onto its shoulder to the hard ground.

Winters got the machine upright and mounted it with its red and blue police lights flashing indefinitely. The first thing his eyes noticed was the black and white officer's helmet, which was cleverly attached to the right handlebar. It was chained by an industrial pair of police-issue handcuffs, a slick maneuver from the owner to avoid a possible helmet theft. He studied the bike for a moment in an attempt to explore the fancy gauges and gizmos. It was a key start rumbler, and luckily, the ignitor piece remained inserted into the keyhole of the rozzer's cycle. He'd figured that whoever ditched their bike, did so in a hurry.

From the closest intersection near Stone Street, charged three mammoth sphinxes and one humanoid. The posse of fiends was lightning quick in their pursuit and muscled forward on four animal legs apiece. It felt like time had stopped from Damien's perspective, as he watched the freaks click-clack their claws and feet in rabid pursuit.

They were hairless and had reddish exteriors of abhorrent creep. They owned feline-like faces with hulking athletic builds. Horns protruded from each of their abominably foregone surfaces.

The almost-human was a female in a light-colored hospital gown, another unfortunate straggler from Mason. The she-thing was stationed in the center of the pack, barreling full speed ahead toward the hardened Winters. Her usual eyes of civility had been erased from her head, and replaced with sickly albinos of antediluvian destruction. She appeared possessed, running wildly in the endless black on two bare feet, with hands up in the air that flailed all about herself.

The batch converged at a blistering pace of extra disturbing offense. Winters looked down at the inserted key in the cycle's ignition and turned it, with passion, to the right. The engine sputtered beneath him, then died out.

He turned his face back into the pack in time to catch the gowned former patient bending over and beginning to gallop on all fours while mirroring her beastly counterparts, the hospital nightie changing from white to orange as the horde neared the flaming bus in the background set piece.

The man tried the key again, with only a pathetic sputter.

"Come on, baby. Come on," he said aloud as he shot another glance at his attackers nearly there, geared up to consume his attractive spirit for the remainder of a doomed vacuum of nihility.

He turned the key all the way off and gave the bike a kick with his left boot. He cranked the starter a third time over, igniting the police engine into a glorious racket. Damien looked down at his rifle on the crisp asphalt next to him, but it was laid out just beyond his reach. He gave a final darting gasp at the breed with the waxy woman patient leading the rotten charge, only feet from the bike and the defenseless person.

Winters rumbled the throttle with no choice but to leave his stoic Winchester behind in the cold boulevard, plunging the motorcycle out into the open Heatherton downtown. The lady sphinx took flight from her animalistic and archaic stride, launching at the bike but being greeted with nothing but smoky Colorado air.

He had escaped just in time, while suddenly he and the constable's cycle operated as one fluent unit. He tore off in the wrong direction, away from the ghastly convergence, but farther apart from his darling Leigh.

The pack of demons continued the charge; however, they couldn't keep up with the breakneck motorbike and its new leather-jacketed operator. Damien knew he had to turn around and get back home at any cost.

In a dexterous exercise, only a practiced rider could substantiate, the man swung his new copper chopper around in a full 180-degree whip and faced the stampeding family of ancestral foul head-on. Helmetless and darting a look at the handcuffed hat that was affixed to one handlebar, he wiped a hand to his face and removed a tuft of dark locks from his dizzying line of vision.

Winters yanked the throttle and released the clutch. The bike tore off with a screeching sound of rubber shaking hands with asphalt in an unhinged chicken-like maneuver, barreling headlong into the oncoming perversion. He looked down and locked eyes with the siren button on the front-facing dash of the bike. The motorcycle's lights remained on, flying blue and red impressions across the boulevard while his speed and roaring motor increased noteworthy severity.

He switched the siren up and active, booming the raucous law whistle. Offering enough of a distraction and pulling off yet another nifty maneuver, Damien mounted the curb on Main Street as stores and businesses in his beloved town whizzed by in blurry pixels, along with his wavy hair flying behind his helmetless and dangerously exposed skull.

One of the atrocities didn't take the bait and converged on his on-the-fly tactic. Before the beast collided with him in mid-ride, Winters broke off to the right.

The motorcycle caught several inches of air as it lurched and jumped back down from the curb, piercing through the pack of hellhounds with only inches of dead space to spare between them. The legion continued their rumble from behind, forcing him to switch gears and rev the bike to a howling rate of blistering torrent. He turned his head on a swivel back toward the creatures, while he removed a hand from the left bar for a view, watching the diabolical monstrosities grow smaller and further away in the wake of the blues and reds of his screaming cop machine.

The remaining businesses on Main shot by in obscurity of neon and fiery dark. He'd, at long last, come upon the two-lane forest drag that headed straight toward his secluded cabin home. The road was desolate as the clear cerulean hue of airspace mixed seamlessly with the extra bizarre moon and its mystifying atmospheric circles. He maxed out the speed on the lawman's chopper, ripping through the very foundation of the night itself.

I'm coming, Leigh.

Hold on.

The thought flooded through his brain as the wind whipped his chiseled face. He had once more found himself on the very same stretch of roadway where his nightmare first began. Damien dug even deeper into the motorcycle's guts, finally turning off the deafening siren that aided his improbable escape from town. The blue and reds insisted with their intrusive beams, providing trustworthy enough illumination to help navigate the comfortless forest up ahead.

He was nearly there. His lone rumination remained that he absolutely had to save her.

XXXVII

H E SOMEHOW MANAGED to arrive unscathed at the cabin on his stony police wheels. He remained forever alone and dreary, hoping to a God or any other presence of warmth left on watch over his chaos-filled planet, that Leigh remained alive and unchanged. The lovers had been an on/off deal for the duration of just over four years.

It was mostly on, to be forthright and honest.

Leigh Hutchinson was a true small-town girl, living the entirety of her twenty-seven years in Heatherton. She and Damien had that life intrigue very much in common, with him vacating his coastal burgh in California for an even tinier Colorado settlement to call peace and home. Heatherton was astronomically smaller than California's Carmel, and Winters admired the fresh mountain surroundings for most of his up and down adult life.

He untimely flashed back to an initial story in a moment's past of him wanting all the way out out of his Colorado town. He couldn't quite understand the powerful intuition, until right then as he hit the driveway to his log house in the newly forever brood.

THE COUPLE HAD first met at the good old burnt to the ground ashes of Mason General Hospital one gothic evening closing in on Halloween, dozens of moons ago.

He had been on a back to back shift, attempting to enjoy a full hour lunch break in the fine dining mess hall of his geriatric care center that never slept. Kip had come down with a rotten case of the flu that week, and with the dwindling available crew members at his disposal, he'd had to operate more than half of the double by himself. His relief had thankfully arrived, and he was starved half to death. He also needed to piss like a bloody racehorse.

It had been a weekend duty and all but closing time for the 1st-floor tasteless cafeteria slop house situated one floor up from his basement dungeon. That night's special was a decadent compilation of slimy Meatloaf Surprise! It looked and tasted more like dog vomit that a sickly pooch had hurled up, eaten again, and barfed up a second time for a little added flavor. Damien could never find a way to warp his mind around the fact that the inpatients were allowed to suck down such offensive food during their hospital stays.

On a positive note, Mason General's cafe did manage to close down somewhat generously, allowing an extended 10 pm weekend shutoff time. Winters was sitting alone around 9, doing nothing more than staring down at his puppy chow for meatloaf, struggling to cool his jets from the fire alarm panel that had been blaring in his face for a good seven hours in his cellar room, along with three Rapid Responses he alone had to tackle only one-half hour ago. The young man sat adrift in a dazed state of la-la land, peering at his tasteless grey slab of turkey, when a voice filled with milk and honey broke his trance.

"Excuse me?"

Winters gazed up in his obnoxiously lit cafeteria, drenched from head to foot in his usual black hospital scrub suit of the night. His wavy brown hair nearly covered up his coffee-coated eyes, which for the scrubs he'd concluded never failed to make him look like a mixture between an aspiring priest in a chincy Hollywood flick or a high school janitor that couldn't get enough Johnny Cash in their miserable life.

Leigh was standing tall and over him, the brimming and wholesome goddess managing to sneak up without notice during his somberly hazed mind escape. He didn't reply at first, so she continued.

"You obviously work here... umm, when does this cafeteria close for the night?"

He exuded a smirk out of stunned innocence that he'd been blindsided by such a magnificent creature. It had been unusually warm on that backtracked October evening in Heatherton, and the hospital restaurant was more or less sweltering. For all Winters thought back in those days, the big wigs upstairs had gotten extra stingy and decided to skip out on the old air conditioning billy bill for a month or two to save up for backyard Jacuzzis that cleaned themselves and flaunted rainbow light displays for their army of stupendous offspring.

At that time of night, the cozy mountain town had remained a solid 85 degrees outside. The hospital had always given the impression of running extra uncomfortably, causing a luxurious Dante's inferno vibe that the then scrubbed man loathed.

Damien gave Leigh a quick once over with his overworked eyes of mahogany, noticing first that they were very close in general age. He was, in fact, a few years her elder, but what had sucked him into her atmosphere were her striking hazel eyes and medium-long auburn hair. Her locks had a natural spunk of curl to them and hung down and around just past her graceful clavicles. She wore little squares of gray and white patterned shorts along with a white Danzig t-shirt with black lettering. Leigh also had on a pair of wayfarer sunglasses nestled adorably up top of her invigorating forefront.

He'd wondered for a moment if she'd forgotten that they were up there, with it being dark outside for several hours and all. Her summery look was finished with a simple pair of white flip flops. Her toes were painted the darkest of blues, and her short fingernails owned a shimmering sable coat of contrasting polish.

Her enchanting face offered the most gorgeous freckles that dappled throughout her distinctly profiled cheeks and forehead, like dark glittered magic that pushed forward into her sultry olive skin. She was chewing slowly on a stick of bright green spearmint gum when she'd approached the weary worker with her question.

Leigh had surprised him, as again, the young Winters gave her another blameless look before finding something rational and coherent to reply. He was floored at how sexy her legs looked standing above him in her checkered and skin-absorbing hot pants. Another guiltily random thought that perhaps she was a swimmer in her flavorsome spare time crossed the man's marbles as he dropped his fork on top of his enigma meat and spoke in a serious connotation of jazz.

"10 o'clock. You, unfortunately, made it just in time," he'd said, as he finished chewing a bite after locking on once more with her piercing greenish-brown jewels of exploding shimmer.

"Unfortunately?" a confused Leigh replied, as she then shifted her standing weight mostly onto her left leg, forcing the thigh muscles inside it to come forward and bulge in an almost painfully enamoring way.

"Yeah, well now you're gonna have to endure some of this ground chuck from hospital hell like I am," as Winters then took the plastic grey knife he held in his other hand, placed it to his temple, and performed a suicide by plastic knife gesture with a smile.

After she revealed an authentic pearly white grin in return, he had wound up buying her the finest tuna on wheat with pickles that Freddy, the slop house chef on duty, could whip up behind the sterile cafe counter while they sat together as the only two patrons left in the joint, until Damien finished out his much needed nightly meal break.

Leigh's grandmother had been very ill, forcing her visit to the hospital that warm night in the forever distant nothing. Granny had been one of the inpatients that Damien coded while working his shift on the first leg of his double. Leigh was visibly distraught over her cherished relative on that hot and dark evening in Heatherton, with Winters attempting his best display of witty charm with the little free time he had left, to convince the cherubic woman he couldn't believe he'd only seen for the first time in town right then, that her grand-mother was in excellent hands at Mason and she'd pull through just fine.

Sadly, that blind inflection of optimism was not the case, with his overpowering intuition knowing all the better.

He switched off the police cruiser and finally figured out how to turn off the damn flashing lights. Winters dismounted and rolled his life-saving machine up the driveway's initial stretch, toward his secluded cabin sanctuary. He parked it a safe distance away, keeping the bike hidden within the surrounding Colorado foliage. His log house was a compact one-story chalet on the northern outskirts of town.

The sky took liberty upon itself to perform another brazen switcharoo of far-reaching heavens and morphed into a swirl of richly layered colorings. Reds, greens, oranges, yellows, and purples inter-twined in a dazzling picture of churning upward welkin. He could make out choppers and planes flying around in hysterical fashions off and yonder in the nearer inky distance. Flashbangs and echoed pitches of sound could also be heard, likely from feasible gunfire and other forms of defensive carnage, out there somewhere in the ludicrous anonymity.

Luckily, it all seemed to be unfolding at a safer distance away from the scrappy mortal's immediate location. His cabin was situated off of the infamous two-lane roadway that led in and out of Heatherton, with it being disguised by magnificent Douglas firs and other lavish greenery. The endless night scenario remained constant despite the circus act laying wrath in the breezy supremacy above him.

Upon approaching his front porch steps, the entire wooded structure took on a moody unveiling of an array of colors in the remaining light, dominated by a deep reddish-orange of a glow. Winters prayed silently to himself that Leigh was inside with one of his weapons by her elegant yet lionhearted side. The straightforward fact that he'd actually made it home, and was on top of the same location he'd left her last, deemed hopeful and dizzying all at one frightening speed.

Leigh had her own set of keys and would let herself in and wait for Damien to get off work most nights. On the latter days of the week, she would sometimes have a midnight dinner sprawled out on the square wooden table next to the inside kitchenette.

Right before trying his cabin front door, his unruly imagination bent and jagged to one particular night, in a not so distant timeline, that was finished and gone away for good. Leigh had ordered pepperoni and pineapple pizza from Larry's Pizzeria, which was located a block past Maple downtown, and was pouring a glass of vino for the both of them when she'd heard his motorcycle come roaring up the woodsy driveway. He had unlocked the door to find her in the kitchen palming two full glasses of red and wearing an old Jim Morrison t-shirt he would put on during one of his off-the-cuff creative bouts of artistic expression.

Leigh wore only a flossy black thong below the waist that covered next to nothing, but offered her boy toy a satisfying presentation, with the men's rock n' roll shirt being transformed into the world's skimpiest mini dress. The fiery lovers had ended up eating cold pizza and heavily rested Merlot on that memorable Colorado evening. It had always been those spontaneous sorts of little things that had mattered most to Leigh and her damaged gentleman in their spicier days of partnering souls.

Especially to Damien.

THE FRONT DOOR was locked, so he went for his keys in his left jeans pocket.

They were nowhere to be found.

He then thought about going around back to try a window, but he stopped cold in his movements while huddled on the front porch near the door. A scream shot through the house and torpedoed through the barrier, one that pierced his young and bleeding heart; then a sloppy crashing noise ensued from someplace deep in there. It sounded like a woman's shriek.

Operating with a panic-stricken display of emotional strife, while foreshadowing a sequence of unspeakably wicked thoughts, the man reached around for his trusted Smith & Wesson knife in his other tattered pocket. His heart skipped a shuddering beat when he realized there was nothing inside, except hollow desperation.

Empty.

He must've lost his blade with his keys along the way out there in the forever dark. Or maybe he'd never had either of them at all since waking up strapped like a raving psychopath to that fucking hospital bed back at the villainous Mason. Another robust crash from the inside met him, then a gnarly foreign snarl, and a second desperate cry out in strict succession.

Winters shuffled a few steps backward and ran full steam ahead into his locked front door, leading with his freshly shot and abused right shoulder. The sturdy wooden frame budged no more than an inch.

"Leigh!?!" he cried out.

He took one giant step back, then front kicked the bastard door as if it were his most brutal enemy. It gave a bit more, as the hinges wobbled, with the thing beginning to feel the crazed human's desperate display of wrath. After a second booted strike, the door flew open with a sheepish form of forgiveness, all in one fail swoop.

The mixture of fear and adrenaline that churned within him then were impossible to grapple with. Damien's body was riddled in a full shake, but he faced the impending dread with a thrashing heart of impenetrable steel.

The almost certifiable man darted terrified eyes around his cabin's living room quarters. The one-story setup was on the smaller side, but the inside landscape appeared large and spacious due to being edgily furnished and inviting. With Leigh and himself there most nights, the chalet was blissfully artistic and extra cozy for two hopeless romantics.

The kitchen area was positioned to the left of the airy living space, along with the master bedroom with an inviting shower tub, which was inside the large enough connecting bathroom off on the right. There was another smaller room at the very back of the hallway, but that was strictly for Damien's art studio and supplies. His random inspirations of sculptures, paintings, and photographs lined the overall square footage of the neat log cabin.

Make no mistake, the totality of the grounds was nowhere near cluttered.

It was more like an organized form of creative expression, especially in the very heart of his art studio. An oil painting of a sweeping Montana landscape ate up the wall that divided the living room with the kitchen, which took Winters months to finally put down his knife and brush and call that one finished. The striking piece on Plexiglas was textured with beautifully saturated reds, blues, and greens.

There were also a few substantially sized windows that were scattered around the inside perimeter of the house, with the largest one being straight ahead of him, reflecting the colorful ensemble of sky show outside. No signs of a struggle seemed apparent in the living room, and nothing appeared broken or out of place upon initial entry.

Wait.

An otherworldly grunt and a petrified howl echoed out with wretched clarity from the log homeowner's master bedroom.

Again, finding himself weaponless and filled with a gross gradation of powerless desertion, Damien Winters dashed for his one and only bed-chamber. The door rested propped and wide open; no problem presented upon his own getting in there.

Nothing stirred.

A gurgle of incontestable dismay broke the strained silence, close by, coming from the bathroom inside the room. He went for it with his entire body fit to explode with a maximum overdrive of fervid anxiety. He then noticed that the bathroom door had been ripped down from root to stem. It remained in shards, as chunky pieces were thrown around the tile flooring like a tornado had just touched down out of thin air.

Thick steam devoured the sleek washroom world, while the vintage bathtub water ran full blast and scorching. What the barely holding it together man saw next made him question what remained of his fleeting right-mindedness. It also mortified him beyond any degree of sound comprehension.

One of the more abhorrent and incredible organisms from out of the night was there, but not settled down on all fours, instead choosing to tower with a nauseating sense of overpowering prowess on two archaic stalks. It owned a burly blanket of nappy hair; however, the creature wasn't covered in enough of the scraggly thicket. It was patchy throughout its ungainly body, dark in tone and gristly appearing. Through that, you could witness the real and utter monstrosity of the freak. Horns protruded from each cheekbone, as the deformed cat face conjoined with an extraterrestrial nightmare one would be forced to wake up from screaming in the witching hours of the blackest night.

The disgraceful presence was huge, an overbearing frame of insanity that overshadowed the man as he stood paralyzed in his washroom's door jamb. It drooled from its overgrown feline mouth with sloppily salivating jowls that flowed an unidentifiable ropy liquid, anticipating its next soon to be feeble and human conquest.

Leigh was also there.

Leigh, his baby doll, with her devastatingly beautiful reddish-green hazels being locked up with the sphinx's carving and bugged-out milk circles. It grasped his naked deity by the throat with one claw-filled and gnarly paw of inevitable destruction. The outlandish leviathan's mouth was opened up extra wide, revealing a sprawl of despicably rotted and foreign alien shards of grimy bone. The sphinx nearly touched its oversized skull to the bathroom ceiling in a showing of morbid and unrelentingly perverse size.

Then, his darling Leigh began to melt.

"Jesus, Leigh! NO!!" is all that Winters could roar.

His voice was both stern and terror-stricken together while he posed in his lanky tracks, unable to move or comprehend what was transpiring in front of him. Leigh could not avert her gaze and remained limply hypnotized within the bastard varmint's soul-feasting pustules for eyes. The skin from her alluring face began to boil and redden, dripping and snaking down her nude and perfectly voluptuous femininity.

The sphinx must've surprised Leigh while she bathed in the tub, barreling down on his defenseless goddess while she lay at her most tender and vulnerable. The bedroom window was open halfway when Damien entered the room. The latch did work, but it had been spotty as of late.

The fucking bastard had slithered right through at the exact perfect time.

As his femme fatale unhinged a blood-curdling cry toward him, one that the broken man would never, ever be free from within the darkest confines of what remained of his pragmatic bearings, the appalled man charged with empty hands, alongside a heart of pure fortitude, in an attempt to tackle the prehistoric killing machine.

With only a few feet from sudden impact, the reprobate swatted a free left hand of claws across its cursed and unholy body, striking Winters on the left side of his already beaten up and bruised face. The force from the blow was show-stopping, sending the six-foot, 180-pound man to catch air and career backward into a heap out of the bathroom doorway. He hit the hardwood floor in a smash and landed on his leathered back, smacking the top of his skull on the sideboard of his bedroom's California king for a tart and bitter cherry on top. Damien sat up instantly, somehow remaining in a state of foggy coherency, and watched the horror unfold inside the steamy washroom of sadistic malfeasance.

The sphinx continued to corral Leigh by her slippery neck with one ugly and giant deformity. His water-beaded sweetheart began to convulse violently in the hellhound's grip, as the remainder of her wet skin of olive silk cooked clean off, exposing bleached white bones and veiny skeletal anatomy. His paramour shook so violently in the murderous grasp that what was left of her teeth ground and chattered inside her caved and evanescent mouth, giving way and falling to the bathroom tile with bijou clicks and clacks.

Her bright red lifeblood and other bodily fluids deluged the oversized bathroom walls, cutting through the stuffy fog like hot spaghetti sauce that had no choice but to bubble over and erupt down a hot kitchen stove. Her eyes exploded within her elegant framework, as his sugary muse then began to disintegrate within the Sphynx's rebellious grip of abhorrent supremacy.

The medieval brute sucked up her healthy human tissue and charred substance ash into its outstretched demagogic trap for a mouth, along with her soul, her irresistible and heavenly aesthetic life's essence, which then shot into a projection directly into the putrid sphinx's hungry eyes, in a simultaneous display of vile evil.

And just like that, his goddess, Leigh, was gone.

XXXVIII

HIS GUN.

IN a terrorized state of dismayed panic, Damien thought of his revolver on the other side of the king-sized bed. Winters owned a Smith & Wesson .357 Magnum with a 7 shot round capacity. The long-barreled handgun was composed of silver-coated stainless steel with a muted custom rosewood handle.

The weapon had been passed down from his Grandfather, Joe, on his foster dad's side of the family. Grandpa Joe was an old-fashioned city slicker cowboy who'd migrated as an amateur boxer to California from a small island in Portugal, ages ago. Joe meticulously wore either a white or black cowboy hat, even at the dinner table, and a boyish Damien had nothing but the fondest of memories of the cool and collected old-timer. Joe had taught him how to shoot, and the city slicker was graced with being a more patient teacher than Ernst ever was.

Damien adored hanging out with Grandpa Joe out on the border of California and Oregon, where he'd lived on a small plot of land. They'd line up beer targets in an old gravel pit close to Joe's home and fire away until the sun went down way off behind the snow-covered hills. Damien would swipe Granddad's cowboy hat from his head of snow-white every so often, and shoot a hell of a lot straighter with the good luck charm on his own head of chocolate brown.

Winters had purchased a worn and forgiving black leather gun belt for the revolver, with an undercut holster that exposed part of the extended six-inch barrel while the cannon remained nestled inside.

He owned two pouches attached to the belt that supplied a pair of seven-shot speed loaders by a brand named Bumblebee, which were fully loaded within it, and lastly, a pair of industrial police issued handcuffs that were black chrome in color and scruffy shade. The cuffs were a gift from Leigh for those extra kinky romps between the sheets.

Those passionate nights with his better half were forever lost in time, and so was she. He couldn't save her; all of his strengths couldn't quite match up to the daunting task at hand.

The flooding memory faded away from him, giving back to the present moment of the actual Leigh, which the young Damien had just watched die forever.

Severely concussed and down on his back, Winters turned over on his gullet and tried to crawl under the bed toward the left side corner where his weapon resided in its leathered belt holster. He'd almost made the crawl until a giant hand got hold of his dirty right boot. It dragged him with pathetic ease straight back to his starting position. The flailing man shifted his weight and offered a quick glance at the attacking thing.

He settled crushed human eyes on the shocking creation in all its undisputed hideousness and swung a kick with his free booted sole up into the head of the beast with all of his might. The scuffed through wellington landed right between the piercing death stare of the sphynx, sprawling it backward into the fizzing bathroom of what remained of Leigh's fresh blood and gore.

Damien sprang to his feet, huffing knackering gulps of screaming log house oxygen. He dove headfirst over the bed for his holstered apparatus of dignified steel. He overshot the narrow clearance from bed to wall and slammed a good portion of his body into the hard bedroom partition, sending an attached candle and its holder tumbling down next to him. The quaking force also knocked a beautiful black and white framed portrait of his sugar babe that he'd taken during a previous year's Christmas party, a time before human existence was headset for terminal extermination.

He scrambled around and found the belt. Winters palmed his weapon and yanked it with authority from its loose leather. While kneeling on the floor in the tiny cramped space, while paying no real attention to what the alien was plotting behind him, he went for one of the speed loaders with seven large magnum rounds inserted into each cylinder inside the belt.

He then unlocked the wheel of his empty .357 and proceeded to load. His hands rocked and shook during the entire maneuver, but the tottering man endured and lined up the bullets, slammed the powerful lead trinkets flush into the revolver's open-wheel, then removed the loader and snapped the assembly back into a ready position with a left hand.

With no more hesitation left to give, he awkwardly got to his feet from the corner enclave of his tarnished hive and whipped the gun at the insidious bathroom door.

What greeted him next almost made the crumpling spirit drop his heavy firearm to the bedroom floor. Leigh stood settled and plain as day in the bathroom doorway, but it wasn't his enrapturing Leigh at all.

Not anymore.

It was nearly half of her, while the remainder was a morphing experiment of a godawful sphinx. Half-evil and half-angel stood before him in a scene of antagonizing horror. It almost looked as if Leigh's very soul was wrangling and wrenching with the foregone demon from the inside, attempting to win a human struggle that could never be won.

"It's so much better in here, Damien," she exclaimed.

It sounded like Leigh's warm and honeyed undertones, but the voice was a meld that honed a much more ominous key.

She continued, "I don't feel a thing in here, Winter Bear."

Leigh would call him the catchy nickname in a joking manner in a place somewhere back in time. He had never minded the silly moniker from his enamoring soulmate.

"When we've got you weak enough, we're going to devour you and every other useless piece of human filth left on this diseased little world," she hissed, but strangely in her seductive demeanor that the mortal man was all too familiar with.

The seductive blob in front of him convulsed and made a snap, crackle, and popping noise, as his provocative angel infused with the Sphynx on an outright level. The murdering wretch raised its unfortunate crumpet toward the shuttering cabin ceiling, deciding to project a screeching squeal of unhinged magnitude, and bolted headlong for the crushed and massacred soul of Damien Winters.

Up until that dreadful moment, he had never pointed the gifted magnum revolver at anything living, unless you counted the brown bear cub that hung around the cabin in late February of 2018. The fuzzy little tike had attempted to loot his trash box one night when Damien happened to stumble upon him outback. He'd had the gun on hand due to the commotion and raised it in the general direction of the curiously aloof animal, but did not shoot. The famished cub fled off into the woods, never to bother him or his home again.

With the revolver outstretched in his sturdy hand, Damien used his thumb to tick back the weapon's dark silvered hammer. The gun quivered as he completed the action, while he struggled to clench any form of grip on his overloaded nervous system. He reached his other hand up and cupped it over the left like any amateur firing instructor would insist on day one.

The beast was almost at the opposite side of the bed, lumbering on two tree trunks for legs in the warm cabin ambiance. The man closed his eyes out of sheer terror and prepared to fire, but opened them back up again for a reason he couldn't understand. In front of him again, while standing ever tall, was his sultry Leigh.

It was every square inch of her as the sphinx monster had vanished altogether. She stood naked and trembling on the other side of the wood structure's modern sleep chamber. Leigh had no eyes of the human kind in her gorgeous skull of olive skin, but didn't own a single scratch on the entire canvas of her sensuous body. Winters blinked in disbelief and would've trusted it to be his curvaceous beauty if it weren't for her thirsty and menacing abysses of deadly whites.

She screeched out from somewhere deep and beyond the average realms of logical human assimilation.

"DIE!!," and sprung for him.

With hot tears welling to a stream down his chiseled and beaten half to death mug for a face, Damien opened fire. The magnum revolver was a powerful assembly of force. When discharged, a small flame would exit the long six-inch barrel to show off its intimidating man-made prowess.

The bullet struck Leigh in her right shoulder at severely close range, nearly blowing the reaching limb clean off her scandalous imposter's body. The vigor of the shot made the entirety of her frame spin around half swivel and give way unto the oversized bed, only to then writhe in a performance of primal and aboriginal agony.

The expended magnum's sound in the close-quartered cabin was thunderous, with Winters almost losing his basic senses due to the ripping resonance. He staggered to the head of the retirement, tripping over the bedpost in his clunky black boots. With his heavy gun in hand, he scowled forbiddingly upon the billet.

It was all beast again, holding its shredded wreck of a musculature, while a dark green substance excreted from the gaping bullet wound. With the shakes out of his system, the steadfast mortal unloaded again, as the creature barreled a death stare into his brittle and appalled sense of human aura.

POW!

Another quick cock of the hammer soon followed.

POW!!

The second shot hit the alien's sternum area, causing the sadistic animal to begin puking and gagging up its own foreign mucus. Some of the discharge sprayed Damien on his neck and clothes, but he remained unwavering in his prime objective of exacting revenge.

The final shot from the dramatic silver slugger silenced the sphinx for good, blowing apart it's head like a ripe watermelon. The brain matter went splash all across the headboard, as the deviant laid there dead in its own rotten carnage. Only then did Damien lower his handgun with a heavy sigh and was sent down to the bedroom floor. The crushed lover was too traumatized to even shed another tear.

The cabin washroom had been shamefully transformed to look as though Moses and a fedora toting psychopath with knives for fingers had a battle royal to the death in the usually spotless space. Murky water poured from the porcelain tub, overflowing while it ate up the surrounding tiles of enigma.

Chunks of flesh and coagulated crimson showed the walls and flooring who was boss, like a sticky gothic art piece painted all forms of nothing but red. The sphinx was sprawled out motionless and continued to seep its own reeking blood throughout the cool gray sheets on the bed.

The tortured man had been painfully familiar with losing loved ones before, but nothing could have ever prepared him for what he'd just been forced to endure. The out of nowhere automobile accident that killed Sue and Ernst had nearly broken him, however as the years dragged onward in Heatherton, he'd appeared to be making a sluggish pull toward something of forward progress.

In his utmost moment of despair, the losing human found dark clarity within his ruined mind to circulate the more devastating losses of his then-felt rotten existence.

DAMIEN HAD BEEN very close with another former co-worker over at Mason General, a true brother in arms. The pair were even more tightly knit than Winters and Wells ever were, and would relish many nights out after blowing off the usual hospital steam over at Dell's Tavern in the central hub of the neon downtown. They played cards every other day and took scenic motorcycle rides up and down Colorado. Kip would tag along here and there, but Damien had a strong conviction that Daniel's unfortunate aftermath had actually brought him and Kip closer together as future colleagues and friends.

Daniel was a fine and uncommon man, but in downright honesty, he'd possessed terrible life habits. He drank heavily and wound up dipping into the illegal drug scene. It started with weed, then cocaine, and finally crystal meth, which absolutely took hold and consumed his troubled soul. Meth was a powerful drug that could effortlessly bring the toughest of minds straight down to their knees, praying for nothing more than a ludicrous chant of murder death kill. Crystal had an uncanny ability to switch a friendly and charismatic personality into a raging wacko in an unbelievably short duration.

Unfortunately, Damien had witnessed that vicious cycle with Daniel. He was with him, and by his side, every step during the heartbreaking merry go round of his eventual and inopportune destruction. Winters had tried to help along the way, of course. He even offered to take him to see a shrink or drag his ass to a live-in rehab center to help find clarity within. During that time, the trouble was that he really didn't know how or what more to do for his out of control friend. Damien was also consumed within the processing stages of his own personal grief over his foster parent's tragic deaths. He had felt powerless with witnessing such a valued confidante sink morbidly into that kind of rabbit hole, a dark one, which only ended up leading to a cold and rotten place.

He'd seen all the warning signs of his good pal's consequent fate and even had a strong intuition of what Daniel would eventually do to his ailing and unpredictable self.

Daniel wound up renting a chincy motel room one devastating night, one of those rented by the hour types of sleaze.

It was the month of July.

Daniel had smoked some meth that night, along with a few other devilish concoctions to conjure up a radical cocktail. All alone, Daniel contemplated major life choices along his warpath toward the end of his days.

He then scribbled random biblical passages all over the walls and mirrors of that shit sty dank room in Boulder, and whipped out his little filed off serial numbered pistol that he'd bought off another crankster up by the bridge out at the very neck of town. He pointed that unassuming gun to his shattered dementedness and pulled the fucking trigger.

Daniel died alone in a slaughterhouse cesspool, all the way out of his mind that night, snuffed free from the confines of time due to the demons becoming too powerful and great to wrangle with from inside his black and moonless animation. Damien had never forgiven himself for Daniel's awful suicide. That was just how Winters' mind worked. He thought that if maybe he'd been more aware of the situation, along with his own premonitions back then, that perhaps he could have intervened along the way and saved the day for his friend.

Played the God damned paper hero.

Yeah, that would've been just fine by him.

The shadiest truth of all, though, was that there was never really such a thing as saving a spoiled and overthrown soul, such as Daniel's. An ill-omened mind like that, to snuff out from the world, had more times than not been made all the way up, usually for a longer period of time than any saner minded individual could ever attempt to reasonably indulge. Like flies to shit, the only direction left to go happened to be straight down to bloody Chinatown.

That's precisely what Winters' treasured ally, Daniel, ended up doing to himself that one warm Colorado midnight back somewhere in July.

THE BLEEDING SOUL of Damien Winters managed to conjure a brief inkling of gratitude that his loving parents, along with Daniel, did not have to entertain such a horror as the Sphinx. He also wondered, grimly, how his own fate would soon pan out.

How much time do I have left?

XXXIX

DAMIEN NEEDED A drink.

A big ass drink.

He finally peeled himself up off the bedroom flooring and set out to the living room of his then blood-soaked house of wood. He strapped in and left his gun belt on, a subtle form of defense against what appeared like insurmountable odds.

A full bottle of Redemption Bourbon sat untouched in a diamond-shaped decanter atop the kitchen bar table ahead of him in the shallow, lukewarm luster. Two large and fancily cut whiskey glasses were positioned beside it. Winters preferred ice with his sipping bourbon, but straight to hell with all that jazz. He pulled off the crystal decanter top and poured himself an AA sized amount of the fiery spirit, then plopped straight down into the faux leather loveseat in the majority of his dimly lit living space.

He sat alone and drank the tough juice, trying to catch his breath and hold onto the remaining lucid fractions of what remained of his disjointed identity. He pondered over his next moves, but the depleted soul found himself in no real or sudden hurry.

He lost himself with each new swig of the glass-made crystal, with his chocolate eyes staring straight ahead into nothing substantial at all. The deathly silent aura of the cabin laughed crazily at him, reminding the gritty human, over and over, of what he'd had to do in the next room over to his devastating left.

His Turkish manufactured Weatherby shotgun was put away in a locked gun safe in his art studio at the end of the road hallway past the bedroom. He knew he'd have to raid the safe for more firepower. The hidden away lockbox had multiple cartons of diverse ammunition for his revolver, both magnum and .38 specials, to change up accuracy and stopping power flavors.

He couldn't recall exactly how much ammo he had stashed away, however, a hollow comfort mixed with a stupid liquid courage began to worm through the warmer pit of his wrenching insides. He understood that the weapons at his disposal could injure and potentially kill the soul-crushing enemy.

Damien was intricately familiar with his revolver and the shotgun, both of which were registered in his name. He took some more steady gulps of the iceless bourbon while perched in a much-appreciated moment of silence, all the while put under a spell at his own dark reflection in the smoky unlit screen of the Samsung television that was positioned right out before his eyes.

He peered down at his holstered revolver that sat hanging by his left hip, and couldn't help but chuckle at how abnormal it all felt with wearing the heavy cowboy gear around the house. Any other time he'd worn the bulky assembly was strictly for outside shooting practice and fun, plugging full cans of cheap soda and horsing around out in the middle of nowhere land. Damien did hunt here and there, although that had been dedicated mostly to his childhood years with Ernst and Grandpa Joe.

The looming state of affairs that dangled in front of him had become life or death for the very fate of the remaining human condition. The days of popping off deer and wild pig with the comfort of knowing that the human hunter with a gun was the superior organism, were long dead and over.

The imposing magnum revolver that dangled by his side had become a stalwart utensil only for defense. Defense of his own life against the purest contours of a warped and imposing legion of evil. The cold steel had become an embracing part of his very human survival. Winters slung another generous gulp of the stinging liquid, as he brought his attention back to the powered-off television at his eyesight level.

I wonder what the media slack jaws are saying about all of this. Am I gonna turn on this here tube and catch the local weather girl babbling on about a pandemic of acid rain and viruses named after imported beers with no fucking eyeballs inside her bloody head?

Will she have a lion's tail and devil horns protruding like a nightmare from her blighted skull?

The drink was starting to kick in a little bit.

He fumbled for the remote next to him on the curvy wooden end table, and took yet another sling of Redemption with a grunted grimace of inference, then switched on his television set. A reporter's face came into clarity inside the square box of babble. He was dressed in a ridiculously mundane business suit and looked like an ordinary vanilla type chap with perfectly human eyes; all dolled up in his shallow monkey suit with his poufy white hair and short matching beard.

**This is a CWW Special Bulletin: There have been multiple catastrophes on American and foreign soil. London, the Netherlands, and a legitimate chunk of the United States have been under attack from an unknown catalog of rebel terrorist organizations. In the United States, the National Guard and other close-quartered military branches have been deployed to specific areas in the direst of needs for special governmental assistance. ISIL has claimed responsibility for the majority of the attacks on our domestic lands. Citizens are being urged to stay in their homes and lock their windows and doors. Have trust in your country and ride out the storm. **

Winters switched off the Blitzen puppet guy in his wooden clothes with an animal for a first name.

Typical, he thought.

Slews of his kind would be huddled around their holy television screens, listening intently to local and major news stations while following every instruction given as if their very lives depended on sucking it all in. Damien had figured that the glorified media of 2020 would mention nothing of the actual catastrophe that was flattening his Earth.

He couldn't block away from his brain how many more victims there would soon be while they stood in their warm kitchens and dryly decorated living rooms, all the while following such horseshit instructions.

Just wait by your tv with no defenses at all; that'll save you.

Keep listening to your tv God.

It knows what's best for you.

When the tv says jump, we humans are supposed to say how high.

Thank you, tv.

I'm sure our pleasurable and everlasting Commander in Chief has all the righteous answers to everything we demand.

We should just wait for him to give us the God's honest truth of all the pressing human matters at hand.

The spinning man gave his head a vigorous shake where he sat. Then he envisioned an army of sphinx rotters busting down a flimsy door of some cookie-cutter family home in a snazzy neighborhood of rural suburbia yawnsville, scorching down their unsuspecting flesh to a goopy pulp, then sucking up their puppet souls like hungry heifers at a Vegas buffet, while moving right along into the next romanticized brick mansion.

He tried to remain sympathetic to the incoherent victims that would fall for such classifications of blatant governmental bullshit brainwash, but he became enraged instead by the entire premise that had solid control of his fractured state of being.

The human race was, in no question cursed, and it was time to pay the God-forsaken white-eyed piper in full.

THAT WAS PARTLY the reason why humanity had fallen so hard from any degree of clinging grace within itself. Social media and news outlets had become more God than ever, as people's attention spans were always plastered into telephone bricks and electronic tablets, searching for answers that resided in front and within their zombified and confused veneers.

The entire world could've been burning to the ground all around them, and they'd be sitting in the flames searching for a solid Wi-fi connection to boot up as to why. Technology had served its stalwart considerations up until that fateful year of 2020, but the idea of tech had become more so consumed by its fiendish and outlandish cyber-terroristic ideals.

Damien's mind bent and twisted where he sat brooding, contemplating a grim hypothesis of a notion that human evil had been outweighing the noble and righteous side of things for many years up until the endless night he was being forced to entertain. As uncontrollable nausea set into his stomach with painful authority, he ricocheted his thought processes back to his darling Leigh. The overrun man couldn't help himself.

He had just shot her dead.

No, he had saved what was left of her forever condemned soul.

The fact was, both answers made him feel equally horrible. Leigh had been stolen away either way he sliced it within his pulverized and sinking confines, and he understood the way she had been taken, from him and their earthly world, was of the most horrific exhibits of despicable insanity. Winters snapped away from the mental dark and finished his glass of drink while contemplating his next moves.

HE BIT AWAY at more of his booze in the soft luminescence of his living room quarter. The pummeled Damien had withstood incessantly up until his exacting breaking point, to where the all of a sudden pleading hurry to accomplish anything new and spontaneous had run its course.

Leigh was lost to the nothing, and Kip remained nowhere to be found.

He listened within his four walls of shallow comforts for any signs of human life or sphinx death that could be out there to surround his cabin. He'd personally destroyed the front door while breaking in to try and save Leigh, with the remnants of the blockade spilled out on his floor in the front entryway where it lay dead. Again, Winters reminded himself that he'd have to gander off to his art room safe for more weapons, but he also questioned what even the fucking point was to do so any longer.

He fought torturously from the inside and knew that he had to keep moving and continue making big decisions, but he just couldn't find the audacity to rise up from the couch that had managed to grasp full control over him. The whiskey felt good going down, as he struggled valiantly to tackle his mind in finding a substantial reason to continue tolerating his leaden avalanche of a quest.

What was the noble argument to any of it, anymore?

He didn't stand a chance against the Sphynx, who had landed like ungodly cockroaches in his sleepy mountain town. For all Winters knew, he was only but a select few sorry sons of bitches who were left still resisting the inevitable, while the abominations were loading up their gluttonous pustules and securing their revenge, taking back what in their ancient intellects had always and justifiably been theirs from the beginning of all things.

He couldn't help but recall what Doctor Boudreaux had said way back during his shackled waking beginning inside the abhorrently unfeeling Mason General Hospital. The surgeon had claimed that his kind, the Sphinx, had been around and thriving well before God had ever existed.

Could that even be possible?

The spine-chilling physician had also declared that the sphinxes did, in fact, create humanity's idea of a Christian God. That particular slice of information proved the most unnerving to the panicked and overburdened thinker of a man.

If a God or a Jesus had created all of humanity, where is He now?

Damien and the remainder of his inferior kind needed Him more than ever during such a callous attempt at their brutal extermination.

Did God even give a damn?

Was He secretly rooting for the beasts to decimate and obliterate at will?

Did He even have a second thought regarding humanity's initial goodness of intentions or their intellectual processes for the fate of their earthly world?

Instead, the ancient demagogues were in full command and winning the war with ease. They were picking off humankind in infinite waves. For the love of everything holy and left standing, the fragmented Winters could not comprehend how his God could refuse to interject at such a time and desperate need of His own fragile creation.

How could it be that he was left alone in his crumbling cabin to fend for himself against such a darkness?

The fuming human poured another drink from his shimmering decanter, making a clinking sound of two greeting sections of glass butting heads with one another. The log chalet had fallen into an exceptional quiet, a grim degree of isolation, which swirled around his unpredictable forethought.

He could have cared less if he continued to sit there on that comfortable sofa, until the wooden walls caved in all around him, like a suffocating and crushing vice of absolute destitution.

XL

FROM OUTSIDE SOMEWHERE and unsettlingly close in proximity, there spawned an odd rustling. It sounded off right and out near the front door vicinity of the once flourishing log house. Damien set down his whiskey glass on the glossy wooden table at his right, forgetting how long he'd just slumped in the same spot like a stone rock.

Have I been here thirty minutes?

An hour?

Three hours?

He couldn't recall, in fact, but the minuscule time frame had become the least of his gushing forward set of worries. He listened intensely, zapping all of his wits back to the doomsday reality. The off-putting clamor persisted, approaching the destroyed barrier of his home's front door. While remaining seated, Winters pulled the heavy silver revolver from its holster at his left hip. The cold steel felt mythically close to him then, like an old friend shielding his vessel with a reliable comfort inside a whirlwind of grueling chaos.

The scurrying quit for a second or several, then churned back up again. It sounded like footsteps approaching, although, he couldn't tell what was out there. He cocked the hammer of the Smith & Wesson with a pointing and outstretched left hand.

From the dark and iridescent doorway lighting appeared none

other than Kip Wells in all of his malfunctioning glory. Kip stumbled and staggered straight through the entranceway, practically falling headfirst to the rustic living room floor. He settled on his knees and stared up at Winters, but his frantic gaze caught the front-end barrel of the overawing revolver.

"Well, look who decided to join the party," voiced Damien in the last remaining stitch of sarcasm that his torched through mind's goopy vault could feasibly entertain.

He studied Kip for a sequence, piercing his unsmiling glare right into his good old friend. Wells looked exhausted and more or less batshit terrified. Most importantly, Kip remained very much human in overall functionality. His grayish hazels darted around in flutters, resting on the domineering barrel of the unnerving hand cannon. The leathered man lowered his weapon, while gently releasing the gun's hammer from firing with a swift click of a slender thumb. He holstered it away and pawed for his tabled glass of bourbon. He then took a slurping swig of the elixir and set it back down on the lacquer with a clink.

"I didn't know where else to go," huffed Kip.

He continued hysterically, "It's crazy out there! The whole town's gone mad! I'm so sorry for leaving you back at the diner."

Damien scowled down at his friend, forcing Kip to avert his eyes out of a self-conscious and childish showing of discomfort. Winters spoke, "Yeah, well... I killed Thelma. I had no choice. She was one of those things out there. I really could've used your help back there. Why the fuck do you keep bailing on me?"

Kip got back up to his feet and started to peer back into Damien's face. His black scrub suit occupied even more holes in them, and his curly coal-colored hair was drenched with sweat.

Wells replied, "I heard something outside over at Thelma's. It sounded like a plane or a chopper or something. I ran out to see what was going on, then some of those monsters came after me. I've been through hell's half acre trying to get here!"

Damien crossed his arms, and his leather coat made a crunching sound with the closing off maneuver. He hesitated a moment, then spoke, "Ya' know something, I also saw that same chopper. The pilot's dead. I narrowly escaped with my own fucked up life."

Kip followed back, "Shit, D. I'm sorry."

"Leigh's gone, too. She's in the other room," Winters snapped while reaching for the liquor glass on the maple slab after swallowing down a choking sensation that slithered forward inside his suffocating throat.

Kip remained standing in the middle section of the softly lit living quarter. He peered his eyes over toward the master bedroom. He then took a squishy sneakered step in the direction of the single main hallway.

"Please, don't," voiced Damien, almost lovingly.

He was only trying to protect his friend from a scene he would never forget if he laid his fragile eyes to its loathly carnage.

Winters proceeded, "Sit down and relax, man. You look like you're gonna fall flat on your face from exhaustion."

Wells complied reluctantly, plopping down next to him on the plushy wood house's sofa.

"How in the hell did you even make it here?" asked Damien while turning his head toward his hospital colleague.

"I mostly ran," answered Kip out of breath. "I couldn't find the helicopter; then those creatures were all up on me. Once I lost them, I found this lame BMX bicycle I boosted before hitting the main drag to ride up here. I knew you'd be here, D."

Kip studied Damien, sitting next to him on the sofa, taken aback with Winters sanctioning his loaded gun belt around his waist inside the lusterless cabin.

"You want a drink?" asked the leathered man out of left field.

Kip nodded while Damien grabbed the other upmarket bourbon glass on the woodland table and poured another spirit. He handed it over to Wells.

"To surviving the chaotic shit show of life," said Damien with a wink and the wryest of little smiles.

Kip also managed a grin as they clinked glasses and drank together in the illustrious half-dark.

Another hour ticked by with both men lounging on the cabin couch, while the entire world continued its abysmal descent around the outskirts of their barely holding it together Colorado mountain town. There wasn't much conversation between them, mostly just sips of the robust Redemption, along with half-cocked intentions on listening to what new terror would manifest outside. Damien broke the ice from a long and soothing block of comfortable silence. "We need to raid my gun safe. The shotgun's in there along with a decent amount of ammunition."

Kip looked over at his friend after a large sip of the browned bourbon. "You still got that big ol' Weatherby in there? I thought you were gonna size down to a smaller Benelli?"

Damien rejoined, "Still have the Weatherby. I like that big old mother."

"You think all of this madness will ever end, Damien?" Kip chimed back almost embarrassingly.

"Hope so, buddy," Winters replied while he turned toward him, providing an ordained smile with chilling undertones.

"The safe's still in my studio. Remember I was thinking about moving it to the bedroom a few months back? But hell, it's one heavy son of a bitch," Damien said to Kip as he rose from the couch, throating back the last sip of whiskey from his crystal glass.

Kip remained weaponless, armed only with his forever tattered hospital scrub suit and grunged over copper hands. Kip got up from the couch when Damien did, setting down his quarter full glass of drink next to his friend's empty one.

The men were buzzing from their dry bourbon binge, but nowhere near drunk and disorderly. The lighting retained its warmth and relative nature of invite from inside the wooden sanction, with the one noteworthy table lamp next to the men doing all of the moody evanescence.

"Let's at least get you a decent weapon," Damien tapped his friend on the shoulder while they both headed back toward the art studio.

Winters incessantly strived to block out what had become of the blood-splattered remains of his dismal master bedroom. He didn't even want to offer a look in the general direction of the space, and he again ordered Kip to stay away and not go near the haunting scene of atrocious horror. They hung a left in the hallway and moseyed down into the last room on the right.

The door was ajar, with them both entering the creation.

A small window rested in the far-left corner of the room, that gave off a bright green fluorescence in the darkness of the artist's den. Random paintings and drawings that Damien had been tinkering with in his valuable spare hours sat scattered around higgledy-piggledy. Tubes of acrylics and oils were piled high on a paint-covered and meaty chunk of table wood nearby. Two metal landscape prints he'd photographed while backpacking with Leigh in a picturesque Yosemite swallowed up an entire sidewall.

"I could never get over how messy of a starving artist you are, Winters," voiced Wells while shaking his head and scanning the colorful studio. "Talented, no question. But messy as shit," he finished with his own sarcastic compliment.

Damien replied dryly after he switched on the ceiling light. "It's called organized and dysfunctional chaos, Wells."

The leathered man's eyes darted to the closet door in the far-right corner of the room. There was a small bookshelf with true crime novels and other helter-skelter types, along with random artistic textbooks right beside it. He opened the door to reveal his hidden away gun safe. The lockbox took up the entire closet. It weighed hundreds of pounds and was teamed up with a numbered combination lock to reveal its precious and dangerous contents.

"Nobody's ever known the combo to this thing besides Leigh and myself, but I suppose it doesn't really matter now, does it?" said Damien as he turned back toward his smaller colleague.

Kip watched while Winters leaned in and punched home the

six-digit number code. The clunker made two consecutive beeps and released the impenetrable lock from inside. The door swung open a crack, and Winters opened it to reveal everything in the vault. It was almost dark in the closet space, and there also wasn't any substantial lighting to assist with the rummaging of the mammoth locker.

It wasn't a problem for Winters, since he knew his way around more than fine. He grabbed the Weatherby shotgun that stood off on the right, armed with a rope lock attached to the trigger, and handed the lurking firearm over to Kip. He gave up the tiny key to unlock the weapon for proper bang bang.

He then pulled out two boxes of slug rounds for the shotgun and another two boxes of magnum bullets for his holstered revolver. He did have .38 specials and birdshot tucked away near the bottom of the vault's barrel, but on that diseased night, he hunted solely for stopping power of sphinx perversion, leaving the inferior bullets alone to die in the blackness.

The invading sphinxes, whether disguised in human form or owning up to their rawest forms of beastly decay, were a real bitch to take down. Even with Winters' classical firepower, the task would deem difficult. Deep down, both men knew the overwhelmingly callous scenario. However, they continued on with fleeting droplets of hallowed human courage.

A leathered arm dove in again and pulled out the small hand ax that Grandpa Joe had given him on a snowy Christmas eve back in one yesteryear or another. He removed the protective covering from the sharp battle ax and tossed it aside. He then placed the chopping weapon's handle downward and stuffed it into his right jeans pocket.

Next, Damien reached into the safe one final time, resting his hand on another blade he'd almost forgotten had ever existed altogether. He pulled it out of the locker with care, as it dawned on him what he then ultimately held.

It was a first-rate machete knife.

The overlong blade was holstered inside its own dark and protective enclosure. That specific mold of steel had a multitude of powerful sentiments to the empathetic blueprint of Damien Winters. It happened to be the only material piece of anything that he'd ever been given from his actual blood parents.

Ernst had received the knife from Damien's biological father right before he kicked off from too much drink back when Damien was only a boy. He'd managed to mail the knife to Ernst and requested he give it to his son later in life when he was grown up and able.

The manly Winters turned back to Kip and stared into him, while the smaller scrubbed man held the intrusive shotgun. The Weatherby was a pump-action blaster with a gunmetal matte finish through and through. The intimidator's barrel was astoundingly long, more of a hunter's shotgun than a close-quarters, home defense pedigree of shooter.

"I've always hated this whopper of a thing, Damien. It's way too bulky for me," said Kip as he stood there open-legged in his barely holding it together hospital outfit.

The shotgun did appear funkily large attached to his friend, but Damien knew in his heart that Kip could handle the firearm with a steady sense of righteous poise. They'd been out shooting infinite times and many moons ago, and although Kip had always complained of the colossal Weatherby, he had become a pretty darn good shot with the girthy thing. The shaggy-haired man became deathly serious while he replied to his closest friend.

"You're gonna have to make it work. I've seen you with it. Piece of cake, right? Listen, there is one new thing about it, though..." The jacketed man turned and chucked a heavy box of armor-piercing shells into Kip's exposed stomach region. He caught them fancily with the shotgun held in his other hand. "Those are slug rounds. You've only fired bird and buckshot through that sucker in the past, but right now, we need the slugs. They're gonna beat up your shoulder like a mother when you shoot, but it's got killer stopping power, and it's better off than being melted down sphinx meat."

Kip gazed down at his handful of goodies while he managed only a, "Right..."

"One final thing," Damien said as Kip began to turn around away from him and begin loading his shotgun. "I want you to have this. You may need it out there if the Weatherby fails you."

Winters handed the machete in its protective casing over to Kip.

Wells placed the shotgun and bullets down by a tub of paint thinner on the studio's carpeted floor. He took the knife with wonderment from his colleague and removed its slick vinyl enclosure. The long blade was two-toned, a stunning construction of silver with a matte black lining. Six grooves ran down the edge of the gaudy and impressive cutting edge. It was intrusive to the naked eye and devastatingly sharp. The cold steel had a sheen to it inside the ceiling bulbs of the innovative art room. Kip studied the base of the knife for a second or two before saying anything.

"Hey! There's a D inscribed on the end of the handle, looks like someone carved it in there. That stands for Damien?" Wells said, as he looked up at his mahogany eyed confidante with a boyish form of innocent intrigue.

Damien had never mentioned to Kip that he was an orphan, and he'd also never shown him that particular knife that his abandoning bastard father had given him on his deathbed through the gracious efforts of Ernst Winters.

"Don't know. Never noticed it before." Kip seemed perplexed with such a response, as Damien shot in again with a purposeful face aimed squarely at his finest main man. "Take good care of it, Kip. It's yours now, old friend."

"Thanks, Damien. It's a real beauty," Kip gleamed a smile in the direction up at him.

Winters gave his friend an easy wink in response, never uttering another word to anyone about the powerful family heirloom.

More time went by in the studio while the men loaded up their guns. Kip maxed out the slugs into the shotgun, emptying most of the remaining shells into his hospital garb pockets. As for Damien's passed down machete, Wells placed it back into its sleeve and tucked the six-inch blade into his tattered work pants at the waistline by his left hip.

Damien unlatched the wheel of his revolver, picking out the spent casings he'd already used to murder Leigh. He then replaced them with live rounds and took a second to restock one of his empty speed loaders. His gun belt had individual ammunition holders already built into it, so he filled the few vacant slots one by one with chilled and active lead.

Next, he took the remainder of just under a quarter box of .357 magnum hollow points and jammed them into his coat and pants pockets.

While Wells and Winters continued their frantic and haphazard stand of defense, faint explosions and scattered gunfire rang off from somewhere near their gloomy wooden abode. Then something of an airstrike or raid ignited, followed by a distant crash bang that cut through the outside air in the closer existence.

Those were all blind assumptions from the two preparing men, being that they couldn't be confident as to what was authentically unfolding out there in the decrepit Colorado darkness. Then all of a sudden, everything went suffocatingly quiet again.

The friends stood together like stiff scarecrows in the painter's den, staring back at each other with wild, but most importantly, striking human eyes. With Kip being armed with the long pump-action shotgun and sharp as hell machete knife, Winters holstered his maxed-out revolver and resituated his hand ax.

They gave each other a final silent nod, one which only close companions could accurately interpret, and stormed out of the backroom toward the main living quarter.

Damien was again left with no choice but to pass by the bedroom where he'd executed his voluptuous girlfriend.

No, it was the bygone sphinx that consumed her and then replicated her perfect human body that I killed.

Right?!

The man's brain waves were in such turmoil, to the point of barely knowing any longer what was reality or the land of insidious make-believe. He longed to step inside his master bedroom and see her there curled up inside the cool sheets, sleeping like a sublime little thing, waiting for him to arrive back from a tough night at the buried, but somehow still alive and breathing Mason General Hospital.

He wanted, agonizingly, to feel her again, to caress her olive silk and pull her head close to his when she needed his touch, while he thirsted even more for hers. Instead, Kip and he passed right by the infamous room of despair and never looked in again.

They beelined it straight into the large clearing of the main cabin's living room. The house's subtle lighting held its gleam, giving off the faintest glow of warmth in an otherwise morbidly dark area. The broken-down front door was straight ahead of them, as the men found themselves standing side by side. The kicked in framework, courtesy of Winters, was positioned away from the entrance, half on the floor and still on a hinge in a severely cocked position.

The rectangle opening that showed the outside world changed over in a vibrant unexpectancy. A multiverse of blue, then green, and finally, an orange vividity manifested into a morphing pattern in succession unto the forest madness. The three luminescent variations highlighted the morose living room when they all cycled at random, adding more drama to Damien's claustrophobic cabin fortress.

The jacketed man glanced over at his friend, who remained shaking by his side. With being a few inches shorter than him, Kip's hair found itself eye level with Damien's umbered jewels of shameful dread. His short curls were wet and matted down, more or less glued to his overwrought face of medium brown. The shotgun in his grasp trembled, and his legs looked extra wobbly underneath what was left of his nerve-wracked balance. Kip stared back at Damien with a carnal fear that began to creep in and bubble over to overwhelm and consume his right-hand man.

"Stand your ground, Kipper. Believe in yourself. I always have."

A sincere notion escaped out from Winters, while the wacky color scheme continued its satanic dance around the vacant doorway entrance.

XLI

AN ENORMOUS CLATTER began to kick off from outside the cabin walls. It sounded like an all directional onslaught of strange and unusual variations of incredulous white noise. The rustling of leaves and the tumultuous roaring of aircraft could be sensed right on top of their isolated vicinity. From around the very back of the house, or perhaps veered off toward the side someplace, forged a spine-chilling roar.

It was not a single ungodly pitch, but more so a classification of a screeching symphony. The resonance could be heard as neither person nor animal that could have belonged to anything remotely civil inside a crumbling human world.

It had to be the Sphynx.

The out of tune shrieks seeped through the wooden perimeter, trying as it might to bleed through the thickly coated stucco. The archaic motif infiltrated through and encompassed all sides of the usually serene Colorado refuge. Through the insane outside winds and the howls of impurity, clomping footsteps became raucous and intense within the gusts. They were boisterous and frantic in their famished and possessed giddy-ups.

By chance, the steps could have been manifested by an ordinary earthly animal, or even a human being. There was just no surefire way of telling.

Each uncertain uproar grew closer and closer!

Louder and louder!!

The unnerved log cabin felt as suffocating as ever, as a graphic red hue decided to enter the othered mixture of outside forest saturations. The change of richness lit up the sitting duck cabin dwellers like two trembling flesh lanterns.

At that very instant, Damien's home might as well have been stuck in its own throaty trash compactor, ready to be squeezed and crushed to a certain death into the wood chipper of a slivered oblivion.

Kip was growing antsy within himself, shuffling his feet from side to side, becoming victimized inside the awful grips of primal angst. He wanted to take off and run, run like the wind for the Colorado mountains for all he cared. He just wanted out of his currently perceived jaws of inevitable doom.

Winters peered over again, pulling his revolver from its forgiving holster of leather with a left hand. He cocked the weapon's hammer and reached over to grab Kip by the shoulder in the very center of his living space.

"NO," is all he uttered while shaking his head and booming fierce eyes straight through his counterpart's unsteady humanity.

Wells nodded with unease and ceased his jittery shuffle, as the back-kitchen window came imploding within itself in the crashing blink of an eye. The invasion was deafening, and in like a flying malady, came a rancid and spine-chilling experiment of sphinx.

It slammed into the refrigerator on entrance to the modern cookery, knocking over some vitamins and a cold cereal box that were atop of it. The loathsome creation rose to two muscular frog-like legs, while it stood hulking with dreadful confidence a solid foot taller than either Damien or Kip.

Winters flung around with his revolver to face the evil, right as a jet-black uniformed soldier came hustling through the vacant front door. He was weaponless and armored from head to foot. His helmet remained on, but the dark shield visor was hoisted up, revealing what remained of his sorry face. Cozied up in the protective hard hat were the eyeless orbs of albino dominion. The sickening globes scanned the cabin from deep inside the trooper's skull, priming to rest its gooped up jawbreakers on the cowering men, while the thing came barreling soullessly toward them.

"NOW!!" Damien screeched.

The defending men fired in unison, as a slug round from the Weatherby shotgun blew the former militant's right leg clean off its housing. Damien shot twice in the opposite direction, striking the full-on beast that entered his cooking area once in the chest and another in the head.

The creature laid disabled in a mangled vision of fright on the floor, but remained very much alive and unsavory. Winters holstered the long silver cannon and pulled the hand ax from his jeans pocket. He approached the demon as it snarled and spat an unadmirable gunk, trying to inflict a showing of ancestral mind control while it grasped its gaping wounds.

Damien powered through the primordial perversion of wits, instead bringing his sheening battle ax down in breath-stealing succession several times over. The oversized head gave way and separated from the crude animal body, sending a flood of contrasting dark matter spilling in jetted streams to the cabin's usually clean lower surface.

Once the muscular legs of the deformed lion stopped thrashing, Winters lurched his head toward Kip in perfect timing to see his comrade bring the butt of the clunky shotgun down on the soldier boy's overtaken face. The yolky discs exploded on impact, forcing the commando to fall lifelessly limp.

The hospital colleagues scrambled to a regroup in the center of the quarter. They both breathed heavily with Damien's stoic lionheart almost bursting through his rugged leather jacket. More pitter-patter of footsteps commenced from the outside perimeter.

Pitter-patter, pitter-patter.

Converging upon the quaking human beings like the final plague left on a tired and almost giving up planet Earth.

Just like that and in through the front doorway, rushed three creatures all at once. Two led the way with the third clustered closely behind. Full sphinx or human sphinx or half-human hybrid sphinx mattered no longer. Kip cocked the heavy shotgun, flinging a red round to the area rug while loading the chamber with another.

Head-splitting gunshots erupted in the tight cabin air, a brain-melting explosion of primal and manmade chaos. The men unloaded on the alien trio with rapid-fire, cutting the monsters down to pieces and into the log structure's inviting undertow. Once the shotgun and revolver ceased in unleashing their unbelievable fury, the weapons were left hot and smoking in the palms of the two Heatherton heroes.

The posse that had barged through as a rank unit were scattered in a broken heap of chewed up meat and ancient death, never able to consume another soul for the remaining ticks of a cursed eternity.

The cabin sat stifled in gun smoke, with the rotting corpses of the dead strewn about the jumpy partners like a medieval gothic forest parade. Damien's revolver hung empty in his grip, while the six-inch barrel plumed steam from its wild and vengeful exertion.

He popped open the wheelgun, sending spent cartridges cascading to his hazy cabin grounds. He gritted his teeth and reached for a speed loader in his belt, finding a full cylinder of a ready to go lucky seven. He pawed for it and plunged the live rounds into the magnum's thirsty chamber with the weapon's barrel facing straight down. He replaced the empty loader to his belt and smacked the wheel back in place with a swift flick of his right wrist.

Kip rummaged through his pockets for more slugs, racking a few into the Weatherby's smoking guts. It could be perceived as if a full army of decay were chomping at the bit outside, bobbing and weaving in the unpredictability and strangely colored pines and firs. It reeked to high heaven of gunpowder and alien blood, as the piping firearms were loaded again in the arms of the mountain town cronies. Damien spoke for the first time since the initial cabin bloodletting. "We're gonna have to move outta here real soon."

Before Kip could breathe an answer, a crazed child in a Mason hospital nightie charged from the hallway, slithering in from the bedroom where Leigh lay slain and gone forever. The pint-sized thing was bald and came across as looking emaciated and genuinely unwell.

The poor little dude was an escaped chemo patient. What were left of his windowed circles of withered away humanity were utterly transformed into a bulging soup of a mess, which allowed his mint green hospital garb to droop awkwardly and appear twelve sizes too large for his papery little frame.

The moving bag of hairless bones took off in a bound toward Kip, springing with a sinister purpose from the hearty log foundation. The hardwood bottom made a creaking snap with his reprehensible dismount. Damien zeroed the flying Q-ball at the last possible moment, as he leaned into the scene and shoved Kip aside with force, nearly spilling his friend to the messy and blood-soaked shallows.

The gangly hellion flew right past them both, landing on its scrawny feet up near the kitchen entrance. Winters unloaded on the milky creature with one outstretched left arm, his revolver sending a glorious roar throughout the isolated abode. The single powerful bullet struck the gowned sphynx's right goopy disc, stopping the former child patient dead to undeniable rights.

The thin sick baldy folded to the floor without a peep and began to rot. His flesh melted away in a twinkling revolt and opened up to reveal wiry tendons and fragile muscles. The inflicting man stood and watched the horror unfold, grossly entranced at the absurdity with his hulking revolver pointed down at the disintegrating sphinx corpse. When only a miserable pile of calcium remained on the leathered man's corroded deck, the frail nanoscopic skeleton exploded into a cloud of powdery dust.

It could be seen as if someone had clapped their hands together while they were covered in a heavy dose of baking flour.

Poof, just like that.

A vicious boom of the Weatherby bellowed out right next to Damien's left ear. The sound ripped through the tortured soul's mind and made him curl up in a cringe where he stood racking, snapping him out of his temporary daze of decaying obscenity.

Kip regained his footing and had taken aim at an auto mechanic in a greasy white jumpsuit who'd managed to gain entrance from the back-sliding door. The slug round missed the intended receiver, as the car tinkerer's brick shithouse of a frame came barreling straight for him. Wells tried to ready the oversized pumper again for firing, but his rushed effort was uncoordinated. He leaned down in a defensive position to brace for impact with the charging human imposter.

He looked up in time to catch Damien enter the frame from nowhere, only to blow the left side of the mechanic's face clean off with his revolver, causing the auto man to spill over and smack the good side of what remained of his skull on the corner of another wooden end table.

The grease ball had almost gotten to his friend, so close, in fact, that flying brains and skull bones from the magnum blast peppered Kip's face and shirt. Another fierce demonstration of ultra-violent magnitude erupted without warning from somewhere outside in the unknown shadow world, rattling the entire foundation of Winters' once prized Colorado cabin.

More ear-splitting sphinx vocabulary rang out from the forest from either the north or northwest side of all things fucked.

Or maybe it was coming from the due east and due west directions.

"We need to get the hell outta here!" hollered Damien.

The men both bolted for the front door, tearing through recklessly and wide-eyed back into the hazily infested apocalyptic warzone.

They jumped the cabin porch with their weapons in hand, right on queue to look up at the partly cloudy skyward way, and to take hold of a flock of fighter jets whizzing through the gravity above them. The planes zoomed right over the house like heat-seeking missiles and were gone in an insane flash of an instant.

"Jesus!" shouted a huff from Winters out of a simple character display of holy shit.

The sky bent and turned sinisterly red yet again, a deep crimson color that bled and descended upon the immediate vicinity from the churning night creep. The atmosphere's change provided a makeshift light source, making it visible to trek through the woodlands without the desperation of a flashlight.

"I ditched a copper's bike up the driveway over there a bit," Damien exuded to his colleague with a head nod. "This way!" as they broke for the hidden police cruiser that he'd used to harrowingly escape from town.

The jaunt wasn't far, and they converged on the hidden machine unscathed. Winters holstered his revolver and got on the bike. He turned the key that he'd left in the ignition and fired her right up.

"Hop on, buddy!" Winters hollered to Wells after a group of sphinxes in mostly human arrangements materialized from a bunch of nearby Ponderosa pines.

Kip got on the back of the chopper and stuck the giant shotgun in a slot within the motorcycle's machinery, offering a sort of makeshift holster for the bulky firepower.

Damien switched on the red and blues and tore off down the remainder of his driveway, just as the pack of hellspawn just about collided with them, almost stifling their amazingly great escape.

XLII

THEY'D DITCHED THE hungry herd and made it back out to the infamous two-lane forest drag on the outskirts of their town. The bulky police cycle charged dead ahead with its two gritty survivors. The heavens oozed down, causing the luscious full moon entangled with the awe to turn full-on black.

Winters headed north, in an attempt to completely escape town. Once they crossed over the geriatric Bixby Bridge, they'd enter Anderson County. The two riders decided to take their chances in exploring the neighboring avant-garde territory. Anderson was four times the size of Heatherton, however, that sole fact deemed refreshing.

Maybe things looked better for the human condition over there.

It couldn't possibly be any worse off than their destroyed dink of a settlement.

Could it?

Was there an outside chance that the remaining human masses were rising up and fighting with all they could muster, while hopefully evening the score against the foregone exterminators?

What if the military had a base or had set up camp somewhere over there?

What if the people had found a better way to fight the sphinxes?

What if the sphinxes were the only things left standing all across the globe, an entire fortress of bastard varmints on the brink of wiping humanity off the face of their bountiful and ever forgiving planet?

What if Kip and Damien were the last two survivors in the whole state of Colorado?

What if a giant anvil fell on their heads mid-ride, causing their endless nightmarish miseries to swiftly come to a satisfying conclusion?

What if, what if...

For several minutes, there was a crisp break in the incessant damnation. Only the winds and the rumbling motor could be heard in the night. Damien's mind twisted and raced with negativity that bordered on total defeat as he commandeered onward, but he and his counterpart remained very much inside the cosmic fight. A morsel of what could be coined as peace came over both young riders while they charged through the insipid woodland road.

They found themselves at the stage in their journey where they'd take it any way they could get it, because it sure as hell couldn't possibly get any worse.

Towering trees lined both sides of the familiar two-lane blacktop. The deformed galaxy's magenta tones opened wide and reigned super-lative from above and beyond the thicket of sumptuous foliage, gelling with the reds and blues of the State Police motorbike that screamed from the ground. When the blue half of the cycle's flashing bulbs entered to say hello every other second or two, the icy contrast was welcomed frankly, although chillingly out of place.

The famous Bixby Bridge was a quarter-mile of distance straight up ahead of them.

The sky would not stop shifting on the bizarro fly. The full moon cookie had lost its stranger than fiction rings of atmospheric haze. The rose matter hue in the vaults of heaven made the Earth's alien planet remain frighteningly black in contemptuous richness. Stars littered the azure, as the Milky Way swirled together with another unknown galaxy, showing off an unfathomable sight to the two well-built survivors.

Bixby was, in her defense, an ageless thing of a bridge, being that she almost collapsed down to the river for good way back in 1908.

The state of Colorado had saved the bridge that year and attempted to rebuild it. 1908 was also the last time that any degree of substantial maintenance work had been done to her. The classical way over still donned the exact same sea green and weathered color palette, teamed with uncertain hinges and rusted out bolts that peppered around the entirety of the clunky overpass.

The Colorado River gushed one hundred or so feet underneath Old Bixby, providing the one and only way out of their ravaged and bloody borough.

Wells and Winters were nearly there.

They were moments away from all the way escaping, but most importantly, surviving their town's heinous destruction. They were on the brink of getting out when there was nothing left for their beloved Heatherton to give them, besides death and a horrific void of engulfed annihilation.

The elusive earthly sun's lightning in a bottled essence had become a thing of the past, its fiery warmth held down and suffocated by a river of desolate dark.

Damien switched off the police lights and braked hard in a startling maneuver about a shallow field's length away from the tired old bridge. Bixby was ahead of them, along with being fully on fire in the shallow distance, engulfed in a dancing and hysterical inferno of crushing delirium. A rear section of the timeless viaduct disintegrated before their eyes, suddenly careening down in slow motion unto the hypothermic river charge below.

The helmetless heroes dismounted from the motorbike, with Damien turning off the engine and striking down the kickstand with a bloodily tarnished boot. They stared at the burning bridge in the yellow centerline of the mirrored road, with mouths agape and flooded in a state of shocked dismay. Winters managed to remain somewhat rational within the confines of himself at the unpleasant scene, but Kip was seriously starting to lose his shit.

"I'm never getting out of this place. We're dead...we're all DEAD!"

Wells paced back and forth in a kind of hissy-fit, with him circling the narrow blacktop road.

Damien stood affixed to the roadway pitch, studying the flames in silence with his warm eyes while they hopped and skipped in the gloom, adding an orange crush of vibrancy to the already red sea of sky abyss.

A fracas unexpectedly echoed out from behind Winters as he heard his friend call out his name. However long the absorbed man had been hypnotized by the cremation of dear old Bixby, he couldn't have known.

The commotion broke his distraction, so he turned around very slowly. His exhausted eyes forced a squint to adjust themselves, while he saw his esteemed friend being held at gunpoint by another trooper in black, who had popped from the shadowed tree line from behind them. The stealthy attacker wore arrant riot garb, along with a brawny helmet and midnight black visor, that shielded a vital section of humanity that Winters absolutely needed to see.

The soldier had on a fancified flamethrower pack, identical to the psycho woman soldier's assembly back near the burning bus carnage down on Main Street.

But she was stone cold dead.

No use crying over spilled milk, right?

The actual thrower was extinguished, dangling by the side of the eerie foot soldier. A decent-sized Beretta handgun was, instead, palmed inside a black-gloved hand. In their other arm was Kip in his withering away hospital scrub outfit. More importantly than the condition of his obliterated work clothes, Wells was without the Weatherby.

He'd left it inserted in the police bike's chasm before commencing his tantrum over the barbecue at Bixby. The masked gunman had the military issued pistol pressed to Kip's temple. Wells squirmed for a moment, but fell limp as the piece was jammed deeper into his face. Damien raised both of his blood entangled hands to the air and spoke with a steady demeanor of envious calm.

"Don't shoot him, please. Show yourself. Let's just talk about this a minute."

The leathered man used a lukewarm style of talk, primarily because he had a deep intuition that the individual who had his friend was nothing more than a scared and desperate human being, just like them. Winters took a smart and easy step forward into the sudden hostage situation.

Then another one, with his worn boots setting off a grinding crinkle on a cluster of loose gravel underneath the shiny noir asphalt out in the middle of nowhere.

The blacked-out soldier took a full step back in response, still wrenching a sturdy wrangle upon Kip Wells. He removed the pistol from his head and instead turned the gun on Damien.

"Not another step," the shadowy figure replied in a muffled audible through the thick visored mask.

Winters had an even stronger conviction that it was an ordinary fella underneath all the fancy armor.

Damien stopped advancing.

"Show yourself. Listen, why did you burn down the bridge? Both my friend and I barely made it out of that town alive. Why did you take away our only way out?"

The soldier said nothing while holding the Beretta in the direction of the beaten up yet forever standing leather coat. Winters tried again.

"Look, take me as your hostage. Just let him go. This is ridiculous. It's us versus those things now. Don't you see that? You're making a grave mistake."

Damien then raised his hands even higher skyward, attempting to give the commando even more situational confidence.

It worked.

The man in black took the same hand that held the pistol on the pleading mortal and drew it toward his face, swiping up the smoked through helmet visor. Just as Winters had suspected before responding, "You're no different than we are. What the hell are you doing, soldier?"

The hostage-taker replied, "Orders. For containment."

Winters shook his head in dismay, but managed an almost

sympathetic laugh before retorting. "There is no containment for what this is. You think what you've done here will change anything out there? Your orders are dead wrong."

The commando released his aim at Damien and returned the handgun back to Kip's throbbing temple. Wells gave a grimace when the cold weapon met his head once again, as he glared out after his friend with the sincerest desperations of a, please help me.

"Nothing can leave here," the soldier went on.

He looked frightened inside his elaborate suit of armor, taking each passing second as a moment to moment sequence of heightened unpredictability.

Winters proceeded.

"This isn't an isolated incident, is it? It's happening all over, and you know it. You're just scared. We're scared, too. Let my friend go, and we can forget all about this. We can even work togeth--"

"Nothing can leave here!" The commando snapped in an instant.

The man in his fancy military duds was shaking, while again, he decided to turn the gun back on Damien. Kip sensed the gripping fear that overwhelmed his captor, and without a single warning's notice, even to his good friend and colleague, Wells lurched an elbow smack dab into the stomach region of the lone wolf trooper.

A shot from the Beretta called out for Damien, but instead, it skipped on the asphalt a few feet away from striking him. Out of a purist poise of enhanced instinct, Winters pulled the revolver from his hip and exploded a round from the extended barrel without even nicking back the hammer. It met the upper arm of the helmeted vigilante, forcing him to shout out in a grueling surprise and crash backward to the ground in one failed swoop.

The magnum bullet narrowly missed the flame pack he was wearing, grinding the magnum's lead through and through the fleshiest meat parts of the very edge of his shoulder blade.

Kip was left dazed and standing straight up in the roadway, with the dropped Beretta resting by his feet. He picked up the pistol and ran forward to situate himself behind his charismatic friend.

Winters, alone, approached the wounded commando, laid out on a dirt portion of roadside, slinking his hull backward and forward while grasping his destroyed shoulder. The gnarled leather coat on two rugged boots approached the wounded man and stood over him with his giant hand cannon barreling down on the writhing party, like a brooding force of steady menace.

"Are you really this dense, soldier? This is an extermination. Of all humanity. The only thing you've accomplished here so far is assisting the other team with their blatant fuckery."

The twenty-something man in his riot helmet remained down, as he swayed quite uncomfortably. "Piss off! I have orders! Nothing…"

As the soldier breathed and paused his rant, he reached into a side pocket with his one good arm, and drew another small grayed-out brand of handgun. Before the screwball commando boy could even raise his other surprise, he was fired upon. The bullet from Winters Smith & Wesson smashed the toy soldier right between the eyes, muting his pathetic delirium for good. The sneaky gun that the trooper had yanked fell with his hand to a mirrored spot of black tar, after he was shot gruesomely at close range. He maintained a grip on the weapon after his brain exploded out the back of his forefront.

"Yeah…" Winters responded before turning around and trudging his way back toward Kip and the motorcycle.

Bixby continued on with her sizzle, transforming into a complete blanket of fire with no way across. A helicopter could be heard off in the distance inside the larger area of town that would never be reached.

"You killed him?" Kip turned to look at Damien, as his leathered companion holstered his bushwhacked Smith & Wesson.

"Had no choice. He pulled another gun. The boy was crazed," he spoke back without looking at Wells, instead choosing to glaze his eyes over to remain fixated on the smoldering vintage obstacle.

Kip then tried, "Yeah, but…"

Winters broke away and looked his way with a burning stare that was interwoven with sympathy and sad eyes. His medium brown optics appeared to almost sparkle within the jumping reflections of raging bridge flame.

"Forget it. Thanks for always being there for me," Kip concluded with his head craned down toward the pavement.

Damien smacked his friend lightly on the shoulder, offering him a 'you're welcome' of a muted sort. Winters then began to peer around, where the two men stood. Daring to attempt a swim across the glacial Colorado waters may as well have been inevitable suicide. It was too daunting and frigid of a journey for the barely surviving paragons. A whimsical and match-stick idea entered Damien's brain just as he revved up to speak. "Perhaps we should..."

His comment fell off into nothing when he scoured further down toward the riverbank nearest the very beginning section of the disintegrating crossover. He nodded at Kip to take up his own gander at what he was studying. On the soft soil bank, down a stubby little hill, just off a bit from the initial bridge entrance, were more flames.

Bonfires, in fact.

Makeshift structures were clustered all around the separate and haphazard fire pits. The area had an overall layout of a relaxed beachfront from the colleagues' distance, where surfers and campers would lounge around all night drinking rum and beer while exchanging ghost stories on a fog riddled ocean night.

Wells spoke first, "Hey, that lame homeless encampment is still down there?"

Kip was zeroed in hard on the barrels of blaze while standing next to his taller friend. The neighboring county had made loose and recent plans to come out and shut down the rickety city around six months ago. However, the effort had fizzled, much like the unfortunate crumbling timepiece that wept hot tears in front of them. Neither Kip nor Damien had been as far as Bixby those months, but they'd known the intricate details of that particular encampment.

Every citizen of Heatherton did, for the most part.

The Bixby brigade was made up of down and out drifters, hipster agitator types, along with unfortunate and erratic schizophrenics. The vagabonds who cozied up next to the bridge had a knack for smuggling drugs and other illegal paraphernalia into the small timey Heatherton micro-city. A number of hospital crew over at Mason, which consisted of anyone from janitors to security personnel, and even a handful of medical assistants, had all been well aware of the lucrative dump and the totality of its worthy backwater appeal.

Both men had seen the camp roughly eight months ago, but it seemed to have evolved over those dragging months from their then on looking perspectives. Somehow, the camp had tripled in size, swallowing up most of the left side of the embankment right off and away from the churning Colorado River.

Damien squinted to see further down, as the ever-ludicrous sky night switched to a bright green essence, changing his perception of the things manifesting inside the distant black. The transition from red to green was fluent, sweeping the evocative landscape like a wave of creepy sludge. The bridge continued to burn mercilessly, throwing its own spicy oranges and blues into the color wheel of primarily sable.

Winters stretched his neck forward a bit for a more provocative view, then placed his left hand on top of his holstered revolver, while executing a body lean. The posture made him come off as looking like some genre of rebel anarchist, or a shaggy-haired biker cop staring down the last jelly donut in a ransacked apocalyptic box of a baker's dozen.

The jacketed man could faintly make out various movements and random shadowy activities carrying on down there, while things dipped earthward in the heart of the Bixby down and outers. What appeared to be human beings were scurrying around the general vicinity, shuffling in an abnormal and off-putting wave of frenetic conduct.

THE ALL-INCLUSIVE HOMELESS crisis during the ripe old year of 2020 had become worse than ever, a metaphorical festering of sorts that spewed throughout the United States of salute-worthy America. Arizona and

New Mexico were the top two culprits of the toxically jinxed spillage into Colorado's eventual streets and cities. Larger conglomerates, such as Denver and Aurora, housed massive amounts of those less fortunate, but smaller sectors were getting blindsided at will by the hapless human plague in more recent years.

Ten or so years ago, around 2010, things shifted for America and their boiling gutter war on poverty. California was the flamboyant problem child during that time, sparking the eventual out of control and catastrophic insurgence of unsteady knockabouts. The city of San Francisco had become enraged as a whole back then, because of laughable inflation in the state's housing markets and steadying unpredictability of technological progression.

The Financial District of SF had gotten so raunchy that, eventually, the sweaty suits and ties gave up, and would instead step over their fellow citizens who were laid out shooting up in the alleyways, or watch and stare as the destitute masses relieved themselves on the glossy front doorsteps of a major tech company's main lobby of former prestige.

Businesswomen and men slothed throughout their oh so salient workdays, unconsciously walking right on by zonked out overdose victims, with needles protruding from their rotting and diseased arms and legs. They'd carouse along while humming some overrated Beatles tune, refusing to make eye contact, as a homeless kid no more than fifteen years old sat Indian-style on the piss-filled pavement, scraping away at a gaping leg wound with blackened fingernails, which was the result of horrendous and god-awful needle addiction.

As the streets became dangerously overpopulated and even more radically unjust, along with the country snaking downward into dangerous levels of never before seen divisiveness, the government pricks continued to apply their foolproof and cringeworthy smokescreens of flimsy patchwork.

They would concoct and cluck away with their swankiest jargon and scripted televised concerns, aimed at the sorrier puppets of the immediate public.

But it only continued to feed the decaying open sore that truly plagued the root of the common people.

There needed to come a freezing fork in the road someplace, where the average people could no longer blame the sorrowful individuals who were derelict and addicted, while they rotted away in droves on the city's hot pavements.

They could, however, lay a meaty chunk of that blame on the jackals and bloated puppet masters of an infernal society that continued to enable and enrich such outrageous sinfulness.

The typical working stiff wound up coming home early from the stuffy daily office uptown, bitching and carrying on to high heaven, angered to the gills about how the bums and deadbeats were taking over their precious little street corners in pristine suburban hell. The paper educated city officials would continue to administer those ill-omened souls of degeneracy with desirable needle clinics and warm shelters with steamy showers to settle down their downtrodden and confused compasses of existence.

The icing on the shit cake, in fact, was that everything was executed on the people's dime, the working schmucks that were gouged with festering taxes to continue fueling the glaring misconducts of their supposedly decorated officials.

The California government's beautiful attack plan on the crisis with the vagabonds kept society's underbelly higher than a fucking kite around the clock while also wildly unstable in the overall functioning marbles department.

Enabling authoritative tactics, such as those, would result in the slow and eventual ticket to the destruction of a civilization that had finally been checkmated by their own incredible stupidity.

A plethora of underlying issues into the primal root causes of homelessness, things like erasing moral structures within the acting government, along with an alarming spike in mental health disorders, continued to go unnoticed right up until the bitter end.

Even primitive human values around the last decade, which led to the fateful year of 2020, had already suffered incredulously, as people wound up turning their backs on the most basic codes of genuine ethics and positive outlets of spiritual civilities.

Straightforward fundamentals and noble principalities for a human being to remind themselves that stepping over your neighbor to make an extra penny for the payment on that crappy BMW or to swallow up anything in the shortest time possible was also another form of tyrannical human suicide. This came to the belief that we all only get one shot at life because God is dead and we're all doomed.

People had turned off and mutated into the sturdiest shills of over-indulgent consumerism, while brushing off any negative consequences or administering creative brain prowess to tackle the larger pictures of their peculiar existences.

As for the hobos and the streetwalkers, more than half of those unfortunates were more or less cerebrally unhinged. Schizophrenia and depression had become shoulder shrug-esque epidemics all across the country, even with honest and 'noteworthy' TV outlets having stated that 2020 had, downright, become the age of overall human mental collapse.

All the while, the shit and piss continued to swirl a warpath throughout the country's green clusters of high-rise city districts and illustrious banks, weaving their acrid rancidities to settle down and root in sleepy and untapped mountain towns of simple intrigues, such as dear old Heatherton.

Self-entitlement ran amok like rats in a chemistry maze with the deletion of fundamental moral upbringings within decent homes and solidified school systems. Sure, numerous hobos were beaten down on their luck and out of the game; however, some remained in their dire situations completely of their own free volition.

Menacingly enough, an insufferable number of able-bodied remnants of fractured human beings wound up becoming those grungy slugs on Hyde Street, slithering behind some bus stop, begging for a nickel from the pretty foreign exchange student on the corner, who, for the sloppy duration, wanted nothing more than to blow lunch once the stink got too close to her nose.

Much of the droves of the American homeless population had become their own worst undoing, but more so than anything, the society they'd been entangled with along the way had failed them without mercy long ago.

It didn't happen overnight, and the down and outers had always existed.

But never quite like 2020.

Not to such a skewed and frightening scale. Camps like the one attached to Bixby were swathed like a raging pandemic in every state near and around the attacking year of the Sphynx, puked out and littered with a constant reminder that the supposed 'civilized' world was anything but civil.

A grave cue that humanity, at the snap of a finger, could become violent and corrupt and turn the other cheek, while the entire country beneath them was slowly consumed by the cataclysmic doom.

Winters broke his gaze on the camp of wayfarers and walked back near the toy soldier he'd just shot in the face. He stood over the corpse, briefly hypnotized at what was left of his helmeted head. The man's mouth was stuck wide open, with his tongue resting to one side, like a deer that had yakked its last breath from a hunter's precise kill shot. A puddle of crimson slime pooled near the exit wound behind his exploded fragments of skull.

Damien knelt down and shifted the stealth commando onto one side. He removed the fire pack and thrower gun from the carcass, then rested the dead weight back down where he was shot. Kip had gone over to the leaning motorbike in the middle of the road. He grabbed the Weatherby shotgun from the machine's insides and strolled back into position to have another look at the far-off bum camp.

Damien scrutinized the coal-black apparatus and attached inferno shooter, deciding to sling in his right arm and settle down into the loaded assembly. Strapped and secured to his back, he studied the thrower part of the slick military issued weapon. It was connected by a hose that ran down and back to complete the heater's overall functionality.

The weight was burdensome; however, Winters welcomed the added protection of immaculate firepower. It was a straightforward hand unit, just a meaty metal tube with a trigger attached to the underbelly.

The curious man pulled the flamethrower up into his face, rotating it from one side to the other, with an on the fly intention to inspect the intimidator's every nook and cranny. He brought the flame piece back down to waist level and placed his right index digit on the cold trigger. He squeezed it into himself gently, nearly halfway home.

The gun's tip ignited after a surging sound, along with a controlled orangish blue flame of sear. The man then released the spring device as the fire went out lickety-split. He squeezed a second time halfway, sparking a conflagration that swept an awed look across his chiseled and stubble-filled overlay of pure shadow.

Extinguished again, he mozied his way back over to Kip.

The distraught companion stared over at Damien, armed like a leathered Ghostbuster with the hellacious fire weapon, and managed a smile.

"It matches your coat. She looks good on you, Winters."

Damien smirked back but did not look upon his confidante.

He, instead, peered down in the distant direction of the bustling homeless campground and said, "Follow me."

XLIII

THEY SCALED THE simple hill, which led down into the grungy barracks. The air was molten as the fiery Bixby raged beside them. It burned alarmingly close to the men on their immediate right, with embers spraying with fierce anger all over the misty green night.

Initial entry to the camp proved a breeze, with the colleagues strolling right up to the front of the hopeless city. Wells and Winters looked like two modern cowboys headed straight for a dilapidated ghost town on the very edge at the end of everything.

That particular grunge section, which nestled close by their fated bridge, remained populated, however supernatural and frigidly felt down to the bitter human core. Upon forging ahead to the camp's wide-open clearing, they both halted as if made of stone, while they perched like statues in the shuddering Colorado soil.

From the upscale skyward abyss, and without any noticeable degree of warning, bursts of starlight and intergalactic space dust sparkled and collided with the never-ending nighttime. The spirited humans aimed their faces high, becoming lost within themselves and into the stunning picture show.

From the cluttered grounds ahead of them, ramshackle homes made of cardboard and soggy wood were assembled in arbitrary fashion. Worn out bicycles and tipped over shopping carts were tossed here and there as if a deck of cards had been squeezed from a card shark and sent flying across the borough. It was a ruined mess of a deranged looking world; although, the knockabout realm did solidify a sense of organized, but nevertheless haywire ingenuity.

Thick and loose strands of gnarled Christmas lights powered a few of the mini cardboard shanties, along with several dated television sets that beamed on full power, projecting nothing except marbled electric static. Garbage and debris were strewn out and piled high like a disturbed beaver dam consistent with perfectly shit out of luck humanity.

The most startling aspect of the disorderly scenario was, without a doubt, its occupants.

The camp was stretched out like a generous football field in overall length, but only half as wide. The figures darted and swayed from middle sections to corners in the demented psychedelic gleam, sometimes colliding into one another and tripping over themselves.

Kip took a brazen move forward and stepped on a belching piece of dry branch in the process, sounding off a foreign distinction in an upcoming sea of forlorn senselessness. A handful of the crepuscular shapes took notice and stopped shuffling in their sooty tracks. Another nearby clump began to scorn and hiss in bizarre broadcasts, while their tattered robes and grunge worthy appeals weaved in the iridescent showcase of Colorado night bright. Their offbeat grumbles and random screeches called the others forward, all stopping their obsessive-compulsive behaviors and settling fixated on the armed intruders at the doorstep of their smutty hell that crept up from the netherworld. Kip stood mortified with the shotgun chattering inside his medium-sized and calloused over brown hands.

The skyward spectacle took a sudden breather, dimming the entirety of the scene ever slightly. The atmosphere remained breathtaking and freakishly unnatural. However, the army of beings in front of them took center stage, while stirring up the most polar feelings of mortally diseased dread.

Each moving creature in the herd came across as all the way human, but they were not for all of God's remaining sake.

The leaky and bulbous eggs for eyes were exploding from each infiltrated and mud-caked stew, parched to the gills for the last remaining souls of the living inferior. Damien looked beyond the first impromptu hut of muddy boards and interlocked sinister eyes with a sphinx woman cradling a mangy infant. The child also was without its human windows of innocence, and the ordinary looking lady was licking the baby's head and body as if she were a tiger or some other feral beast of purely wicked burden.

The slobber came off in strings with each swipe of the thing's sandpaper tongue, and could be seen clear as daylight in the offered pungency of the lime green blaze. The female sphinx wore a dirtied caliber of a thickly knitted stocking cap. The wool lining was darker in shade and gave off an almost sympathetically weathered and beaten down appeal. The creature was nude, except for the headdress, with her wiry body baring all but a cruddy mess of once upon a time sorrowful depiction of gristly poverty.

The armed humans looked on with awe and terror at what was an entire horde of human sphinx replicates, padded up in a thin straight line along their flattened home's riverbank. Hundreds of former vagabonds and bindle stiffs had become radically transformed into soul swallowing abominations, set out to erase the remaining essence of a thoroughly weakened Mankind.

A baker's dozen of the first wave of heathens goggled at Kip and his jacketed partner in a ruling and alien way, an overpowering offense that would have lit most other humans up in a snap like malnourished Christmas trees.

Winters shook off the ancient death glazes with his gifted and unusual workings of mental precision, but as Kip began to tremble in place and break out in alarming perspiration, Damien ignited his newfound flame gun.

The second wave of devils joined the telepathic onslaught, causing Wells to smoke all over, his tattered scrubs beginning to disintegrate and flake right off his body due to the unbelievable hotness.

Winters advanced in an instant, plunging his right finger down to the fire trigger's bottom floor.

An aggressive burst of flame shot far and wide from the device, setting a handful of the already then erased transients into a reddish-orange magma. The intended targets stood at home while continuing forward with their preternatural mind game, never shifting a muscle, even under fire in the ancient effort to convert Kip down to their primordial level of eternal damnation.

Damien continued his own raging destruction throughout the pathetic grunge, never easing up his slender digit from the weapon's glorious trigger. The flame pack continued to administer a hellacious cloud of conflagration in an insanely brutal directional formation.

His boots of blood pressed forward through the flimsy huts and soggy box overhangs, obliterating anything and everything that moved in front or around him.

The filthy sundowner city entered a Bixby Bridge empire of predestined inferno in a matter of minutes.

The human sphinx *maestros* remained steadfast while they burned, only being sent down to the dirt when their undyed whites melted down and popped from the blistering thrower's heat. Winters was sweating through his jacket due to the violent outrage, narrowly catching ablaze himself as he whipped the torch every which way.

When he reached the very end of the engulfed bivouac, the man extinguished the flamethrower and began to remove it in a huff from his fatigued back. The device had become intrusive at that point and was smoldering from its extensive efforts in assisting with decimating the overruled mud hut for a town. Certain sections of his sterling coat of leather were singed and stained from the pack's blistering upheaval. He could smell the burning material of his beloved cape of cover at disturbingly close range, along with burning sphinx meat and hot garbage.

He made a sudden hitch with his long body as the entire assembly dropped hard with a clunk to the dirt canvas in front of him. He then pulled his silver steel from its sweating holster and bolted back towards the opposite way where he hoped Kip still remained alive.

He took off in a lumbering revolt, avoiding flame and raging inferno at absurdly unsafe quarters.

One partially ignited sphynx had jumped out and managed to block his narrow escape route. The thing was smoking from head to foot by a pile of charred and burned out rubble. The mortal fired his magnum in mid-stride, as the seeking bullet connected with the burning head region of the intrusive depravity. The fiery body was sent to the muddy deck with a crunch, while embers from its carcass poofed through the air on sudden impact.

Winters kept his relentless pace authentic, an exhausted excitement peppered with rage and basic survival beginning to course nearing insanity throughout his human framework.

The naked woman with her sideshow infant were positioned by a barbecue pit near the initial entryway of swagman camp Bixby. The baby sphinx's eyes erupted first, causing the senior melting wench to aim her gawk upward and screech some degree of ancient bloody murder. Her yolky discs streamed right down her naked chest as Damien rolled by in half stalk, sending the thing to her knees and forward, to burn on what remained of the doomed child and her own mangled face.

Once he'd made the initial set of Christmas lights in the first cardboard home at the very front of the onslaught, which remarkably managed to be intact and was also one of the only structures left not in flames, he damn near collided with Kip in the clearing of the non-threatening hill they'd descended from to reach the unholy opposition.

Kip was down on his knees with the shotgun sprawled out by his side. His body no longer smoked, and his face was down close to the dirty Colorado floor. Winters approached him in a frenetic fury, outstretching his high-powered revolver towards the robust back of his friend's unassuming skull.

"Hey," the leathered man exhaled as he stopped and brought his right hand over to assist in aiming his magnum.

Wells strained within himself and peered skyward towards Damien. Kip's eyes remained betwixt inside his own soul of tragically abused. His muted hazels looked to be on the verge of shatter beyond a reasonable doubt from deep inside, a pain that Winters had never witnessed in such magnitude within the very essence of his closest friend.

He holstered his weapon and rushed over to him.

He dropped to a knee and spoke in a labored vein.

"You're alright, Kip. Up you go now, soldier," while he pulled him back up again to his shaky sneakers.

Kip unreliably complied but managed to right himself once more on his own choppy sea legs. Damien picked up the shotgun from the grot and handed it back over to his wounded partner.

"Dropped something?" He questioned with a sarcastic smile and a wink.

Kip wrapped his hands around the Weatherby once more, with an uncertain vitality that managed to keep on swirling with a little push from a mythically resilient friend. They labored backward into the direction of the road and the waiting police cruiser. The men needed to get back to their own destroyed Heatherton town.

Tearing straight through her heart and plunging southbound had become the only way out.

XLIV

THE SKY MAINTAINED its cloudless green while a subtle mist of fog descended on the otherwise pitch-black Colorado roadway. Lightning smacked through the welkin, a clownish oddity entering a blank atmosphere. More than three-quarters of the Bixby Bridge had collapsed, without pity to its untimely death, into the icy river. There was no viable way around or across the destruction, with the charred embankment they'd just survived from offering only more arctic black water just beyond it.

Attempting to scale Colorado's daunting depths was certain death. The swim alone was too damn far. The churning water rush was thirty below zero in the endless October dark.

"Let's light this sucker up and smash back to town. Hell, maybe something forgiving will be there for us this go around," Winters said as he mounted the police chopper.

Kip had that look on his face, that mask of ugly pessimism that he never failed to wear so well. One of those cringe-worthy looks where his mind had already been made up and nothing good or even maybe good would ever come from it.

Fat chance, Winters, was precisely what swam through the mind of Kip Wells before joining the maverick rider back on the presumed dead officer's law machine.

The motorcycle's operator knew in his heart that he had to try something as he fired up the familiar rumble. He switched on the aqua reds and used his left thumb to ignite the blaring siren. Kip took a moment but managed to hop on with him, replacing the shotgun in the handy dandy slot within the bike's housing and placing his hands behind his back to grasp hold of a special bar for a single riding passenger to latch on to.

The throttle of the cycle was pulled, as they screamed away in a tear back through the very path they'd come for escape. The dead night winds of change whipped ferociously against the grain, while a brisk October airstream pushed off from the helmetless veneers of Wells and Winters.

With the towering pines cascading in bokeh blurs on each side of the renowned drag of forest, the coast looked clear and vacant for only but another moment. In a half-mile or so, they'd have reached Heatherton's once welcoming and inviting Main Street of annihilated neon.

The thrashing gusts made visibility daunting for Damien in rushing sequences, never having the luxury of a visor or helmet to grind down the cutting force. The police person's riding hat remained forever attached to the right handlebar, cuffed in place like a plastic prisoner that would never escape.

Winters offered up a long squint ahead, shooting his jewels of worn through mahogany into the piercing narrows of the exact same stretch of road that nearly killed him once before.

The man suddenly slowed the motorcycle to a crawl, all the while killing the siren and halting to a stop in the center divider paint strip on the grainy concrete.

"What is it?!" Kip shouted out from behind with his hands gripped to the bar at his back.

"LOOK!" His driver echoed while throwing his right hand away from the steering bars and projecting it straight ahead into the murk.

Up the road befell nothing short of a fucked-off army.

From a human being's perspective, it could have been seen as a wall of moving figurines sloshing their way up the roadway exiting town.

There were hundreds of them.

They blocked the two-lane access road, filling it to its slender brim of usual beauty. The occupants advanced forward in strange ethos movements, more like a cockeyed absurdity that revolved within the obscurity of their distrusting gaits. Kip leaned forward on the bike a hair, assisting his leather-jacketed colleague with a fresh set of watery eyes.

"They don't look friendly," Winters scoffed.

A section of the horde seemed average and genuinely harmless, but they'd all been sucked up and replicated for some time then. Others remained downright and ungodly beasties, sticking out within the crowd while roaring convolutedly throughout the pack.

Out of, more than likely, half of the remaining townsfolk of duly departed Heatherton, neither Damien nor Kip could settle their eyes on a single figure that bore remotely human or even animalistic earthly peepers. Each individual of the advancing legion owned the albino whites of obliteration and was forging ahead with vulgar guile of ancestral poise straight for the loaded copper chopper.

A dozen degenerates separated from the army. Clearly extra famished for satiation on quite possibly the last remaining survivors of their dwarfed Colorado settlement.

"Hold on!"

Winters unloaded as he flooded the engine to four or five thousand RPMs. He twisted the handlebars in a switcharoo maneuver that only a crafty rider could even dream of smacking off, causing the bike's wide tires to thrash and skid with inspiring robustness. Smoke entered the incessant night due to rubber inflation burning on the gritty asphalt grain.

The heavy cycle whipped around in a full 180 degrees of incredible and powerful precision. With no siren active and only the blue and red bulbs bleeding out as a stoic guide into the blackened abyss, the scrappy hospital workers screamed ahead in the other direction, away from the horrendous legion of ravenous parasites.

The charred remains of what was left of dear old Bixby was again rapidly approaching, as Kip peeked behind himself to check up how the clan was making their overall progression. The moving mass was behind them and closing, but Damien had done a fine job at separating themselves from imminent danger.

Mere feet before what would have been the usual bridge entrance to the next over county and town, Kip clutched a little tighter on the heavy metal bar at his back.

He knew exactly where they were detouring.

Winters cranked the motorcycle right, picking up gravel in the process and chugging the hefty machine down a side dirt road adjacent to the obliterated carcass of the classical bridge of fire. They made haste toward the town's one and only cemetery and graveyard. With plausibly being the last unchanged beings left in the entire great state of Colorado, the two men attempted a finishing gasp of refuge in an all-too-familiar house of the ghouls, while being hunted without mercy by something far worse than anything ever buried or expired by the liberties of silly human merits.

It had become their final chance at survival.

XLV

SERAPHIM STONE CEMETERY proved to be the only existent hope of escape. With Bixby barbecued to a crisp, and the sea of monstrosities oozing their death brights up the only woodland road that could access Main Street, the off-course jag in the ricocheted direction was the one possibility for a safe haven.

Seraphim had prevailed at being the gaudiest cemetery in the whole state of Colorado, gushing with timeless stone works of marbled rustics that dated way back to the early 1700s. The divine mausoleums inside the lavishly panoramic grounds were nothing short of a haunting, yet breathtaking spectacle. Slathered about and lined in off-kilter formations up and down the grandiose graveyard's unorthodox foundation, the anthropoid remains of the once upon a time living lay dormant.

The forgotten people rested safely and nevermore underground, allowing the Earth to do its transformative job on their spent and finished bodies of human existence. Unfortunately, the deceased of Seraphim Stone possessed a luxury that Winters and Wells did not have.

The graveyard's flesh and bones from down under had died off naturally, under a God perhaps, or even by the beautifully artistic circle of Mother Nature's complicated splendor. Those fortunate underlying residents were not being hounded for extermination, to be destined only and forever onward into an abyss of never was and never could be again.

Above all, the sphinxes' lone offer to the human race appeared to be the endless black of the deepest shades of a nothinged damnation.

Damien had fostered a shoddy belief, in a time not so distant ago, that the cemetery was pretty much the safest place in the world to be. He would visit the very same grounds he then rode toward, armed with his film camera and laptop computer, roaming the sanctified place to fire off a few grainy black and whites.

Or to hunt and peck something frightening, with a bottle of beer perched on the grass by his side, spiraling into the electronic notebook while resting his back up against a crucifix tombstone under the early evening sun.

The oldest 17- and 1800-year sensations had never ceased to fascinate him in the utmost of inspirations. He'd marvel at their misunderstood beauties and ponder about how the chiseled cuts of precision had managed to withstand the tests of time for so many tireless centuries.

Damien had found a grounded level of splintered and chipped moments of peace for his hyper-anxious imagination in such a place of morbid traditional grandeur.

BUT THIS NIGHT *is different and awful.*

Nothing will escape or be safe here, ever again.

"Stop it," the leathered pilot muttered back underneath his breath at his own ghoulish festering, while he rode with his trusted passenger through the off-beaten dirt road near the river.

They kicked up rocks and gravel the entire way over, with the motorcycle bumping and rocking due to the unpaved and fickle ground workings. There was an atmospheric haze manifesting in front of them like a vaporous wall, while they continued the journey to the neighboring dead lands.

The men found their dilapidated selves up nearest the entrance gate, as Winters brought the police cruiser to a skidding halt in the choppy dirt just before it. He flicked off the blue blood lighting effects, killing the motor down to a whimpering sputter, then to an eerie dead silence.

Kip jumped off first and grabbed the clunky shotgun from its form-fitted slot. Damien followed suit and had to adjust his gun belt after his own laborious dismount. The brawny gate, which was wrapped in a daunting chain padlock of impenetrable iron, scoffed at Wells and Winters while they slammed into the cemetery barricade at full force.

"Looks like we're climbing," Damien exhaled with his stubbled face, exerting rough and awkward heaves in offbeat succession.

Kip nodded his way as they began to scale the lurid metal, appearing like two spent convicts attempting a daring early morning escape from a stormy Alcatraz Island. Winters reached the elevated midway point first, with his motorcycle jacket glistening on his out-of-breath sternum in the uncanny moonlight.

He surveyed the immediate surroundings from his way up vantage point and gave one or two more grinding exhales while shooting a quick gaze at the always changing skies. The moon had ballooned forward in a full-circled and obnoxious mood of crater cookied magnificence. It spewed a crimson glow along with peculiar aquamarine rings that surrounded the intriguing foreign rock. The rings resembled that of Saturn when a pimple-faced punk would skim a boring science hardcover picture book back in their deformed high school days.

Even in the face of a running scared stifle of desperation, the young man somehow managed a brief amazement, one which projected itself upward into the fantastic audacity of such an exciting and endless solar system, one that then, more than ever, scoffed hysterically down upon him.

Damien held his satisfied transfixion at the teetering stage of the cemetery barrier, for a lasting and longing moment, peering like a boy at the evocatively prepossessing, yet unreal scene of the night.

Kip went back down to the ground and handed over the shotgun to his counterpart, right as he snapped out of his trance, so that Wells could begin his own climb up. He reached the same midway mark and settled right alongside Damien.

As one cohesive pair, they swung their right and left legs over the gate and leaped for the sacred grounds below.

The drop back down to Earth was a good six-and-a-half-foot nosedive. Winters landed on both of his boots, but Kip crashed down from feet to shoulder in a shocking instant. He winced and uttered a mild profanity, as his coated colleague helped him back to his feet and handed over the matte black Weatherby banger.

It took some exhibitions of fresh and nimble agility, but they'd doggedly made it downright inside of Seraphim Stone Cemetery.

The sable void of seemingly endless torture remained alive and festering all around them. A freakish yellow fog blanketed the grave-yard's floor, and to the hospital chums' fatigued sets of eyes, appeared to stretch outward for nothing short of several depressing miles. Seraphim was around an eighth of a mile wide, a loftier garden of remembrance for such an itty-bitty mountain borough.

The Sphynxes would be arriving at any moment.

The horde would be starved and extra motivated, primed for a traditional objective to melt and erase what remained of an obliterated section of unfortunate Earth.

"This way, up to that mahogany mausoleum up that first hill!" exclaimed Winters.

He knew Seraphim well and felt right at home with its uneven and unpredictable layout. He had written several short stories during off-work hours at the exact destination that the heroes were gunning for.

They ran for it, slicing and dicing through reddish and acid green illuminated headpieces that were frosted like stone cakes in the end of the world starlight. The fog made things tricky, but the substance remained thin enough where one could see twenty or so good feet in front of them.

Wells and Winters could only hear their own footsteps squishing through the muddy terrain all the way up until they reached the premeditated mausoleum. The name carved atop the swanky stone structure in their perceived line of vision read, 'LLEWELLYN.'

They'd accomplished the jaunt, with Damien collapsing to the front step and focusing his face upward toward Kip.

"I just need a minute to think," Winters heaved wildly.

"This shit's unbearable, D," replied Kip, with his hands rested on his scrubbed hips and the shotgun leaning into him, a controlled demeanor managing to channel through Winters' counterpart.

Wells continued, "How can the world just be all of a sudden coming down to this hell in a handbasket? I guess it was bound to happen sooner or later, but I never thought I'd witness the shit firsthand with my own two eyes."

"There has to be a better way to fight them," exerted Damien in response.

The lean man was athletic-looking on the outer surface compared to his friend, but running for his life had never been a strong suit for his worked-over windpipes. Also, his hyper-aware nature had his overwrought vitals chugging and twitching on an exploding redline.

They could only enjoy a measly scrap of a huffed and puffed moment of silence before catching the sound of a nearby rumble or stomp. Off and out there, coming from their immediate right.

Somewhere beyond, yet not too distant in the foggy crimson dark, a discomfort that loomed too close for their sinking human comforts.

Then another, and yet another series of blistering click clacks.

Kip bolted up the last five mausoleum steps and huddled himself by Llewellyn's closed and gated door. Damien sprung up jaggedly with ice cubes in his veins and joined his oldest friend at the rusted green and gold mausoleum entrance.

The footfalls grew with rapidity every other second, while more seemed to spawn out from nothing, as if termites had overrun the blessed hollows and were all swarming toward an inevitable spot of anguished sufferers; right then and there, primed and ready to swallow up the remainder of infernal beings left on their miserable planet.

THE MEN WERE just so worn out and beaten to the bone at that stage in their gripping odyssey.

They had endured impossible odds, both alone and by each other's side. Being boxed inside the chilled Seraphim yard on the outskirts of town felt like an ironic ending to such a constant barrage of piercing misery.

Damien suffered where he stood, being cursed as an authentic empath down to his very being's heightened core. He'd struggled to stay alive while continuing to make proper decisions inside his own damaged head along the way. He'd fought back against the detestable insurgence from the very beginning and scuffled in each and every step to save the people he'd cared for and loved.

He'd even attempted to aid a complete stranger, with Rose's straight auburn hair projecting into his brain along with her uncontrollably gushing blood.

All Winters had left was his own life's imperfect heart, along with his best pal, Kip.

He was not going to fail again and let anything happen to his most cherished friend.

Damien had an uncanny ability to fend off the sphinxes within the confines of his mental prowess, in a way, even he couldn't conceptualize, a luxury Wells didn't seem at all to possess. Winters pondered if other people were out there in what was left of his broken down and ravaged world, who also owned such an abnormal dexterity.

He'd hoped more so than ever, while something graver than the darkest depths of a terrifying oblivion was moments away from suffocating down on them.

CRUNCHED UP TO the iron throne of the cold Llewellyn crypt, the men reloaded their exhausted firearms. Kip filled the shotgun's chamber to its brim, while his colleague picked out spent magnum bullets from his wheel gun and replaced the empties with fresh ones.

They stood perched on the final step up, with the locked and closed mausoleum door at their shivering backs, providing a half-assed safety net for a final last stand. Damien's almost black leather coat remarkably held poise throughout it all, with its thick and rugged material casting a reflective sheen due to the afflicted moonlight. Kip's scrub suit was plundered to a pulp in multiple areas, but all in all, the clothes were holding up the smaller man well enough.

The pounding footfalls of the degenerate Sphynx blew up and around in painful frequency, causing a surrounding pattern that charged and squeezed the cowering humans to death right then and there. Wells and Winters darted their skulls this way and that, intent only on making out any exacting direction of the incoming insurgence.

The frantic efforts proved to be of no foundational degree of any good use.

They were two sitting ducks out there, with the only method of fighting back, becoming purely reactionary. Spine-tingling defense mode was the abiding strategy the fixed buddies had at their disposal, crammed up to the brink inside the moss-covered walls of the dead.

XLVI

THE NEFARIOUS MONSTERS entered the scene first.

They were larger than any common man and boasted a definitive and insidious form of frightening agility. The all-out devils were the most ravenous of the aggressors, a horrendously thirsty breed of doomed solitude that had yet to taste the pleasures of an original human spirit. From out front, among the scattered stones, the bygone creatures converged on their two gutsy targets.

The dark substance ash of steely grey snow began to descend from the skies, while unpleasant cloud formations rolled on in along with it. The atmosphere boomeranged and turned to an ominous rose matter, with the flaunting blood moon nearly becoming swallowed up. The immediate surroundings grew more dramatic, with only crimson and black to guide the men against the indefensible attack.

Kip unloaded first with a powerful blast that torpedoed from the shotgun and yanked a sphinx head clean off its wickedness. The thing continued forward in stride after it was shot, not yet comprehending its soul-stealing goops and protruding horns were no longer attached. It lost all motor functions and slid contorted near the bottom steps in front of them, smacking it's hairy and loathsome body into a meaty crucifix headstone for good measure.

It was then Winters turn, as a two-handed grip engulfed the base of his unhinged revolver of rage.

It took three pulls from the mighty weapon to stop a flying hairless wretch, with her lioness mug and perky naked breasts, dead set for the remainder of all things living. He'd shot her during her launching effort, sending the abomination badly off course and careening to the earth beside them.

The stratosphere had become taken hostage by intrusive masses of water vapor, as bellowing cracks of thunder punched the immediate area with a force of untimely wit. The color saturations turned over to the brightest of oranges, for a neon hue of fire-charged and bloodied fright. The ashes of mankind continued their cryptic fall from the ether in a controlled and gorily exotic descent. It then started to rain. A steady deluge of puffy droplets turned the active heroes from dry and limber to soggy and weighed down in a matter of moments.

The sphinxes carried on without mercy, barreling down in heathenish waves from each and every imaginable direction.

Another large fiend appeared, towering like an ancient hellion right next to Kip. It grabbed for the very top of his head with a gangly clawed appendage while he stood crouching to fire, lifting the decent-sized man off the mausoleum steps. Wells turned the wet shotgun upward, aiming more or less in the general vicinity of the famished creation's shifting animal mug. The devil puffed a sour haze of carbon dioxide that cut through the cemetery air, with the smoking steam of the beast trying to drown out Kip's soggy and terrified face. He cocked the large weapon, with Damien looking on beside him.

The cold and slick trigger was pulled within the grasp of the evil, unleashing a wicked boom throughout the sacred land. The sphinx's skull exploded into a pink mist, sending fragments of soupy matter onto Kip's hospital scrubs, and making its diabolical delights all the way onto Damien's precious coat.

The big cat dropped Wells to the turf, just before it was sent falling backward and down the mausoleum stoops, only to clobber itself good into the watery labyrinth.

Winters shuffled over and picked his friend up with a vacant right hand, aiming his revolver outward with a grimace into the shadowy Black Death with his other. The fired upon sphinx made a splash on impact, while dirt and blades of green welcomed the headless disgrace. Winters discharged four more rounds from his stirring handgun, clicking the weapon into the storm, providing a signal that he was, in fact, out of ammunition. Kip thundered off another slug from the Weatherby before Damien glared back his way with a fury.

"RUUUN!" Winters hollered into the crumbling soul of his most trusted ally.

They broke off together with the human imposter waves of sickness making their fashionably late revealing out of the marshy and fogged-up abyss. Winters and Wells jumped the small flight of stairs where they'd made their feeble defense and frantically took to the rain and chiseled granites of the expansive Seraphim Stone.

They remained neck and neck, while sawing and jagging throughout the underlying deceased in a sloppy frenzy of madness. They re-loaded as they ran, with Damien grabbing for a speed loader in his gun belt of drenched black leather. He emptied the revolver's wheel in a full sprint, spilling seven spent cartridges to the muddy shallows below. He smacked the Bumblebee into the empty barrel, primed and ready again for more sphinx's blood.

Kip fumbled for shells in his soaked through scrub pockets. He dropped a few while he lumbered forward, finding a home for a couple extra rounds in the big ass Weatherby shotgun. The horde gave chase alright, chanting and snarling their own unbearable tune in a rampaging and tireless pursuit.

The air turned icy in conjunction with the rain, causing each breath to exude a visible heated vapor from the mouths of the final two humans warring against the incorrigible eyeless fuckers. With doing nothing more than running for their very lives, a saturated lab coat from out in no man's land took a massive lurch toward them.

The thing had manufactured a way to climb a tall grave piece and use its bastard new sphinx agility to accomplish such an unthinkable spring. It was female and tight in overall frame.

It, no, she was without question, a former Pharmacist from the very foundation of the gone but never dead Mason General Hospital.

She latched onto Kip's back as he tried to scamper away, stopping him cold in his mud-soaked sneakers. She began clawing into his back, where he stood upright and center. He flailed around while holding the shotgun, trying in sorry desperation to fling her/it off of him.

Damien emerged from the depths with his revolver holstered, and his hand ax clutched in his right hand. He brought the sharp object down with one swift stroke, finding a home on the very top of the revolt dressed up in a hospital overcoat's water-logged skull. She or it or whatever it was, snapped toward him after the unsavory head chop, remaining affixed to Kip, with the ax plunged grossly into the highest point of her soggy noggin.

She hissed rancid death while sucking in a breath and greeted Winters with a calculated whack of her own across his sturdy, but battered down and beaten veneer. The force hit him like a freight train running psychotically with no brakes, picking up the young mortal and sending him cascading into a heap to the sacred mud-caked earth.

As the crazed former pill crusher reached for the cleaver in her crown, Kip flicked his slick body with enough human exertion to fling the thing off of him, to where they both stood separated and facing off with each other. He took the butt of the shotgun and smashed it off her germ cell pales, sending the despicable sphinx onto a monolith grave that was constructed into the shape of a large stone bed. There were two names inscribed into the granite berth tablet.

'Here lies Karla and Stan McCutchen.'

Both died only three months apart, sometime in the year 17 something or other.

Kip flipped the Weatherby back around again, as the overlong barrel became outstretched in front of him. He cocked the wonderful weapon and squeezed down the trigger. The pharmacist's brains splattered all over the fancy bed-chamber tomb, with the legs of the fuck kicking wildly, as Kip rushed over to help Damien back up to his feet.

They embraced leathered forearm to wet brown skin that made a smacking sound on impact, while they both used vigorous efforts to get each other upright again. Labored breaths and audible exertions from Winters graced the moist dying air.

"Thanks. Keep going."

They resumed their demented cemetery dance, with the leather-coated man unholstering his fully loaded magnum revolver one more time.

The rain fell down in sheets, with an orange glow to boot, that sent painful shivers down the remainder of what was left of the giving up world. Winters and Wells remained stride for stride, struggling not to break too far apart from one another.

"Stay close!" Damien howled as they trucked and weaved through the messy garden of the dead.

A scattered group of sphinxes popped up in the forefront that slanted outward, facing west. Winters rang out a shot while continuing the gripping escape. The magnum bullet missed everything important, instead, nicking off part of an angel's wing of an admirable early 1900s masterpiece.

"This way!" he again shouted out toward Kip Wells.

Damien broke off due east in the exact opposite direction of the seething convergence. Kip, however, continued straight up the middle in an unfathomable display of a type of chicken maneuver. The drenched gunslinger noticed their separation, so he slammed on his boots in between two reddish-orange glows for stony marbled tablets.

"Kip?! Kip, Goddammit!!" he hollered after his brazen and ludicrous compadre.

Kip paid no attention to the urgent plea; instead, firing a thunderous slug into the chest of a youngin human sphinx who was destined only for a pathway to something worse off than Hell. Winters swiveled his head around in mucky desperation, with his shoulder-length mane becoming a flinging and dripping mess.

He noticed he was being collapsed on in every moveable direction. A slew of beasties and human imposters were only fractions of seconds from having him. The man sprang off again, hurdling a shallow grave in the process, and jumping over another crucifix made of a beautifully rough and textured hunk of cut quartz.

A clodhopping outrage almost got a hold of him.

While he hustled away from certain death, the monster slung out a heaping hand of claws and offered the fleeing man a swipe. The brute was covered from head to foot in mounds of matted hair, with the horns gouged from the cheekbone areas, along with the sickening saucers for eyes deeming visible. It grazed Damien, missing his body but ripping off a section of his cherished coat of arms.

It didn't slow him down while he kept up the slushily charged mad dash.

He zig-zagged the condemned terrain, avoiding another herd of deadites and beginning to distance himself from permanent doom within the archaic set. His lungs screamed at him, along with his jacket and lengthy stems becoming as heavy as one of the ever forgotten 1800-year stone classics. The rain pummeled without ceasing from the sky of maddening unpredictability, as the man found himself soaked through from the incessant downpour.

Winters had to think on command at full tilt speed and needed a moment to remember exactly where he was inside the substantial cemetery artistry. He'd visited Seraphim many times over the years, so it took him another second to decide where to bolt for next.

There was a haughty pyramid-shaped sepulcher that belonged to a rich Colorado business type who'd demanded something ancient and Egyptian, along with obnoxiously elaborate, to decorate his final resting place once he met his undeniable maker. The last name on the domineering structure was easy for the young man to remember.

'HILL.'

The most intriguing aspect about that particular graveyard vault was it always remained open, there was no door or locked gate blocking entrance into the showy triangle's starless innards. Mr. Hill happened to be buried in the floor below the center workings of his intricate pyramid piece. Damien had come to presume, whether accurate or nowhere near, that Hill had perhaps wanted living folks to roam around freely inside his stone triangle, and maybe even check up on him from time to time after his passing.

The pyramid was just up ahead on a slight incline in the soupy and uneven sod. With a ceaseless ditch of drearily spent hope, alongside wheezing lungs damn near ready to explode from his body, Winters cut through the night for the shallow opening refuge to Hill's exalted pyramid. He completed the crazed intention, more or less diving into the harsh uncertainty headfirst.

The triangle structure swallowed the human man up in a blink, protecting him from the ghoulish elements, providing a makeshift shelter from the constant brutality that had become his outside world. He was so horrendously out of breath from the demanding jaunt that he couldn't even manage to settle his mouth closed to breathe through his own showering nostrils. Damien panted and coughed, while giving audible stresses of passionate resonance, in a flimsy attempt to wrangle even a fraction of graveyard fresh oxygen.

He managed to calm down his insides while pursing his lips together and sweeping a section of dangling damp chocolate away from his glassy brown eyes.

His handy battle-ax was gone for good, and so again, was Wells.

HE SAT ALONE in the triangle black with his water-leaden leather coat pressed up against the farthest wall of the confining crypt. His slick revolver remained gripped in a slim left hand, ready for anything without the benefit of a soul to dare and come slithering in.

He craved only a few minutes to contemplate his ruminations and catch his breath. The pyramid could have easily been a death trap if he was found, but the raw comforts of it during such a moment of delirious exhaustion was worth the hefty price of demise. He worried for Kip out there, but he also couldn't understand why he'd broken away from him and plowed full speed into the swarming parasites.

The irksome cloudbursts poured through the narrow rectangular entrance of the pyramid haven, with the persistent orange neon fighting, as it may, to sneak on in after him. Winters found himself vanquished inside the sappily dark confines of the graveyard crypt.

He rummaged and checked ammo inventory on his sagging leather gun belt.

Only seven shots remained.

A full load of his tired magnum was all he had left to give.

He quietly clicked open the wheel of the Smith & Wesson to double-check his grim calculations. The armed seven that rested in the raindrop-glitter silver circle was, in fact, all she wrote. He pressed the mechanical portion of his thrilling weapon closed again with a gentle sweep of a left hand.

He was sitting against the back wall of the tomb, with his knees halfway up and the rear of his head pressed to the cold stone behind him. He pondered away for an aborting sequence that he really didn't give much of a shit any longer if an army of the unfathomables crawled their vile and rancid delights right on inside and just let him have it.

Melted his body down to nothing and stole away everything unique and original that he ever had or would never become.

If the sphinxes came knocking with their salivating eyes and digested every nuance of his freest pleasures and darkest fears, he'd be erased from the drawn-out timeline of the totality of human existence. His valiant efforts and rugged charms during the infinite hours of hopeless malice would go down unnoticed, never meaning a thing to anyone or anything remotely important.

His eyes began to well up with moisture of defeated sorrow, but mostly, they were functioning with fires of inexplicable rage.

The hollowed-out impermanent never felt so alone and vulnerable in his entire careening existence. The gravest of thoughts began to seep and chatter their clucking ways into his wrenching and overwrought frame of being. Rapping considerations, things like all the grappling and persistence against the outside nihility was in nothing but vain. An inevitable null and void of assured obliteration from an emotionless legion of the first-ever lifeforms was only to be, at long last, looked forward to.

Any previous perceptions of himself or anyone he'd ever encountered would be slurped away from the constructs of the remainder of time. Such rushing sequences of intrusive thought processes frightened Winters the utmost, as his chilled steel revolver remained gripped in a dominant left hand.

It caused the drowning man to, again, condemn his God for allowing him subjection to such an elaborate spectrum of damaging and diseased frames of thinking.

How could He just flump idly by while the entire human world was being burned to the ashen ground?

Was He second best all along, created even before His own time by a superior organism that never dared to make His gravest mistake of all?

Did He make His own selfish abomination when he created the very first human specimen?

Winters sulked and sank against his will into another realm of presumptions that perhaps his kind, the humans, were getting the shortest end of the proverbial shit stick. The war that he had been fighting up until that painstaking moment should have belonged to the devils and the gods all along, not the resulting mortals and their erroneous human condition.

The sphinx's wrath was for a god to fight, having no place for an ordinary man or woman to attempt to overcome. Damien had never asked to be mentally gifted or even to be born into such a world, however, rivers of agonizing suffrage and tremendous feelings of loss had landed and burrowed their despicable practices into the narrowest trenches of his darkest fears.

He sat for several minutes more, hoping at least the rain would provide a mini-break and let up its annoying onslaught. He stared ahead limply and devoid of any life at all in a half-seated position, peering out at the rain from his sizable pyramid mausoleum.

A RACKET OF activity rocked his body rigid and could be heard converging closer from nearby outside. He couldn't tell what the source was or how far away it was operating, although it didn't feel to be right there on top of him just yet.

While he sat glaring ahead at the opening in his ice-cold burial chamber, the rain stopped itself on a dime.

The orange sherbet atmospheric tonality shifted to an even richer scheme of deep and vivid purples. It was the color of a highly powered black light, an aggressive magenta of neon that spiced with vivacity over the lost and gone grounds of the ageless forgotten. Winters listened for anything that could help his cause, but more than anything, a sign from Kip.

"Damien?"

A voice on command cracked out from off in the closer distance.

He concluded that it was coming from the outside right portion of the pyramid of solid stone. He wanted to spring up from his position and holler out his friend's name, but he had to be sure it was authentically him. He waited another agonizing moment.

"D-Daamien!" rang out close in frightening proximity.

The unfamiliar voice calling for him seemed right outside the pyramid's vacant doorway. Damien rose to his boots and crept toward the entrance with his throaty steel hung down low. A shuffle of mushy outside footfalls, more or less, attacked his brain from a claustrophobic inky distance. The open entrance was high and long, to where the cautious slender man could perch up with no problems, while he inched his way into the unknown clatter.

He stepped all the way out from his granite safety net and plunged into the new black light, sweeping his head around to look for any sign of his rightful ally.

Maybe Kip had miraculously found him.

Winters was only half of a second from uttering his companion's name in a relieved state of cautious exasperation.

But all of a sudden, inside the swirling night creep, a figure surprised him with a quick startle, one that appeared squared up and straight in front of his confused face of damp soot. A deep and unforeseeable agony, cycled with pure human shock, flooded throughout Damien's entire vessel. The man's adrenaline spiked off the charts, providing him with the most ravenous extremes of basic survival instincts.

It was, in fact, Kip Wells.

He did appear to be alright.

Kip's muted eyes were darting wildly, and he'd managed to lose the Weatherby and Beretta handgun. The men stood squaring off after more or less running into each other by the dark-lit entranceway to Hill's triangle tomb. Damien gazed his eyes below to where Kip's hands were situated in front of himself. They were both down around his sides, with one of them extending outward.

Kip had plunged the extensive machete into the hollow meat region of Damien Winters' lean and heaving gullet. The exact blade he had been gifted hours before at his murderous cabin. The disbelieving man dropped his revolver to the slick blades of graveyard green, while he placed his left hand on the stony machete's handle, as it became a part of him through and through. Kip's stabbing hand remained affixed to the weapon, as the two men's bare hands shook for a freezing second, with them both meeting the knife for the first time as a cohesive unit.

Kip let go as Winters took a staggering step back away from him.

"Oh, God!! Damien?!" Kip's heightened tone cracked through the air as a bolt of lightning obliged in the skyward shadows, with his sturdiest friend standing aghast before him, with his own knife gored into his insides. Damien choked twice, spilling a jet of warm blood from his pursed mouth of bafflement.

He grabbed for Kip but found nothing as he plummeted to the floor on his side with the knife protruding out from the other.

The horrifyingly wounded man managed to pull himself up on his back to the front side stone workings of Hill's vacant entryway. The initial shockwave from the attack subsided from within him, and was replaced with the most heinous degrees of physical human torture. Kip remained lurking over him, frozen stiff in his barely holding it together hospital scrub outfit.

"Damien, I'm sorry! I didn't know it was you! Please!!"

Winters reached a limp hand up toward his paramount friend, as the boisterous pitter-patter of the degenerate Sphynx became audible. The herd was gaining ground and could smell the blood and mortal fear.

Kip looked around insanely in the night, with his wet hair of curly-q's flicking off of his medium brown skin. He gave a lasting look down at Damien on the cemetery turf, with his leathered arm outstretched up and into him. The man's revolver lay by his side while he moved his other hand to affix onto the knife that had just been gouged through him. Kip supplied one final focus at his gravely wounded running mate, seconds before a screeching and animalistic howl rang true that could be heard from several miles.

Wells left Winters arm reaching up into nothing, while he bolted off running like a Judas in the blood-curdling night. Kip fled away like a frightened canine, leaving his devoted friend to die in the dreadful graveyard of doom.

Damien gathered enough strength to tilt his head skyward and look out into the direction Wells had run off to, watching his double-crossing silhouette disappear into the disgraceful haze of dark purple.

"K-k-i-i-p," could be barely heard over a whisper from the crimson saturated mouth of Damien Winters.

He'd been left alone and injured at the very hand of his most valued brother in arms.

Left to perish and die.

XLVII

KIP DISAPPEARED FROM view with his cowardly deed being carried out in full. His most genuine colors had shown through at the bitterest of endings, when everything was on the line and mattered more than ever before.

Sure, Kip had run off before, and his antics were nothing juicy or original, but the dreadful final time was more complex in a glaring sense of indignant severity.

Ghastly mutilated, the wavy-haired hero managed to pick up his revolver from the glistening graveyard earth. His hands trembled with the effort and were soaked through in his own lifeblood, smearing the rosewood handle and parts of the magnum's beautiful steel with his own oozing vermilion. While, somehow, being able to prop up on his back against the front entrance of the lofty pyramid house, the forever gritty man pushed with all his might to shimmy his way backward into the triangle's gritty viscera.

He cried out in deep-pitched anguish while he moved, inching his way back on one elbow into the impromptu safety of the shapen tomb.

Betwixt inside the consuming darkness, with the betrayal throbbing like rotten vinegar inside his overwrought frame of being, Winters stoic mentality began to catch up and blackly tango with the overall goodness of his mind. He had finished the laborious crawl back and was settled up against the deepest side wall of Hill's godless sanctuary.

His legs were sprawled out straight in front of him, along with the red-splashed magnum, which rested in his lap. He scowled below at the rancid knife that stuck like a nightmare from his seeping core. The pain was unbearable at the sight of it all, but he continued the war within himself to remain conscious and thinking.

His mind bent away without hesitation into graphic tales of gory hypothesis.

Storylines such as, perhaps that razor-sharp instrument was always destined to rest inside him, a metaphorical thorn in his side, which was excreted down the pipeline from a troubled bloodline that was destined to drain the brilliant life force from his solid and dependable framework.

He thought of smarting and damaging emotional states of his fellow humans such as exploits in fate and rocky relationships, but above all, love.

He pondered how those three insatiable philosophies imprinted into his kind had always come with surefire and gut-wrenching consequences. The more trust one offered to another, the bigger possibility that very trust would be turned against them when push came to shove. The more love one dished out to someone else, the more that same love could and would be twisted and turned against the giving initiator.

Those agonizing reminiscences were facets of the darkest, yet most authentic displays of thought-provoking intentions within the overall human spirit; introspections that Winters thought deeply of as he lay bleeding out inside the leaking stone walls of ill-fated chaos.

His vision began to fog and blur, while the black ash fell with poise outside and beyond the lofty pyramid house.

The purple-black radiance transitioned on a whim to a striking shade of eye-catching blue. It was made up of the showiest turquoises of genuine splendor. The arctic tones crept into the stone triangle, sending a glacial chill through the shattered heart of the withering away Damien Winters.

The piercing shrieks from the everlasting Sphinx could be heard from off-beaten directions in the then ice-colored cemetery confines.

The hellacious screams didn't seem to be close, but during that specific moment, the dying man could've really cared less.

HE TURNED THE gun on himself, moving the bloody revolver to the direction of his grizzled chin.

Damien tilted his head into the neo-noir ceiling of granite, feeling the rawest emotions of betrayal and horrific loss stream down his beaten down silhouette. The mortal man only wanted his unrelenting madness to end, to simply cease and desist.

The festering anguish had become too burdensome to withstand.

The spinning saga felt cruelly all for naught in one surging moment of chaotic bliss.

He placed the intimidating barrel of his indifferent firearm underneath his defined jaw of scruff and grime. With two hands wrapped around the large revolver's cherry wood handle, he nicked the hammer back with a steady right hand. His finger caressed the sensitive trigger ever slightly, massaging it back and forth while toying with centimeters between certain life and despicable death.

A voice abruptly crept in on him and filled up his mind, while the demented soul wanted nothing more than to squeeze that trigger in the dank and miserable black. The voice clawed its way home at the very marrow of his disturbed and crippled demeanor. It was not a nagging or perverse intrusion of a presence, more so an inviting warmth of familiarity that was becoming of the invisible royal tongue.

The voice wasn't even recognizable, neither male nor female in definitive resonance. It remained with him and provided the faintest of beacons, barely filled with a slivering light in the deepest crevices of his disintegrating gray matter.

It knocked at his brain and instructed him in a decibel over a murmur to please keep on going.

To never surrender the fight.

To admire his valor and his insatiably enlarged heart, along with his scarred and unrelenting human guile.

To have confidence in knowing that he'd still go out of his way to help someone in need, even if they'd had the nerve to stab him in the back for a thanks a million, in return.

That unassuming and mellow yellow input had been there throughout his life, but could have been drowned out altogether if the young man's powers of reasoning hadn't always been somewhat admirably in tune. His overflowing despair remained constant and sharp throughout, as all other exits pointed toward the firing of his foreboding handgun.

The tears welled to the brim as he scowled upward inside the empty vault of the triangle black.

His filthy and bloody index finger remained rested with a steady indignance on the sensitive hair trigger.

Winters went to offer the fatal squeeze, with his warm mahogany eyes opened up wide and fleeting, when a faint sob rushed to the surface and saturated all over him. It was the subtlest phenomenon of a purely raw emotion, and he'd never heard such a thing escape from him before in all of his adult life. The man had become so intensely accustomed to locking everything away, to being coined the cool guy under any degree of hardened life pressure.

He slowly pulled the gun away from his face, disengaged the hammer by pulling it back, then squeezed the trigger to desensify it. He placed the cold steel beside him within the void, as the weapon made a grinding sound when it scratched the crypt's suddenly comforting floor. He placed that same hand around the machete handle that impaled his gut and rendered a despairing and intense grimace. The blood continued its flow, but the mighty blade that persisted inside him seemed to slow down the inevitable draining.

He removed his slender duke from the indelicate sharp object that bore his name and placed both of them to his mournful and exhausted face, covering it almost completely.

He cried silently in the dark.

THE AIR TURNED over and shifted to an arctic cold, one which settled in nicely with the frosty color scheme. Damien's broken breaths could be noticed in front of his own eyes, a wheezing, gasping rhythm joining forces with the incoming blue abyss of the outside remainder of his reeling world. He gave his head of damp chocolate a good and healthy shake, trying to unwind the cobwebs of his seeping through and hollow spirit.

Get up.

It's time to move now.

He was never going to just sit there and rot away like a frightened rat in a dingy hole. It wasn't in the man's nature for such a surrender. The ash fragments of his fellow humanity plummeted with passion from the outermost heavens as he rose to his feet. He winced and ground his teeth the entire way up, using the cold stone concrete at his back to assist with his wobbly ascent.

On instinct, he pawed again at the sunken blade, which was cemented into his right sidewall. It physically, but more so emotionally writhed like something rabid, but the darkly ironic dagger remained forevermore throughout the entirety of his being.

Kip's clumsy stabbing effort had missed his venerated leather coat, instead tearing right through his thin mangy t-shirt, to resolve somewhere inside his toasty guts.

He reached down toward the floor and grabbed for his blood speckled Smith & Wesson. The young man made contact with it in an unorthodox way, righting it together with a red left hand.

He stood erect while leaning against the wall for a full minute, doing everything that was left in his fleeting human prowess to seize a morsel of calm and rational bearings. He tried a booted step, then a second dragging shuffle of his other scraping foot. With a final choke of confidence for the fact he could still operate his arms and legs, he trawled along like something undead to the triangle's chill-factored open vacancy.

Winters' life magma poured and dripped from his grisly trauma with each cautious step, gracing Mr. Hill's pyramid with an alive richness that only a dead man could envy.

He raised his trusted steel painted in blood water up near the side of his handsome skull, aiming the barrel into the oncoming and ever-changing skyscape.

He cocked the hammer back with a left thumb and tore off in a labored trudge back out into the frightful graveyard.

XLVIII

S T. DOMINIC'S CATHOLIC Church had become the endmost structure in the general proximity that could offer a living, breathing human body for seven strong miles in any direction. The holy house was affixed to the central-most spot of the panoramic Seraphim Stone.

The undersized church looked as senior as some of the underground occupants, covered with centuries of shoveled over soil inside the sweeping yard. It was a two-story structure, but was a bite-sized sanctuary for such a stretch of sacred land. Dominic's home of prayer cowered in size to several more elaborate crypts belonging to the graveyard's more well-off dead residents.

The church was covered year-round in a thick and imposing density of moss, with the beat-up exterior boards peeking through for a breath of fresh air once in a rare blue moon. A crucifix was planted on the rooftop, where the two lined arches met in the middle. It wasn't a complicated cross perched atop the front rafters out in front, although it did have several bulbs inside the symbol that glowed a reddish spark in steady intervals for a little showing of added intrigue.

The more striking pieces of antiquity happened to be situated inside of the olden place of controversial worship. One monumental aspect of St. Dominic's that Winters had appreciated was her stained-glass windows. There were six of them in alluring totality. They lined the left and right sides along the perimeter of the little place of small-town grandeur.

The beautiful and overbearing moss of forest green never dared to cover up the garish glass art, one task the sole priest on duty always made sure to cut down if the fungus ever got too cocky. They were magnificently fused together with colored chunks of painted mirrors, featuring three elaborate Heaven scenes on the left, along with an exacting opposite of a trio from Hell on the right.

Being an authentic artist by nature, Damien remained a sucker for such a medium of timeless creative expressionism.

The church's operation functioned with Sunday masses and the occasional wedding or funeral consuming her insides during the finished times when humanity reigned supreme.

Maybe Father Markus will be home.

Damien believed in his debilitating mind haze that Markus had been the newest man of the cloth in charge during that tragic year of 2020. The priesthood gang seemed to be a revolving door of elusive sorts. A nun or priest would stay and practice at a specific church for a year or two, then pick up or get picked up, and move on to another new parish.

Winters didn't know what year Dominic's had first been built, but the place had endured its fair share of harsh Colorado weather over countless seasons.

Maybe Markus was boarded up in there, ready to be called on to become a decent and terminal slice of biblical humanity, to open up his doors for a miracle kind of rescue.

Or perhaps Markus had already fled away and gone, or been scorched down to nothing and sucked up into the yolky purgatory of unspeakable Sphinx.

With the pressing man's usually inviting eyes of umber growing steadily dim, along with his overall thought processes increasing in alarming grogginess, Damien knew that for his one remaining sake, he had to get there.

WINTERS FOUND HIMSELF whirling around in confused circles inside the heartless cemetery gates. He thought he knew exactly where he was, but in such a gravely weakened condition, he'd forgotten his most basic senses of general direction. Dominic's church was supposed to be a short hike east, which was the route he thought he chose after exiting Hill's triangle, but he must've made a mistake along the way in his morose daze.

He labored on alone with his head on a swivel, dripping his own precious fluids behind him ever progressively. On occasion, the lengthy hero would use a random headstone to right himself steady from falling down to the blessed turf of Seraphim Stone. He jagged and crossed around the funereal maze with the cold aqua intensifying all around him, as scattered cloud formations began to roll right on in. The still full moon transformed into a deep and gory crater of enriching red.

A smack of lightning and a beastly howl cracked damn near simultaneously, whipping Winters around in the imprecise direction of it. His hot life source jetted from the blade that gored him as he turned, defacing another headstone owned by an alcoholic Irishman he knew from town that'd kicked off prematurely from another fermented case of liver disease.

A monstrosity of an animal was barreling straight for him.

Damien found himself standing open-legged by a medium-sized gravesite right before he zeroed the evil.

'Here lies Norma Jean Wiley. She outlived while outsmarting all four of her greedy and dumb ex-hubbies.'

The sphinx stood prowling on a veiny pair of stalks and ghoulishly advanced toward the sinking young man.

It wasn't a sprinted stride from the abomination, but more of a slithering rumble of a spine-tingling gait.

The bastard thing was consumed in hair with a set of horns that catapulted from the cheekbone regions of its overgrown lion face.

Damien leaned up against old Norma Jean's stone and offered her some more of his leaking human vermilion.

Another bolt of lightning pinballed out from the intensifying sky space as the mutilated Winters fired one-handed with his virtuous revolver, striking the approaching demon in a milky right eye of superiority.

It grunted something foreign and worse than awful while continuing its gallop as both human and sphinx mouth smoke became primed and destined to collide. The shaking man cocked the hammer again for a more precise shot and unleashed another bullet into the charging mutation. It caught the other gross peeper and slipped straight into the profane monster's skull, exploding out the back of the hulking son of a bitch.

The beast stopped dead in its unsavory tracks and squealed up high and far toward the blood black moon, while it began to combust right where it stood in front of the man's endlessly fighting eyes. Boils and vomitous open sores broke out on the big cat's veneer, along with an unidentifiable viscous discharge that crept through and seeped from its blanket of dark fur.

In a hunched over position with both clawed hands outstretched, the entire oafish body detonated into nothing but gelatin liquid. The mucus flung all over the night, covering the ground and scattered resting sites with hot alien sludge.

Damien turned away in a huff and headed on while moving westward, thinking it was the proper direction to land at Dominic's precious doorstep. He was moving even slower in the ailing moonlight, slouched to one side with the smoking revolver down low in his governing left hand. He would occasionally bring his other paw up to check on the bleeding, reminding him in a fuck you kind of way that it would never dream of stopping even for a second.

He climbed a shallow hill as the sky shook its head of pitch-black dismay and turned the exact same color as the cardboard cookied moon. Scarlet red ruled over the lay of the land, stifling everything in its calamitous and terrific wake.

Damien then fell down hard to the grass.

He had tripped over the corner of an unassuming resting place, one belonging to an infant with only the name of, 'Our Darling Boy.'

The dying Winters braced for the inevitable tumble, throwing out his free hand to catch himself from going down all the way. He kept a grip on his gun and looked up while halfway to the turf from one skinned knee.

St. Dominic's was there, alright.

The relentless mortal cringed again as lightning smashed down with crazed brutality, careening off a tree way out in the distance beyond the church. It sparkled and fizzled on sudden impact, nearly catching a flame to add a glorious degree of orange to the already steady flow of crimson. He pulled himself back to his bloodied boots, with an agonizing outward cry of desolate effort buried within virtue, and muscled his exhausted way forward.

The church sat right up ahead of him.

The mossed over sanctuary was boxed in by its usual and unoriginally colored picket fencing. The fence had been painted hundreds of times over the years, but it was always determined to settle on a slightly different shade of bleach than the last coat. The uneven and bent wooden boards were four or so feet high while being buried somewhat straight up from the soil; however, the walkway loomed open in front where the Catholic church's main door sat like a shot in the dark beacon of hopeful fragility.

The entire house took on a reddish-orange hue right before his bloodshot and brown eyes of despair. The once magnificent stained-glass windows glowed creepily with the evil outside color scheme, which continued to swallow up his poor tiny town.

From the underneath crack in the church's front door, Damien thought he could make out a white-colored light source coming from somewhere in there. Something welcoming and pure was deciding to peek through, giving off a wafer of yearning that something sterling and optimistically human resided there, no matter how false of a misperceived notion that may have been.

Winters yanked himself back to his feet and labored on to the sanctuary's fenced in front opening. He peered off to his left as thunder rocked out right above his soaked head of cracked grit.

Two uniformed police officers from way back in town popped into view, out in the shallow distance, and were dashing in a sprint from the very direction Winters had looked upon.

The fine officers of the law had one surefire objective.

Their characterless chalks for eyes pulsed and fiended, grossly streaming down their contorted faces and settling onto their pressed and fancy monkey suits. They bolted like unlawful lunatics for the leathered man, while they licked and smacked their famished sphinx traps. The two former coppers wore their customary on-duty khaki pants and button-down shirts, courtesy of the purposeful Heatherton police force, accented with a contrasting tint of molten brown for added civility.

They each sported their heavy utility belts around the waist, while Winters could actually hear the various police toys crackling and popping together as the anomalies rushed at him. The one sphinx cop on the incoming far left was massive, with his extra dark skin almost swathing out what was left of the brutish insanity that would never end.

His partner hurried alongside in modest and dwarfish fashion, a fiercely uneven tandem out for the ultimate fresh slice of humanity left within the Colorado graveyard.

Damien considered firing upon the changed public servants; however, ammunition had become the utmost lordship. His bloodied steel was just about empty, less than a full load left in his defaced, but never wavering faithful hand cannon.

While continuing to gush from the treacherous knifing, and almost crashing to the muddy earth one more time, the staggering human found himself at the church's entrance just as the two uniforms were geared up to corral him.

With laborious and chopped half to death heaves, Winters slammed into the wooden church door with his right shoulder, in an absolutely final chaptered effort of a chance pulled straight outta Hell. It was meekly in hopes for nothing short of a supernatural intervention.

The barricade gave way with his noble weight and whipped open with ease. He entered St. Dominic's palace right as a human-looking paw grazed the collar of his jacket, attempting to wrangle him from entering the divine sanction. The man fought through the calloused grip and entered the confines. A protracted and imposing gothic candle holder greeted him a tick out toward his left. The large display piece was three-headed and stocked with a cluster of bright white and burning candles, which dripped runny wax from the sides and down the provocative twisted metal.

Damien awkwardly holstered his revolver and picked up the candle piece with both of his blood-saturated hands. The lit blocks of wax cascaded down to the hallowed floor, sending smoldering candle remnants and hot sparks to the thirsting underworld.

He turned back into the doorway in time to catch the smaller of the two cops standing in the open entryway. The teeny cowboy was foaming at the mouth, while a watery substance poured like a waterfall from his open stew. The little fella's entire body glowed a bold magenta, a prime result of the crazed and demonic outside ambiance.

Damien rallied all of the God-given strength he had left in the tank and turned the clunky candle holder sideways. While using a javelin motion, he met the heavy illuminator to the copper's corrupted face. The thing screamed a sound of prehistoric malfeasance in response, before spilling the little dude to the outside porch steps.

The daredevil man then reached out for the metal ring door handle, while managing to keep hold of the girthy candle weapon in his other arm, appearing like a leather-coated lumberjack hoisting a massive tree log.

He slammed the church door shut just as the larger of the two officers opened it right back up again.

The entrance barrier flung open with incredible force, with the raw strength of the larger sphynx proving unbelievable. The overmatched Winters could no longer hold the solid candle object. It tumbled to the floor in an impish crash, as the human being and mountainous sphinx stood face to face in the St. Dominic's churchway entrance.

The ungodly entity towered over the lengthy mere human specimen. It reached a meat hook for a hand at the inferior and gravely injured young hero.

Damien ducked under the sloppy attempt, raging back up with a right hooking punch of his own that connected to the left side of the granite chinned rock formation in a uniform. The mutilated man cried out in agony with the sudden burst of shuttering offense, as his knife sawed more savagely into his leaking gullet, in an avant-garde showing of a fuck you revolt.

The titanic officer took the mean strike with an all but laughable poise, while its swelling goops darted this way and that in a lurid attempt to lock themselves on with Damien's struggling and perilous brown eyes. The hulk reached out again, finding a happy home around the blood-encrusted and perspiring neck of Damien Winters.

The impossible to keep down man grabbed at the officer's forearm with both of his crimson covered bare hands, wrapping them up, but not even fully around the meaty imposter's lower arm, as he was lifted off the church's flooring like an unruly bastard stepchild.

Winters could feel his throat being slowly crushed inside itself within the classical and despicable clench of ageless power. Seconds later, the frightener cop yanked him straight back out of the doorway of St. Dominic's, while pulling his punished face horrifically close to its white orbed gawk of bygone death.

Damien reached down frantically with a left hand and managed to pull his revolver from its loose leathered holster.

A fraction of a moment before his lights went dark, Winters brought the weapon up into the giant chin of his alien attacker. He fired a ringing shot at sickeningly point-blank range, with the bullet exploding from the barrel and lodging somewhere in the granite head workings of the impenetrable monstrosity.

With viable surprise, the thing released its grip in full, spilling the broken-down soul to the rough porch floor.

Damien found himself back inside of Dominic's hollow refuge. From the heart of his back to which he landed, he pulled himself backward and inside. The muscular magnum bullet from his thunderous cannon barely did a thing, causing zero damage to the uncanny specimen that stood stalking at the church's front stoop. He raised the revolver again at the beastly uniform while being laid out on his back, while the sphinx took a half-step attempt to try and gain entrance into the atmospheric divinity.

Damien nicked the hammer and was prepared to unleash another bullet when the creature unexpectedly paused where it stood while foaming at the mouth. The eyeless agent scowled toward the floor and glared left and right, then up, and finally down through the intimate insides of the moss-covered abode.

While remaining on his stern, with the savage blade of his closest friend's execution jutting from within him, the spent human being shakily held his dreary weapon on the blasphemous curse that loomed in the church's no vacancy.

It again swung its balloon head around and back to the floor. The rancid dastard rested a dominant leer downward upon Damien, while the injured entity altogether assumed that the telepathic chess match would surely commence. He held the piercing stare down from the overgrown sphinx, dressed fancily in its spiffy monkey suit for several painstaking moments. However, his ravaged body never became oven-like or boiling. His thoughts remained with him, and his mind sat attached to his own wrenched through spirit.

The overgrown horror offered a chilling grin at the prostrate man, with its oversized pearly whites nearly consuming its shiny ebony skin. The officer thing puffed a few extra intensive breaths of Colorado night crisp, only to disappear sideways back out into the cemetery chasm.

THE RAIN BEGAN to fall again from the outside world, as all snarls and shrieks from the immortal Sphynx fell away and subsided.

The fresh antics of precipitation had a sideways turn to it, causing Damien to slant his own head with it to line up the falling pattern. He lowered his gun and set it down to the church's blessed floor. The revolver had become substantially more imposing in a short duration, as the courageous man's physical strength and fiery moxy faded with every new drop of leaking gore.

He stared at the empty doorway for what felt like nothing short of an eternity.

When his neck and shoulders screamed out his name in a please help me surrender, he lowered his head to the floor and glazed with eyes half-closed at the holy house's simple ceiling that watched over him. He wanted more than anything to let go and drift off to sleep, almost shutting his eyes into the safety net of Dominic's presence.

Before drifting off to rest, a rest the spirited Winters knew would probably be his last, an irregular tone of voice sounded out from way off behind him. It was more profound within the church, undeniably a woman's aura of dignified enrapture. The notes bordered on delicate impressions with friendly undertones that swirled within it. It sounded as if there were sweet honey and an authentic warmth in such a voice, which called out for the man's undivided attention.

It paused, then spoke again.

"You've made it, Damien. Now it's time to die..."

XLIX

HE CONTINUED PEERING upward into the ceiling interior, disregarding the threatening declaration due to the last remaining breaths of vigilant life the young hero clung to. The lighter shaded rafters crisscrossed in a uniformed pattern way up and beyond the lofty church's high tower.

A puzzling ruckus broke out coming from the front of the house closest to the church's main altar. Winters coped to gather enough strength to stir his head and body around from his defeated position, straining with ruthless effort to get a gander at what the hell was breaking off behind him.

A displeasing whimper followed by a grisly human scream ensued, forcing the clinging grounded man to palm his bloody gun a final time from the underground, and turn over slowly to right himself steady.

The sheer pain was excruciating to even budge another inch at that pivotal moment in the journey, with the unmistakable feeling of the dagger biting through his insides with every miniature gesture. Damien rose to his boots and faced up with Dominic's simple and trite altar.

A woman stood at the foot of it, dressed in a boundless robe of the most striking ivories of glossed white. Her mythically long-lasting and straight raven hair obscured her facial structure, blacking it out altogether while providing a mask of sorts to her fair and strangely transparent complexion. The figurine was leggy, even from his cool distance, proving to be an unprecedented specimen of a woman.

Damien shot a glance toward the left of her remarkable positioning and settled his umber eyes on a man that stood off beside her. His hospital scrubs were wilted and worn, with the left leg material almost fully gone to hell, while revealing his medium brown tones of scruffy flesh. His curly hair lay matted and damp upon his uncertain framework.

The secondary figure at the very altar of St. Dominic's Catholic was none other than Kip Wells.

Kip had implausibly found a way to arrive at Dominic's oasis, remaining blessed with his amicable and sinful human form. He had acted out his decrepit betrayal and altogether survived, only to burst in alone and frenzied to the green moss-covered refuge of the saints.

In her sweet ivory of lace, the leading lady took a gangly and skeletal hand of her own and raised it hypnotically into her shadow for a face. She removed her raven blanket that was used as her mask, revealing a bony, yet structured appearance that was grotesquely dominated by unspeakable yolks for seeing windows.

The larger than life entity in her gown that lurched before the two fractured colleagues, was the same apparition that had flooded into Damien's former dreamscapes on countless sleepless nights.

His dream terrors, more than anything.

Pleasant dreams and happy go lucky wishes were only reserved for the overall innocence of a damned human species and a dying mortality. The severity of nightmares where the man could never quite be certain if he had been in a hopeful dreamland all along, or inside an actual living travesty of an intense pseudo-reality. A state of mind and being where he would end up stifled and paralyzed with dread, in a showing of jaggedly sharp angst, while wheezing to the sounds of his own altered carbon in the murky abyss of his frigid bed-chamber.

Winters had dreamt of her for several painful years, with her initial visit coming shortly after he'd moved to Heatherton to search for a new life and to take up permanent residency at Mason General Hospital. The abhorrent sight of his most intimate and unwanted desires, who slacked with stagnant confidence next to Kip, nearly made the leather-jacketed hero buckle and collapse to the floor, only to beg for the swiftest mercies of a justifiable death. To have an unprejudiced and righteous God come right on down from a land high and mighty, and whisk him up to all the angels and shimmering harps that danced freely in the heavenly cosmos.

She wiped away her sable mane in perfect timing to stare Kip straight down through his vulnerable and pitifully tainted aura of humanity. His whole body began to writhe and twitch insanely on command, in the warm candlelit vigil of the aged Catholic home of unheard blessings. Damien's unforgettable friend and ultimate betrayer's earthling vessel became rigid where he stood writhing and racking, and was lifted straight away from the altar's simple felt flooring. With Kip exuding the faintest of glances that projected toward Damien, flooding with regretful and pathetically human eyes of muted hazel, his entire body of work went up in a complete and total hellfire.

Winters exploded his magnum revolver from his sophisticated distance and began approaching the consecration table from the backside region of the olden church. His glorious handgun sang true with a blasphemous vengeance, sending echoes and shattered vibrations throughout the supposed house of peace and prayer.

His aim was perfect and deathly accurate, striking the murdering sphinx woman in all parts of her rangy and slender body. The rounds entered her clothes of pencil-thin silk with ease, spraying a black flavored ooze in puddle formations out of each gaping entry wound. Another bullet nicked one of her tyrannical eyeballs of yore, shooting the milky horror onto her powdered face and flinging outward behind her.

Once Winters stalked his way halfway down the churchgoers' pews, advancing his firing approach, his sterling Smith & Wesson finally clicked a tired display of all the way empty.

The crumbling man ceased his progression, as his weapon no longer shot lead, yet he continued to squeeze the trigger, only with more mechanical clinks to follow in the direction of the unstoppable thing that nauseated his disbelieving eyes.

The brute offensive he'd inflicted on behalf of his friend had done nothing to the abomination.

The unsavory woman commenced her callous glare down upon Kip with a swift forward cock of her mysterious skull, melting the traitor's body down to nothing but a steamy and bubbling pulp. He screamed with raging horror the entire way to death while his face melted to the floor, exposing a bleached bright skeleton with a jawbone outstretched in the widest of gangrenous shrieks.

The Sphynx at the altar slurped his remaining human soup up and into her eagerly awaiting gape, then shot the precious vapors of Kip's grievous soul, which hovered hazily in the holy climate, into her balloon-shaped nothings of irrefutable damnation.

Damien remained tall and standing in the center aisle of the moodily lit church, with his left arm authoritatively outstretched, firing an empty gun into the direction of the invincible dark pelt. The dreary revolver popped weakly with each new trigger pull, as lukewarm pain salt cascaded down the face of the barely holding on Damien Winters.

The sphinx god turned over to face him after she siphoned up his most esteemed brother in arms, then provided the man with the wryest twitches of a court jester's delight of a sinister snicker.

The drowning mortal fell to his knees in the middle of St. Dominic's center aisle, flinging his forever empty Smith & Wesson magnum revolver ragefully off to his immediate left.

It struck a solid wooden pew several feet away, causing a decent sounding thud to ring out and signify the valiant young man's authentic last stand.

Kip was permanently gone.

There was absolutely nothing left of him.

He never was, and would never be again.

Wells had become another countless victim of a consuming and all-out oblivion, an eternal euphoria of a blank slate that only bled the color of primal jet black. The grievous noir shade of infinity that had always been destined to be surrounded by an endless loop of unrelenting dismay.

Up until that bitter and ultimate ending of fateful destiny, Damien had struggled with every nuance of his own tortured being to save his closest alter ego. They'd protected each other along the gripping warpath, but the more loyal being remained alive, if not only for another moment.

With the sharp machete dagger protruding without failure from his dripping and throbbing sidewall, the one that the nevermore Kip Wells had placed unwanted forever there, Winters had still fought for his fellow human's imperfect perseverance.

As the blinding realization that Kip's ill fate had come full circle and been hopelessly sealed to burn off in the void of the menacing black, it made the hardened young man grind his teeth almost to bits in a jarring display of grizzly agony.

L

THE TERRORIZING APPARITION that slithered her ways into the indigenous realms of the darker spectacles of human imaginations shifted her unyielding and actually beautiful veneer toward the dying, yet somehow forever going Damien Winters.

He knelt down on both knees in the centermost aisle near the halfway marker facing the unmerciful altar. Ultimately weaponless and endlessly bleeding, the mortal man sat down with a muffled gripe on the dreary soles of his boots, while he glared up at the robed entity, doing his very best to avoid the vile and famished eyes of domination.

"The entirety of your feeble and unsavory Mankind has nearly been extinguished. Your resistance up until this inevitable fork in your intended pathway has been utterly pointless, destined forever to be erased away and forgotten into Our insatiable realm of savory nothingness," she declared.

The jet-black mane of flowing sable had been swept back behind her face and ears, as a false caring expression decided to wash over it instead, with dying anticipation for a human man's angry response.

"Not to me!"

Damien's dynamic voice boomed out and echoed throughout the hallowed walls, with a choke of warm crimson filling his mouth after the explosively intense exertion.

He spat his life's liquid to the floor and stared down at it for several moments.

"In a short time, your Earthly world will belong wholly and forevermore to Us," she continued.

"Don't you see it is better Our way? The majority of the human race has become such a plaguing pandemic for the pleading exhibitions of this beautifully lavish planet, a planet, which your infernal and weak species seeks only to destroy. We have experienced a plethora of alluring celestial bodies among thousands of countless galaxies; however, they all perish to the longing We have of what you piteous humans call Earth. We are accustomed to a sentience of bleak simplicities and desolational principalities that remain flawlessly inside a void worthy structure—a peaceful first order where nothing else exists but Us. Your overly imaginative mistake of a species will officially be no more. You are no longer allowed to take as you please, destroy as you please, and design as you please. Do you not understand that humanity has become a cancer to themselves and to this overly tired and infected region of absurdly decimated and trampled through space?"

Winters remained silent while engrossed in a mournful daze at his bubbling and mucus-filled vermillion.

"You can't have me," the young man finally sighed.

He turned a coppery grave ogle toward the altar, just as the long-lasting woman broke out in a surprising scoff of an inhuman and otherworldly laugh. The cackle sounded human at first, but quickly transitioned into something chilling and monstrous.

It was a resonance not meant for human ears to be forced to entertain.

It belonged buried away thousands of centuries ago in the blackest pits of an empty cosmos.

The raven voice snapped back to a soft and nurturing inflection.

"Such arrogance, little man. We know all about YOU. Your gifted strengths of imagination have kept you going up until this very encounter. Your luscious and plentiful soul is highly sought after for the famished masses of Our superlative kind. You are, in no way, a perfect human specimen. However, you do manage to see the grander scheme of overall existence, do you not? You've even seen ME... Tucked away and hidden inside your ever-vivid human dreams."

Damien scowled at her pristine albino gown and awed at the rangy thing's immense presence with a hopeless sense of frightened confusion.

"This isn't possible. How could you possibly know that?"

She resumed her lecture with thin arms resting by her sides of snow-white.

"I do assure you, this precise moment right here and now, before your inferior human eyes is no dream. You were able to view Us for several fleeting fractions of the slightest infinitesimal flashes of your earthly Manmade time due to your sharp and intricate mind workings, without you even fully understanding why you were doing it. Your human dream scenarios and nightmarish composites allowed you to tap into and access Our forever realm of governing sovereignty. Only a special human imagination could conjure such premonitions while forging a temporary collision with Our prevailing and labyrinthine intellect. Nevertheless, your skillful foreshadowing has inevitably led you to this undeniable truth. Humanity has lost the war to their utmost and superior elders, and justifiably so. Now, YOU will taste all the sweeter!"

Damien twisted his heavy head into the wooden rafters high above him and pleaded in the most murderous of displays.

"What the fuck are you?! Oh, God, please help ME!"

Another bloated guffaw escaped from the velvety slender woman, more beastly than human with the second offering.

"Your God is weak and an infernal coward. He's quite flawed, to be plainly honest—just like your feeble kind and you. His initial creation of your flat-lining species has been His most dire of wrongful doings," she interjected while spitting and hissing within her adopted human vocabulary.

The abysmal creature proceeded with delight.

"He does exist, there's no doubt about that. Jesus Christ, the man and son, also existed during a microscopic window of a forgotten time. Not all of your human biblical stories are complete make-believe. Although humans have ironically made lucrative justifications throughout your narrowly extended timeline to debunk the spiritual and holy beginnings of your very own tumefied existence. Your God has always been an expendable pawn wrapped up in a dominated grander scheme from the beginning, you pathetic little thing. A pawn in Our game. We created Him, and He went ahead and made a choice to go rogue and create You. When the vast and distant of all the galaxies were nothing but an endless vacuum of lavishly rich chasms, WE resided peacefully within that vacuum of nothinged blackness. We eventually created Him simply to spice things up. He added imaginative creations, such as oceans and mountains, to various worlds that We've conquered and resided over until this monumental second in your trite little manmade realm of animation. At first, We admired His ingenious Holy Spirit, but along the way, He introduced another side of Himself to Us. He forged ahead and created other angels in His own exacting image, angels that rebelled against Him due to His original and powerful inventiveness. He then decided to create Man. And finally, He gave Man His insatiable ability to reason and dream and think for themselves. He initially wanted to give you only but a taste of His glorious free will, along with His divine depths of boundless imagination; however, even He didn't fully reason without a transparent doubt before He went ahead and started creating. Such magnificent and vivacious gifts of original choice reside within the human spirit, yet most of you remain constantly clouded by dreadful and merciless ways of diseased thinking. We stood idly by and watched this game amongst your kind versus His fighting angels and glorious demons for multiple centuries. The truth of the matter is that nothing undoubtedly lasts forever. Except for Us... OUR Legion! The gross fallacies of Man will forever be righted. You can now find a comforting moment of nevermore solace in knowing that you are one of the remaining last of your subservient kind."

The debilitated man chimed in after the lengthy monologue, as a sarcastic and demented tone finally escaped from him.

"That's a riveting story, lady. But you still can't have me."

Winters drifted his glassy eyes over to the very last spot where he'd witnessed Kip being scorched down to slime.

He sat up straight on his knees and shot those warm brown eyes of his up into the standing sphinx woman that dominated over everything inside the blessed realm of the earthly St. Dominic's. He managed to proceed with an excruciating agony that swooshed throughout his every lingering fiber.

"If I'm dying tonight, it's on MY terms, you unholy tyrant! Humanity may not be a perfect breed, but by listening to your talk and resting my hateful wrath upon you and your kind, your legion of destruction is really no different from us. You may have been here before everything else, but your kind is just as relentlessly starved for lusting power and equally as vicious as we are. Just as fragile, as well, it seems. I've slaughtered many of your repulsive eyeless army during this endless and God-forsaken nightmare I've been thrown into!"

The slender white woman needn't appreciate the latter comments from the shaggy-haired and dying hero, sending a wretched growl pulsing toward him into the center aisle of the fading church warmth.

Damien shot a look past the incredulous wretch of his innermost terrors to rest his draining, yet without question, mortal eyes on the boisterous six-and-a-half-foot wooden crucifix statue that perched with majestic vigor behind her. It was by far the most enamoring piece of decorative antiquity that all of St. Dominic's had to offer its visitors.

A dying Christ was affixed barbarically to the sturdy wooden cross, nailed down like a savage murderer by his wrists and ankles. His body was laid out contorted and vulnerable, showing off a beautifully intricate depiction of a mortal man surrendering himself over for the sake of others, with his own fatherly God.

When Damien visited the olden green moss church in days gone by, surrounded inside those very cemetery gates, he would occasionally lounge alone in silence at a front-row pew, while wearing his number one leather bomber's jacket, and lose himself within the detailed woodworking and sinuous craftsmanship of the gorgeous carving. The crown of thorns He wore was painfully involved and stunningly detailed in execution, slanting toward His left and burrowing into His exhausted skull of medium brown matte.

Painted droplets of leaking blood trickled down His face, with His eyes enraptured in a skyward succumbing of freeze. The crucifix exhibit was both haunting and arresting inside the seeped in and current red raw ambiance of the sullen holy place. The nailed up wooden Christ appeared almost as monumental as the towering robed sphinx that was plonked in front of it. The inferior crucifixion piece was somewhat dwarfed inside of her domineering silhouette, although, it remained just visible to the imploring hero from back in deep of the distant shadows.

DAMIEN OFFERED ONE final darting scowl into the disgusting and viscous pustules of the lanky woman that owned him.

The sphinx grew orgasmic with his bold approach, plunging her two jelly-like saucers into his tough as nails original human grit. As his body temperature redlined, Winters pawed for the gnarly blade that was cemented like a bad habit inside his damp and soupy gullet.

He fought back with a gripping force of mental clarity and broke free from the brazen black look of the superior god, instead choosing to slant his face downward upon the knife's wooden handle.

He grabbed his biological father's jagged machete with both of his gorily marinated hands and yanked with the last remaining morsels of inspired human might that the man had left to provide. The knife slurped out from inside him with one slithering stroke, making a nauseating *squish* sound of surrounding new flesh being greeted with unnatural razor-sharpness. His stomach caved inward with the effort, while Damien was left with no choice but to howl out skyward in a gut-wrenching display of painful madness.

The steel thorn in his side dropped to the church's abyss in front of him. Jets of fresh and newborn ichor poured like a sieve from the openly inviting gouge.

In the very back trenches of his expiring subconscious, he thought to grab at the wound with his hands, with the intent to stop the killing and continue battling with his unrelenting quest. Winters was an authentic fighter, so that grievous decision of insufferable yield proved to be the most dire and consequential of his entire destroyed existence. He refrained from the primal instinct to seal the gaping wound, as his remaining life force spewed in warm flooding streams. With a darkly fogged over conscience of unrelenting artfulness, Damien brought his face back upward toward the gowned temptress in white.

"I'm dying my way, not yours. I already told you, you can't h-h-a-ave me-e."

A jellied scab of crimson oozed from the hero's mouth again, causing it to bubble and pop while he spoke up to the goddess.

He took a look toward the crucified statue that was submerged behind the exclusive and unbeatable thing. The mortal's eyes grew increasingly heavy, as he could sensationalize the last gutsy pages of his earthly life, draining without mercy from his battle-hardened and majestic human vessel.

The discernment was genuinely authentic in nature, however, surprising.

There was a strangeness to it, where for a split second, he believed one could only comprehend such a feeling if they'd experienced it from within their own personal accord. His life's essence wasn't being stolen away from him by something altogether foreign. His final decision felt oddly unalloyed and intoxicant, the right thing to do when there was nothing left to functionally fight for.

The wretch of a goddess grew infuriated by such a deceptive and unpredictable human maneuver. Her syrupy piercers began to glow menacingly, white death lights that projected an incomprehensible oppression from her own overdrawn head. Through an overriding display of ancestral mind manipulation, the imperfect man was forced to keep his eyes glued wide open while he stared into the villainous fiend.

As his human mirrors of sight met the sinister orbs of, in all probabilities, the first-ever Sphynx to grace the blackest void of everything and anything ever-existent, the scrappy Winters was hoisted straight up off the floor in a dastardly fashion of inferiority.

From the man's downed positioning, his knees nearly snapped from beneath him, as he was lifted into the fresh and sacred airspace. The raven's telekinesis was leaps and bounds more electrifying than any other attempt from her other fellow abominations. It felt grossly offensive and as primeval as ancient death ever was. While hovering several shocking feet from the blessed floor inside the mossy church aisle, his arms began to outstretch all by themselves. Damien tried to resist the bludgeoning; but the imposing force field was too great, even for his stellar human prowess.

The man grew weaker by the second, barely clinging on to any degree of rational or cognitive consciousness. His upper appendages were crudely snapped out and away from his body, to fully extend the profane posture. His beloved jacket of leather crinkled and caved with him, as Winters found himself in a midair crucifixion of his own, being outsmarted through and through by the intrusive rapscallion that had wreaked havoc inside his grimmest of waking dreams.

His remaining drops of scarlet oozed to the carpet, while the knife wound gaped open even wider.

It had become a classical race against time for the crumbling Damien Winters.

A war of sorts between dying within himself under the graces of his own merciful God, or being thoroughly obliterated into the darkest of oblivions by a force made up of the most diabolic atrocities of the purest forms of forgotten evil.

THE STARE DOWN intensified as Damien was forced to behold the macabre transfixing. His mind jumbled heinously under the raw magic of the elder Sphynx. He struggled and clawed within her overpowering enrapture, unbelievably breaking off his eyes to again rest on the nailed-up state of Jesus Christ behind her.

The abhorrent insidiousness then hunched over, while the entirety of her slender back began to snap and crunch like a pumpkin being carved, then squashed under a teenager's foot on a chilly Halloween night.

The stained-glass windows all around the rich red ambiance of the moody environment imploded within themselves. Shards from the saturated masterpieces shot everywhere, inviting insane gusts of echoed winds from the outside world to gain access and make their gleeful presence known. The pews on the left portion of St. Dominic's began to shake where they were positioned strongly, rattling up and down then side to side.

They clicked and clacked an incredulous tune, as if a Celtic Irish tapping team had turned wooden. The remaining wax candles blew out within the sheltered main hall, while thunder ripped off from the outside graveyard.

The elder forced Winters' gaze back to her glutinous and lionizing eyes, just as her face shifted into Leigh's forever devastating arrays of beloved magnificence.

His vixen was right there in all of her alluring superiority.

It looked exactly like her, barring the rancid and unavoidable mucous jawbreakers for seeing membranes. He grimaced at the scene, as little Rose's face morphed inside the oval frame in astonishing replacement. Leigh was washed away like rain, while sweet Rose became front and center within the soaring lacy menace.

She spoke inaudibly at him, without providing the horrified human an ability to clarify anything rational that the young dead girl was attempting to plead. The man's ravaged down and pummeled body was crunching like a weak match stick within itself, as the strain of being held above ground in such a rudimentary and sacrilegious fashion became unendurable.

Without a second's warning, the Rose face swirled and twisted like jelly to form that of Kip's.

Wells appeared as an oddity, with the sweeping raven mane of the initial woman clouding most of his brown face, but it was without question, Kip Wells. His medium complexion gave off a searing magenta hue inside the remaining church light. His face was contorted in a miserable display of a ripping scream, with the mouth being several sizes too big, eating up half of the shapeshifter's unforgivable forefront. Two jagged horns of rugged bone protruded from the cheeks, revealing the truest colors of the eternal and savage beast.

While Kip's face was deleted as quickly as it had come, and then ghoulishly replaced with that of an overgrown falcon, another rip and crunch from the gangly monster beckoned with hateful resonance. Gargantuan bird wings emerged from the bony shoulders of the svelte sphinx, folding up behind her with their initial backward protrusion. The unfathomable flying mechanisms crept up behind the domineering figurine, gaping wide open and flapping in the holy winds, with a jaw-dropping display of otherworldly brutishness.

With her alive and gray-feathered pinions, the entire crucifix statue of Christ became swallowed up by the forward flapping demagogue. The sight was both marvelous and horrific, with the lionhearted man barely able to fathom the severity of what he was seeing.

With a sick caw from the ugly fowl's mouth, her gown proceeded to be pecked away in rough order by the mountainous and despicable thing. It tore away at its own earthly garment until there was nothing more left to cover, as another set of frightful horns dug through and up from its hideously oversized bird head.

It squawked a second time, bringing its blackened stare back to the hovering and dying Damien Winters.

The atmospheric haze from the outside lands held the deepest colors of splendid carmine, creepy crawling like a possessed centipede into the vacancies, where the luxurious stained glass used to reside. The monster could be seen as a huge bird of prey, with most of its face being consumed in a thicket of rangy feathers. When the Sphinx opened her beak wider, its tongue appeared slimy and blackened from the man's dying perspective. The wingspan was enormous and stretched out, occasionally giving a whip of a winged feather to demonstrate a meticulous degree of narcissistic command.

The one remaining facet of the former raven-haired slag, which could pass as being even remotely human, was its snake-hipped body. It remained female in sex and nauseatingly fetching. The legs endured as curvy and meaty for the thinner frame of insipid fright. Not fat, but more sturdy like tree trunks and long in overall design. The thing's overbearing breasts were neither saggy nor firm, but held a supple medium of pompous voluptuousness. The human nipples were as hard as rocks, giving off a surefire signal of primal arousal from an overly bellicose race of bygone species.

WINTERS AGONIZINGLY ATTEMPTED to move his body in midair, trying to lower himself back down toward the church house's floor. With all of his righteous efforts, he could not, and instead remained frozen in his ribald mid-air posture.

While the eyes of the beast went to feast back inside his overwrought blood shots of brown, the man yanked his head hard and skyward. The aghast mortal called out for his God to interject on his behalf, or at the very least, do something to help His fragile and nearly exterminated creation. Or to just let the tired man bleed out and offer up his spent and damaged soul with no further questions asked.

On incalculable command and without forewarning, the ceiling of the rickety old structure birthed wide open. Debris rained down upon both man and Sphinx, missing both entities by fractions of torturously close quarters. The sphynx bird clawed into Winters' mind even harder, as her radiating discs became evermore blindingly brighter, jumbling the hero's thoughts until the point of total and complete madness.

As the vanquished man's most irreplaceable leather coat began to ignite all around him, a celestial scene unfolded directly above St. Dominic's Catholic church. It was a full-fledged battle sequence playing out unleashed between the clashing realms of the outermost heavens. He could no longer be aware if he was envisioning something distant or current in overall time and space, or if he was being offered a fleeting hallucination from the alarming status of near death. Or if the Sphinx was overloading his brain wires with anciently superior smoke and mirrors.

It seemed and appeared real, along with being an incredibly vivid upward spectacle.

A full-on war between all the angels and all the demons throughout the history of human creation erupted in the heavy gray clouds, high above the falling down Colorado church. Tridents were swung while majestic swords found homes in the thickset skulls of the misunderstood gods. Heads wound up on spikes, while God Himself and the immoral wiles of the Devil duked it out in the middle ground, for a final settlement of cosmic and spiritual rule.

The broken man cried out once more with clinging desperation, while the saturated scene blazed on in a dreamlike stupor from up above and beyond.

But nothing ever came to help, or to interject, or to try and save him on that incredulous forever night.

No divine force or angel with a halo on its crown of sterling pearls entered his thought processes, while the almighty Sphinx climbed in instead, building a nest of noxious doom into his innermost workings with unsavory satisfaction.

In the definitive truth of it all, the gruesome battle between the mighty angels ended in an ugly cat's game of a pointless tie. God and Lucifer were both vanquished, while their fighting and following forces all perished alongside Them. Between the opposite conundrums of the devils and the angels, to which humanity had numbly pondered over for countless centuries, even They had been second best all along.

The ever first and all predominant Sphynx stood strong and

confident before Winters from the ground, thrashing its hellacious wings with scrutiny as the blood-soaked good for nothing skirmish in the clouds ended in a meaningless purgatory.

The vision ended, revealing only darker formations of puff followed by a sinister flash of angry lightning. The zigzag bolt entered the church moss arena and landed just beyond the winged fowl woman, blowing the enormous crucifix of Christ to splintered smithereens. The blood continued to drip from the pierced through stomach of Winters while his body became drained dry of every last morsel of red.

But despite everything, the gritty young defender was never dry enough.

It was not to be that kind of finishing tale for him.

In the obligatory endings of all things, nobody ever wins much of anything.

Especially mankind.

Each person and every-thing remain stifled and locked away within their own fleshy prisons throughout the entirety of their fleeting lives. The fact of the matter is that everything eventually dies out and away— nothing can escape that harsh truth of inevitability.

The last man standing gets no pity.

And at that very moment in the ageless skies, more so than ever before, death had become evermore fickle and grim.

If the devils and angels had all been killed off in the kingdoms of the cosmos, then the only things left to rule anything and anywhere were the immortal sphinxes. They were an immaculately operating force, destined to erase the roguish wrongdoings from the very face of the Earth itself, along with boundless other galaxies out there and beyond.

The bygone race of Sphynx did nothing of any kind to save a soul. It did not allow safe passage into a Heaven, some glittering gate, or even a Hell with its raging fires and awful brimstone.

From the beginning, those eyeless things were ever and only just plain old hungry.

Hungry for obliteration and the savory consumption of lesser and inferior organisms.

A single objective to gobble up the spirits of the weakest links, allowing them only to rot away in an endless abyss of the gravest blankness right alongside them.

The clinging man's greasy head of wavy chocolate was snapped back forward against his will, ordered to carry out his destined scowl upon the repellent and divine bird beast.

As his skin boiled and his clothes melted off and away, he did not utter even a scream. The physical pain was perverse and archaic. However, the emotional trauma that raged within him reigned overriding in gripping totality. Winters could feel his thoughts being plucked away from his tired soul, with all his dreams and terrible fears of past, present, and futures being wiped away like a metaphorical blackboard.

While fully ablaze, Damien struggled with an imperishable effort to wrangle and house his most painful and precious ruminations, to hold them in only for himself. He managed to reminisce of everything he'd done up until his catastrophic and bloodthirsty ending, and finally realized a calming satisfaction that shone somewhere vastly internal, while his clothes were stripped away and his olive skin oozed and liquefied from his terrestrial human vessel.

The remainder of the burning man's thinning convictions were of Leigh, Kip and Rose.

He pondered if he truly was the final human organism left on his planet to be destined for such an imposing and eternal doom.

His vivacious spirit became utterly erased from a forever existence. Still, his mind miraculously maintained and abstracted on past regrets and earthly human decisions, and how brave he had always been to continue sacrificing for the people he'd cherished in his quaint little mountain town called Heatherton.

As the very last charred remains of Damien Winters' body floated above the hallowed church grounds of St. Dominic's Catholic church, then nothing but bare-bones and soot, the final sequence the man could conceptualize was a rich **triangle of black**, somewhere out in the boundless interspace, with two piercingly bright illuminated eyeballs sucking him in.

THE END

AFTERWORD

I LEAVE YOU WITH one absolute truth regarding the creative process of *Triangle Black.* As your author, I did in fact, have a vivid dream one night in my mid-thirties. It was haunting and explicit, at the same time-bone chilling. When I awoke from my affliction, I wrote a poem.

It was from that poem, the first one I'd ever written, where I eventually manifested the many pages you've graciously digested. I scrawled that poem in frantic cursive inside the half-dark, subsequent to my shuddering "visitation."

So it goes:

'Apparition'

Wake, Wake, Wake
Unchain yourself from the sweet abyss;
Wake, Wake, Wake
Rise up from your slumbered bliss.

In a bed surrounded by the pitch of black,
You struggle to decipher fiction from fact.

There truly is no need to fight,
You will soon again regain your sight.

Wake, Wake, Wake
Allow you now with the dead of night. Don't you dare sink;
You are almost near the truth and light, or so you think.

Wake, Wake, Wake
Eyes now open, at last fully alive?
Piercing in the dark corner of your hive.

She is there, in that very corner. She simply cannot be.
Am I still in dream, what God Almighty do I now see?!

A woman in white, in plain sight.
My heart now a stone cold fright.

Crouched on haunches with knees pressed up to a shadow for a face,
Brooding ever so lowly in her white gown of lace.

Figure rocking, back and forth.
Why will she not behold my haunted way? Her face transfixed in her
own dark dismay.
Back and forth, back and forth..

She surely cannot be real. I am uneasily certain this is merely but a
specter.
Raven hair masking her face like a blanket of black steel.

Blink, blink, blink your frightened soul's orbs.
Back and forth, back and forth..

O' the horror! I cannot avert my vicious gaze.
Finally here the elusive blink, now she's gone vanished in a heart sink;
Ripped from sight like a delicious evil haze.

Wake, Wake, Wake…

Made in the USA
Middletown, DE
15 March 2021